Misfortune's Daughters

BY THE SAME AUTHOR

Misfortune's Daughters

JOAN COLLINS

Doubleday Direct Home Library Edition

HYPERION

NEW YORK

This Large Print Edition, prepared especially for Double-day Large Print Home Library, contains the complete, unabridged text of the original Publisher's Edition.

**This Large Print Book carries the
Seal of Approval of N.A.V.H.**

For my darling husband Percy—
never ever change

PART ONE

Laura and Nicholas

CHAPTER ONE

Nicholas Stephanopolis had always made his own rules. When his schoolmates were only fantasizing about girls, he was out to deflower them, and more often than not he succeeded. By the time he was fifteen, he towered above his contemporaries not only physically, but in style and confidence.

Fear seemed to have no place in his vocabulary. When he was only fifteen, he went down the deadly Cresta sled run in St. Moritz with awe-inspiring boldness. Lying flat on his stomach, he negotiated the deadly twists and turns of that treacherous track of black ice as skillfully as experienced skiers twice his age. But Nicholas was at his happiest when riding one of his Arabian steeds on his father's private island, or when making love to one of his many conquests.

High spirited and volatile, Nicholas's moody personality was seasoned with an outrageous wit. He could reduce a roomful of sophisticates to helpless laughter, and was utterly irresistible to women of all ages. His combination of looks and charm was deadly.

Nicholas was the sole heir to the Stephanopolis shipping empire. His mother, Lady Anne, from an aristocratic English family, was imposingly authoritative, with the erect carriage that came from her class. His father, Constantine, was so busy with his complicated business affairs that he had left the rearing of his only child to his wife. His empire had grown enormously since the Second World War, and in addition to his fleets of tankers, he had holdings in major companies everywhere. When Constantine died in 1957, he was mourned by his many employees on both Stephanopolis Island and in the business capitals of the world.

Stephanopolis Island would be hard to find on any map of the world. It was just a tiny dot, separated by a few miles of sea from the southern coast of Greece and from which, on a clear day, the rocky mountains of the Peloponnese were visible in the distant west.

The island was completely closed to all outsiders and heavily guarded by patrols of uniformed security men, and landing was by invitation from the Stephanopolis family only.

Although it was only seventeen miles by ten, the island was full of lush vegetation and a haven for birds, butterflies and exotic insects of all kinds. In the center was a small forest, where the scent of the pine trees and wild thyme filled the air. Wild boar, peacocks, foxes and deer roamed free and teams of gamekeepers saw that they flourished.

On the southern coast of the island stood the magnificent mansion that was the Stephanopolis residence. Surrounded by olive trees, umbrella pines and oleander bushes, the emerald lawn edged with rolling sweeps of lavender led to a golden beach.

With over a hundred rooms and an indoor staff of fifty, the property, which had been part of the family dynasty for over one hundred years, was an amalgam of styles: some ancient, some modern.

The enormous marble-floored entrance

hall and the lavishly decorated formal reception rooms were of massive proportions with vaulted and frescoed ceilings in shades of pink and gold, which created an ambiance of power. Much of the exquisitely carved furniture was eighteenth century and priceless.

By contrast, the first floor, comprising the family's living quarters, was furnished in contemporary style. Huge terraces from every bedroom let in the blazing sun, but cool, white curtains and modern air conditioners guaranteed that their inhabitants would always remain comfortable.

Nicholas had started learning about the family empire as soon as he left Cambridge, so by the time his father died he was ready to take over. With his vast fortune, expanding business empire and personal charm, Nicholas soon became one of the most eligible bachelors in Europe.

He was eclectic in his choice of women. Princesses and shop girls, actresses and chambermaids, mature married women and nymphlike virgins were all to his taste, but not one of them ever managed to fully capture his heart.

With Constantine gone and no one to hold him back, Nicholas gave new meaning to the word reckless. No stunt was too dangerous for him, no sport too risky. He drove any one of his fleet of sports cars so perilously fast on the twisting mountain roads of Greece that the locals eventually complained to the police.

He built a show-jumping arena in a paddock on the island, where he put his purebred horses through such alarmingly unsafe hurdles that the trainers threatened to quit.

With only enough air for an hour he would explore the unknown depths under water, delighting in confrontations with particularly fierce denizens of the ocean bed. It had been rumored that he had fought and won a battle with a shark, although he himself modestly never mentioned it.

Nicholas was a prime target for matchmakers, and ambitious hostesses would go to tremendous lengths to wangle an invitation to any event to which he had been invited, then bombard him with requests to attend dinners, parties and balls all over the world.

His mother despaired of his hedonistic lifestyle, but Nicholas was damned if he was going to marry some silly princess or heiress just to please her. He was content with his life. He had women for all occasions. Sexy women with whom he made love, passionately and often cruelly; athletic women with whom he rode or scuba dived; intelligent women with whom he could share the philosophical and political conversations he relished; and then of course his socialite women—glittering glamorous creatures who dressed in the height of fashion, danced, drank and gossiped until dawn.

But the only kind of woman Nicholas didn't have in his life was one with whom he spent the night. In his bedroom, dark as a cave, the only arms he slept in were those of Morpheus. No one ever shared his bed, and he fully expected it to remain that way, for in his heart he believed that he could never really fall in love.

CHAPTER TWO

There had seldom been a more desirable and lovely movie-star than Laura Marlowe. From the moment she lit up the screen in her debut movie *The Most Beautiful Girl in New York*, audiences couldn't get enough of her blonde ice-maiden innocence. Although Laura had always known she was beautiful, it had not affected her sweetness of character or her sunny disposition. In an industry whose *modus operandi* was cutthroat bitchiness, her niceness endeared her to everyone except the most jealous of actresses.

Throughout the early sixties, the teenager went from strength to strength, and even though her movies were of the candy-floss variety, no one came close to her in popularity.

By the time she was twenty, Laura was at the top of the heap, the ultimate star. She had made eight films since *The Most Beautiful Girl in New York*, and had managed to rescue her studio from the string of flops that had dogged it through the previous decade. Her cool, ladylike, girl-next-door beauty was the coveted goal of women the world over.

For Laura's latest film, a slapstick comedy called *Monkey Time*, one of her co-stars was a trained chimpanzee, Mr. Bongo, who did practically everything except talk. She was playing a girl shipwrecked on a desert island with two men and an ape who all fight fiercely for her favors. When she is finally rescued, she chooses the ape rather than either of the men.

It was a lighthearted romp giving Laura plenty of opportunity to show off her gorgeous face and body in a variety of revealing outfits, and she threw herself into the comic role wholeheartedly.

She liked Mr. Bongo, Mr. Bongo loved her, and the two of them sometimes strolled across the studio lot together, hand in hand.

Wearing matching blue-and-white-striped sweaters, they caused much amusement in the commissary. Mr. Bongo usually munched on a banana, grunting to anyone who spoke to him, but Laura hardly ate at all for she had been warned by studio boss Lew Irving to watch her waistline.

"Nobody loves a fat girl, kiddo." Lew regarded his studio's major asset critically, with cash-register eyes. His gray toupee was perched askew on his head, like the pelt of a dead rat, and he was wreathed in an aureole of blue smoke.

"You're twenty now, Laura, that's a fine age and you're in your prime, kiddo. But in five or six years' time you'll lose that bloom, and there'll be other gals yapping at your heels— younger gals—with firmer tits, rounder asses and fresher faces. The public loves new faces, Laura, believe me. We're always looking for 'em and we'll always find 'em."

Laura was well aware of that. The competitiveness with the other contract girls and the stigma of aging had been instilled in her by her mother, Pauline. She had already seen other starlets dropped by the studio when they edged close to the dreaded twenty-seven-year-old mark. She knew the lies they told in publicity to stave off a couple of years and she'd observed them in the mirrors of the makeup rooms, anxiously examining their youthful faces for traces of wrinkles.

So she watched her weight, took care of her skin, didn't touch alcohol and got plenty of sleep. But although men flocked around her and she dated occasionally, Laura never lost her heart, and certainly not her virginity. Pauline saw to that.

Pauline, having been dumped by Laura's father, was desperate for her little girl to remain innocent. She had filled Laura's head with tales of the fickleness and deception of men since she was a child and it had worked, for Pauline's words were always ringing in Laura's ears.

"When you marry, honey, you'll bring your husband the greatest gift in the world—your virginity."

Everything Laura did made news, and although the studio contrived a few public romances—just enough to keep the fan magazines happy—her private life was just that—private. Laura radiated an innocent sex appeal and youthful, clean wholesomeness as fresh and American as apple pie, which was desperately attractive to all the young men who flocked around her, but she wasn't interested in any of them.

Kevin Bentley was just one of the young contract actors who harbored a crush on Laura, but he had managed to control his desires over the years, and enjoyed a close friendship with her.

Kevin was acknowledged as the handsomest actor on the lot. Six feet tall, with thick brown hair which fell uncontrollably over his forehead, his eyes were a luminous green so unusual that no Technicolor camera had yet been able to do them justice. His cheekbones were high, his nose Roman and the sexy cleft in his chin made his female fans swoon.

"Dimple in the chin, Devil is within," Pauline admonished Laura, the first time she saw Kevin. "Stay away from that boy, honey, he's trouble."

She needn't have bothered to warn Laura against Kevin, for although they adored each other they had managed to keep their relationship platonic.

Kevin's looks and versatile acting had entranced America since his first movie at the age of twenty, *Summer Daydream*, with Coral Steele.

Soon after, he played an upper-crust boy

in *Dirty Tricks*. Then he had donned rags and, barefoot and grubby, took the lead in a film version of a John Steinbeck novel for which he was Oscar nominated. Over the next few years he portrayed a variety of roles in everything from comedy to high drama, and starred opposite some of Hollywood's most beautiful leading ladies. The gossip mills said he'd bedded them all and since all the contract actresses fancied Kevin Bentley, as did most American women between the ages of sixteen and sixty, his batting average was excellent.

One Friday night, after a grueling twelve-hour shooting day, Kevin picked Laura up from her dressing room.

"It's party time." He handed a cellophane-wrapped orchid to her dresser, who pinned it to the shoulder of Laura's pink chiffon gown. "Time to bop till we drop, paint the town red and live it up, my lady fair."

"I really don't want to go tonight." Laura sighed. "You know the usual boring crowd will be there, all of them older than God."

"Then we'll go to a nightclub later," said Kevin.

"Ooh, yes please!" Laura smiled. "I don't want to stay long at the Irvings."

"But we've got to go, sweetie. Orders from the boss. Take you to his party, show you off to the guests, and after, if you spread a little sweetness and light with the numero unos, we'll creep off and twist the night away. Let's hit Mocambo, deal?"

"Deal." She smiled. "You sure can charm the birds off the trees, Mr. Kevin O'Bentley."

"Yeah." He grinned wickedly. "That's why I'm a *star*, sweetie."

"You know who'll be at the party tonight?" Kevin asked as they relaxed in the back of the limousine.

"Who?"

"Nicholas Stephanopolis."

"Who he?"

"Only one of the most notorious playboy billionaires in Europe. He has a *terrible* reputation with women. Stay away from him, honey, he's a wolf who eats pretty blondes for breakfast."

"Kevin, you of all people should know I couldn't care less about men, let alone wolf-men."

"Men," squeaked Kevin à la Jack Lemmon in *Some Like It Hot*, "rough, hairy beasts all of 'em, who only want *one* thing from a girl!"

Laura giggled. "And *you* better behave yourself tonight, or Lew may not renew your contract. You're twenty-six, remember, so try to be cool for a change and stop chatting up all those old producers' wives. It makes the husbands so jealous that they'll pass you over when they're casting, and soon it'll be 'Whatever happened to Kevin Bentley?'"

"I assure you that won't happen," said Kevin confidently as the car drove up the winding driveway. "I told you I'm going to become a producer myself."

The party was in full swing as they greeted their hosts, Lew and Ivy Irving. Kevin gallantly kissed Ivy's hand and zeroed his piercing green eyes into hers with the familiar look that never failed to entrance women. Ivy Irving seemed no exception and soon they were chatting animatedly.

Then Laura was introduced to the man who stood beside her.

Nicholas Stephanopolis admired the ravishing creature before him and formally extended his hand. "How do you do," he said.

"Hello." She looked up at him. He was certainly handsome, and there was a devilish gleam in his eyes, the kind of gleam her mother constantly warned her about.

"I feel we've met before." Nicholas's voice was deep, with a faint accent.

"I'm sorry, I don't remember."

"It was at a cinema in London, several years ago. I saw a film about a beautiful girl in New York and you were the girl in it, I believe."

She looked up at him through her forest of lashes in the way that most men found totally irresistible. "Yes, that was me."

"Splendid. You gave an excellent performance. I remember my mother mentioning how surprised she was that such a young girl was such a good actress. Are you still acting, Miss Marlowe?"

Was she *still* acting? Well, really . . . Didn't he go to the movies? Didn't he read the newspapers? Or the magazines? Probably not. He was a tycoon, and tycoons obviously had more important things on their minds than the movie business.

"Oh, yes, I'm still working." She gave him her most ravishing smile. "All the time. I never stop making movies."

"Excellent. Well, do keep it up. I shall look forward to seeing your next film." He looked into her eyes, then took her proprietorially by the arm. "And now perhaps you'll join me in a glass of champagne on the terrace?"

Laura turned and gave Nicholas the winning over-the-shoulder glance that had graced a thousand magazine covers. "No, thank you, I don't drink," she said and, removing his hand from her arm, glided over to Kevin.

As Nicholas tried to follow he was grabbed by Rita Raven, a fading star done up to the nines in black sequins and an ostrich-feather boa that had seen better days. Extending a multibraceleted wrist to Nicholas, she cornered him and, with a final glance at the dazzling Laura, Nicholas was forced to listen to her self-serving anecdote.

Throughout the evening he attempted to capture Laura's elusive attention, but she ignored him and appeared to have eyes only for her escort, Kevin Bentley. But he had covertly observed her with great interest. The thrill of the hunt beckoned, and there was nothing Nicholas Stephanopolis relished more.

CHAPTER THREE

The boy stood outside the strip joint hawking the tawdry wares inside to the cruising sailors and tourists, entreating them with enticing sweetness to enter the portals of the sleazy dump where his mother and sister worked.

"Come see the pretty girls, *señor*, please." His falsetto voice had not yet broken into the deeper growl of his adolescent comrades, but at twelve, Kristobel was as tough as they were, and in a brawl would usually win. You had to be tough to work the streets of Tijuana, and Kristobel was getting tougher every day. Using all the force of his wiry arms he shoved aside the street vendors hawking their trays of matches and chewing gum, and followed his prey along the street.

"Beautiful girls, *señors*, very beautiful." He tugged at the Hawaiian shirt of a beefy Texan sailor who cuffed Kristobel away as if he were a horsefly. Undeterred, the boy picked himself up from the gutter and continued his spiel, directing it at a swaggering bunch of college boys in from San Diego for a good time.

Traffic, both pedestrian and mechanical, was loud and aggressive and, although it was barely dusk, the bars, clubs, and dives on Revolucion Avenue had been in full swing for hours. There were swarms of peddlers and hawkers offering the tourists a variety of goods: silver crucifixes, bright paper flowers, cheap cigarettes and gaudy velvet sombreros encrusted with glittery braid.

Kristobel's best friend, Gilberto, two years older, also worked for Juan, the club owner, who told him that if he couldn't entice his quota of customers into the club, he would be out on the streets. There were plenty of other boys in Tijuana who could do Gilberto's job just as well. Too many.

"And me with six brothers and sisters to

support," Gilberto said gloomily as he and Kristobel sized up the seething mass of tourists, who waddled and swaggered along the gaudy ten-block strip of shops, bars and restaurants in search of excitement and adventure.

"We've all got brothers and sisters to support," answered Kristobel, his sharp eyes constantly searching the faces of the throng as he chatted to Gilberto.

"And mothers and grandmas and cousins and babies," said Gilberto glumly. "I need to keep this job."

Kristobel shrugged his puny shoulders then suddenly darted into the crowd. He had spotted a live one. A middle-aged man, already half drunk, and with the porridgey complexion of someone who spends his days hunched over ledgers, was lurching down the street.

Kristobel's spiel worked and the customer went unprotestingly into the club. Kristobel earned an approving nod from Diego, the cashier, who took the patron's money and tallied up the number of customers the boys brought in each day. Returning to his station, Kristobel selected a pack of chewing gum from the tray of a wizened seven-year-old girl. Ava-Maria's tiny tray was suspended from her fragile shoulders by two striped canvas straps. She smiled a shy gap-toothed grin as Kristobel threw a couple of pesetas at her and patted her matted black hair.

"It's too slow for Friday night," said Gilberto glumly. He didn't have Kristobel's animal instincts for spotting the good customers, and he was gloomily aware that if he didn't pull at least ten more people by midnight, he would be on Juan's firing line.

But Kristobel had darted into the crowd again and was looking beseechingly up at the faces of a young couple.

"Meester, Meesis, come with. You see things you never see before," he said enticingly, noting the flush of excitement that appeared on their young faces. "Nice girls do naughty things with whips and chains. Show their boobies too. You'll love it—*si*?"

With a conspiratorial giggle the couple disappeared into the cavernous darkness of the club, and Kristobel pocketed the coin they'd given him. He wished he could make enough money in this job to get his mother out of here. His heart broke every time he saw the frail woman hunched over a stool in the powder room. Such a grand name for what was almost an outhouse, with one pink lightbulb, two toilets—one without a seat—a cracked sink and an abundance of cockroaches. It was Anunciata's job to keep the cockroaches away from under the tiny dressing table. The patrons never noticed the bugs scuttling across their feet as they sat gawking at the strippers strutting their stuff on the rickety stage. But as soon as one of the women saw an odious creature in the ladies' room, she would hastily grab her escort's arm and escape in a hurry. It was worth it for Juan to employ Anunciata for sixty pesetas a day and all the measly tips she managed to collect, just to keep the ladies' room cockroach clear.

"Is it all clear, Mama?" whispered Kristobel.

Anunciata looked up from her work, smiling at her son as he peered around the door of her domain.

"All clear, Darling. Everyone's watching your sister."

"I brought you something." He handed her a *taco* filled with stringy chicken.

"Thank you, son," she said gratefully, putting aside the embroidered dress she was working on.

Anunciata never stopped working, sewing with tiny delicate stitches on white cotton dresses. She bought the material by the gross from the woman next door and transformed it into a riot of color. She laid the fabric out on the cramped floor of their tiny apartment and painstakingly cut out simply shaped dresses.

Kristobel loved helping her do this, and quickly became so good at it that he soon had no need of the paper pattern guide and swiftly cut out the dresses by himself.

After sewing the pieces of a dress together on her rusty sewing machine, Anunciata would draw flowers on it with a pencil and painstakingly embroider it with multicolored peonies, lilies of the valley and hibiscus.

They were her works of art, and she worked diligently as she edged the necklines and hems of her dresses with rich flowering fantasies. In the past she made only three or four dresses a week, but since Kristobel had been helping, she had managed to almost double that amount, and the ones that Kristobel cut and embroidered were far more fanciful and exotic than hers.

Anunciata then sold the dresses to the

woman down the street, receiving the equiv-
alent of four dollars a dress for her efforts.
Both Anunciata and Kristobel thought that
this was scant payment, but on the few occasions when they had protested, the
woman had shrugged and suggested that
Anunciata go elsewhere with her wares.

A tiny fragile woman, with brittle limbs,
sunken cheekbones and the huge, burning
black eyes that her son had inherited, Anunciata was barely thirty but looked almost
twice that age. Life had been even more difficult for her than for her children, as her eldest
daughter, Carmen, was also her half-sister,
the father of both unfortunate women being
Anunciata's father.

With her own mother's tacit knowledge,
Anunciata's father had slept with her on a
regular basis since her eleventh birthday, but
when at thirteen Anunciata had given birth
to a little girl, both parents had kicked her out
of the house, berating her for her sinful
ways. Penniless and starving, the young girl
had walked with her baby from the outskirts
of Tijuana to the sprawling colorful inner city
of sin, sun and fun.

In the early 1960s, Tijuana was still fashionable and full of promise. Tourists flocked

there from across the border, encouraged by gambling, duty-free shopping, live sex shows and cheap booze. It was a magnet to many, where a good time could be had for a minimum output of cash.

But for Anunciata and her baby there was no fun. She had sat on the streets of the city begging for a few pesetas to feed her hungry infant. Knowing no one, she slept under the stone arches of the Caliente Race Track with other young mothers of similar fate, tramps, drunks and derelicts—all the sad souls that this city spawned.

When Carmen was one year old and crawling around her mother's skirts on the filthy pavement where she squatted every day, Anunciata was approached by a well-dressed, mustachioed man wearing a clean white suit and a Panama hat. He asked her if she had any dance experience.

"Of course," said Anunciata, her young face lighting up with excitement, her enormous black eyes flashing. "I dance all the time, *señor*, when I can. I love it."

"Good," said the man, admiring her youthful prettiness and slender but curvy shape. "I'll give you an audition, and if you're any good, then I think I can use you in my club."

He took off his hat and bowed politely. "My name is Juan Armendez."

Anunciata soon found herself working in the Havana Club, where taking off her clothes for a living seemed to be less of a sin and more of a blessing, thanks to the accommodation the job also provided. This consisted of a tiny room in a rickety building in the street next to Revolucion Avenue, with a small bed, a cot for the baby and a washstand. There was a high window through which Anunciata could see if she stood on a chair, and although it was a dump, to Anunciata it was heaven.

She was happy for the first time in her life. The old woman whose house it was gladly looked after Carmen while she was working at the club, and when Juan came to ask for a little physical reimbursement for his largesse, how could she refuse? He was such a nice man, after all.

By the time she was nineteen, Anunciata had given birth to four children, and—although Juan had been kind, giving her months off at a time when her pregnancies began to show—when Victor, the youngest, had taken what was left of her breast milk, her body was no longer juicily enticing enough to titillate the tourists. She was given the job in the ladies' room. For this she was even more grateful to Juan, her mentor and still occasional lover.

Juan repaid Anunciata's gratitude by allowing her eldest daughter to start stripping in front of his clientele at the ripe age of thirteen. Since Carmen was not Juan's, he wasn't bothered by her extreme youth one bit, and the patrons certainly whistled and shrieked appreciatively at her succulent young body as she writhed suggestively around the tiny stage, clad only in a G-string, stilettos and an ingenuous smile. He considered that he had been more than fair to Anunciata, Carmen, Kristobel and the rest of the brood. Times were hard and he had many mouths to feed.

Carmen was, after all, born on the wrong side of the blanket, and since Juan had four daughters and a son to support from his bovine wife, he lost little sleep over his fatherly duties toward his three children with Anunciata.

Anunciata had been reading one of the glossy fashion magazines that she loved. Her friend Sanita worked as a maid at the Casablanca Hotel and saved the thumbed copies of *Vogue* and *Harper's Bazaar* that tourists left behind. There were piles of them in the family's tiny two-room apartment, and Kristobel was as fascinated with the gorgeous models who posed in their elegant costumes as his mother was.

He was eagerly flicking through the latest copy of *L'Officiel*. "Wow." He breathed. "Look, Mama, at how beautiful is this dress—isn't it wonderful?"

"The embroidery is so pretty," she said. "So beautiful and fine. Oh, Kristobel, how I wish I could work on dresses like that."

"You will one day, Mama," he said, smoothing prematurely gray hair off her lined forehead. "You will. I'm going to go to New York as soon as I'm old enough, and I'll get a job in a clothing factory, and as soon as I have enough money you'll come and join me, and then the other children will come, and then we'll both start designing clothes. Then Jackie Kennedy, Maria Callas and Audrey Hepburn will all want to wear our dresses and we'll be rich and famous."

"Silly boy." Anunciata smiled at her young son's enthusiasm. "Such big dreams you have, my son. You know they can't happen."

"You *must* have big dreams, Mama," he

said vehemently. "If you don't have dreams, you won't ever get anywhere in life. Anyway, I'm not waiting. I'm not going to stand outside this old club for the rest of my life. No sir."

"I know, Kristobel. I know how much you hate it." Anunciata sighed, and suddenly her body shook with a deep, wracking cough.

She hadn't told her children that recently she'd been coughing up blood. She was worried about it of course, but what could she do? She had been to a local doctor, who took her sixty pesetas and said that there was nothing wrong with her.

But she knew. If it was God's will that she die, she prayed that Kristobel would be able to look after her two youngest children. God knew their father, Juan, wasn't going to.

CHAPTER FOUR

Laura, more gorgeously sexy than ever, was in London starring in a film being made at Pinewood Studios with Kevin Bentley.

The excitement of 1960s London was palpable. With the recent sexual liberation of women, the city was the center of where everything innovative, hip and young was happening. The shops of King's Road were cutting edge, the electrifying music of the Beatles thrilling, and Mary Quant's mini-skirted fashions the height of shocking chic. London fashion was more originally outrageous than anywhere else, the music newer and louder, and the *joie de vivre* and exuberance that the young exuded was a heady mixture.

Every Saturday at lunchtime, at the Club-del-Aretusa on the King's Road, many leading entertainment and society figures would linger over their *pasta e fagiola* often until teatime, table hopping, drinking wine and occasionally smoking substances more potent than cigarettes.

The private dining club was a mecca for the rich and famous. And it was there on a hot summer afternoon in 1967 that Laura Marlowe met Nicholas Stephanopolis for the second time.

At first, Nicholas observed her from afar. She was sitting at a long table, part of a group that included Kevin Bentley, two women and several young men, two of whom he recognized as the popular young British actors Albert Finney and Terence Stamp.

Nicholas noticed that all the men tried to flirt with Laura, but although she was charming toward them, she showed no real interest. An older woman, perhaps her mother, sat opposite, occasionally shooting Laura warning glances if one of the men appeared too eager. Half hidden behind a pillar,

Nicholas watched Laura for some time, then made his move.

A waiter arrived at Laura's table, bearing a jeroboam of vintage champagne and a note: "We met last year at Lew Irving's party. I would consider it a great honor if you and your friends would join me for an aperitif on my boat, which is moored on the river, near London Bridge." It was signed "Nicholas Stephanopolis."

Laura passed the note to her mother, Pauline, who scanned it coolly then checked out the handsome man behind the pillar. When Kevin saw the note, he exclaimed, "His *boat*! Honey, this we've *got* to see. It's supposedly the biggest floating thing since the *Titanic*."

"Mama, what do you think? I'd love to go."

"Me too," said Ginny Jones, Laura's oldest friend and personal assistant. "After all, it's not like he's a stranger, you did meet him in Hollywood."

Pauline signaled to the waiter to open the champagne, and then told him to invite the man to join them. Laura smiled at Nicholas as he approached their table.

"Mrs. Marlowe, what a pleasure it is to meet you." Nicholas bent to kiss Pauline's hand with such old-fashioned gallantry that she was immediately won over. He clapped Kevin on the shoulders with a manly, "Good to see you again," and shook hands with the other guests, scattering his charm like confetti.

Everyone was instantly caught up in his spell, except for Albert and Terence, who decided they had better things to do, so said their good-byes and left.

Pauline invited Nicholas to sit next to her while the other three men—Laura's makeup man, her stylist and her hairdresser Benjie— overawed by the magnificence of this macho hunk, whispered among themselves.

"He's gorgeous," whispered Benjie.

"More handsome than Kevin." The makeup artist drooled.

"And *sooo* rich," murmured the stylist. "I've heard that when his mother attends the couture in Paris she buys the *entire* Christian Dior and St. Laurent collection."

They were all fascinated by the handsome Greek, all except Laura who, although sipping champagne and laughing at his jokes, was no easy prey.

And Nicholas sensed this. The more he observed Laura, the more he found her fascinating. Her sweetness and beauty were irresistible. Suddenly he felt that this was a woman who could finally be the one to tame him, and without being told, he suspected she was still a virgin.

CHAPTER FIVE

Although she was working hard in Hollywood, Laura couldn't stop thinking about the
fascinating Greek, and it soon became apparent that neither could he of her. Although
they had only spent two short weeks together in London, Laura relived the memory
of those magical moments. Nicholas had
been a persistent wooer. Although he had
wined and dined her whenever her shooting
schedule permitted, she had not succumbed
to his blandishments.

Laura and Nicholas talked constantly on
the long-distance telephone, and he bom-

barded her on a daily basis with extravagant gifts and greenhouses of flowers.

"This guy's got it *real* bad," gasped Ginny as she ushered in yet another colossal basket of Laura's favorite white roses. "I've counted them, honey. One *thousand* roses. One thousand, I kid you not. I've never seen anything like it. I think the guy must be crazy, but he sure is crazy for you."

"I guess he likes me," said Laura. "And I'm beginning to like him more and more."

"Like you? Honey, you know what this little number costs at David Jones?" Ginny pulled a bloom from the basket and inhaled its scent. "At ten bucks a rose, retail, that's ten thousand dollars! Ten grand. That guy must have more bucks than the U.S. Treasury." Ginny looked at the roses with awe. "A girl can buy a helluva lot of shoes with that."

"I don't want shoes, Ginny." Laura smiled dreamily. "I think I want *him*. For the first time in my life, I really want a man. *This* man."

"You know he's got a terrible reputation with women."

"But he's so gentle and sweet and kind," said Laura.

"Sure, they're all gentle and sweet and

kind when they want to get into your panties. Don't give into him yet, honey, please don't."

"Don't be silly! I don't intend to. You know I'm never going to sleep with a man until I'm married."

"So what does your mother say?" asked Ginny.

"She approves. She likes him enormously. She's even encouraging me to marry him—if he asks me . . ."

"Oh, he'll ask you all right." Ginny smelled the rose again. "If you don't give in to 'em, you'll always win in the end. It works like a charm, honey. But are you sure you want to marry *him*?"

"Yes. He says he loves me, and I think I love him. That's all that matters, Ginny."

"Well, if you think you'll live happily ever after, think again," said Ginny. "He's Greek, remember? They say that Greek men can't be faithful for long."

Laura was uncharacteristically sharp. "Let me trust my own instincts, Ginny. I think he's wonderful, and a good person and he wants *me*, Laura Marlowe. Me, *not* the movie star."

Ginny shrugged. "I shall keep my fingers crossed, Darling, and I wish you only the best."

That night, as Laura was preparing for bed, the telephone rang and the voice that made her heart pound, asked softly, "My angel, how are you?"

"Oh Darling, I'm fine. A little tired, but the picture only has a month of shooting left. Then I'll be free."

"Free to marry me?" asked Nicholas.

Laura couldn't believe he had said it. "But Darling, we hardly know each other."

"It doesn't matter." His voice was calm but insistent. "I knew when I saw you at Lew's party that I could fall in love with you. But could you love me in return, Laura? Could you love me enough to marry me? Please say yes. Please say that you will be my wife."

"Oh, yes, yes, I could, of course I could," breathed Laura. "And of course I'll marry you, Nicholas, whenever and wherever you want me to."

"Then let's do it right away. Let's get married," said Nicholas. "I adore you, my angel. Would you mind giving up your career and just being the wife of a humble Greek businessman?"

For a second Laura was nonplussed, then she laughed. "Would I mind? Well, to be frank, Nicholas, I'm beginning to be tired of being a movie star. I've lived in a fishbowl all my adult life and I'm beginning to hate it. In five years I'll be twenty-six, and my career will be nearly over. In any case, I don't want to act any more, Nicholas, I want to be with you. So yes, I'll marry you, Nicholas. Yes—I will."

"I cannot believe how happy you make me, my darling." Nicholas's voice was cracking with emotion. "You will never regret it—I shall make you terribly happy too, my darling, I promise."

The Stephanopolis family began to prepare for the greatest wedding the Greek family had ever seen. Nicholas, now more in love than ever, flew over to visit Laura in California, but in spite of his entreaties she still wouldn't sleep with him.

"I want to save myself for our wedding night," Laura whispered. "Please understand that."

"I know you are going to be worth waiting for," he said as he stroked Laura's soft hair. "I've waited all my life for you."

"Married? Why the *hell* do you want to marry? You're a major movie star. You're only twenty-one, you'll have plenty of time for that later," said an exasperated Lew Irving.

"I'm in love." Laura now wanted the world to approve of her happiness. "Oh Lew, I'm more in love than I ever dreamed I could be. I never imagined I could feel like this."

"Oh yeah." Lew lit one of his enormous cigars and stared at his prize package through the haze of curling blue smoke. "Just how long have you known this guy?"

"I met him at your house last year."

"Yeah, I remember him. The Greek. He's a known philanderer, honey. He'll break your heart."

"You're wrong, Lew," she replied with a rapt smile on her face. "He's wonderful, special. I know you'll adore him when you get to know him. He's kind, sensitive, funny. And rich of course. Very. His family has holdings in shipping and munitions, publishing, and they control most of the money in Greece."

"Greeks. I know about Greeks. I don't trust any of 'em, especially those bearing gifts."

"Don't be so silly, Lew. Anyway, you can't stop me. I'm twenty-one and Mama has agreed. So what can you do?"

"OK, OK, get married then, if you're so gung ho about it. We'll give you the wedding.

The studio'll get a ton of publicity from it, and we'll even give you a month off to go on your honeymoon before your next movie."

"My next movie?" Laura was genuinely astonished. "I told you, I don't want to make movies any more, Lew. I'm going to marry Nicholas, then I'm going to live in Greece and London with him. His businesses are there. It just wouldn't work if I had to be in Hollywood."

"Tough," said Lew, spitting out a tobacco shred. "Too bad. But as you well know, Laura, there's two years to go on your original contract and we're not about to let you go, kid. No way."

"But you don't own me." Laura was shocked. "You can't. That's inhuman, Lew— you know it is."

"Human, schmuman! We *can* and we *will*, kid." Lew was deadly calm. "You belong to us. To Scalini Studios. Your contract is ironclad, and if your Prince Charming tries to make you renege on it, our publicity machine can make things look very bad for him in the press, very bad indeed, and from what I've heard, your Mr. Nicholas Stephanopolis needs good press right now. I hear that his oil tankers are being given more than a run for their money by another shipping line that's taking away a whole lot of his business. He's in trouble, kid, take it from me."

"It's not true."

"Read *Forbes* magazine," said Lew calmly. "This month's issue. The publicity could be very bad for Nicholas if you ran away from your contract."

"I thought of you as my friend and mentor, Lew. How can you do this to me?" Her voice was full of emotion.

"I *am* your friend, but this is show business, kid. As in there's no biz like it. No, I'm sorry, Laura, but you mean major bucks for this studio, and we have to first think of the stockholders. We've got five pictures lined up for you over the next two years, honey. Five. You know how many actresses would *kill* for that? Liz, Natalie, Barbra—they don't have anything lined up for them, other than another divorce. Our screenwriters are burning the midnight oil creating ideas just for you, my little star. Audiences all over the world are *panting* to see your next movie, you've been one of the top ten box-office stars for more than four years, and we expect you're gonna stay up there for at least six more."

Lew's fleshy face was sweating as he relit his huge cigar and leaned back in a mahogany seventeenth-century chair, reputed to have been owned by Charles II. He surveyed his agitated star across the enormous expanse of his desk. The morning sun glittered through the stained-glass windows of his colossal office, which bore more than a passing resemblance to the interior of a Catholic church, although its incumbent was Jewish.

He was determined to be impartial. She was, after all, simply a commodity, a goose that regularly laid golden eggs, a situation that the studio needed. Sure, Lew loved Laura—after all, she was a big star, but business was business.

"No—I'm sorry, honey." Lew flicked his ash into a thick glass ashtray. "There's no letting you out of your contract now. The studio simply cannot spare you . . ." He paused, regarding the glowing tip of his cigar with a look of intense concentration. "You're much too valuable to us."

A tearful Laura telephoned Nicholas the following evening to tell him of Lew Irving's ultimatum, but he simply roared with laughter.

"How can you laugh?" she sobbed. "I read that article in *Forbes* magazine that implied your conglomerate was in bad trouble and that your shipping line has been losing a fortune. Lew Irving could hurt you, Nicholas. He said he could destroy you if we marry and you force me to give up making movies."

"Darling, darling, darling," soothed his brown-sugar voice, almost melting the phone lines across the six thousand miles that separated them. "He's bluffing, my love. It's the oldest game in the book. That story in *Forbes* is a complete load of bullshit invented by one of my enemies." His voice became harsh and cold, and Laura felt a shiver go down her spine. "I could destroy your Mr. Irving."

"Nonsense," she said. "Lew Irving is one of the most powerful men in Hollywood. He can, and often does, ruin people—their lives, their careers, even their families. No one crosses him in this town, Nicholas. He's omnipotent."

"Omnipotent, my foot. My darling Laura, don't you see that Hollywood is an extremely tiny little fish in the huge sea of world finances?"

"What do you mean?"

"I mean, my sweet angel, that if there is any destroying to be done, it will be Nicholas Stephanopolis who'll be doing it. I've been thinking about it for a while, actually. Buying a movie studio, that is."

"What?" Laura couldn't keep the amazement from her voice. "Nicholas, you *can't* be serious."

Nicholas's mind was already buzzing with all the possibilities. "Deadly serious, my angel. Now, please don't bother that delicious little head of yours with these boring financial shenanigans. Just stay calm and beautiful, finish your movie and continue with your preparations for our wedding. Say nothing to Lew. If he wants to discuss your next movie, be amenable, act like little Bo-Peep with him. Better still, act like one of her little lambs."

"But I still don't understand. What are you planning to do, Nicholas?"

"Hush, my sweet. All will be well, I promise you. You must trust me," soothed Nicholas. "Trust me."

A week later, as she reclined in the makeup chair having her hair done, Laura picked up *Daily Variety* to read:

"Scalini Studios in shock takeover by Anglo-Greek shipping conglomerate."

The essence of the story was that the Stephanopolis conglomerate, which was basically an oil company reputedly worth billions, had successfully bid for and bought Scalini Studios, which, in spite of Laura's star power, had been in dire financial circumstances for some time.

"Major studio executive upheavals are expected," the article continued, "with the present studio hierarchy, headed by Lew Irving, liable to be completely restructured."

Laura stared in the mirror, the flush of victory in her eyes. So he had won the prize for her. Her knight in shining armor had saved her from the inevitable toll of the studios. Saved her from the built-in obsolescence that awaited her when she reached the age of twenty-seven. Saved her to be his wife and to live happily ever after.

But a sliver of doubt sliced through her euphoria. Did Nicholas always get what he wanted so easily? By what means, fair or foul, had he been able to gain complete control of the studio, and so quickly? Well, she would find out. Once they were married, they would share all of each other's secrets; their private feelings and thoughts would inter-mingle. They would be a team. The true love with Nicholas for which she had waited so long looked golden and ripe with promise.

CHAPTER SIX

Anunciata was taking her three youngest children for an afternoon stroll in a quiet plaza when it happened.

With unusual religious zeal, Juan always closed the Havana Club on Sunday, giving his staff some well-deserved time off. Carmen had gone to the movies with her latest boyfriend, and Anunciata and her children were enjoying the charming square, with its tinkling fountain in the middle, and the bougainvillea adding bright splashes of purple as it climbed its way up the gray stone walls of the surrounding buildings.

Busy playing catch, chasing after his two younger brothers on the dusty grass, shrieking with laughter, Kristobel hadn't noticed the drunken tramp as he lurched toward his mother muttering under his breath. He didn't hear her answer:

"No, I have no money. Please go away— leave me alone."

He didn't see the filthy creature grab his mother's handbag from her frail wrist as he snarled, "*Putana*, give it to me. I know you have money. All of you *putas* have money on you."

It was only when Kristobel heard Anunciata's scream of protest that he turned to see the mad eyes of the derelict as he lunged at her, pushing her to the ground with all his force.

As she fell, the man spat at Anunciata, screaming, "Filthy *putana* bitch!" Then he turned, and bolted from the small peaceful square.

Anunciata shouted, "My bag, my bag, it's got all my money in it! Kristobel, go after him, please . . . Oh sweet Mother of God, he's got my money."

Kristobel chased the tramp on wiry thirteen-year-old legs, but the older man

rapidly escaped, disappearing into the labyrinth of shabby back streets and alleys that bordered the square.

Despondent, Kristobel returned to the plaza, the image of the savage's evil face, long matted hair and beard etched in his mind.

A small crowd surrounded his mother, who was lying on the grass, wracked with coughing. Kristobel could see the worried expression of some of the women in the crowd and the frightened faces of his brothers.

Anunciata lay groaning, her white face contorted with pain. Drops of blood flecked the corners of her mouth, and as she suddenly convulsed with another bout of coughing, he saw with horror more blood staining the sparse grass in front of her.

"Call an ambulance, we must get this woman to a hospital at once!" The commanding voice came from a passerby, an American man in uniform, who spoke with the authoritarian air of a man who is used to being obeyed. An onlooker muttered that he would go and telephone for one.

"Mama, Mama, what is it? What's wrong?" Kristobel dropped to his knees, cradling his mother's head in his lap.

"Don't worry, my son," she croaked from bluish-white lips. "I'm all right—really I am—please don't worry."

The military man shook his head in pity and whispered something to the woman next to him who nodded sadly.

"I'm fine," said Anunciata as her body shook with another spasm of tubercular coughing. "Just fine, Kristobel." Weakly she spat into the white starched handkerchief that the major proffered.

"Did you see him? Did you see that bastard hit my mother?" Kristobel cried fiercely to the crowd.

Several of them nodded.

"Do you know him? Do you know who he is?" Kristobel's voice was filled with hatred. "I must find him—he has all our money, and now . . ." He looked at his mother, who, exhausted by her coughing spasm, had closed her eyes and was breathing shallowly. "It's all the money we have for the whole week," he said desperately. "If we don't have the money, our family won't eat."

The major quietly pressed a twenty-peseta note into Kristobel's hand, saying, "I hope that will be of some help. I'm very sorry

about your mother, but I'm sure that she will be all right once she gets to the hospital."

"Thank you, *señor*." Kristobel smiled with genuine gratitude.

"If my wife and I can be of any help at all, we are staying at the Casablanca Hotel," he said. "My name is Brown. Major Gordon F. Brown, United States Army, at your service."

"Thank you, *señor*, you are very kind." Kristobel stroked his mother's head tenderly. Her eyes were closed now and he saw the tiny blue veins on her eyelids and the faint pulse that beat in her left temple.

"Here comes the ambulance," said Major Brown, and with the organizational skill born of years of duty, he helped Anunciata and her sons into the back.

She lingered for three days. In between feverish bouts of coughing, Anunciata's burning eyes stared into those of her children, who had gathered around the narrow hospital bed to watch their mother die.

"You must take care of your brothers now, Kristobel, please," she whispered. "You are the head of the family now. Promise me you will look after them."

"I promise, Mama," he sobbed.

The somber major, accompanied by his wispy, pale wife, came to visit often, as did Juan and his portly spouse, Florinda.

When Anunciata finally died, surrounded by her few friends and her children, everyone wept when the doctor closed her eyelids with dispassionate thoroughness. As Kristobel held on to his mother's lifeless hand, he felt as though his own life had ended.

During their vigil at Anunciata's bedside, Florinda had become extremely attached to Kristobel's younger brothers, Pepe and Victor.

"Let them come and stay with us," she had begged Juan. "They are so young and they have no parents at all. I will look after them."

Juan grumbled, but nevertheless gave in. It would be nice for the motherly Florinda to have some children around now that their own were grown up. Only he would know that these were really his children. Now perhaps Florinda would stop smothering him and devote more of her time to those poor boys, who looked as if they could do with a good wash and a few square meals.

"I shall move in with Carlito," announced eighteen-year-old Carmen, hanging on to

the arm of her young electrician. "I am expecting his baby and he wants to marry me." She blushed through her tears, and the boy squeezed her arm encouragingly.

"And what about you, young man? What will you do now?" Major Brown put a fatherly hand on the weeping Kristobel's shoulder.

"I suppose I'll stay on working at Juan's club—if he wants me to," he stuttered.

"Of course you can stay," said Juan. "You're a good hustler. Stay as long as you want."

"But one day I want to go to America," confided Kristobel softly to the major, wiping his eyes with the sleeve of his torn shirt. "I want to work there, and make beautiful dresses. Mama said that I had the talent to do that and I know I could. I must do that. Mama would want me to."

The major smiled and handed Kristobel a small engraved card. "If, or when, you get Stateside, young man, give me a call at this number. I might be able to help you. My son-in-law owns a factory that manufactures ladies' apparel. I'm sure I could get him to give you a job there—if you're prepared to work as hard as I think you are."

"Thank you, *señor*," Kristobel said huskily. "I shall never forget your kindness, and when I come to America, *señor*, I shall definitely telephone you."

CHAPTER SEVEN

As her wedding day approached Laura was immersed in grueling rehearsals for a big musical number for her latest movie and so had little time to spare to prepare for her nuptials. The rigors of the fourteen-hour shooting day, and her utter exhaustion at night, gave her little time for anything other than to work and have fittings for her exquisite wedding dress.

The world's press was eagerly reporting Laura's every move, even staking out the studio at five o'clock in the morning; she now needed two full-time security guards to protect her from the avid media, greedy for any snippets of news about their favorite girl next door and her playboy tycoon.

To add to the excitement of the romance, there was now the fillip of his company having bought Scalini Studios. With the major shake-up of the studio brass, Nicholas Stephanopolis now owned the contracts of the studio's entire stable of stars, directors, producers and writers.

It had taken him little time to send one of his colleagues to rearrange the studio's power structure. Lew Irving was unceremoniously dumped, much to the delight of many of the studio personnel, and Nicholas appointed Hal English as CEO and head of the studio. An ambitious young filmmaker, he was considered to have a brilliant future.

Laura was immediately released from her binding contract, and all that remained for her to do was to finish her current picture, and then to devote all of her time to starring in the most glamorous movie-star wedding the world had yet seen.

In the week before the marriage, hundreds of guests arrived by helicopter and private plane to Stephanopolis Island. The wedding was to be Greece's social event of the year, and Princess Margaret, King Constantine of Greece and almost every minor European royal were expected, along with many of Laura's Hollywood friends and co-workers.

There was an egalitarian atmosphere on the island as munitions magnates, press barons, courtesans and career girls rubbed shoulders with noblemen and society hostesses, cigar-chomping Hollywood producers and glamorous actresses, all of whom were helicoptered in from the mainland.

Laura had always admired the designs of a young couturier, Raymond Bolan, and when she left for Athens two days before the wedding, he flew with her, along with Pauline, Ginny, Sadie, her hairdresser, and the designer gown itself, packed in a box the size of a coffin.

Laura's movie had gone over schedule, so when she arrived on the island in the Stephanopolis helicopter at dusk, she was simply too physically and emotionally drained to appreciate either the beauty of the island or the magnificence of the villa. She spent only an hour at dinner with her future husband and their countless friends, already there for the pre-wedding festivities.

"I cannot wait for tomorrow, my love,"

Nicholas whispered to her as he escorted her from the enormous dining room to her cool suite of marble-floored rooms. "This is the last night we shall spend apart, my darling—from tomorrow, we will be together always."

Their lips met, and she looked into fathomless dark eyes that seemed to shine with love. All doubts flew from Laura's mind as she gently stroked the shadowed curve of his chin.

"I can't wait either, Darling," she whispered. "I simply cannot wait to be your wife."

The day of the wedding dawned hot and gloriously sunny. Ginny and Pauline brought Laura's breakfast to her on a wicker tray, covered with a Porthault cloth of green and white lilies of the valley, a pattern repeated on the matching breakfast set.

"I simply couldn't eat a thing," Laura said, pushing away the croissants and fragrant coffee with a sigh.

"How did you sleep, honey?" Pauline looked at her only child with the universally anxious expression of mothers about to lose a daughter to marriage.

"Really badly. I had a *horrible* dream. But it doesn't matter, it's over now."

Sadie sat on the edge of the bed, and started to brush Laura's hair with long expert strokes.

"Y'know, I told you May twenty-second wasn't good for the wedding." A gloomy expression crossed Sadie's lugubrious features. "You know what they say about a wedding in May."

"What do they say, Sadie?" Laura asked. "I don't believe your superstitions."

"Married when bees over May blossoms flit, strangers round your board will sit," Sadie intoned.

"Oh, stop being such a pessimist, Sadie," admonished Ginny. "How can you say such a horrible thing today of all days?"

"I told you May is the unluckiest month of the year to get married in. You should have waited until June. It's only a week or so away. That's the best month, and the luckiest."

"I don't believe a word of it." Laura bounded out of bed to the bathroom. "It's all just silly old wives' talk and since I'm not an old wife, I'm not going to take any notice of you."

"Atta girl." Ginny nodded. "Why don't you shut up, Sadie? What the hell's gotten into you?"

"Listen, girls," said Sadie. "I, like you, had a terrible dream last night, and this place really gives me the creeps."

"How can you say that? This is the most gorgeous house I've ever seen," said Ginny. "You must be going crazy in your old age, Sadie."

"She is." Pauline looked at her oldest friend and shook her head. "Crazy and senile too, aren't you, Sadie old girl?"

Sadie crossed to the window and stared at the glorious view. She didn't have premonitions very often, but when she did they always seemed to come true, and she would always just blurt them out to whoever was around to hear, without even thinking.

She had known with absolute certainty when Laura started at the studio that she was going to be a huge star. Now, she felt with the same icy certainty that this marriage was doomed. Something horrible was going to happen, she just knew it. Maybe her hunch would be proved wrong. She certainly hoped so.

But she'd never been wrong yet.

The Greek Orthodox church, on the north side of the island, had been built by

Nicholas's grandfather in the early twentieth century. Today the interior had been draped and festooned with thousands of white blossoms—lilies, gardenias, dahlias, orange blossoms, and at enormous cost, Laura's favorite white roses had been helicoptered in from the mainland, along with teams of florists and designers, who had toiled throughout the night to transform the simple chapel into an enchanted place.

The floral extravaganza filled the church with its heavenly scent, the pews were packed, and six hundred famous faces watched in fascination as the massive paneled doors opened, and the bride entered to the music of Mendelssohn.

Sunlight filtered in, from tall stained-glass windows, and hundreds of votive candles cast a luminous glow on Laura's golden hair. She looked ravishingly beautiful and the congregation drew in its collective breath as she walked slowly down the aisle to the altar where Nicholas waited for her.

Laura's dress was a masterpiece of the couturier's art. The lace was vintage and so delicate that much of it had had to be painstakingly repaired.

It had been specially woven for a bride a

hundred years before, and there had been more than enough material to make a long flowing skirt and gossamer train which was supported by six little girls, distant cousins of Nicholas's. The gown was embroidered with thousands of seed pearls on the bodice which then trailed down the skirt on to the train.

On her hair Laura wore a tiara of white rosebuds and lilies of the valley, thickly entwined with real pearls. And even her skin seemed pearly in the soft light. The absolute perfection of her face and simplicity of her blond hair was an optical feast.

While the eyes of the congregation devoured the vision of Laura, floating out at sea, half a mile from the island, the world's press sat fuming in a motley fleet of motor boats, launches and dinghies, gnashing their teeth over their lost photographic opportunities.

Only one photographer had been allowed to shoot the entire proceedings and, after carefully vetting his contact sheets, the bride and groom would then allow selected pictures to be given to the media.

Nicholas slipped the simple gold ring on to Laura's finger and kissed her gently, then bride and groom left the church hand in hand. The church bells tolled, and the one hundred and fifty employees and servants gathered outside, cheering and throwing copious quantities of rice and confetti.

At the glittering reception Nicholas and Laura mingled with their guests, but all they really wanted was to be alone with each other. They could hardly wait until it was time for Laura to change into her Chanel cream traveling suit. As she threw her bouquet to the crowd to be caught, amid peals of laughter, by Ginny, the couple flew by helicopter to begin their honeymoon in Venice.

The wedding pictures appeared on the cover of practically every newspaper and magazine in the world, making Laura into even more of a desirable cover girl than she had been before, and her wedding gown was given a full page in *Women's Wear Daily* and copied by brides for years to come.

They flew from Athens in Nicholas's private plane to a crumbling but romantic palazzo on the Venice Lido.

On her wedding night, Laura, wearing a delicate white chiffon nightgown, waited expectantly for her bridegroom in the vast and elaborately decorated bedroom. A bottle of vintage Krug and crystal bowls of strawberries and cream were laid out on a table in front of the blazing fire, for although it was May and the sun was warm during the day, there was still a chill dampness in the ancient palazzo at night. But when Nicholas came to her, held her in his arms and told her how much he loved her, the chill and dampness were forgotten, as Laura finally gave in to his embraces. He was tender and caring, making sure he didn't hurt her and he was absolutely thrilled to discover that she really was a virgin.

The following morning he was full of fun and laughter and they spent the day in their private cabana on the Lido beach, enjoying the weather and whispering to each other the promise of the delights to come.

On the second night the couple dined by candlelight at Harry's Bar, then traveled by gondola along the romantic black waters of the Grand Canal. Laura, wearing a filmy dress of pink chiffon, looked more gorgeous than ever as they lay back together in the gondola, serenaded by a golden-voiced gondolier.

She gazed at the decaying buildings in the

bright moonlight, then turned to her husband. He was the most charming, affectionate and loving partner, and she was totally in love. She lay back in the gondola, gazing up at the inky starlit sky, and listened to the gondolier's poignant voice, and to Nicholas murmuring in her ear how much he adored and wanted her.

After they returned to the palazzo they went straight up to their bedroom. Nicholas looked deeply into her eyes with a look of hungry longing and, slipping Laura's dress off her shoulders, gently pushed her on to the bed.

His lips covered her body with kisses as he murmured her name over and over again. When she felt she could no longer live if he didn't make love to her, he took her, thrusting his powerful body into hers.

"I love you, Laura," he murmured afterward as they lay entwined together. "I love you now and always. You will always be my wife. Our lives are forever tied together and you'll always be mine. You will never leave me."

A year after their wedding Laura gave birth to a tiny dark-eyed girl with a head of thick black hair.

Nicholas held the mite in his arms joyfully.

"We shall call her Atlanta," he crooned. "My daughter Atlanta, after the Atlantic Ocean, where my tankers rule the sea, she shall take her name. Atlanta, it's a beautiful name, Laura, don't you think?"

"Yes, darling," Laura answered dutifully. "It is a beautiful name."

Since their marriage, her husband's behavior had become increasingly erratic. Sometimes inexplicably absent for weeks at a time, when he returned he could often be cold and distant, although most of the time he was kind and loving. During their honeymoon he had attempted once or twice to introduce some rough sexual games—"a little playful bondage," as he called it—but Laura would have none of it and was quite outraged. That side of his nature he soon enjoyed with his other women. Because, of course, there were still other women.

When Laura began to suspect this, she had confided in Lady Anne, her mother-in-law, who had tried to give Laura some insight into the mind of a Greek man.

"They are not like other men, you must realize that, Laura. Not like American men, or even other European men. You must never expect that a Greek husband will be what you want him to be, or that he himself would ever want to be under a woman's thumb. He is seldom a faithful husband. He is proud. He thinks of himself as omnipotent, his word is absolute and a Greek man expects his wife and his children to think the same."

Having spent much of her life complying with the demands of a male-oriented studio hierarchy, Laura attempted to tolerate and understand her husband's sometimes irrational and unaccountable ways.

Although she would have liked to have spent more time with him, she soon realized that his work came first. However, Nicholas never talked to her about his business affairs and when she attempted to discuss them he would irritably change the subject.

"It's man's work, Laura, and none of your business."

To the outside world Nicholas was a seemingly devoted husband and doting father, and to Laura he was still the most dashingly handsome man she had ever met, who could still make her heart melt. But there was something dark and mysterious in his character that she knew she could never reach.

CHAPTER EIGHT

In the early years of their marriage, Laura was kept constantly occupied with the organization and planning of the lavish dinners and parties that Nicholas insisted on throwing whenever he was at home. Three times a year, the most important and influential people would be invited to join them on Nicholas's giant yacht, the *Circe*.

In the forties and fifties, Constantine Stephanopolis had entertained the *crème de la crème* of the social, political and entertainment worlds, from Winston Churchill and Noël Coward to the Windsors and the Roosevelts.

Now his son was determined to indulge

the elite of the era in equally glittering hedonistic voyages. Aristotle Onassis and Maria
Callas, Elizabeth Taylor and Richard Burton,
Prince and Princess Rainier of Monaco,
even the Vice President of the United States
had partaken of Nicholas Stephanopolis's
legendary, leisurely cruises, and an invitation to a trip around the so-called Turkish
Caribbean or Galapagos Islands was a coveted prize for even the most cynical of the
haut monde.

Laura was a dutiful wife, but she now
knew that Nicholas was not entirely faithful.
As the years passed, she realized that turning the other cheek was the only policy. On
the few occasions she had confronted
Nicholas with her suspicions, he had gone
into a towering self-righteous rage.

After her mother returned to California,
having confessed that she found life in LA
more interesting than life on a Greek island,
Laura's confidante became Ginny Jones.
She needed a companion, as Nicholas often
left her on her own for weeks on end. Ginny
settled happily into her life as Girl Friday, and
although she still missed her mother, Laura
came to lean on Ginny for support, friendship and trust.

"Are you sure you want to stay stuck on this island for the rest of your life?" The pair were flicking through scripts as they sat in the drawing room after dinner by themselves. "You're young, Laura, and you're still getting offers. You're wasting away here. You've got a lot of life still left to live."

"But I love it here," said Laura. "It's the most beautiful place in the world. I have my horses, my dogs and my little girl."

"God! This is *such* a great script," mused Ginny, scanning the pages of the fourteenth script to have arrived that year for Laura. "It's a wonderful part, honey, I've heard that *everyone* in Hollywood wants to play it. Audrey, Sophia, all of 'em. But you're their first choice. It's a helluva role. Got Oscar written on every page."

Laura didn't answer. With an enigmatic smile she continued looking through a magazine.

"I just don't understand why you don't want to work anymore. Nicholas wouldn't mind—would he?" wheedled Ginny, who occasionally yearned for Hollywood.

"Ginny, for the *umpteenth* time, I am not interested in acting anymore. Being a movie star is a dreadfully boring life. And Atlanta needs me, and Nicholas needs me, in spite of what you think. Don't forget, darling, that I'm expecting another baby and all my duties are here. Can't you understand that?"

Ginny chucked the script onto the pile of magazines, sighing. "Sometimes, Laura, I think you're some sort of saint. Most actresses would kill their agent for a role like this. The studio would wait until after you had the baby, I'm sure they would."

"Ginny, I'm not an actress anymore. I haven't acted for five years and I'm simply not interested. I hadn't been interested for a long time before I quit. Besides, I'm too old now."

"Too old, my foot!" Ginny exploded. "You're not even twenty-eight. That's not old today, honey. Look at Audrey Hepburn, Liz Taylor, they're much older than you."

"Well, I wonder how long they'll enjoy it," murmured Laura, who had been wondering rather a lot lately, about her husband in particular.

Before she became pregnant again, he had still made love to her on a regular basis, but as soon as she told him that she was expecting, he had stopped totally and even moved into another bedroom.

He had been like that when she had been expecting Atlanta, so although it bothered her, she thought perhaps it was just another of the idiosyncratic characteristics of the Greek male. Although he had hardly made love to her then, he had at least still been warm and reasonably affectionate.

But, in the past weeks, his affection seemed to have waned. He was loving toward his daughter, thought Laura, observing the two of them, so alike in so many ways, rolling on the grass, tussling to pick up a ball, or splashing each other in the swimming pool. Atlanta brought out Nicholas's inner child, and he was enjoying teaching her to swim.

Yesterday Laura had remonstrated, "It's too dangerous, Nicholas," as he took the tiny girl's hand, insisting that she jump in at the deep end.

"Nonsense." He laughed. "It's good for her. Toughens her up. Makes her a true Stephanopolis, doesn't it, my little darling?"

"Yes, Papa." Four-year-old Atlanta stared down into the swimming pool, which seemed to be very deep.

"Then go ahead, my darling, jump. Go on, don't be a sissy Atlanta, *jump*!"

Atlanta started to cry. She was frightened, and her heart was beating so hard she thought it would burst.

"Well if you won't jump, I'll throw you in then," announced Nicholas, and he picked up the tiny girl and threw her into the middle of the pool.

"Nicholas, stop it!" cried Laura as her daughter spluttered and screamed in terror.

"Don't worry, she'll be fine," said Nicholas testily, before diving into the water to rescue his child as roughly as if she were a dog.

"You're a good sport, my darling." Nicholas beamed proudly at his shivering daughter as a disapproving nanny patted her dry with towels. "A wonderful sport. Papa is very, very proud of you, and he is going to give you a lovely present tomorrow."

"Thank you, Papa." Atlanta's little face lit up with joy. How she loved praise from her father. He was so strong and superior that words of approbation from him made her glow.

She loved her mother too, because she was sweet and gentle. But not with the same passionate devotion she felt for her father. He was like a god to Atlanta.

After lunch, when Nicholas left by helicopter, Atlanta felt as though the sun had gone in.

"When will you come back, Papa?" she called sadly, waving to him as he strode down the wide graveled pathway, lined with cyprus trees, to his helipad. "I'm going to miss you so much, Papa."

"Soon, my little darling. Papa will be back very soon." He blew a kiss to her, and she blew a dozen back.

"I cannot wait until I see you again, my darling. Papa is going to Rome, but he will be back very soon, I promise you . . ."

CHAPTER NINE

"Hell, shit, damn, *stronzo*!" cursed the darling of the Italian tabloids.

She had been trying to clasp a choker around her throat, but it had broken and beads were scattered all over her dressing-room floor.

"Fuck it," she snapped. "I didn't want to wear the stupid thing anyway. It doesn't go with this outfit."

Her hairdresser retrieved the scattered pearls quietly as Helena the wardrobe mistress murmured, "It doesn't matter, *signorina*, it was not your fault." She instructed her assistant to bring a different choker to Stefania's dressing room, but when it arrived, the actress waved it away impatiently.

"I won't wear it—I'm supposed to look sexy, not like some *stronza* grandmother who wears a pearl choker to seduce a man."

Sycophantic nods greeted this tirade. They knew who was boss in this dressing room. The bitch needed constant attention and even if the attention was not always flattering, Stefania still craved it, otherwise she felt unimportant. She required lots of attention to make her happy.

Stefania loved nothing more than to see her photograph in the magazines and, for relaxation, to sleep with as many beautiful men as she desired. It didn't matter what they did for a living, they could be street cleaners for all she cared, as long as they were magnificent young studs with gorgeous faces and firm, lean bodies who could give her what she needed. Rome was full of young men like that, and Stefania had her pick.

Stefania adored being loved. She was in love with the idea of love, and her need had to be constantly fed. But after the initial euphoria, a day or a week later, she became jaded by her conquests and went on to the next affair, and the next, and the next. Now, in between lovers, she was bored and irritable.

"*Basta*," she snapped at her dresser, who was attempting to do up the second choker. "Enough, *stupida*. It's time to get dressed. We mustn't keep them waiting."

That was a joke, thought Helena, glancing at the hairdresser conspiratorially. Keeping the cast and crew of her movie waiting was Signorina Stefania Scalerina's speciality.

The amount of hours she spent gazing at her reflection, primping before a mirror, while the director and crew fumed on the set, was legendary. Even during her first movie, two years ago, when she was only eighteen, she had made people wait for her.

Plucked from the chorus of a third-rate touring revue, she had caused a furor in Italy, France and Spain in *The River*, playing a simple peasant girl, toiling knee-deep in water, implausibly, in the rice paddies of Sicily. Her voluptuous teenage body, in shorts and skintight, low-cut sweater, her face shining with perspiration, tendrils of gypsy hair escaping from a kerchief, had driven male moviegoers wild with lust. Stefania knew what men liked and she knew how to use what she had; and use it she did, to sensational effect.

"You remember today we have the visitor." Helena handed her a pair of sheer black silk stockings. "Signor Giancotti said to please be nice to him, *signorina*, he's a *very* important man."

"Of course I remember," snapped Stefania, attaching lacy black garters to her stocking tops. "He's some boring old industrialist Carlino wants me to charm so maybe he'll put money into my next picture. Oh well." She sighed as she wriggled into a tight black satin-and-lace basque, groaning as Helena laced her waist to the required 21 inches. "If I charm him to hell and back, maybe he won't stay too long."

"Maybe," said Helena cryptically, as she surveyed Stefania.

"How do I look?" asked the actress, expecting the right answer.

"*Bella*," said Helena dutifully. "*Molto bella, signorina*. As always."

"*Grazie*," said Stefania, graciously. "*Andiamo, bambini*." And she swept off to the waiting set, her followers loping behind her.

* * *

Nicholas was becoming impatient. He'd had a long, boring lunch with Carlino Giancotti, the head of the studio that his advisers had suggested he consider buying, to add to his other entertainment assets, and he was itching to get away. But it was only polite that he stay to meet the star.

He'd heard of her vaguely, Stefania Scalerina, latest sex goddess of the Italian cinema. More than a rival to Lollobrigida and Loren it was said, and more temperamental than both of them put together. Nicholas couldn't care less.

He glanced at his Breguet watch. Four o'clock. He had a five-thirty meeting in Rome, and the actress was already an hour late. Of course, he'd heard that she had a reputation for being impossibly unpunctual. She'd almost made a career out of it but it hadn't hurt her—in fact, sometimes it seemed the more demanding some actresses were, the more in demand they became.

Carlino was making yet another excuse when the EXIT door at the back of the set was thrown open and Stefania swept in.

Nicholas pursed his lips in a silent whistle.

No wonder she was the movie magazines' flavor of the month. Tall, with a body that was pure carnality. Her dark red hair, the color of chestnuts, tumbled over creamy shoulders; her eyes smoldered and she oozed raw sex appeal and youth.

Every man on the set stared at her even though they had been working with her for two months. She wore black stockings and stilettos with ankle straps on endless legs, a basque on her hourglass body, suspenders covering firm white thighs, a Gestapo officer's cap perched on her head at a rakish angle, and over everything an ankle-length golden sable coat, which slid casually off one shoulder.

A cigarette drooped from her lips. On most women this would have looked sluttish, but on Stefania it only seemed to enhance her sexual allure.

"I should like to present Mr. Nicholas Stephanopolis." Giancotti's voice was deferential.

"Signorina Scalerina, a pleasure." Nicholas bowed low over her hand.

"*Piacere*, Signor Stephanopolis," Stefania said huskily, feeling the heat of his lips on her hand.

"*Molto piacere, signorina*," he answered, and their eyes locked.

* * *

He didn't leave the set all afternoon—so much for his meeting.

Although barely twenty, Stefania was a practiced mistress in the art of seduction and she knew how to keep Nicholas interested. She found him gloriously handsome, if not as young as the men she usually fancied, but he oozed incredible power, and this excited her.

She was playing the mistress of a Gestapo officer who in today's scene was trying to seduce his fourteen-year-old son. The way she played the scene that afternoon ignited every man watching and none more so than Nicholas Stephanopolis.

He was fascinated by the way her body moved. She undulated, seeming to melt into the velvet sofa as she sank into it. Her long legs were draped sinuously along the couch, and she tossed the sable coat around her almost in slow motion until finally she enveloped both herself and the teenage actor in its furry folds.

"Cut," yelled the director. "*Bene*, Stefania. *Molto bene.*"

"OK—it's a wrap. *Finito gente*," called the assistant. "*Domani, alla siete—buona notte tutti.*" The unit called out their good-byes and began to pack up their equipment and leave the set.

Stefania didn't need to glance over her shoulder to know that Nicholas's eyes were glued on her. Dressers and wardrobe personnel fluttered around her, taking her coat, fiddling with her cap, chattering in Italian. She stuck another cigarette in her mouth and waited.

"Are you free for dinner tonight?" Nicholas asked as he lit her cigarette, watching the smoke wreathe lazily up around brown velvet eyes.

"I am never *free*," her voice was deep and husky. "Never. In fact, I can be very expensive." She stared at him challengingly and for a second he was taken off guard.

Then she laughed.

"I'm sorry, Signor Stephanopolis. I don't mean to shock you. I am not free tonight but, I shall *become* free—for you." She dismissed Helena and her hairdresser with a wave of her hand, then turned and walked off the set.

"Come, come follow me," she commanded Nicholas, who followed like a little lamb.

Stefania leaned against the wall of her

dressing room, a cigarette still dangling from glossy lips.

"Close the door," she whispered. "And lock it. Unless you would like someone to come in and catch us."

Nicholas did as he was told, then walked toward her, mesmerized by her fathomless tiger's eyes.

"But maybe you would like that?" she whispered. "To have someone watch us."

Nicholas shook his head, feeling himself grow hard. He looked into her smoky eyes and could smell the musky smell of her sex as he moved closer to her. Without removing the cigarette from her mouth she put her hand on his rigid cock and stared boldly into his eyes.

Slowly he caressed the smooth flesh of her thigh, his hand moving up to where the silk of her underwear cut into her cleft.

"Jesus," he muttered as his fingers found her ready.

She removed the cigarette from her lips with her free hand and placing her mouth on his, slowly exhaled the smoke into it. Then her tongue darted into his mouth like a snake.

"Jesus can't help you now," she whispered as his tongue met hers. "Only I can, *caro*."

In his whole life Nicholas had never been with a woman who had aroused him as much as Stefania.

In spite of her beauty and sweetness, since their honeymoon Laura had never made him feel truly sexually aroused. There was something too intrinsically good and innocent about her, and she had never really liked the tricks he attempted in bed. But Stefania certainly did. She was like an animal, and she made him feel like a stallion, a stud—and he couldn't get enough of her.

CHAPTER TEN

"Do you think Nicholas will be back in time for the cruise next week?" Ginny was skimming the latest pile of international newspapers and magazines that were delivered each week to the island. "We've got two of his Greek shipowner rivals, and Stefania something . . . that Italian actress, on the list. Do you think Nicholas will be coming?"

"Of course." Laura turned the pages of *Gente* absentmindedly. "He always comes back in time for a cruise or a party. You know that."

Nicholas had been in Rome for several weeks longer than expected, and he hadn't let her know when he would return. But that was not unusual, he often did this and Laura was used to it by now. Suddenly she stopped flicking through the magazine, as her eyes became riveted to a photograph.

It seemed innocent enough. Nicholas, flanked by two beautiful girls, at a party in Rome. Not an unusual sight, since women flocked around him wherever he went, as men still did with Laura. But there was something about this particular picture that was different, and instinctively Laura knew it.

Nicholas faced the camera laughing, his arms thrown carelessly around both women, whose cleavage and tumbling hair proclaimed them as film starlets even before Laura read the caption:

"Nicholas Stephanopolis, 39, the Greek shipowner and industrialist, enjoys a joke at the Carioca nightclub with actresses Stefania Scalerina, 20, and Giovanna Vittorio, 24." Wordlessly Laura passed it to Ginny.

"Oh, it's just a paparazzi shot, the kind of thing that everyone's had taken a thousand times," said Ginny.

But Laura shook her head, and stared at the photo intently. There was an expression in the younger girl's eyes. A sly, proprietorial gleam. She looked like the cat that had licked the cream, finished it off and wanted more.

"That woman is sleeping with my husband." The words came out of Laura's mouth before she could stop them. "I'm sure she is."

Ginny glanced at the photo again. "Nonsense." She laughed. "He wouldn't go with that slut. Everyone knows she's had half the men in Rome already, most of them teenage boys. It's apparently all she likes. Itsy bitsy meat. She'd *never* be interested in Nicholas, he's much too old."

Laura continued to stare, mesmerized, at the photograph, her mind a whirlpool. Although she had become reluctantly educated to the fact that, however much he loved her, a Greek man is not always faithful to his wife, this was the first time she had come face-to-face, as it were, with Nicholas blatantly entwined with a rival.

"Even if she has been screwing him, darling," said Ginny, finally taking the magazine gently from Laura's hands, "it doesn't mean anything, does it?"

"Not really I guess." Laura sighed. "It's just upsetting when you're slapped in the face with it, particularly if she's known to be such a notorious tramp."

"Hey, *wait a minute*." Ginny scrutinized the photograph with a frown. "She's coming on the cruise next week, I think. Isn't she the one whose name was on the new list that Nicholas's secretary sent yesterday?"

"Oh God—yes, that's her. He must have met her in Rome last month."

Laura studied the picture more closely. The girl had curly red hair, wild and gypsy-like, with highlights of gold running through it. Her nose was almost too big, and her slanted dark eyes outlined in thick black kohl had a salaciously sexual glint. Her lips were full of sensual promise, parted in a wide smile to show predatory teeth. Her head was thrown back as she looked up at Nicholas and her perfectly shaped breasts strained against her low-cut blouse, which showed the outline of her erect nipples.

"She's certainly sexy, a real man trap," Laura said flatly.

"Forget it. She's not so hot. She's just young—wait until those tits fall. Besides no one ever comes close to you," said Ginny loyally. "What man would want that tramp, instead of you, honey?"

"Oh, you'd be amazed." Laura tried to make her tone light. "You'd be quite amazed, Ginny darling, if you knew what I now know about what men want—especially Greek ones."

Stefania raised her head from the pillow in which she had buried it, whispering dramatically, "*Oh cara mio, ti amo, ti amo.*"

Tiny drops of sweat dripped from Nicholas's forehead as he moved ever more rhythmically inside her, then with a cry fell back onto the bed.

Nicholas and Stefania had been making love now for over two hours, unflaggingly, and Stefania's face, which had been contorted into extreme arousal, became suddenly impassive. She lit a Disque Bleu and lay back, satiated, one arm behind her head staring at the ceiling, thinking.

Nicholas was certainly a tremendously exciting lover. He knew what turned her on, knew that when she reached the peak of her pain threshold she would climax, many times, and more moans of ecstasy would issue from her throat.

Nicholas's excitement matched hers because he realized that when he slapped her and tied her up she really enjoyed it and wasn't just pretending as so many women had done.

She had heard that he had been a great lover in his youth; now, even by her standards, he was still tremendous. Considering he was going on forty years old, the fact that he could, in one afternoon, cause her to reach greater heights of pleasure than she usually attained with men her own age, or younger, was a testament to his virility.

He looked rested, not at all tired. His deeply tanned body was muscled and his thick black hair, tinged with flecks of iron gray, was tousled on his forehead, accentuating the devilish gleam that always seemed to lurk in his dark eyes.

He took the cigarette from her fingers and inhaled deeply. He had stopped smoking fifteen years ago, but his willpower was such that he could take the occasional drag without feeling tempted to start again. Besides, Stefania made smoking look so erotic.

He smiled at her, then consulted the platinum watch with the leather strap that he never removed.

"Eight o'clock! My God, time flies when I am with you."

"I know." She smiled and let her silky red

hair brush against his chest. "It's never long enough though, is it, *caro*?"

"Never," he said, pulling the silken ties that held her legs to the bedpost tighter, enjoying the tiny grimace of pain that crossed her face. "Do you want me to take these off now, or shall I just leave you here for the maid to find?" He smiled.

"Take them off now," she whispered. "But when you come back tomorrow, tie them tighter."

They had been lovers for several weeks now, but Stefania still knew little about him, other than that he was rich, successful and married—happily, so they said.

Ah, if only they really knew, she thought. Truly happily married men do not plunge themselves into passionate affairs. She could tell his wife didn't satisfy him. An all-American girl-next-door type couldn't possibly pander to Nicholas's exotic tastes, and from the looks of Laura, butter wouldn't melt in her mouth, let alone anything else.

Stefania had heard rumors about Laura. That her ice-maiden façade had never been pierced, before or since she married Nicholas and that her reputation was as flawless as her face.

It was obvious that Stefania had discovered how to satisfy Nicholas the way he truly liked; discovered the secrets that unlocked his bizarre libido, often enough sometimes to make him lose the control he relished.

In Nicholas Stephanopolis she had finally found a man who fulfilled all her kinkiest fantasies, and he, in return, had found a woman who relished the bizarre sado-masochistic games he loved as much as she did.

Nicholas untied Stefania and bounded quickly out of bed. As usual, whenever he was going somewhere or doing something, he did it with purpose and definition. "Another damn meeting with film people. Sometimes I wish I'd never got into the media business," he muttered.

"Whatever you do, you do so well, *caro mio*," murmured Stefania in her silk-stocking voice. "And now that you own this studio you will make even more money with my movies and buy me even more beautiful things." She stretched and raised her arms in front of her, admiring the wristful of diamond, sapphire and emerald bracelets with which he had showered her. "If you keep on giving me all these bracelets, soon I shan't be able to raise my arms." She smiled.

He leaned over and kissed her lingeringly. "Eight is enough," he said. "You'll even break me. From now on it will have to be just flowers, or would you prefer whips and chains?" he whispered.

"I'll settle for just you," she said huskily. "I don't want anything else for now, but bring the whips and chains—just in case."

Nicholas dressed swiftly. Gray flannel trousers, pale blue cotton shirt, silk socks from Charvet. Black oxfords from Lobb, ink-blue blazer from Brioni. He unstrapped the plain leather strap of his Breguet watch and fastened it over his buttoned shirt cuff, a style he had made his own. With several swift strokes of the pair of tortoiseshell-handled brushes that Stefania kept on her dressing table just for him, his hair was subdued again. He leaned over to kiss his mistress's glorious bare breasts. "Tomorrow," he said huskily in a voice that was never argued with. "After lunch."

"Of course." She smiled up at him through her wild tangle of hair. "Of course. After my interview I shall be waiting, my love. With more surprises in store for you."

"I can hardly wait," he breathed.

CHAPTER ELEVEN

Stefania stopped at the bottom of the *Circe* gangplank, looking up at the towering magnificence of the huge vessel in awe.

"*Madonna mia,*" she breathed to her escort, Bruce Winters. "It's a floating palazzo!"

"I've never seen anything like it." The young designer was even more impressed. "Not even in the movies."

One hundred and eighty-five feet long, the Stephanopolis super-yacht had three decks, a swimming pool, and nine state rooms, each one more lavishly appointed than the next. It had a launching pad for a Sea King eight-seater twin-propeller helicopter and on board were a sleek black Riva speedboat, three fully equipped lifeboats as authorized by Her Majesty Queen Elizabeth's Royal Navy, six Jet Skis that could race across the waves at twenty miles per hour, fifteen different kinds of water skis, fifty assorted sets of fishing tackle and equipment, and a fully stocked wine cellar that could rival that of the Ritz.

Bruce followed Stefania as she regally ascended the steps of the gangway. Assorted crew members in crisp white uniforms gawked as she stalked up the narrow passage, in unsuitable thigh-high white stiletto boots. Her pale blue suede miniskirt, designed by Bruce, had sleeves edged with white leather, as did the buttons of her jacket.

Behind her, seven crew members carried her matching leather Gucci luggage banded with the familiar red and green canvas stripes, on which Stefania's initials were embossed in gold letters three inches high.

Stefania's hair was teased into an intricate mass of copper-colored curls. Her eyes were covered in huge white-framed sunglasses, and over her shoulder was slung a three-thousand-dollar white alligator Hermès bag, a present from Nicholas.

From a secluded corner on the top deck Laura and Ginny watched the actress's arrival. "What a tramp!" Ginny said in disgust. "Look at that outfit. She looks more like she's going to pull johns on the Via Veneto instead of going yachting."

"Mmm." Laura quietly assessed the girl, whom she instinctively sensed was her rival, then giggled. "I can't *believe* she can walk up that gangplank in those boots, *look* at them—it's ridiculous."

"If all her footwear is like that she'll break a leg on this trip for sure," crowed Ginny.

"Let us go to greet the *signorina*," cooed Laura, smoothing down the folds of her delicate flower-printed caftan.

"I wonder if she knows you're seven months pregnant," Ginny asked, as they walked toward the main deck.

"Who cares?" Laura shrugged. "I'm sure she doesn't give a damn about me or anyone else. Why should she?"

"Bitch!" hissed Ginny. "How dare she show her face here."

"It's not her fault." Laura sighed. "It's Nicholas's. He's the one who asked her here."

"Is that the boyfriend?" asked Ginny,

catching sight of Stefania and Bruce Winters outside the main salon, looking with wonder around the opulent vessel. "He looks gay to me."

"Of *course* he is; he's just the 'beard'," whispered Laura, as she glided toward her new guests. "How do you do, Signorina Scalerina." Laura oozed the dazzling charm of a perfect hostess. "I'm so glad you could make it."

"*Buon giorno*, Signora Stephanopolis. How do you do?" Stefania's English was not her strong suit; neither, Laura noticed, was her skin, which from a distance, looked like peaches and cream, but close up revealed the faint remaining scars of adolescent acne behind the heavy foundation.

"I'm Laura Stephanopolis." She extended a delicate hand to Bruce, who suddenly saw that Stefania looked cheap in the clothes that he had designed.

"How do you do. Bruce Winters." The young designer shook the hand of the fabled movie star, and wished he could design clothes for her subtly elegant style—even when visibly pregnant —instead of the flashy outfits Stefania insisted upon. Never mind. Maybe he would have an opportunity on this voyage to show Madame Stephanopolis his portfolio of designs and sketches which, in his mind, were as beautifully stylish as anything by St. Laurent or Dior.

"Come into the salon," said Laura, leading the way into a fifty-foot-long room. "I want you to meet the rest of our guests."

Bruce admired the subtle chic of walls hung with heavy, ribbed pearl-gray silk, and matching sofas striped with burgundy grosgrain ribbon. The portholes were twice the size of a normal yacht and were edged in a thick rim of silvery gray malachite, which matched the coffee tables and the tables each side of the couches. The white and gray marble floor was covered in gray, peach and cream Persian carpets, and the lighting, from recessed alcoves in the ceiling, was muted yet bright enough for him to observe the glittering, scintillating guests who were assembled.

"May I present the Duke and Duchess of Wyndham," Laura said smoothly. An extremely tall man, slightly stooped, with receding hair and a chin to match, stood to attention and extended an aristocratic hand to Stefania.

"Teddy," he said, his smile revealing English teeth, his eyes riveted to her cleavage. "Please call me Teddy."

"And I'm Conchita." The duchess smiled, although her expression looked more like a scowl. A fiery Spaniard, she had managed, against all odds, to capture the eligible duke, heir to one of the finest fortunes in Great Britain. She watched over her catch like a mother hen and her claws were immediately out for Stefania, as she realized she must not drop her guard for one second on this voyage. She noticed her husband's appreciative, randy scan over Stefania's lush body, and mentally gritted her teeth for the fray ahead.

"Why do guys always dig high-heeled boots?" whispered Ginny. "It's such a cliché." Laura ignored her as she steered Stefania to the other side of the salon, where Coral Steele, sophisticated and *soignée* in white silk jersey lounging pyjamas and matching turban, an amber cigarette holder clenched between perfectly capped teeth, extended a languid hand as she cased the Italian girl with one piercing glance. What a slut. As an ex-actress, Coral was well aware of how her profession too often encouraged the wrong type of person to enter it. This girl might be the current toast of the European cinema, but to Coral's selective eye she looked like one of the dime-a-dozen starlets, draped on the counter at Schwab's drugstore, whom she had observed when she was a child star. In tight sweaters and heavy lipstick, they had all hoped to be discovered, but apart from Lana Turner, few of them had been. Stefania might be the *fille du jour* in Italy, but her attraction would be ephemeral, Coral thought. In a year or two, she would be yesterday's news, and a newer, younger model would take her place.

"She'll have a short shelf life," Coral told Laura, *sotto voce*, as an ogling crewman escorted Stefania and Bruce down to their staterooms. "Those kinds of trampy girls *never* last, darling, you know that, surely, of all people."

Laura shrugged, watching as Stefania sashayed across the room. "But while they're around they're lethal," she murmured.

Coral, having heard the rumors about Nicholas and Stefania, had observed the chemistry when he had come in to greet her. It had been so palpable that no one in the cabin needed to be drawn a picture of what the two of them had going for each other.

"Don't worry, darling." Much-married Coral was an expert in the way of men's sexual behavior. "It won't last. She's just a cheap slut. I don't see what he could *possibly* see in her."

The cheap slut's eyes opened even wider when they clocked the magnificence of her cabin, then they narrowed, and a tiny secret smile crossed her lips as she saw the intricately carved ivory bedposts that supported the silken canopy of the bed.

Nicholas had planned this room especially for her, she had no doubt about that. She wondered exactly when, tonight, he would take her. When their eyes had locked in the main salon, she knew he would come to her tonight, tie her legs to those creamy posts and ravish her. Was this cabin close to his wife's? Would Laura be able to hear Stefania's cries of ecstasy as Nicholas made her come, over and over again? Stefania shivered with anticipation at her fantasy.

The cover of the bed was cream-colored mink edged with caramel suede. The walls and carpet were of the softest yellow, as was the en-suite bathroom with its sunken marble tub and solid gold taps and showerheads.

Such opulence was rarely seen in grand private houses, let alone on boats, thought Stefania. She wondered what she should wear tonight. A maid had already unpacked her suitcases, and she surveyed the silks, satins and sequins hanging in the mirror-fronted bank of cupboards. The mirrors, she grinned to herself, reflected the bed. Nicholas was a clever boy.

Something diaphanous for tonight, she thought—something transparent and very, very sexy, something that would make all the women hate her, and all the men desire her. Especially Nicholas. She wanted him now, even though she had glimpsed a few gorgeous young sailors on board. But her usual type no longer tempted her. It was Nicholas she wanted, and she knew she was going to have him tonight.

An elegant feast was served on a long teak table, polished to within an inch of its life and adorned with cream linen mats appliquéd with the blue *Circe* motif. The heavy silverware was Georgian and the royal blue goblets were of rare eighteenth-century Venetian glass.

Down the center of the table six silver candelabra, evenly spaced with military precision, cast the soft glow of their dripless beeswax candles onto the assembled diners.

All the women looked stunning, but none more than Stefania, who exuded a special inner sexual aura that every man in the room was aware of. Her sexuality was like musk and she held the rapt attention of both her dinner partners with effortless ease. Ever since she was eleven, men had been rubbing themselves up against Stefania, trying to get close to her, trying to get into her pants, and she had learned how to handle them expertly since then.

From the other end of the table Laura watched her husband's reaction to this siren with well-concealed sadness, while she chatted to the Duke of Wyndham on her right and the British ambassador to Greece on her left.

There were fourteen people on this cruise. Apart from Laura and Nicholas, Stefania and Bruce, the Duke and Duchess of Wyndham, the Greek ambassador and his wife, and Coral Steele, there was Coral's latest escort Gerd von Panzer, the eligible and handsome heir to a French car company.

Gerd and Coral had been lovers for several months now and rumor had it that he was about to become the glamorous actress's husband number four. But tonight he too seemed to have fallen under Stefania's spell, gazing at her from down the table with a bewitched schoolboyish look, much to Coral's disgust.

Philip Skorpios, the Greek shipping tycoon, rival and old and trusted friend of Nicholas, was with his inamorata of several years, the famous opera singer, Ariana Giannetti.

As soon as the diva clapped eyes on Stefania she loathed her, and at the sight of her perfect, almost nude breasts thinly veiled by the brown chiffon folds of her gown, Ariana could barely contain her jealousy.

"That bosom will drop soon enough," she hissed vindictively to Hal English, co-owner with Nicholas of Scalini Studios.

Hal laughed agreeably, secretly wondering if he shouldn't sign this girl to a studio contract. Although the studio wasn't signing many new stars these days—only making deals with established superstars—Stefania was so hot-looking that maybe they should make an exception in her case. He'd certainly like to screw her, he thought, and glancing around the table at the fascinated expressions of the other men, he was well aware he wasn't the only one.

After dinner, the party adjourned to the main salon, where the diva sang an aria from *Romeo et Juliette*, accompanied, rather pedantically, on the enormous white grand piano by Philip.

Stefania lounged on the gray silk sofa, arms behind her head, a cigarette hanging in her wet carmine lips, conscious that every man's attention was on her, and not on Ariana and her magic voice.

Ariana was aware of it too, and her normally pure tones quavered on the high notes, as she saw the lascivious eyes of her lover feasting on Stefania's beauty.

All of the women, even Hal English's no-nonsense, tennis-mad wife, were inwardly fuming at the flagrant way Stefania flaunted herself.

"How dare she show off her bosom like that," seethed the Duchess of Wyndham to Coral as they primped in the pale green onyx womb of the ladies' room.

"She's just a trollop, dear—here today and gone tomorrow," said Coral in her knowing way. "Don't fret about her, she's not worth it.

Besides—it's not your Teddy she's interested in."

"But Teddy hasn't taken his eyes off her since she came on board." Conchita's voice became shriller. "They bulge out enough as it is, but when he saw those tits tonight, I thought they'd pop out of his head completely."

"Men!" Coral shook her wise sleek head, and adjusted a pearl-and-diamond parrot earring. "Just a bunch of little boys, darling. The sooner you realize that the better. Come, let's go to the discotheque. The third act is about to begin."

This cruise was to mark the opening of Nicholas's new discotheque. With its black glass dance floor twinkling with underfoot lights, flashing pink strobes, an enclosed disc jockey booth where a full-time hipster was installed, and a state of the art hi-fi system, it was an extraordinary oasis of hi-tech super-chic. Few, if any, yachts, even the most lavish, had a discotheque.

"How divine," breathed Stefania, who loved to dance, especially if an appreciative crowd was watching. Grabbing Bruce by the hand, she pulled him onto the dance floor, her hips pulsating to the sound of the Bee Gees' "Stayin' Alive." Stefania writhed and wriggled in front of Bruce, and most of the men watching felt a stiffening in their loins and a mad desire to join in.

Soon, as the champagne flowed and the other women temporarily forgot their envy of Stefania, everyone was gyrating around the tiny floor, even the duke, who had managed to wrest Stefania away from Bruce, much to Conchita's fury.

Laura slipped away. She wasn't feeling at all well and she didn't want to observe the inevitable, her husband dancing with that brazen hussy. It was time to bow out gracefully.

Before she retired, she went to look at Atlanta, sleeping soundly in her little bed. She kissed the child gently on her forehead, then went to her stateroom. What was the point of worrying about Nicholas and Stefania? He was going to do whatever he wanted with her anyway. Laura couldn't prevent it, no matter what she said.

He hadn't made love to her now for six months, ever since she had informed him that she was pregnant. Well, she would just wait, and hope that after the baby was born, her marriage would return to some kind of normality.

The party lasted until after three, when finally, amid much joviality, everyone tottered off to bed.

Stefania stood in the muted lamplight of her bedroom removing her chiffon dress, which was damp with sweat. She had not locked the door and soon, as she had expected, without knocking, Nicholas glided in.

"Good evening, my lord." She turned her body to him, naked except for the gold and amber beads that still draped her neck, shoulders and breasts.

"What can I do for you, my lord?" Her eyes were narrowed, her half-parted lips held a cigarette. One hand lazily caressed her nipples and Nicholas caught his breath. It had been three days since he'd had her last. Much, much too long.

"My God, my God," he said, closing the door and looking at her exquisite body, bathed in the golden light from the recessed sconces. "What do you do to me, you witch? You are unbelievable."

"Thank you, sire." She smiled, slowly

pirouetting so that he could feast his eyes on every flawless curve. "You like?"

"I like," he said huskily, his hands reaching for her firm young body. "I like a lot. Too much—much too much. But you must be punished. You've behaved very badly to-night, flaunting yourself in front of all those men. Remember, you are only a slave. My slave."

"Good." Her tongue flicked into his mouth. "Punish me now, my lord. Punish me, lord—as much as you want to—I know I deserve it."

"Oh, I'm going to," he muttered, reaching into his pockets for two silk ties. "I'm going to tie you up so that you cannot move—slave—then I'm going to fuck you all night."

"Yes, yes," she whispered eagerly, her dark eyes shining as she undid the buttons of his shirt.

"I know I have done wrong, my lord. You are my master, I am your slave, so you can do what you want with me. Anything. Anything you want."

She lay on the bed, looking up at him with lustful eyes. "Are you going to punish me now? I deserve it, sire."

He took one arm and tied it to the carved ivory post. She writhed as she pretended to resist, but he was too strong for her; forcing her kicking legs apart, he started to tie them to the bedposts.

Atlanta opened her eyes. She thought she heard something, a sound like an animal in pain. Climbing down from her bed, she opened the door of her cabin and listened. Yes, she could hear faint cries. Where was Nanny? She knocked on the cabin next door, where Nanny Scotty, having imbibed a few too many whiskies at the crew's table tonight, was dead to the world. Atlanta tried her door but it was locked, so she started gingerly down the long corridor toward the commotion.

The door to the yellow stateroom was closed, but she could hear noises coming from inside and a voice that sounded as though it was pleading for mercy. It was scary. Slowly she opened the door, peering into the dimly lit cabin.

A red-haired lady lay facedown on the bed. Her legs seemed to be tied up, and she was moaning. Standing over her, Atlanta saw the back of a man who was slapping her and every time he hit her she gave a little cry.

Atlanta let out a gasp of shock as Nicholas turned to see his four-year-old daughter, frozen with fear, standing at the open door.

"Get out of here, Atlanta," roared her father in his most frightening voice. "Get out at once."

Atlanta fled on rubbery legs, tears streaming down her face, terror in her heart. What was Papa doing? Why was he hitting that lady? Where is Mama? Why wasn't she there? Why won't Nanny wake up?

She threw herself onto her bunk, cowering under the covers, covering her head with her hands, sobbing breathlessly.

Several minutes later the door opened, and her father, out of breath and wearing the ship's white toweling bathrobe with the blue *Circe* logo on the pocket, entered.

Nicholas sat on the edge of the bed and put his arms around her quivering body. Atlanta snuggled into their comfort.

"Now Atlanta, you must forget about what you have seen tonight," he said harshly. "Do you hear me, kitten—forget about it—completely."

She nodded and took her thumb out of her mouth. She knew how much Papa hated her to suck her thumb, but it gave her solace.

She knew she must obey Papa. But how could she forget what she had seen?

"It didn't happen, you see," Nicholas droned, rocking her softly from side to side. "You just had a nasty dream, my little kitten, a nightmare. It's over now, and you will forget it. You saw nothing, you heard nothing and you will remember nothing tomorrow—all right, Atlanta?"

"All right, Papa," she said in her tiny voice, wanting to obey him.

"Now drink this." He handed her a glass of fizzy yellow liquid.

"What is it, Papa?"

"It's just a little drop of champagne," he soothed. "Drink it up, kitten, and tomorrow you won't remember a single thing about tonight."

"All right, Papa," said Atlanta, and dutifully drained the champagne, which her father had spiked with half a crushed Valium.

"Now you will sleep, kitten." Nicholas put her head on the pillow and pulled the covers up over her neck. "I'll see you in the morning. Sleep well, my darling."

As he closed the door, Atlanta put her thumb in her mouth and soon drifted off into a dreamless slumber.

The following morning, when Nanny Scotty finally managed to rouse Atlanta from the deep sleep she had been in, Atlanta felt very odd. A vague memory of some horrible dream lingered in her consciousness, but by the end of the day, as the hazy blue mountains of Sardinia hove into view, she had forgotten about it.

CHAPTER TWELVE

Atlanta's earliest years were secure in the devotion of her mother and father. Surrounded by servants and nannies, her golden summers were spent on Stephanopolis Island, where from the end of March until the beginning of November the family was based, and although Nicholas spent most weekdays at his desk in Athens, London or New York, Laura dutifully stayed on the island with her infant daughter. It was an idyllic life, and Atlanta's first four years were extremely happy.

She learned to swim like a fish in the

shimmering blue-tiled pool and the open sea, often racing with her father, who would sometimes even let her win. When that happened Atlanta felt her heart burst with happiness. He bought her a pony for her fourth birthday and encouraged her to ride it, but Atlanta was frightened of horses and didn't like riding.

Nicholas was fond enough of his only child to want to be with her whenever possible, so sometimes Atlanta would be allowed to go on the fabulous cruises. Although he spent little actual time with her, the brief moments she was with her father were the happiest of her young life.

"Where is she? Where's Papa's little darling?" crooned Nicholas, striding into the nursery and scooping the squealing child up and away from whatever she was doing. "Who's Papa's best girl in the whole world?"

"I am, Papa," she cooed happily, nuzzling her dark head into his neck. "Me, me, me."

Papa always smelled so nice. He smelled of tobacco and the sharp tang of cognac, and the cologne he always used lingered in the air long after he left the room. Atlanta used to creep into his bathroom sometimes, when he was away for weeks at a time, and rub his cologne onto her arms, keeping his scent with her, all day long.

"Who do you love best in the world, my little darling?" he would whisper softly into her baby ears.

He had been worried about her ears when she was born. They had seemed too large; she had appeared almost jug-eared, in fact. The doctor had assured him that this was nothing to worry about and that, by the time she was five or six, they would have settled in closer to her head.

"You, Papa. I love you *bestest* in the whole world." Atlanta excitedly hugged him as tightly as her plump little arms could.

Atlanta's plumpness had also given Nicholas cause for concern. She seemed to be fatter each time he saw her and although the battery of nurses and governesses assured him that it was perfectly natural for a girl of four to weigh 45 pounds, he himself wasn't so sure.

As Atlanta's baby fat increased, so did the black hair, not only on her head, but on her chubby little arms and legs, which were becoming covered in a soft, dark down.

Nicholas had always been a fastidious

man who appreciated beauty in his women, and he was beginning to find his little daughter's hairiness worrying. The contrasts between this child and her glorious mother were becoming more marked and, in spite of himself, Nicholas found it repelled him.

The day before her fifth birthday was the saddest day of Atlanta's young life.

Laura had gone into labor and was rushed by helicopter from the island to a hospital in Athens. Nicholas and Ginny accompanied her, leaving Atlanta behind with just Nanny Scotty, her grandmother Anne, and the servants.

Hearing all the commotion outside, Atlanta ran to her bedroom window, where she saw her mother being carried into a waiting helicopter, whose huge rotors were turning at full speed.

"Cancel Atlanta's birthday party tomorrow," Nicholas called over his shoulder to Nanny Scotty as he raced along the tarmac, the wind whipping the silvery-black tendrils around his face. "Call everyone and cancel it right away."

"But Atlanta will be so disappointed." Nanny waddled behind him, trying to keep

up with his strides. "She's been looking forward to her party for weeks."

"Do as I say, Nanny," Nicholas yelled
above the deafening noise, climbing into the
helicopter where a white-faced Laura was
being comforted by Ginny.

"There will be no party. It's not the time to
celebrate now, not while her mother is in labor. When our new child is born, then we'll
celebrate—we'll have a double celebration.
Tell Atlanta that. All right, Nanny?"

"Yes, sir," called Nanny, the noise of the rotors drowning her thin voice. "I will, sir—but
she'll be so disappointed, sir."

The huge machine rose into the air and,
with a twist of silver steel, skimmed across
the water to the mainland.

Atlanta had run down the stairs to the helipad as fast as her little legs could carry her,
but she was too late to say good-bye to either of her parents.

She clutched Nanny's hand and watched
the helicopter disappear into the hazy blue
horizon. Tears streamed down her face.
"Papa didn't say good-bye to me," she
sobbed. "Neither did Mama. They just left.
They didn't look at me, or say Happy Birthday. Why, Nanny? Why?"

"Hush, dear. Papa's worried about your mama. She's sick. But she will be all right, dear. In a few days' time Papa and Mama will be back, and they'll have a nice, new little baby for you to play with. Won't that be fun, dear?"

Atlanta sucked her thumb glumly. "I don't think so, Nanny."

Atlanta stared with loathing at the hateful pink creature crawling across the rug. She suppressed a strong desire to raise her boot and stamp on her baby sister, but she contented herself merely with a sharp nudge of her boot to Venetia's diaper-padded bottom, which caused the infant to topple over onto her back like a beetle and wail piteously.

"Oh shut up," said Atlanta unsympatheti-cally. "No one's around to hear you crying, you horrible baby."

Provoking her little sister always gave Atlanta perverse satisfaction, for Venetia was a crybaby. She cried for the slightest cause. If she was wet, if she was hungry, hot, cold or just plain cranky. The cherubic pink-and-white face would crease into a screaming mask of fury, and nannies and governesses

would rush from every part of the house to
tend to her needs.

Well, no one was around to hear her yell
today, thought Atlanta gleefully. It was Nanny
Scotty's day off, and the number-two rein-
forcement was doubled up on her bed with a
bad case of cramps, so Atlanta was temporarily in charge.

Atlanta gave Venetia another sharp kick.

"Scream your head off, monster," she
shouted, her eyes flashing. "No one's going
to hear you, so there."

Suddenly, the baby stopped wailing, and
looked up at her sister with a little coo. A
dribbling gummy smile suffused her face as
she smiled at her angry sibling.

"Goo-goo-goo," she gurgled excitedly.

"Oh, goo-goo yourself," snapped Atlanta.
"You're a horrible baby, so don't you goo-goo
at me, 'cos it won't do you any good at all."

The baby gave another grin and waved
her pink rattle in front of Atlanta's cross face.
Droplets of spittle trembled on her rosebud
mouth, and she rocked back and forth on
her padded bottom, her eyes following her
sister.

Atlanta ignored her and, flouncing over to

the sofa, picked up one of her children's books and busied herself with it. She glowered at Venetia over the top of the book. For the rest of the afternoon, the baby amused herself by thumping her rattle, while her sister buried her head in the illustrated tales of Hans Christian Andersen.

When nanny number two arose from her bed of pain to collect her charges for supper, she was delighted to see an unusual harmony and peace reigning in the nursery. She was followed by Nicholas on one of his rare visits to his children's quarters.

"How's my darling? How's my little princess?" he boomed in the deep, rich voice that always gave Atlanta a pang of excitement.

She looked up from her book as he strode in. He had obviously been riding, for his black hair streaked with silver highlights was rumpled, there was a faint sheen of perspiration on his mahogany skin, and he smelled faintly of the horses that he loved.

"Da-Da!" cooed Venetia, as Nicholas scooped her up in his tweed-clad arms, nuzzling his head into her soft baby skin.

"Hello, Papa," Atlanta said meekly, the

smile evaporating from her face as she realized that her father was, as usual, cosseting
her sister.

"Gorgeous, what a gorgeous little girl you
are, aren't you, my petal?" Nicholas was
holding Venetia close, crooning softly, hug-
ging her to him. The baby girl tugged at his
silvery-black curls and gave a beatific smile.

Atlanta ground her teeth. Burying her
head back into her book, she pretended not
to notice as Nicholas carried Venetia to the
wide french windows that overlooked the
spectacular view of manicured emerald
lawns edged with profusions of flowering
blossoms and shrubs. The sea shimmered
brilliantly in the late afternoon sun.

"Look, kitten, there's Papa's boat. Isn't it
pretty?"

Venetia hit her father's tweed shoulder
with her rattle.

"Say 'boat,' darling," coaxed Nicholas. "Say
'Papa's boat,' Venetia."

"Da-Da." The baby pounded harder on his
chest with a dribbling smile.

"Da-Da's boat," persisted Nicholas patiently. "Say it, my petal, Da-Da's boat."
Nicholas pointed to the *Circe*, which lay at
anchor in the bay, the sun glittering on its

blinding white magnificence. To simply call the floating palace a boat was a vast understatement.

"Boo," gurgled Venetia. "Boo-boo." She gave a little hiccup.

"You *clever* girl." Nicholas hugged his favorite daughter excitedly. "That's *right*, my darling, my clever little kitten. Boat—boat. Now my darling must have a special treat." Nicholas held Venetia at arm's length, admiring her peaches-and-cream skin and her beautiful curly white-blonde hair.

"She shall have some *very* special ice cream tonight after supper. Specially sent from America. Nanny, see that she gets the strawberry."

"Of course, sir." Nanny glanced over at Atlanta, who had put her book down and was staring at the three of them with her thumb in her mouth. She started to give a tremulous smile as her father turned his attention to her for the first time.

"Oh, and give Atlanta some, of course," he said. "We don't want them getting jealous of each other, do we, Nanny?"

"No, sir," said Nanny as Nicholas gently deposited Venetia in her arms. "We don't, that would be a terrible sin, sir—indeed it would."

"Bye bye, beauty," Nicholas said, softly nuzzling Venetia's pink and cream cheek. "Bye, my precious kitten—Papa'll see you soon."

Nicholas glanced at Atlanta, who was grinding her teeth together so hard that Nanny gave her a pinch. Nicholas blew his eldest daughter a perfunctory kiss and Atlanta's face lit up, as she bounded from the sofa and trotted to where her father stood.

As she attempted to get the hug she craved, he patted her on the head like a dog, said, "Good girl, Atlanta. I'm glad to see you're studying," and turning swiftly, left the nursery.

Atlanta looked after him, her plump little chin trembling. "Bye, Papa," she whispered softly. "I love you."

Nicholas took no notice. His tall figure disappeared into the inner recesses of the enormous villa and Atlanta heard the sound of his riding boots clacking on the burnished marble corridor.

"Da-Da," crowed Venetia happily. "Boo-boo."

"Oh shut up," said Atlanta wearily and, throwing herself onto the sofa, buried her nose in the exploits of *The Ugly Duckling*. "I hate you, Venetia—I really hate you."

*   *   *

By the time Venetia was two years old, Nicholas Stephanopolis and Stefania Scalerina were no longer a scandalous couple, they were almost establishment.

For a few months after Venetia's birth, Nicholas had contrived to retain some semblance of a normal marriage with Laura, even managing to make love to her occasionally, but as Stefania invented newer and more fascinating sexual games, he found he had no desire to sleep even in the same bed as his wife. Sexually, she no longer interested him.

The only interest he had now in his family was Venetia, his beautiful blonde daughter. Atlanta was so plain, and becoming more difficult and sullen each day, and Laura was merely a decorative armpiece, necessary to show publicly but to whom he barely gave the time of day when they were alone.

Sadly, the realization dawned on Laura that she had lost the love of her husband. However much she tried to interest him, it didn't work. She knew now that, for the sake of her children, she would have to remain trapped on the island.

CHAPTER THIRTEEN

She had always known that she wasn't the prettiest. Shortly after Venetia's birth, Atlanta became aware of her lack of beauty compared with her sister, who had inherited all of their mother's golden looks. The fine blonde hair, creamy complexion and slender limbs of Laura's North American forebears were hers, and from the time she took her first faltering steps, Atlanta couldn't help but see the admiring looks that Venetia received from everyone.

Little of Laura's beauty had been given to Atlanta. Where Venetia's features were a mini version of her mother's, Atlanta's were an accentuated version of her father's. But what was handsome and distinguished in a man was almost ugly in a girl.

Atlanta's skin was more yellow than the golden olive of Nicholas's, and in her round face, his darkly smoldering eyes were like black pebbles. True, her eyes were fringed with double rows of jet lashes, but her thick eyebrows almost met in the middle. Her nose was like Nicholas's, long and fleshy, but the protuberance at the end of it owed allegiance to neither parent; a bad gene from some long-forgotten grandparents. Her mouth was too thick, Nicholas's sensual lips unbecoming on her young face.

When she was a toddler, the faint dark hair on her chin, upper lip, and arms and legs had begun to show, and by the time she was ten, the beginning of acute hirsuteness started to appear. Many young girls from Mediterranean climates suffer from this embarrassing condition, but Atlanta soon became convinced that she was as hideous as a witch.

Every morning, locking her bathroom door, she would rip off her nightgown and gaze horrified at the hairs all over her body. Her arms and legs were a forest of feathery dark hair. Of course, it all could be covered by clothes, and Atlanta made sure that shorts, sleeveless blouses and swimsuits were banished to the back of her closet. Eschewing the dainty frocks that Laura wanted her to wear, Atlanta wore only boys' clothes, jeans and shirts, and on the occasions when she had been forced into white knee socks and a dress to be on show, she would have to be dragged from where she had hidden herself. What she could no longer disguise was the downy black hair above her upper lip that each day grew darker.

None of her various governesses and nannies realized that this excessive hair growth was caused by an overabundance of the male hormone testosterone, produced in both girls and boys at puberty, and no one seemed to worry as Atlanta started to gain weight at an alarming rate. Later, as a teenager, she would shave her legs daily in the bath and use a depilatory on her upper lip, which she would then smother with cover stick. Pleading sun allergy, she kept her arms covered. She also developed a fake cough, a useful ruse; when she caught anyone staring at her she would immediately go into a paroxysm, which caused everyone to politely avert their eyes.

She cringed with embarrassment when she had to meet people who always compared her unfavorably with her beautiful younger sister, who was blissfully unaware of her older sister's problem.

Although she never believed she was pretty, the one advantage Atlanta did possess over her sister was that her hair was marvelous: thick, glossy, blue-black, and curly. She let it grow to below her waist, and used it as a shield to disguise as much of her face and body as she could, refusing to let her crowning glory be cut.

Atlanta's unhappiness with her appearance forced her to retire more and more into her shell, and her favorite retreat was the world of books. She read voraciously—everything she could get her hands on—often continuing deep into the night, using a flashlight under the bedclothes until her eyelids dropped.

As her daughters grew up, Laura's relationship with Nicholas deteriorated to the point where her main solace was, increasingly, the vodka bottle. Although Ginny tried to prevent her, Laura continued to blot out her pain every lonely evening with alcohol. She was too concerned with her own thoughts—or perhaps too preoccupied with shutting them out—to be aware of her eldest daughter's problems.

Much to everyone's amazement, Stefania had managed to keep Nicholas more or less enthralled for nearly six years. What the sexy actress didn't suspect was that, when he wasn't with her, he saw other women.

But when Stefania found out Nicholas had been seeing one of her deadliest rivals, Gabriella Gilardi, she went berserk. "*Bastardo*," she screamed. Her dark eyes venomous, she threw a heavy statue in his direction. "*Stronzo-bastardo*, son-of-a-fucking-bitch."

Nicholas ducked a glass ashtray. Although her aim was bad, things hurtled toward him so thick and fast that one missile was bound to hit him eventually. He couldn't help but admire his fiery mistress, as she hurled objects at him, cursing wildly. She was intensely fuckable then, more so than ever.

He captured her and, in spite of her furious writhing and screaming, subdued her and took her quickly on the floor. Afterward she purred like a cat, then raked his back with pointed nails.

"That's my mark, so no other woman better look at you." She gave a tiger grin. "You'd better keep away from that no-talent bitch Gabriella, Nicholas, or I'll *kill* you—I promise—I'll kill you."

"You wouldn't dare, you're my slave and you love me too much. You'll never leave me; besides, you'd have nobody to throw things at if I were gone."

"Try me." She changed her mood and lay languidly back, lighting a cigarette. "It's enough I have to share you with your wife and kids. If you ever start anything with another woman again, you'll regret it, Nicholas." She smiled through her tangle of hair. "So keep your pants zipped, Mr. Big Shot. *Capisce*?"

When Stefania heard that Nicholas continued to see Gabriella, she decided it was time to go for the jugular.

"It's for you," said Ginny, as she and Laura lay by the swimming pool sipping Pimms from frosty mugs and idly watching Venetia at her diving lesson. As Ginny passed the phone to Laura she made a gagging gesture and mouthed, "It's that great thespian, Signorina Scalerina."

Laura took the telephone gingerly. She was in no doubt about the place Stefania had in her husband's life these days. Their photograph in *Gente* had been followed by dozens more. Every downmarket European publication had run innuendo and surmise about the Italian sexpot and the Greek industrialist, and the gossip mills had hummed. Laura still hoped that the affair would burn itself out and he would tire of Stefania—that she would eventually disappear.

"Hello." Her voice was clear and cool.

"Madame Stephanopolis?" purred Stefania. "I'm so sorry to bother you, but I think that there is something that you should know about."

"If you're referring to your blatant affair with my husband, I already know about that, Signorina Scalerina."

"Oh, Madame Stephanopolis, I'm so sorry, I never meant to upset you. I could never consciously upset you, because I have been such a great admirer of you on the screen, ever since I was a little girl."

Laura bit her lip. The nerve of her. Laura was only about seven years older than this calculating strumpet. If Stefania was trying to upset her, she wasn't going to give her the satisfaction of knowing she had succeeded.

"Signorina Scalerina . . ." Laura's voice was smooth as silk. "Thank you *so* much for the compliment. I'm so sorry that I can't return it, but you see I have never seen any one of your films. Since they are only in Italian, they only play at tiny art-house cinemas, and not for very long. Now what can I do for you, pray?"

Stefania was thrown off guard. Nicholas always told her that Laura was weak and vulnerable. She hadn't realized that there was a sliver of steel in her too. "I thought I should tell you, woman to woman, that Nicholas is being unfaithful to both of us."

"Really?" Laura took a sip of Pimms, intrigued by the girl's gall. "With whom?"

"Oh, I understand totally the *awful* position you are in, Madame Stephanopolis, and I can only apologize again for any pain I've caused you." Stefania had never been much of an actress; her voice sounded fake and Laura could hear it. "But this girl he has been seeing is also an actress. In fact, she used to be a good friend of mine."

"No longer, I suppose?" said Laura, the hint of sarcasm escaping the Italian.

"No, no longer," spat Stefania. "In fact, if I ever see that *puta* again I'll claw her tits off."

"How charming. What a sweet picture." Laura made a moue of distaste to Ginny, who had picked up the extension and was listening with vicarious enjoyment. "Who is this other woman?"

Stefania's voice was thick with disdain. "Gabriella Gilardi. She's almost a porno actress, she's short, fat and not even pretty."

"So what do you expect *me* to do about it?"

"Well—aren't you furious? Don't you want to kill her? She's a bitch, a cow, she's trespassing on our property—you must want to destroy her."

"Strange as it may seem to you, I've never wanted to kill anyone," said Laura calmly. "But if I *had*, *signorina*, it would probably have been you." Her voice turned icy. "Now would you kindly do me the favor of never, ever telephoning me again. What you do with my husband is your affair, for as long as it lasts, which I don't think will be much longer. I have no interest in what the two of you do together at all. I know my husband, *signorina*. He is a man incapable of fidelity. I have known that for many years and I have accepted it. I suggest that you had better accept it too, as he is obviously losing interest in you. So, *signorina*, I suggest, if you are annoyed about his philandering, you take a running jump into the *Fontana di trevi*, because you won't get any sympathy from me. *Ciao*."

She hung up and stared triumphantly at Ginny.

"Bravo!" Ginny applauded loudly. "Bravo, my darling, that's telling her. How dare she call you and tell you Nicholas is screwing someone else—what a nerve." She started to laugh, then saw that Laura's brave façade had crumbled.

"Oh no, don't, honey, please don't." Ginny ran to kneel at Laura's feet. "Please don't cry, Laura. You must fight fire with fire, you simply must. Don't let her rattle you."

"How can I not?" Tears poured down Laura's face and she scrabbled for a handkerchief to wipe them away. "It's bad enough that he's had a blatant affair with that slut for six years, *and* made me look like a complete fool, but then to start *more* public canoodling with some porn star, it's too much."

Laura crossed to the window and looked

out at the dazzling view. The sailor-blue sky
blended into the deeper blue of the sea.
Across the vast lawns the glittering lake
shimmered, as black swans glided on it
proudly. The garden was a blaze of flowers.
In such a hot climate their beauty and profusion was always a surprise to visitors, who
wondered who had the patience and fore-
sight to encourage them to bloom so exquisitely.

Laura did. She was the one who told the
gardeners what to do. Her magic fingers
gave life to those spaces which, when she
first arrived, had been filled only with easy-
to-grow azaleas and rhododendrons. Now,
there were roses, lilies, fragrant lavender,
chrysanthemums, millions of blossoms—a
glorious burgeoning of color and life. Life.
There was so much life growing in that garden, while her own life was going nowhere.

"You've got to get away, darling," said
Ginny. "You need a vacation, to go far, far
away—enjoy yourself—pamper yourself—
forget about Nicholas and his women." Like
he's forgotten about you, she wanted to
add, but feeling sympathy for her friend, she
refrained.

"How can I go away? What about the children?" asked Laura, trying to control her sobs. "They need me. Nicholas never sees them. They're always asking about him. He promises to visit them, then he never shows up. Poor little things."

"They'll be fine," said Ginny, glancing over to Atlanta, who was covered in a long cotton robe and engrossed in a book, and little Venetia, who was splashing happily with her nurse in the pool. "Just fine. Kids are tough, darling. It's time for you to have a holiday, Laura. You're too young and beautiful to put yourself through this torture all the time."

Privately Ginny thought Laura ought to divorce the bastard, but Laura had told her that she would never consider that in a hundred years. It would hurt the children too much.

"All right, Ginny." Laura dabbed her eyes with a damp handkerchief. "You're absolutely right. This time I'm not just going to sit back and let him get away with his women and his carousing, and his contemptuous lack of consideration for all of us. I'm going on vacation and *you're* coming with me."

"Now you're talking, honey," said Ginny. "Let's teach that male-chauvinist-pig husband of yours a lesson."

Laura raised her glass in a toast. "To hell with Nicholas Stephanopolis, and to hell with all men who cheat on their wives." Then she burst into tears.

From across the pool, Atlanta raised her eyes from the book that she had been pretending to read, and stared sadly at her beautiful mother's tear-stained face.

A wave of fury swept through her. It was her father who was making Mama cry like that. It was horrible enough that Papa barely paid any attention to her any more, but the fact that he was doing the same to her mother, her wonderful angelic mother, made the kernel of hate harden in Atlanta's young heart.

CHAPTER FOURTEEN

The African sky was a pale, translucent blue with tiny white clouds scudding in the distance as Laura and Ginny drove from Johannesburg Airport, chattering excitedly.

The landscape was bare and scrubby, edged with mud or corrugated iron huts outside of which people squatted, glancing with listless disinterest at the speeding limousines, while a few skinny goats and chickens pecked at the sparse ground. Then suddenly the view changed as sparkling new white skyscrapers and office buildings became visible.

"You were absolutely right to make me get

away, Ginny." Laura's face was glowing. "I feel better already."

"You bet I was," said Ginny. "I've been telling you to get away from him, for years. You're too damn loyal, Laura."

"Well, my marriage vows still mean something to me, even though it's obvious that they no longer mean anything to Nicholas— indeed, if they ever did."

Laura was facing the hard fact that she had been in a loveless marriage for far too long.

"Do you know, he and his friends truly believe that women should be seen, and only heard when the man wants to talk to *them*. They consider them inferior intellectually, emotionally and certainly physically. The only woman Nicholas seems to respect is his mother."

"And of course, Venetia, he *adores* her," said Ginny.

"Worships her." Laura sighed. "I don't understand how he can love one daughter so much and practically ignore the other one."

"Poor Atlanta." Ginny sighed softly. "I feel really sorry for her."

"Nicholas thinks that if women ruled the world there'd be no great works of art or inventions. We'd still be living in mud huts, like them." Laura gesticulated toward a somnambulistic family group clustered outside their hovel. "There'd be no Shakespeare, no Michelangelo, no Mozart."

"There'd be no wars and no Jack the Rippers either." Ginny sniffed. "He talks a load of crap, I wish you could see that, honey."

"I've begun to." Laura laughed lightly. "Do you think I'd be going on this trip if the scales hadn't fallen from my eyes at last?"

"It's taken you long enough," said Ginny. "About eleven years."

"You're right." Laura sighed. "That's why, Ginny, my darling, we are going to have the most wonderful time on our South African safari. We are going to enjoy every second, I promise you."

The twin-engine prop plane made a bumpy landing on the single runway of what passed for an airport in the jungle clearing. Waiting at the side of the road, two husky rangers stood next to an open-topped Land Rover.

"There they are." Ginny giggled as the pilot helped them down the rickety steps of the plane. "The answer to a matron's prayer, sometimes known as 'The Safari Gods.'"

The two deeply tanned young men came over to greet the women and stow the baggage in the vehicle. They were in their mid-twenties, and both good-looking in a rugged outdoor way. They wore khaki shirts, with rolled-up sleeves revealing muscular arms; on their longish hair, faded brown slouch hats protected their heads and eyes from the glare of the burning sun.

"Good morning, ladies, I'm Steve Baden-horst." The better-looking one with the blue eyes extended a firm, callused hand.

"And I'm Ed Hardy," said the hazel-eyed one. "Welcome to Mala-Mala, ladies. I hope the flight wasn't too bumpy?"

"Not at all. It was exciting really. We got to see quite a bit of South Africa from the air." Laura admired the ease with which Steve Badenhorst hefted her heavy suitcase onto the back of the four-by-four.

"Well, you'll be seeing a lot more here, ladies, if we have anything to do with it." Steve grinned, putting the rickety but serviceable Land Rover into first gear. "I'm glad you'll be staying longer than the usual three days, because that'll give you both a chance to really see this part of the world. As long as you don't mind getting up early; to get a proper good look at the animals, you've got to rise with the lark and get out there before six o'clock, like they do."

"Why is that?" asked Ginny.

"'Cos the animals sleep for the rest of the day, until dusk. As long as you don't mind ruining a bit of your beauty sleep, ladies, we'll show you a lot of wildlife here and a great deal of fun too."

Laura and Ginny had adjoining bungalows at the main camp. Separated by a few hundred feet from the main lodgings, the camp was laid out in a triangular shape—the reception room, dining rooms and bar opened out onto a stunning panoramic view of verdant rolling hills and valleys. At the bottom of the lawn was a small swimming pool surrounded by banyan trees, and as the women ate lunch outside on the covered veranda, they could see baboons and chimpanzees swinging from the trees; in the far distance a flock of impala sprinted through the undergrowth. Laura felt supremely relaxed already in her loose khaki shirt and trousers.

"It's so wonderful here. There's such a feeling of peace and freedom."

"After lunch, if you ladies would like to take

a little nap, we'll take you out on a dusk safari," suggested Steve.

"Great," said Ginny. "I can't wait, can you,
Laura?"

Laura looked at Steve, who was carrying a
tray of coffee to their table.

"No, I can't." She smiled her dazzling smile
at him, and he grinned back.

Steve Badenhorst was not unused to having women flirt with him. Having heard rumors about the handsome rangers who ran
the safaris in the African jungle, many
women came prepared not only for the safari
but for romance too.

Steve hadn't been averse to dallying with
some of these ladies, if they were good-
looking enough. Unmarried and unfettered
at the age of twenty-six, he'd had his fair
share of flings, and as his eyes connected
with Laura's, he thought that he would like to
more than flirt with this lovely lady. Neither
Steve, Ed, nor any of the hotel staff had any
idea of her identity. To them she was Mrs.
Laura Stephanopolis—just another married
woman wanting to experience the magical
sights and sounds of the jungle.

*   *   *

After a fascinating trip through the jungle, they met up with the other Land Rover in a small clearing. It was time to watch the sun set. They set up camp on a huge flat rock surrounded by foliage, where the view of the setting sun would be spectacular.

Two trackers fetched bottles of champagne and cold beer while the tourists stretched their legs, exclaiming in awe at the orange fireball in the sky.

Laura had gone to the farthest end of the rock, partially hidden from the rest of the group by some banyan trees.

"It's beautiful, isn't it?" said Steve, offering her a paper cup of champagne.

"Ravishing," she breathed, "absolutely gorgeous."

"Like you." He smiled, raising his cup in a toast.

"Thank you." Her eyes met his and she felt the beginnings of something that she hadn't experienced in a long time. She couldn't tear her eyes away from his. Vividly blue in the dark brown of his face, they looked like sapphires. He had removed his hat, and his golden brown hair curled lightly on his forehead and over his ears. He was only a few inches taller than her, so they were able to stare into each other's eyes almost levelly.

He smiled a boyish smile that revealed his dimples, and Laura noticed that one front tooth was slightly chipped.

"How did that happen?" Gently she put a finger to his lips.

"In a fight." His tone was of one who doesn't wish to discuss the matter. He brought his face closer to hers until their noses were almost touching. "Do you think it looks terrible?"

"No," she whispered, "I think it's rather adorable."

She could smell his freshly laundered shirt as he raised his hands to touch her feathery hair, and then he bent his lips gently to hers. She felt herself floating, light as a piece of thistledown, carefree and cocooned.

"That's for now," he whispered, drawing back from the gentle kiss and raising his paper cup in a salute. "There's more of that to come."

He came to her room after supper.

They had sat with the other guests around the campfire, drinking sweet local wine, eating several courses, chatting amiably and finally singing fireside songs.

Laura couldn't remember when she had had such a good time, it had been so convivially relaxing, but all evening she had been aware of Steve. He was seven years younger than her and his slim muscular body, in fresh khakis, moved agilely like one of the jungle animals. Occasionally his hands surreptitiously brushed across her shoulders or arms as she sat suffused by a surge of longing and confused feelings.

She wanted this man even though she was married, but what a charade of a marriage it was. Even now Nicholas was probably with Stefania, or some other woman, but tonight, she didn't care. She only knew that she wanted this slim South African man with the jewel-like eyes and a chipped tooth.

She sipped her wine and shivered. Only this magical, tropical night in the middle of the jungle with the faint sound of animals in the background and the hissing of the campfire was real.

Steve was gentle and passionate and his tender lovemaking sent Laura into raptures that she'd never experienced with Nicholas.

"What have I been missing?" she asked Ginny, dewy-eyed, early the next morning as they prepared for their dawn safari. "I never knew how wonderful making love could be."

"You better make up for lost time." Her friend smiled. "It's about time someone made love to you, Laura. It's been far, far too long."

Three days went by. Three perfect days, each one a maelstrom of the enchanted sights and sounds of the jungle, mixed with nights of such searing, tender passion that Laura felt reborn.

They saw every kind of animal on their twice-daily safaris. It was as though Steve, who more than proved himself each night as a lover with Laura, wanted to prove himself the best possible guide during the day.

They saw apes and baboons, lions and leopards, elephants and water buffaloes. They saw a herd of giraffes and one morning, a beautiful young giraffe, felled in a clearing, being feasted on by packs of ravening hyenas, while vultures hovered evil-eyed in the trees. Laura turned away in horror.

They sat in their Land Rovers, silently surrounding a pair of mating lions who rutted with each other every twenty minutes for twenty or thirty seconds.

"They do that for five straight days, continuously," explained Steve. "That's to be quite sure that the female is impregnated. And they normally are, of course."

Laura and Ginny watched, riveted, as the female lion awoke and thwacked the male with her paw, then he immediately mounted her again.

They saw deer and zebra and fleet-footed tribes of impala, and at the river they saw an enormous hippopotamus wallowing in the mud.

Laura watched in awe as a huge female crocodile delicately protected her baby crocodiles from other predators, by taking them gently in her mouth and hiding them under a rock in the river. She was then horrified to see the male crocodile try to eat one of his own offspring.

"Why does he do that?" asked Laura.

"The females have to protect their baby crocs from the males, otherwise they'll eat them all. The survival rate for baby crocs is less than ten percent, and that's mostly because their dads like to snack on 'em." Stoically resigned to jungle law, nothing Steve ever saw in the animal kingdom shocked him.

"Sounds like someone we know." Ginny glanced sideways at Laura.

"There are so many different kinds of wildlife here," Steve told Laura one night, as they lay entwined together. "And you have only seen a fraction of it, my sweet." He stroked the hair off her forehead, kissing her softly.

"You love the jungle, don't you?" Laura whispered.

"I must admit I do, my darling." Steve drew her closer to him.

"Can you ever imagine leaving it?" she asked.

"What?" He looked surprised. "Of course not. I'm a jungle boy. 'Me Tarzan—you Jane.' You like it here too, don't you, Laura?"

"I really do," she admitted. "I've never had such a wonderful time, Steve. I don't ever want to go back to Greece."

"Then why go?" His voice became thick. "Stay here with me, Laura. Why don't you?"

"To do what?" She laughed lightly. "It's certainly an appealing thought—but an impossible one—I have a husband and two daughters, remember."

"A husband who's a right bastard, from what I can gather. Life's too short, Laura. Why do you want to go back to him? Now that we've found each other, come and live here with me, here in the camp. I get leave four times a year—we can visit Johannesburg or Cape Town. Johannesburg's a great town. You can visit your kids whenever you want."

"If I leave him, he'll probably get custody anyway," said Laura bitterly. "That's the Greek way."

"I love you, Laura, I haven't said that to any woman before, but it's true, I really am in love with you."

"I love you too, Steve." The words came out before she could stop them, and affectionately she touched his cheek. "I do, I do, but it's not that simple, darling. Not simple at all. I have so much thinking to do."

He drew her close to him, so that their bodies were like one entity and she felt the flickering flame of desire that she knew he was going to fan.

Laura had extended her holiday by another week, when the telephone call came.

"What the hell have you been up to?" The familiar tones made her shrivel inside. "I've been trying to reach you for two days. Atlanta's sick—and you're off gallivanting halfway across the world."

"What do you mean, sick? What's wrong

with her? I didn't know she was ill—how was I supposed to know?"

"Measles," said Nicholas bluntly. "A bad case that's turned into viral pneumonia. I'm on the yacht outside Athens—Atlanta's in our hospital here. You better get back here, Laura, right away, before your daughter dies."

Laura stood at the bedside of her eldest child with a heavy heart. Atlanta's little face was pinched blue-white, her breathing shallow and sporadic, but at least the doctors said she was out of danger.

"It's been a close call," Dr. Margreaux told her gravely. "We didn't think that she would pull through, but she's a strong girl. Although her fever is still high, we believe that she will recover completely now."

"Thank God. Thank you doctor, for all you've done for her."

After he left, Laura sat for some time holding Atlanta's hand and watching her. The thoughts she had had in Africa were crystalizing in her mind.

That night Ginny went to bed right after dinner and Laura sat silently with Nicholas in the pale gray main salon of the *Circe*. It seemed so excessive and overdecorated. There was such a glut of Meissen statues, ormolu clocks, Sèvres vases, and the atmosphere, thick with the scent of Rigeaux candles, was cloying.

Laura now wanted to eliminate all this self-indulgent affluence from her life. How unimportant and trivial these surroundings were, compared to the simplicity and unfettered freedom of the jungle camp.

She glanced at the darkly brooding visage of her husband, with whom she had once been so in love, and felt nothing. She only wished that she was with Steve.

"What are you thinking about?" As if reading her thoughts, Nicholas looked up from his *Financial Times*.

"Nothing." She felt herself flushing and tried to look into the flickering fire.

"You must have been thinking of something." There was sarcasm in his voice, as he stood up and moved closer to study his wife's face. She looked lovely tonight. There was a glow about her that hadn't been there for a long time. Yes, she was still a beautiful woman. So innocent-looking—so pure.

So different from Stefania. That bitch was giving him problems these days. He hadn't been able to see her in a week because she'd been playing one of her hard-to-get games. Real cat and mouse. Nicholas was becoming irritated by it, but there was no else around who interested him at the moment.

"Did you have a good time on safari?" His instincts told him that he was on to something. If she hadn't been having such a good time she would have returned a week ago.

"Yes, I did." She avoided his eyes and moved away to the edge of the sofa.

"What did you do there?" He joined her, sitting close, folding his hands over hers, aware that she had flinched.

"Oh, we saw lots of animals, took tons of photographs, ate a lot—slept a lot—that sort of thing."

"Photographs? Interesting. I'd like to see them," he said pleasantly.

"Oh, they wouldn't interest you, Nicholas," she said nervously.

"*I said* I want to see them, Laura." His hand tightened its grip on hers. "Now."

Wordlessly, Laura went to her room, and returned with a few of the many snapshots she and Ginny had taken, and handed them to Nicholas.

He flicked through without curiosity, until

he came to a laughing one of Ginny with Steve.

"Who's this?" His voice was cool.

"Oh, that's Steve something-or-other—the ranger—you know, our guide, as it were."

"Ah, a safari Romeo. Yes, I've heard of them." He flipped through more photographs until he came to one of Laura and Steve, arm in arm, an unmistakable look of togetherness on their faces. He studied it intently without saying a word, then turned to her, his face impassive.

"Did he fuck you?" he asked.

"Don't be so ridiculous, Nicholas." Laura tried to laugh, but Nicholas grabbed her wrist and held it in a viselike grip.

"He fucked you, didn't he? Of *course* he did. That's just the sort of pathetic romantic interlude you'd like, isn't it, Laura? A romantic fuck by a campfire in the middle of the jungle."

He was twisting her arm behind her back. It was agonizing. "He didn't, I swear."

"'He didn't, I swear,'" he mimicked. "Oh, yes, he did! I can see it all now, like a scene from one of those stupid movies you used to make. The white hunter and the whiter-than-white maiden, falling in love among the jungle beasts."

He forced her arm back even tighter until she screamed with pain as she tried to wrest her arm away. "Stop it, Nicholas, please stop."

"Mama, Papa, please don't fight."

They both turned to the door at the sound of a child whimpering. Atlanta was standing there, crying softly, her face flushed with fever.

Instantly, Nicholas let go of Laura's arm and strode to the door.

"Go to bed, Atlanta, *now*!" His face was red and his voice harsh. "This is none of your business. Mama and Papa are just talking. Now go to bed—do you hear?"

"Yes, go back to bed, darling, please," said Laura weakly.

With a faint sob, Atlanta ran back to her cabin and Nicholas advanced on his wife as if his daughter had never interrupted them.

"Did he make you come?" Nicholas's breath was harsh in her ear and he grabbed her hair. "You never managed it with me, did you?" His voice rose as he was suddenly overpowered by jealousy. "You always faked it, didn't you? Don't think I didn't notice, that's why I lost interest in you—you cold bitch."

"For God's sake, stop." Laura was struggling to get away, but she was helpless in his grip.

"Admit it—you slept with him, you slut."

"No!" She was surprised by the vehemence in her voice, then by her strength as she wrenched her arm from her husband, and stood wild-eyed in front of the carved marble fireplace.

"Yes," she hissed. "Yes, I did go to bed with Steve Badenhorst. And do you want to know why?"

Nicholas stood staring at her, his black eyes burning with fury.

"Because *you* wouldn't. Because you haven't made love to me, except as a sort of *duty*, for years, Nicholas. You think I don't know—you think a woman doesn't notice the difference when a man makes love to her because he wants to, or just to keep her quiet?" Her voice grew. "A charity fuck, Nicholas, that's what you gave me, for most of our marriage. And even when we did make love, after the first year or so I *hated* it because I hated your perversions and knowing you slept with other women. All I wanted was for you to love me, and you couldn't— you wouldn't."

"Shut up!" He took a threatening step toward her. "Shut the fuck up, Laura."

"*I will not shut up!*" she exploded. "I've been shut up for *years*, Nicholas. I've been shut up verbally, shut up emotionally, and shut up on this boat, and on your bloody island. Well, I'm sick of it. I've had enough, and I'm getting away from all of it and from you too."

"Oh no, you're not." He was very close to her now, tall and menacing in the muted light of the salon. "You're my wife, and the mother of my children—you're never leaving."

"Your children!" she almost spat. "You don't give a *damn* about your children, Nicholas. Oh, you care about Venetia because she's like a beautiful little doll, but you loathe Atlanta because she's not pretty. And don't pretend you love me anymore, because you don't, I know you don't. God only knows why you married me—or why I married you. It was a mistake. But it's a mistake that's not too late to change."

"I don't want to hear any more, Laura, go to your room," he ordered.

"Go to my *room*?" She looked at him in amazement and laughed bitterly. "Who do you think you are? Even if your mistresses obey you, I will not go to my room on your orders, I'll go when I damn well feel like it and not before."

"Oh yes, you will."

"No—I won't." Laura's voice was calmer now. The storm had abated and she knew what she was going to do, what she had to do.

"I'm leaving you, Nicholas. As soon as Atlanta's better I'm going to divorce you. I'm still an American citizen, and I shall cite you for grievous mental and physical cruelty—as well as many counts of adultery—and I'll get custody of my children. No American court will let you have them when they hear what I have to say about you and our marriage."

"You're a whore," he hissed. "You dirty, unfaithful bitch. Don't you fucking threaten me, Laura. Don't you ever *dare* threaten me again."

He raised his hand and brought it down with a vicious chopping blow across Laura's cheek. With a cry she fell and her head hit the corner of the marble fireplace with a sickening crack.

Nicholas took a step back and looked at his wife. Her face had turned bluish white and she was unnaturally still. He bent to feel her pulse. It was very weak. With rising panic, Nicholas knelt and put his ear to her heart. There was only the faintest beat, then she moaned, very softly.

"Jesus Christ," he whispered. "Oh my God!" Laura looked as if she were dying.

There was a fully equipped hospital on board and if he raised the alarm now, surely Laura could be saved. But did he want to save her?

Nicholas sank into an armchair and buried his head in his hands. His thoughts raced around in his head, as the life ebbed from Laura's body: She was the mother of his children, but that was all. He hadn't loved her for some time but she was his wife. He stared down at her ice-white face and could almost see death claiming her.

As the dark sky started to lighten, Nicholas knew that his wife was dead. He was about to summon the servants when the door opened and Atlanta stood there again, flushed and feverish.

As soon as she saw her mother she ran to her and threw herself on her.

"What's happened to Mama?" she cried. "She's all white and she's not moving. What's wrong with her?"

The lump in her throat was so large, Atlanta could barely swallow. She started to sob, her shoulders heaving.

"Nothing is wrong with your mother, Atlanta. She's fine. Now go to bed." Nicholas's hair was in wild disarray, his face contorted.

"Mama . . . Mama . . . Mama   . . ." she wailed. "Wake up, Mama."

Laura lay still as stone, her eyes closed. Atlanta could see the tiny blue veins on her lids. She clutched her mother's body, as her own tears dropped onto the beautiful, still face.

Nicholas watched, sweating hard. He closed the door and poured some champagne into a glass.

"What did you do to Mama?" Atlanta sobbed. "Mama's dead—you killed her."

Oh, sweet Jesus. He must think fast. He must do something, otherwise, in spite of his power, he would be accused of murdering his wife.

"Atlanta, listen to me. You know I love your mama, don't you?"

She didn't answer, as she lay curled up beside Laura's body, like a kitten.

"I am going to tell you something now, Atlanta," Nicholas said urgently. He went and knelt on the thick Aubusson carpet and gently picked up the sobbing girl and held her close.

As soon as Atlanta felt the comforting arms of her father she stopped crying, and he, sensing advantage, held her closer, rocking her comfortingly.

Papa was so big and powerful. She loved this feeling of being held and of being protected by him. Nothing could hurt her when Papa was close to her like this. Nothing.

"Now, baby, I want you to listen." Nicholas's voice was at his most beguiling. "Yes, I'm afraid your Mama is dead, and I'm so sorry," he whispered. "She slipped and hit her head, I was just going to call everyone when you came in." Atlanta began wailing so loudly that Nicholas was convinced she would wake the entire boat. Her face was now bright red and her fever seemed to be rising. He offered her a sip of champagne which she drank so greedily that he poured her another. Dimly he realized that he was probably making his ten-year-old child intoxicated, which with her high fever could be dangerous, but Nicholas didn't care. His only concern now was to save himself from the incrimination that would befall him if the au-

thorities discovered that he had done nothing as Laura died in front of him.

He looked down and saw that Atlanta had
fallen asleep, but her breathing was shallow
and her face and body felt fiercely hot. It was
time to do something. Shouting for help,
Nicholas ran through the dimly lit corridors of
the *Circe* until he reached the hospital room.
The doctor took the child from his arms and
immediately summoned nurses and aides.

"Her fever is 105 and rising," said Dr. Margreaux gravely. "This could be very bad after
her pneumonia." An unconscious Atlanta
was put into bed while cold compresses
were applied. Nicholas watched for a few
minutes then slowly retraced his steps to the
salon, where the lifeless body of his wife lay
where he had left her, surrounded now by
the shocked faces of the crew and staff.

CHAPTER FIFTEEN

The intrusive world press staked out Stephanopolis Island for Laura Marlowe's funeral.

There were so many paparazzi and news
photographers in a flotilla of boats a few
yards from the shore that dozens of extra
policemen from Athens had to be drafted to
help.

Nicholas came out of the church first—his
head bowed, his face grim, followed by Lady
Anne and Laura's mother, Pauline, swathed
in black veils; then Laura's daughters walked
behind with Nanny Scotty.

The policemen lining the hundred-yard
walk to the graveside were red-faced, strain-

ing to push back the crowd. Employees, people who worked on the island, and hundreds of Laura's friends and co-workers, who had wanted to pay one last homage to the beloved star, had come to her funeral.

Some reporters and photographers pretending to be workers had managed to infiltrate the island, and they whispered into mini cassettes while others snapped pictures of Nicholas and the girls with hidden cameras, intent on only one thing: getting their best shot or their best headline. Heedless of family grief, photographers and tourists in the boats offshore yelled and screamed out the names of celebrities.

The congregation followed Laura's coffin, which was draped in the American flag, to its final resting place in the family plot, on top of a small hill. Like sharks in a feeding frenzy, the paparazzi went mad, snapping their cameras at everything they saw.

Atlanta was dry-eyed, as was Nicholas, while Venetia, at five, was too young to understand what was going on, as she held the hand of her godmother, Ginny.

A young man who walked behind the crowd looked at the little girl, thinking how much she resembled her mother. A perfect mini version of Laura. His grief-stricken eyes covered by dark glasses, Steve Badenhorst took grim, measured steps, and ensured that he stayed out of Nicholas's sight.

Ginny's face was drenched in tears. She had called Steve as soon as she learned of Laura's death and begged him to come to the funeral. He hadn't believed any of the Greek police's investigations. Although the case had garnered front-page publicity throughout the world, not one paper had hit upon the truth.

According to the coroner and the police, Laura Marlowe had tripped on the rug in front of the marble fireplace in the salon of her luxury yacht, hit her head and died instantly. Her husband had been questioned, as had all the staff and her children, but foul play was not suspected.

Except by Steve Badenhorst. He knew the Greek police would take little notice of his suspicions, what he truly believed to be the truth. No one would listen to the word of a young gamekeeper who had been having an affair with Laura; not when her husband was one of the richest, most powerful men in the world.

Laura had told Steve before she left the

camp that she loved him and wanted to be with him forever. She was going to tell Nicholas that she was leaving him, and although she was frightened of what his reaction would be, her mind was made up.

Steve thought that when Laura confessed to Nicholas, he had lashed out at her and beaten her, as Laura had confided to Steve that he had before.

As the funeral procession arrived at the top of the hill, and Steve saw Laura's coffin lowered into the ground, he knew that if it was the last thing he would ever do, he was going to avenge her death.

Nicholas Stephanopolis was responsible for it and he was going to pay the price.

PART TWO

Atlanta and Venetia

CHAPTER SIXTEEN

After Laura's death her daughters' lives were ruled by a succession of governesses and nannies, and as Atlanta grew more shy and retiring, Venetia, by far her father's favorite, became more outgoing and wild. From the age of twelve, boys flocked around her, and she reveled in their admiration. Although her looks were fragile and feminine, Venetia had a tomboy's mentality and loved athletic pursuits.

Both girls attended school in Athens in the spring and summer and New York in autumn and winter. Every day after school, Venetia would rush to an exclusive country club, the meeting place for all the rich, young elite. There, she would ride or swim or play tennis for hours, laughing and joking with her gang, while Atlanta slunk home to read her books.

From time to time Atlanta would attempt a conversation with her father about school, where she excelled. When she came home excitedly one day and rushed to tell him that she had received straight A's in all her subjects, he had snapped, "Atlanta, can't you see I'm busy? How many times have I told you not to interrupt me during the day?"

Atlanta had left in tears and then shut herself in her room, refusing supper. She still found it hard to accept that her father didn't love her, even though he behaved with total indifference.

Once, she had a part in the school play, *Twelfth Night*, playing Sir Toby Belch, complete with padded stomach and florid make-up. The drama teacher had complimented her on her excellent characterization during rehearsals.

Nicholas had promised to attend, but as the cast took their bows and she searched the audience for his familiar face, Atlanta realized with a sinking feeling that her father had let her down yet again.

As the years passed, Atlanta became increasingly removed from Nicholas. She was not interested in the macho activities that he and Venetia reveled in. Polo, riding and tennis left her cold and she would develop every possible ailment when they tried to get her to join in. But Venetia always went; from the age of five she sat a horse brilliantly, loved playing ball with her father and was fearless in the water.

Atlanta, however, was still nervous around horses, and those canny animals sensed it, playing up whenever she came near them. Rolling their eyes, rearing up on their hind legs, baring their enormous teeth in her direction, they made her shrink against the stable door in terror.

Nicholas mocked Atlanta for her fears, insisting she mount up, and goading her to follow as he and Venetia galloped over the hills and olive groves of their island.

Clinging breathlessly to her mount, Atlanta would close her eyes as she followed them, praying fervently that this agony would soon end.

Once, at the end of their ride, her father had sneered, "You're such a baby. You behave as though that horse is a dragon, Atlanta. They're gentle, sweet animals who just need a bit of affection and love to make them do your bidding."

Like me, she had thought bitterly.

Atlanta poured her feelings into a diary. She seldom allowed herself to think about her mother's death. That night remained locked away in the pit of her memory, along with all the happy recollections of her early childhood and the feeling of closeness she'd once had with her father before Venetia was born.

She committed the day-to-day minutiae of school life to paper and, during the holidays, she would glean exciting material from the rumors and gossip that always surrounded her father's glittering parties and cruises. As she wrote about them in her diary. she re-created a glamorous, thrilling world for herself.

Venetia seemed born to be a jet-setter and Nicholas indulgently encouraged her in her excesses. He taught her from an early age the art of spending money freely. He gave her an unlimited allowance, and by the time she was fourteen, a platinum American Express card. Venetia threw herself into a he-

donistic lifestyle with easy alacrity and an in-
stinctive understanding for all its rules.

Alain Bartond, the son of a French diplo-
mat, was Venetia's closest friend. He, like
the Stephanopolis children, was one of the
gilded youth of Athens, and his father,
Jean-Noel, was one of Nicholas's closest
friends. The youngsters shared the same
reckless spirit and a love of clowning and
carousing.

At Christmas, both the Stephanopolis and
Bartond families always went to St. Moritz,
where they owned adjacent chalets. Each
morning, Alain and Venetia would be the first
on the highest *piste*, each racing down as
many times as they could.

At lunchtime the dazzling duo would com-
mandeer the most prominent table at the
Corvigla Club, and luxuriate in the fawning
sycophancy of their friends. But it wasn't too
long before the aperitif and the bottle of wine
with lunch and dinner were not enough to
satisfy their young appetites.

One night, when both families were in
Paris for the weekend, curiosity and high
spirits led them to the most notorious leather
bar in France. Located in a dark and narrow

back street, Madame Jo-Jo's was not the kind of place that the locals frequented.

Madame Jo-Jo was actually Joey Johnson, an ex-Marine from Kansas City who had taken his passion for black leather and blond boys to new heights during one long-ago weekend in Cannes. While playing roulette he had broken the bank at the casino so many times that the casino had to have three policemen escort him and his money back to his "pensione."

Joey had used his new money to open Madame Jo-Jo's to a discreet group of homosexuals, and the club soon became extremely popular, developing a worldwide reputation for wild licentiousness.

Although the local authorities had made some attempts to have it closed down, there was nevertheless nothing in French law that considered it an offense to wear leather, chains and an abundance of cosmetics—even if you did happen to be a man. None of the local residents felt the need to complain, because most of the boys and "girls" behaved themselves outside the portals of the establishment.

Alain and Venetia were at the King's Club,

a sophisticated disco. They had been there for an hour and were becoming bored.

"Where shall we go?" yawned Venetia.

"Madame Jo-Jo's," said Alain slyly. "To-night is *La Cage Aux Folles* night. People can only get in if they're dressed as a woman—the more outrageous the drag the better. All you have to do is borrow some of your mother's old costumes and we'll be in!"

"But how can we get in?" she asked, excited at the prospect of a new adventure, which at fourteen was the very spice of life to her. She wanted to experiment—to experience exhilarating thrills. "You know they'll recognise us. Father will be *furious* if he finds out. He doesn't mind us coming here, but Madame Jo-Jo's is the kind of place that's definitely out of bounds."

"You're chicken, admit it," teased Alain. "Didn't you say your mother kept her old movie costumes down in the cellar of your house here?"

"I'm *not* about to raid Mama's closets," Venetia said firmly.

"Come on, we'll just borrow a couple of things," persisted Alain, lighting up a small cheroot. "Those flapper dresses she wore in that twenties movie, with all the beads hanging everywhere. I'd look great in one of those."

Venetia laughed. "You sound really turned on by all this."

"She had those great wigs, short ones with the ostrich feathers stuck in them. C'mon, Venetia. Just for tonight. No one will know. We'll put everything back, neat as a pin, tomorrow, I promise."

"OK. Why not? If the only way we can get into Madame Jo-Jo's is in drag, let's do it. I've always wanted to see what those old queens get up to."

They both looked exquisite. Although Alain was a few inches taller than Venetia, the perfection of the beautifully constructed beaded flapper dresses that slithered over their lithe young bodies made them head turners. Their makeup was immaculate and they wore identical short blonde bobbed wigs and, across their foreheads, embroidered bands of beads that held tall aigrette feathers.

Outside Madame Jo-Jo's the grille opened, and a disembodied voice demanded fifty francs.

Then the door opened and black Ray-Bans swiftly appraised the costumes.

"New here?"

"Don't be silly, *dear*," drawled Alain. "You know us well—but no prizes for guessing. Tell you at the end of the evening."

"And we *shall* go to the ball," he whispered as a bouncer opened the velvet curtains with a flourish.

They both gaped at the scene before them. The tiny dance floor was a sea of writhing male bodies, most of them outfitted in resplendent female costumes.

Marilyn Monroes danced with Dolly Partons, Barbarellas writhed with Barbra Streisands, Dietrichs strutted and shimmered with Judy Garlands.

The two teenagers stood on the edge of the dance floor while a dozen pairs of eyes watched them.

Everyone was dancing, groping, and some were kissing lasciviously. The atmosphere was festive, but there was an undercurrent of sleaze as drugs were passed and assignations were made.

A young reporter had followed Alain and Venetia from the King's Club and then managed to gain entrance into Madame Jo-Jo's by greasing the outstretched palm at the door. She wore a black lace mantilla to cover her head and tried to blend into the background.

Various "girls" kept sidling up to Alain and Venetia, batting fake eyelashes, begging them to dance, but they refused. In spite of their precocious sophistication and the fact that they'd been hanging out in discos since the age of twelve, neither had ever seen anything remotely like this before.

"Wanna toke?" A Marilyn lookalike sidled up, proffering a homemade joint. Alain shook his head but Venetia grabbed it.

"Don't be a drag, you're in drag, so have a drag!"

She grabbed the roach and inhaled it deeply. From behind a pillar, the hack snapped the shutter of her minuscule high-speed camera. Once, twice, three times. "Got it," she breathed. "*Great* shots. The tabloids will love it."

Venetia leaned affectionately on Marilyn's shoulder and laughingly blew a smoke ring into Alain's disapproving face.

"You're crazy, Venetia, y'know that?" Alain could hardly be heard above the sounds of Gloria Gaynor wailing "I Will Survive."

"Oh shut up, Alain." Venetia took another deep drag and passed it back to the waiting transvestite, who gave her a wet kiss on the lips before ambling off.

The reporter watched triumphantly and then followed discreetly as Alain and Venetia strolled into the next room. She used her tiny state-of-the-art camera to surreptitiously take as many pictures of Venetia and Alain as possible.

"Coke, darlings?" An Amazonian redhead, dressed in strapless black satin with matching opera gloves smiled at them, spoiling the Rita Hayworth illusion by revealing bad teeth. "A hundred francs a snort, my loves."

"No thank you, ma'am," said Alain, firmly grabbing Venetia's arm.

"Yes please, ma'am," insisted Venetia, even more firmly, quickly passing "Rita" a hundred-franc note.

"Venetia, that stuff's poison—you're mad."

"Stop *fussing*, Alain, I feel like I'm out with my nanny instead of my best friend. I haven't tried coke yet."

"That stuff'll drive you crazy, Venetia, I'm warning you. You'll turn into a maniac."

"OK, OK—you're a real museum piece

tonight, Alain. Just *how's* it going to turn me into a monster?"

"It will. I've seen people do it. They get addicted right away."

"Well, this girl won't." Venetia grinned, pocketing the tiny envelope. "Let's go try it. I'm getting bored here."

"OK, let's go to my place," said Alain reluctantly. "Everyone's away, we'll be able to chill out there. You're a bad influence on me, y'know that?"

"Hey, coming here was your idea," said Venetia, as they pushed their way through the dancers toward the exit. Outside in the cobbled street, they leaned against the wall and Venetia began laughing hysterically.

"Did you *see* that gross one with the hairy bosoms?" Venetia laughed. "He looked like the Teddy Bear from Hell. What *was* he dressed as?"

"I think he was trying for the Cleopatra look."

Venetia was convulsed by giggles.

"That grass has really had an effect—you're wild."

"You know, darling, you look cute dressed as a girl. I think I quite fancy you." Venetia bent forward and licked Alain's ear, then drew back until their noses touched.

"I've never slept with a boy dressed as a girl," she confessed.

"Neither have I," said Alain huskily, his hands stroking Venetia's shoulder.

"We should try everything at least once. Let's go home and experiment."

As they ran laughing down the icy street, the photographer who had been watching took off her mantilla and smiled. It was Atlanta. She turned in the opposite direction and ran back to her house, eager to develop the incriminating photographs of her younger sister. Atlanta now knew quite a bit about her sister's exploits, although she wasn't planning on showing the photos to anyone. She had also discovered that she really enjoyed acting as an undercover reporter.

"Maybe I'll take it up professionally," she muttered.

CHAPTER SEVENTEEN

As the daughters of the famous and beloved Laura Marlowe, Atlanta and Venetia had always held interest for the world's tabloids.

Neither of them had done anything particularly scandalous or outrageous, so when a telephone call from the Greek embassy in London informed Nicholas that a gutter tabloid had a story on his daughter, he arranged for the offending paper to be dispatched to Paris on the first flight out of Heathrow.

Nicholas and his mother stared at it chillingly.

"What *is* she doing? My God, why is she

being so foolish?" said Lady Anne. "And who is that girl with her—do you know her?"

"It's not a girl, Mother." Nicholas stared grimly at the photograph. "Can't you see it's Alain, and it looks to me as if he's wearing one of Laura's dresses from *The Most Beautiful Girl in New York*."

Atlanta had overheard Nicholas's last sentence just as she was about to enter, and quickly turned away from the door. She had panicked a week ago when she noticed that the pictures of Venetia she had left on her desk had gone missing—but she told herself that one of the maids must have put them away. Now it was clear that someone had sold them to the press. Atlanta was horrified and decided that she had better make herself scarce.

Atlanta heard the dismay in her grandmother's voice as she tiptoed away. "At a gay bar dressed as a girl! Nicholas, have you no control over this child?" Lady Anne threw down the paper in disgust. "She's only fourteen. It's disgraceful."

"I thought I had control, Mother," said Nicholas dryly. "But I think the time has finally come to lay down a few more rules."

*   *   *

Venetia groaned. Her head felt as if it was full of cotton wool soaked in petrol and her mouth tasted as if a family of baboons had just moved out.

"I'm a corpse," she whispered to herself. "Let me die now, Lord, I can't face today."

There was a sharp rap on the door and before she could answer, her father stormed in, brandishing a newspaper.

"Hello Papa," Venetia purred as she tried to sit up. "How are you?"

"What is the meaning of this, Venetia?"

"What are you talking about, Papa?"

"Don't play the innocent with me, Venetia. You know perfectly well what I'm talking about. Look at this disgusting photograph." He threw the paper on the bed and Venetia stared at a picture of two girls kissing in smudged black-and-white.

"Oh Papa, that's only *Alain.*" Venetia started to laugh although her father's face was a thundercloud.

"I *know* it's Alain," Nicholas said coldly. "I recognized him. Unfortunately, the newspapers did not, and even if they did, I think it's absolutely *shocking* that you should dare to borrow your mother's clothes to visit some homosexual dive, then be photographed kissing a girl."

"Oh Papa, there's no harm in kissing." Venetia willed her father to leave. He was making her head throb.

"Your grandmother is also extremely upset with you, Venetia. You've become a laughingstock. All morning my press secretary has had to deal with reporters and journalists ringing from all over Europe. They believe you are kissing a homosexual—a transvestite. It is extremely embarrassing for all of us, Venetia, terrible for my business, and a scandal for our family. Surely you must realize that?"

"Yes, Papa, and I'm sorry." Venetia groaned. Oh, leave Papa, leave, she willed. Go. Go back to one of your offices, make some more takeovers, only leave me, *please*, please *go*.

"I won't do it again," she said meekly. "I promise, Papa, truly I do."

"I'm really disgusted with you, Venetia—it makes you look like a pervert. For God's sake, you're not even fifteen yet."

"It was just a little joke, Papa. We were kidding around like we do. It backfired and I'm really sorry. Tell Grandmother I'm sorry too. Oh dear!" she moaned theatrically. "I feel so sick, Papa, I don't feel well at all."

Nicholas's rare paternal instinct went into gear. "Were you drinking again last night?"

"No, no, of course not," she lied. "It's just cramps—girl's things. I'll be all right, Papa. I must go to sleep now, I really must."

"All right." Nicholas stood up, his stern face melting. "Rest now. But I'm warning you, Venetia, do not ever embarrass the family or me like this again. You know how much you mean to me. Will you promise me that?"

"Yes, Papa," said Venetia meekly. At last he was leaving. "I promise I'll never embarrass you or the family again. I'll be a good girl. Just what you want me to be."

"I know you will, kitten." He hugged her, looking at her almost adoringly. "Your daddy loves you. Don't you forget that, will you?"

"No, Papa, I won't," she said and blew him a kiss.

Like an animal who has tasted first blood, the European gossip columns suddenly found they had new prey to feed on. Newspaper and magazine editors lost no time in making the beautiful Venetia Stephanopolis one of the most written about and controversial teenagers of 1988.

Atlanta's name was hardly ever mentioned and the world knew little about her. She retreated more and more into what she thought of as her unattractive shell, as her father's indifference became more apparent each year.

Boys held little interest to Atlanta and since they had zero interest in her, she was resigned to being alone. That is until the night she met Kevin Bentley again, whom she hadn't seen since her mother's funeral.

Nicholas had been throwing one of his formal dinner parties when, at the last moment, the Duchess of Seville had been taken ill. In desperation, Nicholas had insisted that his elder daughter take her place.

So Atlanta now sat, uncomfortably, in an overly expensive, hideously unflattering couture dress listening uninterestedly to the buzz of cosmopolitan small talk.

Kevin Bentley, who had remained in touch with the family over the years since Laura's death, was seated to the right of Stefania, whose famous breasts were oozing out of her low-cut purple satin dress. He seemed hard-pressed to keep his eyes off them.

Atlanta observed Kevin's attempts to flirt with Stefania with a pang of envy while she signaled to the butler for more caramel sauce for her *tarte aux pommes*. After all, Stefania was not only unbelievably sexy but also one of the most famous actresses in Europe. Who wouldn't desire her?

Stefania was gazing into Kevin's smallish green eyes, which on screen always gave the impression of being larger than they were. He was telling a joke, and they were laughing together conspiratorially. Kevin glanced at Atlanta, who blushed and lowered her head in embarrassment.

Atlanta had never been interested in boys, but Kevin Bentley was hardly a boy. Pushing fifty, although holding the years at bay with a daily program of vigorous exercises, considerable vitamin intake and as much screwing as he could manage, he had been one of America's leading heartthrobs for over twenty-five years and was still in possession of the boyish sex appeal that allowed him to charm as many women into his bed as possible. Never married, he preferred famous women, actresses, heiresses and celebrities, and he never cared a whit if they were already spoken for.

Kevin lived for the chase and the conquest and his string of liaisons with celebrated actresses went back to the beginning of his career, when he had indulged in a torrid affair with a young actress, the daughter of a famous actor. Their romance had been given major coverage in every fan magazine, and guaranteed that Kevin was almost a household name, even before he signed for his first starring role, opposite actress Coral Steele when she was young.

After *Summer Daydream* became a major box-office success, to ensure that he remained firmly in Hollywood's consciousness, Kevin embarked on a sizzling affair with his leading lady. It didn't take long for gorgeous newlywed Coral to dump her young husband and move in with Kevin, which created scandalous headlines, and caused even more people to join the queues for the film.

When Kevin Bentley's movie stardom was assured, he soon developed a network of influential friends—producers and directors, studio heads and agents—and he usually spent most of his day talking on the telephone, pushing ideas for scripts, and exchanging gossip.

During dinner Atlanta found herself unable to tear her eyes away from Kevin, whom she hadn't seen since her mother's funeral. But he would never be interested in me, she thought. At nineteen she was still a virgin, while her fourteen-year-old sister was getting the reputation of being quite a wild child.

Later that night Atlanta stood naked in front of her full-length mirror. It was a sight she hated but she needed to do it. She had to force herself to be objective about just how bad she looked, so that she could do something about it. She shuddered at her reflection. God must have been out to lunch when he was handing out physical attributes the day I was born, she thought.

There was no doubt that she had to lose a lot of weight from all over. Atlanta focused on each part of her body. Her large black eyes were hooded by lids which she thought made her look like a frog. Her lips were too thick. Her teeth were small and still crooked, in spite of the endless dentistry she had undergone. But it was her nose that she considered her worst feature. Thick and masculine, it seemed to dominate her face, casting a shadow over her mouth and chin. "It's so long it comes into the room before you do," Venetia had taunted her when they were children.

Her chin was fine but, because of the extra weight, it was a double chin, and sometimes, if she had been overindulgent in the chocolate department, it was a triple one.

She managed to keep her faint mustache at bay with an agonizing preparation called Eazy Off. But this unfortunately gave her spots, a plethora of which cruised across her upper lip and over her cheeks. As for the hair on her body, she seemed to be fighting an almost daily battle with depilatory creams and razors.

All in all, she was a mess, and it was about time she did something positive about herself. She recalled the conversation she'd had with Stefania in the powder room after dinner. Stefania had looked at her sympathetically as she sighed in dismay while trying to pull down her too-tight gown. "I look like a baby buffalo," Atlanta had exclaimed despairingly. "I *hate* the way I look."

"*Cara, cara,* stop," Stefania had said, stroking Atlanta's long luxuriant hair. "If you *really* want to do something about yourself you can."

"What?" blurted Atlanta, "I've tried a million diets and I end up fatter. What can I do?"

"Have you heard of The Last Resort?" inquired Stefania. "They can do miracles—I know, *cara*—several of my actress friends have gone there and they've returned like new women. Now, *cara*, I'm going to give you some of the best advice a girl ever got."

Maybe, if she looked better, Kevin Bentley might become interested in her. Maybe even make love to her. Atlanta blushed at the thought. If she did something about her weight and spots, then just maybe, *someone* would fall in love with her. It was time to change the dreary pattern of her life.

It was time to take charge.

Three days later, Atlanta bade her father good-bye, saying she was off on her first journalistic assignment in Rome.

Since her father had never before cared about where she was or whom she was with, he didn't really listen to what Atlanta said.

"Good-bye, Father, I'll be gone several months. But don't worry about me, I'll be just fine."

"I'm sure you will, dear." Nicholas barely looked up from his desk. "Don't forget to write." They exchanged perfunctory kisses. "Oh and Atlanta, send Venetia in on your way out, will you?"

"Yes, Father," she said meekly, closing the heavy oak door as a little voice inside her crowed gleefully, "You're free, Atlanta—at last. Time to get up and go, and make something of your life!"

CHAPTER EIGHTEEN

The major had remembered him, even after the years that had passed, when Kristobel had called him from Grand Central Terminal in New York, after five dusty days by Greyhound bus from Tijuana. He had 350 dollars in his jeans and high hopes in his head as he pressed the brass bell on the front door of the smart brownstone house on East 88th Street.

The major opened the door, still very much the military man in mufti. Gray whipcord trousers, blue shirt with stiff white collar, tweed jacket with leather elbow patches and a military tie.

He seemed pleased to see Kristobel and urged him to stay in the guest room until he got settled in New York.

"It's no trouble at all," he insisted. "You remind me of myself as a young man. I know how difficult life is in the city for a boy alone."

The major introduced Kristobel to his wife, Lavinia, who was delighted when Kristobel opened his case to reveal five hand-embroidered and beaded evening gowns that he had painstakingly sewn by hand over the past two years. She had a passion for clothes herself and was keen to show Kristobel her collection. Opening her wardrobe with a flourish, she revealed an eclectic range of vintage women's clothes.

"I collect them," she explained. "After my mother died, I couldn't bear to throw her things away, so I kept them, then when our son-in-law needed some ideas, I went to the thrift shops and looked for some dresses for his collections. Don't you love this?"

She pulled out a 1930s Balenciaga gown, still in mint condition, and held it up against herself. Kristobel made appreciative noises as he admired the outfit.

Later, when Lavinia examined the dresses that Kristobel had made himself, she exclaimed with pleasure, "Oh, I love your things—you have a true talent."

Kristobel lived with the military man and his wife in their brownstone for two years, during which time he worked in their son-in-law's clothing factory. He grew to love them like family and soon became an assistant to one of the designers, Bruce Winters. Bruce, realizing the boy was extremely talented, allowed Kristobel to design some of the range.

Then one day, arriving home early, Kristobel was confronted by a horrific scene: the major's and Lavinia's lifeless bodies covered in blood on the kitchen floor.

It didn't take the police long to find their killer, a vagrant who lived and slept in Central Park. He had crept in through a back window while the couple were preparing supper and stabbed them viciously with the knife with which Lavinia had been gutting Cornish game hens.

During the trial, Kristobel sat in the spectators' gallery every day, watching the loathsome tramp, listening to his slick lawyer whitewashing the truth. The lawyer, provided by New York State, swayed the jury into believing that the homeless man had been of diminished responsibility because he had drunk three bottles of cheap red wine and ingested a quantity of hash.

Kristobel locked eyes with the man as he was led away, grinning, to serve a token nine months for inadvertent manslaughter. Kristobel vowed that he would never forgive him and that he would one day avenge the death of his friends.

The dress had cost fifty-five thousand dollars.

Ten seamstresses had toiled for several months to complete the gorgeous creation. Now it lay crumpled and discarded on the backseat of a cab.

"They said to bring it back here," said the driver, handing it to Bruce Winters, Kristobel's partner.

"Thanks," Bruce said through gritted teeth.

"That'll be seven ninety," prompted the driver.

Bruce handed him a ten-dollar note.

"Keep the change," he sighed, retrieving forty yards of crumpled white embroidered satin from the taxi's dusty floor.

Ten pairs of eyes followed Bruce as he entered the workroom, the dress slung casually over his arm.

"Here you are, girls," he said. "Here it is once again. Your favorite old friend, the wedding frock featuring ten thousand dollars' worth of the best Austrian rhinestones, twenty-five pounds of fine crystal beads and a thousand pearls. And the bitch only wore the thing for an hour and a half."

Disapproving clucking noises came from the long-suffering Hispanic workers, whose fingers moved ceaselessly over swatches of satin, lace and chiffon. They listened to Bruce with a patience born of hard work and gratitude for their jobs. Kristobel and Bruce made it their business to hire as many immigrant workers as possible, and they treated them all extremely well.

"Kristobel will have a fit," muttered Bruce. "A fucking fit. And the bloody father didn't even let us take a photograph of her in it," he snapped.

"But at least we got paid," murmured Carolyn, the head vendeuse, chic and slim in her orange Chanel rip-off.

"Well, luvvies," said Bruce cheerfully, "clean it up and chuck it back in the cupboard with the rest of the stock. They might want it back one day, for one of the other daughters."

When Bruce entered his private quarters, Kristobel didn't raise his eyes from the drawing board.

"Well," he inquired, "how did she look?"

"How the hell do I know how she looked?" Bruce sulkily threw himself into an Empire sofa covered in fake leopard skin and exhaled heavily. "When Carolyn and I arrived at the hotel with the dress at seven o'clock, she was still having her hair washed."

Kristobel stood back from his sketch and frowned slightly. "So?" he said in his almost nonaccented voice. "What's the problem with that?"

"The problem with *that*, my dear, is that her bleedin' hair comes all the way down to her arse and the wedding was meant to be at half past."

"So, what happened?"

"Well, Hugh was buzzing about like a blue-arsed fly—*three* assistants he had, all with fuckin' hairdryers goin' like jet engines. Do you think the little bitch would stand still? Not for a second. She was jumping about all over the place, giggling with all her female entourage."

Kristobel raised his dark glasses for a second and took a step back to admire his drawing. He flicked his eyes briefly to Bruce, signaling him to continue.

"Well, finally Little Miss Princess was ready, having kept the guests waiting for an hour. She goes down to the ballroom, where they must have bought every white flower in New York, and shows up for less than ninety minutes! What a little cow."

"Why don't you go and take a small quantity of poison, Bruce dear?" suggested Kristobel silkily. "It may help to calm you down. And forget about the dress. Next time any of *that* royal family want something to wear, it'll cost them treble."

"Right." Bruce was annoyed. Kristobel was acting like he was boss, when actually, Bruce was in charge. But he had never guessed that his clients would end up preferring Kristobel's designs. Even Stefania Scalerina, who had practically discovered Bruce and had been loyal to him for years, now preferred Kristobel's work.

Oh well, philosophized Bruce, as he stared at a framed photograph of Stefania wearing one of his jewel-encrusted dresses, at least he's good for business. He knows just what the customers seem to want, and besides, the money keeps rolling in.

CHAPTER NINETEEN

Dr. Milton Hoffard had refused to perform any surgery on Atlanta's body until she had lost a lot of weight.

He confessed he was not the best man for breast augmentation anyway. That would be Dr. Kay in Beverly Hills, who was the acknowledged "King of the Bosom," but Dr. Hoffard agreed to do her face after she had lost twenty pounds. On his sophisticated computer he showed Atlanta how she would look with a smaller nose, more shapely lips and surgery on her eyelids.

"Oh yes," breathed Atlanta. "Oh yes—

that's exactly how I want to look. Yes, yes, yes."

Atlanta went to stay for three months at the Last Resort, the spa in Arizona recommended by Stefania, existing on a diet of 750 calories a day. There she lost the requisite twenty pounds—and another ten on top of that. It was a stringent regimen. Woken up at seven-thirty, Atlanta was allowed one cup of sugarless tea, then she followed her trainer and a dozen other suffering women for a three-mile jog through hills and forests. Breakfast consisted of half a papaya or mango and another cup of tea, and lunch was two ounces of broccoli and a piece of fish or chicken so tiny that Atlanta could have swallowed the whole thing in one mouthful. Dinner was only marginally more generous. She often felt even hungrier after meals than before.

So Atlanta suffered. Her body ached from fierce workouts and the endless aerobics and tough exercise regimens.

"Feel the burn!" shrieked the skinny woman in the brown track suit who put everyone through their agonizing paces twice a day and seemed to revel in their

pain, as the sweat poured from their strain-
ing bodies. "Suffer, girls—suffer. No pain, no
gain!"

In the afternoons there were optional
classes: deportment, elocution, makeup and
skin care, and dancing lessons. Atlanta went
to them all, determined to make the most of
every second. At the end of each painful
week of starvation and aching joints, she
could see in her mirror how much better she
looked.

In the back of her mind lurked a picture of
Kevin Bentley, his hundred-watt smile focused on her.

Atlanta was now ready for her plastic surgery. The operation took more than three
hours, and when Atlanta came around from
the anesthetic, she found she couldn't move
any part of her face at all.

"I can barely see," she mumbled in terror
to the nurse. "I've gone blind."

Dr. Hoffard soothed her fears, and assured her that all was going according to
plan.

She stayed at his Malibu clinic for ten
days, at the end of which the doctor took her

into his surgery and slowly peeled off the bandages on her face.

What she saw in the mirror made Atlanta scream with horror. "I look like I've been in a car accident," she cried through blackened lips, which she still had difficulty moving.

"Yes, that's perfectly true, but perfectly normal." Hoffard examined his work with a gratifying smile. "Most people do look dreadful after this surgery. Don't forget you've had as radical a procedure as it's possible to have. You're lucky: only because of your youth were we able to do as much. With older people we must be extremely careful. You've had a complete facial overhaul. We've reshaped your nose and your chin, your lips have been redesigned, and we've inserted silicone implants to make your upper lip fuller. We've removed some of the excess skin from your eyelids and the bags underneath your eyes. We've also given you 'Ava Gardner' cheekbones and taken away that fat from under your chin."

"No wonder I don't feel so good," breathed Atlanta.

Dr. Hoffard patted her on the hand reassuringly. "You're going to thank me a million times over in a few weeks' time. Believe me, Atlanta, you're going to look absolutely fantastic."

Maybe this could be her first article, thought Atlanta. Firsthand face-lift report. It could be a great human interest story. She would describe everything, including the agony.

She reexamined her bloated face, crisscrossed with black stitches. "But how long will I look like this? I look like a road map of Athens."

"Each day you will look a little better. Just be patient. You'd be amazed at what I'm able to do for some of my patients. There is an old Japanese proverb. "You must learn to eat time." Soon you will be a very happy girl, Atlanta. Your whole life is going to change now, I promise you."

A month later, Atlanta left Dr. Hoffard's clinic with a brand-new face and, although it was still swollen, when she looked in the mirror, this new face gave her great pleasure.

During this time of transformation, Atlanta kept in touch with her father by telephone. She never revealed where she was, but wove a web of half truths about her whereabouts.

After her successful facial surgery had healed, Atlanta went to see the highly recommended Dr. Kay, rated the number-one "breast man" in America. She showed him a photograph of Bo Derek in the movie *10*. "These are the breasts I want. Can you make them for me?"

"Of course I can. At the Kay Clinic we make miracles happen every day." And so he did.

Atlanta didn't tell her father she was returning to their home in Paris. She had wanted to surprise him. Arriving in her room in the Avenue Foch via the back stairs, she buzzed Nicholas on the intercom.

"I'm back, Father."

"You've been gone a long time. Where are you now, Atlanta?"

"Upstairs," trilled Atlanta, "in my room. Are you free?"

"Yes, but I'm only alone for a few minutes, I've a meeting at four o'clock."

Moments later, Atlanta tapped on the oak door of her father's inner sanctum.

"Come in," called the familiar voice, and Atlanta entered.

For a few seconds Nicholas stared at her almost open-mouthed in shock, then he said, "Good God! What the hell have you done to yourself?"

"Do you like the new me, Father? Do you think I look pretty?"

"Pretty?" He frowned, and stepped back to inspect her, trying to control his reaction. "Yes, I suppose you are. My God, I would never have recognized you—you look completely different, Atlanta."

"But do you like it?" She hated herself for wanting his approval so much. "Do you *really* think I look good? Isn't it an improvement?"

"It's a shock, I can assure you. To see the child you've known all your life turn into a . . . different person, well—I suppose it's an improvement," he admitted. "Your hair's still a mess, though."

Atlanta bit her lip. Would this father of hers ever be satisfied?

The door of his study suddenly burst open and, in a flurry of floor-length cashmere and sable, Stefania rushed in.

"Hi Stefania," said Atlanta to the woman she no longer resented. "What do you think?"

"My, my!" Stefania smiled. "*Dio*, Atlanta. If it wasn't for your voice I wouldn't have known you, *cara*. You're beautiful, *molto bella*."

Atlanta looked over to her father, who was

at his desk and seemed to have forgotten about her, as he riffled through papers.

Stefania felt a twinge of compassion as she saw the disappointed look on Atlanta's lovely new face. She took a step back, the better to study every detail of Atlanta's incredible new look, then smiled. "Nicholas, don't you think it's amazing? Such an improvement, what Atlanta has done. She looks *fantastico*, no?"

He looked up. "Improvement? Yes, I already told her it is. You look much better than you did, Atlanta."

Stefania gave a deprecating shrug in Nicholas's direction and the two women looked at each other, suddenly sharing that age-old sisterly bond of females against males. For a moment Atlanta had a rare glimpse into what Stefania might also have to suffer with this cold, domineering man.

"What are the plans for tonight?" Nicholas asked Stefania.

"We're dining at Maxim's with the Fabris," she said gaily. "And we're taking Atlanta with us."

Stefania took her lover's daughter under her enthusiastic wing. Atlanta had never had much interest in clothes, but since they were

Stefania's passion, she let herself be hustled off to Stefania's favorite couturier.

"His name is Kristobel. He's new, talented and already one of the best in Paris," she said, as they strolled into the sleek glass-fronted building on the Faubourg St. Honoré, for which a group of rich American business-men had put up the money.

"He will supply you with *everything* you need to wear. He's a magician, aren't you, *caro*?"

"You overestimate me, my dear." Kristobel smiled and came forward to greet them. Although only in his late twenties, he had an ageless look about him, with a smooth, un-lined complexion, melancholy eyes and long, black hair pulled back in a tight pony-tail. His lips brushed the back of Atlanta's hand, his eyes flickering over her expensive but dull gray suit.

"*Bellissima*," he whispered. "Your face is divine, your body excellent, your hair beauti-ful. You are quite ravishing, mademoiselle. I shall make it my business to make you even more so."

Stefania had never had a proper girlfriend for very long, and Atlanta's girlish enthusiasm for everything Stefania was teaching her was infectious.

"I have to go to Cannes next week. My movie is opening." Stefania was admiring Atlanta's reflection as Kristobel pinned delicate folds of pink chiffon to her svelte frame. "Would you like to come with us? I'm taking Kristobel too."

"Oh, I'd love to." Atlanta was mesmerized by her reflection. "I've never been to the film festival before. Mama told me it was wonderful."

"Oh, it is." Stefania, arranging a black velvet wrap on her creamy shoulders, envisaged herself on the Croisette, the focus of all eyes, while the paparazzi fought for photographs of her. "On the one hand, it is the ultimate in glamour . . ."

"And on the other?" asked Atlanta.

"On the other," trilled Stefania, "the ultimate in sleaze."

Atlanta wondered if Kevin Bentley might show up at the festival and what he would think of the new improved Atlanta Stephanopolis.

They flew to Cannes in Nicholas's private jet. Their arrival had been announced

through Stefania's press agent, so the tarmac was awash with press and photographers.

Stefania was admired by European
moviegoers and she fulfilled all the expecta-
tions of the media, who were still hungry for
copy about her. She was a true movie
queen, still beautiful at thirty-six, and still involved in a torrid romance with one of the
leading tycoon-industrialists of the day. So
when she appeared at the top of the steps of
the Gulf Stream II, the paparazzi went into
feeding frenzy. Her hourglass figure was
sheathed in a tight green suit and a matching hat was slanted provocatively over one
eye. Stefania milked the moment for all it
was worth.

At the bottom of the steps, on a short red
carpet, the president of the Cannes Film
Festival waited with various other dignitaries
eager to greet her. A posse of policemen
stood to attention, flanking the carpet, their
eyes riveted to the gorgeous star who
sashayed regally down the steps.

But they did a double take when the last
occupant of the plane descended. After
Nicholas, Kristobel and Stefania's maid had
descended, Atlanta appeared at the door,

the afternoon sun glinting on her glossy waist-length hair.

She wore a simple white cotton jacket, shaped to her body, with gold buttons down the front, a white pleated skirt, and a little white hat like a French sailor's cap.

The photographers' inquisitive lenses followed the two women into the limousine with its smoked windows, and then several of them hopped onto their motorbikes to pursue the motorcade to Cap d'Antibes. But since no press or photographers were admitted unless by invitation to the Hotel Du Cap, the most exclusive of all the hotels on the Côte d'Azur, two policemen shooed them away at the wrought-iron gates.

"The Riviera!" breathed Atlanta, stepping out onto the brilliant white marble of their enormous terrace. "It's gorgeous isn't it, Stefania?"

"Yes, *cara*." Stefania was slightly concerned that she might have made a mistake in allowing Atlanta to accompany her to this madhouse. She looked so wildly beautiful that Stefania could see that Atlanta might upstage her. In fact, Atlanta was such an alluring attraction that Stefania wondered if she might not be well advised to send her home immediately. But she looked so sweet standing on the balcony, gazing in excited awe at the view, that Stefania just didn't have the heart.

"Now, Atlanta, with your looks you know you'd better be careful," she said sternly. "There are predators out there. Sharks. And I don't mean in the sea . . . aren't there, Nicholas?"

"Right." He didn't look up from a handful of telexes. "Be careful, Atlanta."

"Of course I shall, Father. Aren't I always?"

Nicholas was still finding it hard to reconcile the vision of this beautiful girl with the plain creature she had been before.

"Oh, Atlanta might have changed on the outside," Stefania said later, as they lay on their bed after another lovemaking session. "But underneath she's the same little insecure girl—believe me."

Since Nicholas's interest in Atlanta was only ever peripheral, he dismissed her from his mind. After all, she was twenty. Quite old enough to get on with her own life, to make something of herself. Besides, he had business matters on his mind.

*   *   *

Fabio Di Navaro skimmed quickly through the meager pile of mail, consisting mostly of circulars and junk giveaways advertising sex shows and porno flicks.

He had been expecting an invitation to the gala party being given after the screening tonight of the Stefania Scalerina movie.

"Who the fuck wants to see an Italian art film anyway?" he mused angrily to himself. "You do," said his inner voice. "You need to." He had been trying to break into the production side of movies for two years now. With his partner, Marcello Lupe, he had made two cheap soft-porn films, but now they had the rights to a hot new script that could make a great movie, and Stefania was perfect for the lead role.

Fabio had plied Beryl, the plain PR girl, with an abundance of Kir Royal the previous night, as they had sat on the terrace of the Carlton Hotel, surrounded by high rollers, con artists, and film moguls of all nationalities. He had entranced her with an hour of bitchily amusing gossip, for which he was famed on the Via Veneto.

With his witty line of chat, his long yellow hair, and the crinkly gray-blue eyes which oozed sexual promise, Fabio Di Navaro had always been regarded as an A list stud in Rome, a place where young men with dazzling good looks lurked at every open-air café and piazza.

He'd even treated the PR to a *filet de boeuf Perigeux*, swimming in rich truffle sauce, at Felix's restaurant. She had tucked into that heartily enough, plus a large helping of the *tarte aux pêches*, accompanied by poached pears in cassis, for which Felix's was renowned.

The dinner, the drinks, then the taxi to take the silly bitch back to her second-rate hotel at the wrong end of the Croisette, had set him back nearly two thousand francs. Because of that she *should* have sent him the goddamned invitation, which she'd as good as promised him, for tonight's gala.

"I'm in charge of *all* the Italian contingent's industry invitations," she had bragged, her small brown eyes glittering as they ran over Fabio's sinewy chest muscles, barely concealed by the white silk shirt, which he wore unbuttoned almost to his navel.

So where the fuck was that precious white card, engraved with thick black print? Beryl had proudly flashed one last night and, although he had practically salivated for it then, she had laughingly replaced it in her bag and told him that he would receive his, hand delivered, in the morning.

Well, it was already past two o'clock now, and Stefania Scalerina, having given her first press conference, would no doubt be with her entourage finishing lunch on the terrace of the Hotel Du Cap.

As Fabio looked out of his window all he could see of the azure sky was a tiny rectangle of blue, sandwiched between the dull gray stone of the building. This tiny room, at the back of the Majestic Hotel, was a dump, but it was expensive, and it was in one of the only three acceptable hotels to stay in during the festival.

Fabio was beginning to feel as though he had social leprosy. Few of the writers, stars and producers with whom he had hung out and doped up in his nightclub in LA as much as acknowledged his presence here.

"Hi Fabio," they'd say, swiftly turning away from him on the Carlton Terrace, or at the bar at the Moulin de Mougins, where he'd spent all of last Saturday night, hoping to latch on to someone he knew.

The only other people he saw, whom he recognized, were others like himself who were trying to make a killing, and there seemed far too many of them around this year.

He rang Beryl at her hotel, but as he had expected, she was out. Everyone was out. Having fun, making deals, doing lunch, throwing money around. What the hell. He needed some air to clear his brain, which still felt clouded from the Kir Royals and the over-priced bottle of Château Talbot that last night's bitch had made him buy. It was time to take the bull by the horns.

Outside the Majestic he hailed a waiting limousine. "Got time to take me to the Cap?" Fabio waved a five-hundred-franc note in the driver's direction.

"Get in," said the driver. "My clients will be in there for hours, *sans doute*." As they drove out of Cannes and on to the motorway, Fabio thought about Stefania Scalerina. Maybe he should just go over to greet her. After all, they had met in Rome, but would she re- member? When she saw him face-to-face, she surely couldn't give him the frosty stare for which she was famous. She was known to fancy guys who looked like he did; she was known to put out in spite of her rich sugar daddy.

In a white cotton shirt and perfectly cut blue jeans, that clung to his well-exercised rear, he was most definitely a contender in the hot-looks department. His mirrored sunglasses gave him the look of a futuristic young warrior.

At the Hotel Du Cap's security gates, Fabio confronted the ancient gendarme with audacious charm. There were usually two guards but the other one was probably at lunch. Lunch—the French religion for which everything stops.

"*Oui?*" The old man's eyes were faded with time. "*Qu'est-ce que vous desirez, m'sieur?*"

Fabio took off his glasses and threw the old man a dazzling smile. "Fabio Di Navaro," he announced, looking at the man challengingly. "I'm expected."

"Di Navaro, Di Navaro—mmm." The old man looked down his list suspiciously. "*Non*, we do not have your name here, m'sieur."

Fabio, having years ago perfected the art of upside-down reading, noticed only one typewritten name without a tick next to it.

"But you've probably got me down under my professional name," Fabio said easily, "Robert Redford."

"Ah yes—of course, M'sieur Redford."
Suddenly the guard oozed wheezy charm.
"We are expecting you—of course, of
course. Please go right ahead, m'sieur—
your suite is waiting." He looked inquiringly
into the back of the car. "Where are your
bags, m'sieur?"

"My luggage is coming commercially."
Fabio waved airily. "On the six o'clock from
New York."

"Of course, of course, M'sieur Redford,"
the guard gave a broad smile, as he made
a tick next to Mr. Redford's name. "And
Madame Redford and the children, m'sieur?"
he asked.

The limo driver shook his head, amazed
at the *naïveté* of the old gendarme. But it
was none of his affair. If this guy wanted to
pass himself off as Robert Redford, and pay
him to act as chauffeur as part of the deception, what business was it of his? He had
seen many strange things at the Cannes
Film Festival over the years. Strange things
and stranger people. That's what made
these two weeks so fascinating.

"They're coming commercial too," called
Fabio from out of the window. "They'll be

here with the luggage tonight. About seven, I guess."

"Right, M'sieur Redford, *merci*," said the man, scribbling a note next to the name. "Seven o'clock. I will be looking out for them, M'sieur, do not worry."

The limousine pulled up in front of the cool marble foyer of the Eden-Roc annex and Fabio climbed out, nodded briefly to the concierge, and strolled through onto the dining terrace.

Just as he'd thought, Stefania Scalerina and entourage were there. They sat at a long white table, the sun's rays reflecting brightly off the silver and white linen. Cream parasols shielded them from the hot sun and white-coated waiters moved noiselessly among the crowded tables with all the dexterity of ballet dancers.

Fabio stood in the doorway pretending to look for someone, but his attention was focused on Stefania and her group. But when he saw the girl with her, he really stared. Bare brown shoulders in a discreet floral sundress, but who cared about clothes with a body and face like hers?

He couldn't see her eyes but he approved

of the chic harlequin sunglasses, and as if sensing his stare, Atlanta glanced over, meeting only a disinterested pair of mirrored lenses.

Fabio reentered the lobby area and strolled slowly down the marble steps, which led to the swimming pool and changing rooms. He put on a pair of Versace blue-and-white-striped trunks—they'd been much too expensive, but what the hell, the right look was essential in Cannes—and followed the pool attendant out into the afternoon sunshine.

"Down there." Fabio indicated the farthest point away from the pool, but the closest to the sea. "On the rocks."

"*Oui, m'sieur.*" The boy carried Fabio's mattress down to the smooth gray rock, which jutted out from under the white magnificence of the hotel. Fabio tipped him and then strolled over to the edge.

Several girls lying nearby eyed him with barely disguised interest, but he ignored them. Now was not the moment to waste time on cheap and easy conquests. He was going for a prize now. The big time, the big catch—and boy, did he need it.

After discussing the whole situation with

Marcello, they had zeroed in on Stefania. She was a perfect target. Thirty-six years old, in an affair for several years with a man some twenty years older who had given her jewels beyond measure. Rumor had it that she was now bored with Nicholas Stephanopolis. Bored and on the lookout for new and fresh action.

Well, thought Fabio. I can certainly supply that for her. He was in the right place and this was the right time. Stefania could be the catalyst to make all his dreams reality, if he could only interest her in acting in his movie. Providing she fell for him, of course. But she would. In Fabio's mind that was a given. Women had been falling for him since he was thirteen years old. Sometimes it even became boring. But this catch would be a challenge, and he would play it like the experienced and expert fisherman he was.

He knew Stefania loved swimming, so she was bound to come to the pool. But she didn't. Fabio waited and waited, and then the young girl came down, wearing a red bathing suit cut so high above her thighs that her shapely legs looked as if they were six feet long.

She was lithe and luscious, but she was

not alone. An ascetic-looking guy, with long black hair in a ponytail, was with her. Who was he? The minder? What a drag.

Atlanta and Kristobel sat side by side on mattresses near the main pool. After applying a generous layer of Bain de Soleil to her skin until it glistened, Atlanta stretched out for some serious tanning in the late afternoon sun.

Fabio repositioned himself on a raft moored a hundred meters or so from the beach club rocks so that he could watch her surreptitiously, his mind ceaselessly scheming.

After an hour, Atlanta stood up to stretch. The sun had baked her and she was hot and sticky.

"Want a swim?" she asked Kristobel, who was immersed in a biography, under a large umbrella.

He shook his head. "Darling, I never go swimming in the sun. It's a killer for my skin—yours too—but you go. I'm going up for a nap. The screening's at nine and I'll help you with your dress at eight, but we *must* leave the hotel at eight thirty, otherwise Stefania will kill us both."

"Don't worry, darling—it's only five now—

we have plenty of time. I won't be long." She pecked him on the cheek. Kristobel had become a close friend and they had spent many hours talking about their lonely and tragic childhoods.

She swam strongly out to the raft. The water was cold and wonderfully refreshing. Clambering up onto the raft, she noticed that the only other occupant seemed to be asleep. Her eyes flickered along the supine form clad in blue-and-white-striped trunks, but when they reached his face he opened his eyes and stared at her.

"*Buon giorno*," he said in a charming Italian accent.

"Hello." She turned away, looking flustered.

"What time is it?" he asked, his stare strangely disconcerting.

"Oh, about five o'clock," she answered. My, but he was good-looking, and what a great body. She blushed again, hoping he hadn't noticed.

"I must have been asleep for ages." He yawned, stretched and looked at her with a disarming smile. "I'm glad you came and rescued me. I could've fried." He turned his head, giving her the full benefit of his profile.

Wow, she thought, this man was much too

handsome to be ignored. "Are you staying at the Cap?" she asked.

"No, I just came over to have lunch with some associates." He smiled. "I've got to get back to Cannes soon. Got to go where the action is. I'm a movie producer. What do you do?" he asked.

"Me—oh—ah—I'm a student," she stuttered.

"A student, hmm. Lucky girl, college days are the happiest days of one's life—or so they say."

"They lie. I can't wait to leave. In fact, I have left," Atlanta admitted, feeling flustered. God, he was *cute*.

He smiled at her in a grown-up, dismissive way, then looked as if he was preparing to dive off the raft.

Suddenly she felt that she just couldn't let him go like that. It was time to try out her newfound powers of attraction. If she had them. And if she did, would they work on this young man?

"What's going on tonight?" she asked.

He smiled lazily. "What, you mean at the festival?"

"Yes."

"Oh, there's a drinks party at the Carlton

for Sly Stallone, then the new Scorsese film at seven thirty—I guess I'll miss that—and then some movie with that Italian actress."

Atlanta was surprised—he really didn't recognize her, and even if he did, would he care? Probably not. He was a film producer after all, probably knee-deep in big stars all day long. What would the daughter of an industrialist mean to him?

"Are you going to that screening?" she asked diffidently.

"Funny you should say that," he said. "I was invited, of course, and to the gala afterward, but when I was having breakfast on the Carlton Terrace this morning, some bastard whipped my Filofax from the seat next to me. It had all my damn invitations in it, and you can imagine the bother and inconvenience of trying to get another one. Oh well, what's one more party? Parties are like buses here in Cannes. If you miss one there's always another one on the way. They're all alike anyhow, don't you think?"

"I don't know," admitted Atlanta. "I only arrived two days ago." She thought fast then blurted out, "Would you like to come with me?"

"What?" he smiled. "With you? Where to?"

"To the screening, then to the party afterward—I've got two tickets."

"Have you indeed?" he grinned boyishly, enjoying the way she had gone for the bait before it had barely skimmed the water. "I think I'd enjoy that a lot, Mademoiselle . . .?"

"Stephanopolis. Atlanta Stephanopolis. You've probably heard of my father, so I don't mind if you want to change your mind about coming to the screening," she said, her newfound feminine intuition telling her there was little chance of that. She could see he was interested.

"Change my mind! Now why would I want to do that?" Fabio laughed out loud. This had been one of the easiest pulls he'd ever made. She was much more of a catch than the mistress of Stephanopolis. This was the daughter. This could prove to be a real gold mine.

"I shall be delighted to accompany you, Miss Stephanopolis. Thank you very much for inviting me."

Stefania barely paid attention when Atlanta told her that she needed another ticket for tonight. "I'm bringing an escort to the movie—a well-known Italian producer," she trilled happily. "You'll probably know him, Stefania, Fabio Navaro?"

But Stefania, now in the final crucial stages of her toilette—always a galvanizing experience for anyone present—was dithering as to whether it would be overkill to wear a diamond tiara with her ten diamond trophy bracelets. Dismissively, she said, "Yes, I've heard of him," flicking at her upswept Renaissance ringlets distractedly. "He's supposed to be quite a good producer, no?"

Stefania and her entourage ascended the forty crimson-carpeted steps to the main foyer of the Palais des Festivals.

Everyone else had already gone into the screening, but Stefania knew that if she arrived just a fraction later she would receive maximum media coverage. "The bigger the star, the later they are," she joked to a nervous Atlanta, sitting uneasily in the limousine beside Fabio, who was cool, calm and collected.

The crowd craned its collective neck to admire Stefania and the gorgeous girl with her, and there were gasps of appreciation.

Stefania wore Kristobel's red chiffon gown, intricately draped and beaded at the bodice. Sequined panels on her shoulders fell to the ground where they were edged in matching ostrich feathers. A three-hundred-carat diamond necklace, rumored to have belonged to the Empress Marie-Louise, encircled her neck. She looked ravishing, every inch the fiery movie star. She was escorted by the president of the Festival and Nicholas, handsome, as always, in black tie.

Atlanta followed, with the good-looking Italian producer on her arm. Her outfit drew further sighs of admiration. Kristobel had designed a pleated silk pink toga, split in the front to reveal a short, tight skirt that displayed her legs to great advantage. Her jet hair hung sleekly down her back, held off her forehead by a band of pink satin ribbon. She was the epitome of fresh young beauty and style. But despite the applause of the crowd, Atlanta couldn't believe that any of it was meant for her.

The normally stoic gendarmes, ranged each side of the red carpet, were impressed. Stefania was beautiful, yes, a mature woman, but the girl—"*Elle est incroyable,*" murmured one.

When the group reached the top of the steps they turned, and to a cacophony of flashbulbs, slowly made their way to their front-circle seats.

Fabio was in his element. As he sat down between Stefania and Atlanta, he could see out of the corner of his eye several "friends" who had successfully managed to avoid him all week, now craning their necks to see if it was really him with Stefania and her party.

He heard his name called, and turned his head to see Morris Golub, the Israeli producer who had snubbed him only two nights before at the Moulin de Mougins. With a wide-mouthed grin and a wave of his stubby beringed hand, the producer was trying to get Fabio's attention.

Fabio waved back casually, then returned all his attentions to one of the delectable creatures beside him. He bubbled with satisfaction. You play this one right, *ragazzo*, he said to himself, and all your troubles are over.

The movie was received with only lukewarm enthusiasm, but afterward, a chosen few drove to a private party at a majestic villa in Cap d'Ail, decorated by Lorenzo Mongiardino.

Fabio felt a frisson of nationalistic pride that an Italian had conceived this dazzling residence. The sumptuous villa, owned by an ancient Italian count, had been one of the hubs of social life on the Riviera since the twenties. Now nearly ninety years old, the count had been brought out of social semi-retirement and persuaded to host the party.

The exterior of the villa was bathed in crimson floodlights, which illuminated the exquisite neoclassical architecture and turned the creamy stone walls to blood red. In the main salon, hung with priceless Cubist paintings by Braque and Picasso, the guests gathered for cocktails. An immense crystal chandelier was suspended from the ceiling. Its several hundred yellow beeswax candles illuminated the grandeur of the room and its elegant occupants.

Waiters in green and gold livery passed among the guests bearing ornate silver trays, proffering glasses of vintage champagne. For those who preferred, a small bar was set up directly next to the main salon, where a barman dispensed every possible alcoholic drink.

After the guests had eaten the *pâté de foie gras*, the salmon, the beluga caviar and the variety of cold salads and meats, all sumptuously displayed and served on Sèvres dishes, they started to dance to the small jazz band. The photographers hadn't left Stefania alone all evening and she had finally had enough of them.

"Are you ready to come home, *cara*?" she asked Atlanta.

"Oh no, not yet."

Atlanta, flushed with excitement, was hanging on to Fabio's arm and to his every word. "It's not even one o'clock yet, Stefania."

Stefania shot a quick glance at Fabio, who smiled ingratiatingly. He looked as if butter wouldn't melt in his mouth. Those were always the ones to watch.

"Well, we're going to go, *cara*. Nicholas is tired, aren't you, darling?" She shot him a look charged with sexual promise and he gave her a heavy-lidded smile. She certainly still had his number.

Fabio didn't miss this exchange and thanked his stars that he'd been lucky enough to pick the Stephanopolis daughter, and not the mistress.

"Don't worry. I'll take care of her," said Fabio smoothly to Stefania.

"All right. You stay then. We'll see you in the morning."

"Good night, Atlanta." Nicholas gave his daughter a cool wave. "Have fun."

"Oh, I will, Father," she smiled.

"But be good." Stefania shot Fabio her Italian mama warning look and they were off.

"Now what?" asked Atlanta, the gleam in her eyes letting him know that she was ready for some fun. "Where shall we go now?"

"New Jimmy's?" asked Fabio. "Or L'Horizon?"

"New Jimmy's," said Atlanta happily.

"Let's go," he said. "The night is young, and so are you."

New Jimmy's open-air discotheque in Monaco was hot, crowded and deafening. Despite half of the club's roof being open to the balmy May night, Atlanta and Fabio were sweating after only a couple of dances.

She had taken off her long paneled overskirt, leaving her in the pink miniskirt, which gave her the freedom to whirl around the dance floor with abandon.

She had never been so ecstatic or felt so free. The throbbing beat of the music, and the proximity of Fabio, excited her more than she had ever been before.

Soon after Atlanta went to the powder room, Beryl sidled up to Fabio's table.

"Well, well," she said waspishly. "You certainly look like the cat who's swallowed the caviar tonight."

"Beryl, my dear, how *are* you?" Fabio stood up and bent smoothly over the hand of the PR woman. "Thank you *so* much for the invitation, *cara mia*—as you can see, I enjoyed the movie and the party tremendously."

Beryl smiled, revealing pointed teeth and receding gums.

"You're a real operator, Fabio, I'll give you that. I was never going to give you an invitation—surely you must have known?"

"Of *course* I knew, my dear Beryl," he said smoothly. From the corner of his eye he saw Atlanta return. "I'm not quite as stupid as you think. I didn't need the invite, Beryl. I was personally invited by the Stephanopolis family. Oh, may I present Miss Atlanta Stephanopolis."

Atlanta nodded to the plain woman who was glaring at Fabio.

"Goodbye, Beryl," said Fabio smoothly, as she stalked away. "See you at tomorrow's screening." Fabio put his hand gently on Atlanta's shoulder. "Let's dance," he said with a smile. "Let's dance all night."

* * *

When they had first arrived at the party, Fabio had placed a quick call to his partner Marcello.

"You've got to let me borrow your pad tonight," he whispered.

"What?" The Italian had just woken from a wonderfully realistic dream in which he had been accepting the Oscar for best movie from the hands of Meryl Streep and he wanted to go back to the celebrations. "Shit, Fabio, I'm fucking asleep, for Christ's sake. What's your fuckin' problem?" he snapped.

"Our problem, *compadre*, is that I am about to pull Mademoiselle Atlanta Stephanopolis, who I'm convinced is not only a virgin, but who is not going to take much subtle persuading to let me change that condition."

"So? That's your problem, not mine," mumbled Marcello. "You always managed to get that busy dick of yours in where angels fear to tread. What's wrong with taking her to *your* place?"

"*Putz!*" hissed Fabio. "It's our problem because she's perfect for our movie. She's got a fantastic body and she's the daughter of the exceedingly rich and powerful Nicholas Stephanopolis—one step up from his mistress. I can't take her to my place. She's not completely dumb. If she sees that rat hole she'll realize right away I'm not the hotshot producer she thinks I am. I'll be history. C'mon, Marcello, get that fat ass of yours out of bed, leave the key under the mat, and get on over to the Majestic. My room's 173. You can sleep there."

"Thanks." Marcello gloomily hoisted his great bulk up into a sitting position in the rumpled bed. "You really think this chick is a better idea for our movie than the Scalerina dame?"

"I don't think it, I *know* it," Fabio said excitedly. "She's young, she's fresh, she's gorgeous, and she's also Laura Marlowe's fucking *daughter,* for Christ's sake. Laura's movies are on TV every fucking week. She's become a cult figure since she died. Now I need to get a crack at this kid, Marcello. I've been chatting her up all night and I know a lot about her already. She doesn't have a clue what she wants to do with her life. It's fucking perfect. Now I get her panties off, I convince her to do our movie and we've got it made, *compadre*. With her name on the marquee, I know we have."

"All right . . . All right, I'll do it," grumbled Marcello. He scratched his hairy chest. "I suppose you'd like the sheets changed too?"

"That would be very nice indeed," grinned Fabio. "Thanks. *Ciao*, Marcello. I'll see you at lunch tomorrow at Felix's. Make it a late one, I've got a feeling that it's going to be a long night."

She had never danced so uninhibitedly, or drunk so much champagne, or felt so wonderful. The flashing pink strobe lights, the open roof through which she could see the stars and smell the heady scent of the Riviera and, most of all, the attentions of Fabio, who was without a doubt the most amusing and alluring man she had ever met, transported Atlanta into a magical kingdom.

She knew she was slightly drunk with the champagne and the atmosphere, but she couldn't care less, as she whirled with the music, feverishly giving thanks for her grueling months at the Last Resort.

Fabio was the first man she had ever met to take a real interest in her and Atlanta was keenly aware of what might lie ahead for her tonight. Throughout the time she spent at Dr. Hoffard's clinic, she had sometimes wished that she could ask them to dispense with her virginity too. To be a virgin at twenty was like wearing a life jacket in a bathtub, simply unnecessary, and Atlanta was embarrassed about it. She had fantasized for years about how her first affair would begin and tonight all her fantasies seemed to be coming true.

Fabio held her closely in his strong arms while the music pulsed. She felt a tingling sensation in her stomach and down toward a place that was awakening for the first time.

Fabio was fully aware of the effect he was having on Atlanta but he was smart enough not to push it. She would come to him soon enough, he'd had enough practice to know that.

Soon they were almost the last couple left on the dance floor and the disc jockey was yawning in his glass booth, playing an old Ella Fitzgerald number, hoping that it might make everyone leave.

"Would you like a nightcap?" Fabio helped Atlanta into his rented Mercedes convertible with Old World gallantry.

"Yes, I would. But where can we go? It's pretty late."

"We'll find somewhere." He gave her his most tantalizing smile and thrust the car into reverse, then backed down the hill. Atlanta threw her head back and gazed at the stars. Fabio drove slowly along the scenic route rather than taking the motorway toward Cannes. Although it was a winding road, it was much more beautiful.

"Are you hungry?" he asked. He had been watching her out of the corner of his eye. The wind was whipping her black hair into a wild mane, her eyes were closed and she had a beatific expression on her face.

"Mmm, I am a bit." Atlanta never wanted this magic night to end.

The black sea shimmered, its silvery waves breaking gently on the shore. Palm trees waved lazily and the scent of jasmine and mimosa wafted in the air.

Atlanta opened her eyes and studied Fabio's strong profile as the wind tousled his long dusty blond hair. He had an aquiline, inquisitive nose, and a sulky voluptuous mouth which, when he smiled, made her feel as if she was melting. His eyes were luminously gray blue, and his lashes and crescent-shaped eyebrows thick and blond. He had taken off his black bow tie, and the white of his open pleated shirt made a wonderful contrast to the bronzed muscularity of his neck and chest.

God, he was gorgeous. Much more gorgeous than Kevin Bentley, and certainly a lot younger.

A few pedestrians still strolled along the Croisette in the humid night air as Fabio guided the Mercedes into an underground garage of an apartment building. "Here we are," he said. "Home, sweet home."

The apartment was furnished in ersatz Italian modern. There was a small living room with a black leather sofa and a glass coffee table, which held nothing except the latest copies of *Screen International*, *Variety* and *The Hollywood Reporter*, a couple of chrome chairs and a Swedish stereo.

Fabio opened the sliding glass doors to let Atlanta onto the tiny terrace, which faced the sea.

"How does bacon and eggs sound to you?" he called from the minuscule kitchenette, having first checked the contents of the refrigerator.

"It sounds just great," she called over her shoulder, looking up at the moon, which was . . . oh, too perfect . . . it was almost full.

He had put a record on the turntable and she heard the high falsetto voice of England Day singing "Dream Weaver."

Atlanta listened to the lyrics and wondered if it would be true. Would she see the morning light, with Fabio? The thought almost made her dizzy.

"Champagne?" he asked as he came out onto the terrace holding a glass toward her. Thank God Marcello had kept that quarter bottle he'd filched from his lunch tray on the flight from Rome.

"Mmm, thank you." She sipped and they stood close looking at the moon.

Then, slowly, he turned and bent to kiss her and for the first time in her life, Atlanta felt a man's mouth on hers. Light as a butterfly's wing, his warm full lips brushed hers lightly, but the dynamic dangerous sensations that had been building up for several hours shot like a jolt of electricity through her body.

Then she pulled away from him and sighed. She looked up in his face, wanting to swim in the two gray-blue pools of his eyes.

"*Don't stop thinking about tomorrow,*" he whispered, harmonizing with the classic song from Fleetwood Mac, taking away her glass and gently clasping her in his arms.

"I've never met anyone like you, Atlanta."

Corny line, he thought, but it always gets them. Then he kissed her again with more passion this time and she felt his tongue gently probe her mouth.

This memory will be etched in my mind for eternity, thought Atlanta. She wanted to stay forever in the moonlight wrapped in Fabio's arms, on a balmy terrace on the Riviera.

His mouth opened, searching hers, and she felt the hardness in his trousers against her thigh. He attempted to move his lips away but she wouldn't let him go, her hands caressed his hair and she wanted him to bury himself in her.

Then wordlessly, he picked her up, and she, who had always felt as clumsy as an elephant, felt like a piece of gossamer. He carried her into the cramped bedroom, lit only by a low wattage lamp, and placed her reverently on the bed.

She looked up at him, her heart thumping like a jackhammer. "I've got something to tell you," she murmured. "I know you probably won't believe me but I'm a . . ."

"Don't." He stopped her with a kiss of such sweet languorousness that she felt she was drowning in it. "You don't have to tell me—I know."

"I'm so glad." She sighed as his hand unfastened her dress. "So . . . so glad."

CHAPTER TWENTY

Nicholas sat behind his vast desk, bare of papers and excessively neat.

Behind him was a bank of bookshelves and several photographs in leather frames: a large one of Laura, one of them on their wedding day, pictures of Nicholas with various Greek dignitaries and three large photographs of Venetia. Atlanta looked for one of herself and finally spotted it, hidden behind Aristotle Onassis.

"For God's sake, Atlanta. You hardly know this man. How do you know he's really a legitimate producer? Who's putting the money up? Who's his backer? And what sort of a movie is it anyway?" This was an aggravating hiccup in Nicholas's busy day.

"It's a very good script, I've read it and I've seen enough movies to know that it's good. Jodie Foster is dying to play the lead and so are lots of other actresses. But Fabio wants me to star in it."

"What the *hell* do you want to be an actress for? It's a stupid profession and it's difficult to make any money. How do you even know you can act?" asked Nicholas irritably.

"How did Mama know? She started acting in her teens—I'm twenty. No one taught her how to do it, it just came naturally. I *know* I can act, Father. Oh *please*, *please* let me do this movie. Fabio has raised all the financing. Everything is in place—all they need is me, and if they don't get me they'll get Brooke Shields or Jodie or an unknown." Although Atlanta realized she didn't need his permission, she was still yearning for his approval.

"When I married your mother, she was an actress, and it took her a long time to live it down. She told me that the life of an actress is really a very empty one."

"Oh, Father," expostulated Atlanta. "You're making too much of a big deal about this. Acting's just a job—like any other job."

"No, it isn't," snapped Nicholas. "Your mother told me often that the happiness she found with me, on our island, and with her children *far* outweighed the happiness she ever had in her life as a movie star."

"Well, that was her. I'm different. I'm a modern girl, I know I'll be happy acting. And if I'm not, then I'll quit."

"Well, I don't think you should even start it. You could end up making a complete fool of yourself."

"Oh, for God's sake." Atlanta's cajoling charm suddenly gave way to the short temper inherited from her father and that she had recently started using more often. "I'm twenty years old. According to the law, that means I can do what I want now and I'm damn well going to, Father, whether you like it or not. And another thing: I may as well tell you I'm in love with Fabio, and I'm living with him."

Nicholas was stunned by Atlanta's outburst. She had never sworn in front of him before, always been so demure. Her glamorous façade seemed to have given her a new inner fire.

"Ah, so that's it. In love with the producer? That makes everything fall into place. Has it ever occurred to you, you stupid child, that it might not just be your pretty new face and body that this young man is interested in, but something else?"

"What?" asked Atlanta, stonily.

"If you can't see it then you're more of a fool than I thought. Your *heritage,* Atlanta. The publicity that will come from your making the movie. You're Laura Marlowe's *daughter,* for God's sake. The Stephanopolis family is famous. Can't you see what that could mean to a certain kind of man?"

"Look, Father, I asked you because I respect your opinion. If you say yes and give me your blessing, I'll be very happy—but if you say no, I'm going ahead and making the movie *anyway*—because you don't have the power to stop me."

"I see." For the first time in his life Nicholas took notice of what his eldest daughter was saying. There was a silence as he went over to the window and looked out at the serene beauty of the mature garden beneath.

"Very well," Nicholas said. "I'll give you my blessing. Reluctantly, mark you. Because I *know* something of Hollywood, Atlanta, and I know the kind of man who operates there— your mother lived there a long time and told me a great deal about it. If you're a young, pretty girl, you're treated little better than a piece of meat—unless of course you become a box-office star and the chances of that, my foolish ambitious daughter, are slim. Frankly, girls like you are a dime a dozen out there."

"Thanks, Father, for your typically great faith in me." Atlanta struggled to keep the bitterness out of her voice. "But in spite of what you say about me and Fabio, I'm going to do this film. I'll do my best to make you proud of me, but if I don't . . ." She shrugged. "So be it."

There was a knock and Venetia stuck her head around the door. "OK to join you?" she asked breezily. "Hi Papa. Hi Sis."

Atlanta watched her father's formidable face light up, as though someone had thrown a switch.

"How are you, Venetia?" Nicholas hugged his younger daughter warmly.

"Fine, Papa, I'm just fine, but the Ferrari's on the blink again, can you *believe* it?"

"What's happened this time?" Nicholas seemed far more concerned about the unreliable engine of Venetia's Ferrari than about his elder daughter's future career. "Kitten, you go through more sports cars than I go through clean shirts."

"I'm sorry, Daddy, really, I guess you were right, a Testarossa is too powerful for me— maybe I should've had a Jag after all."

Atlanta was forgotten as Nicholas put his arm around Venetia's shoulders and they moved toward the door, deep in a conversation about new cars.

Atlanta watched the two of them together and shrugged. What the hell. What did he care? When had he ever really cared?

"Well, for better or worse, it's Hollywood, here I come," she whispered to herself. "Look out Jodie Foster, there ain't nobody going to rain on my parade."

CHAPTER TWENTY-ONE

Fabio huddled with Marcello Lupe over their cappuccinos at Le Dôme, where the Hollywood power-lunch bunch pushed artichoke salads around jumbo-sized plates. Even though Marcello's name hadn't carried enough clout to procure a table in the exclusive back room, this table in the first section of the restaurant, with its view of Sunset Boulevard, would suffice for now.

"When our picture comes out we'll be sitting back there with the high rollers." Marcello gestured to an elite group of agency bosses at one of the large round tables. "Those bastards wouldn't give you the sweat off their balls. But as soon as they get wind of our project, we'll be fighting them off for representation."

A shriek of female laughter interrupted Marcello's enthusiastic spiel. It came from a corner table at which six overly made-up, bejeweled middle-aged women were tearing everyone to shreds along with their lettuce leaves. "You know what they call *that* table, don't you?"

"No idea," Fabio replied.

"The Vicious Circle." Marcello chuckled. "Those bitches—they just love to destroy people in this town."

"Yeah, well who cares," said Fabio. "Listen, Marcello—this movie is going to be hot—you know that, don't you?"

"Sure, we'll have Ovitz and his cronies breaking down our doors. The majors'll be fighting for our favors," said Marcello, still gazing longingly into the back room. "But you've *gotta* get the girl to do the sex scene, Fabio. If we don't have a fuck scene we don't have a movie—and you know it."

Fabio lit a cigarette and blew three perfect smoke rings. Marcello was right. Marcello was always right. He had, after all, staked Fabio to the Cannes trip for the sole purpose of pulling Stefania Scalerina or someone of equal value for this script.

"How the fuck am I going to get her to do a screwing scene?" Fabio sighed. "I can't even get her to agree to take off her fucking top in front of the camera. She's too fucking worried about her fucking father, and the memory of her wonderful mother, blah-blah-blah—shit."

He blew another smoke ring and glared angrily at the agents who were ignoring them. "Christ, she gets tied up in knots whenever the subject comes up."

Marcello's eyes glittered menacingly as he leaned forward. "I don't care *how* you do it—just persuade her. The film's nothing without that sex scene, *capisce*? We both know that. We gotta have it for the foreign market and for the video sales."

Fabio nodded, his eyes following a long-legged brunette sashaying her way down the aisle. "OK. OK. I guess I'll have to play dirty then."

"Play dirty?" Marcello grinned. "So what else is new, *putz*?"

"Now listen, baby," soothed Fabio. "I know you're nervous. I know you've never done this sort of thing before. But don't worry, sweetheart. You trust me, don't you, babe?"

Atlanta nodded, her eyes wide and frightened.

"You're an *actress*, aren't you? Real actresses do this sort of thing all the time. Look at Vanessa Redgrave—Jane Fonda—Julie Christie—I mean you can't name an important movie actress in the last twenty years who *hasn't* made love in front of the camera. For art," he added. "Always for art."

"But—do I have to take off *all* my clothes? Everything?"

"Of course, you *must*. My God, Atlanta, just pretend it's *me* you're making love to. Can't you do that, baby?"

His hand caressed her leg, snaking up to her smooth thigh. "You've got such a beautiful body, Atlanta—so beautiful."

His voice was becoming husky. Her proximity was getting to him. Better be careful, he didn't want to upset the apple cart yet.

He bent her back onto the shabby sofa in her dressing room and gently kissed her mouth, his tongue and lips full of promise. He knew what she liked and he knew how to give it to her.

She began to respond as he'd hoped she

would. He stopped kissing her, sat up, and passed her a tumbler full of cognac.

"Drink this up, all of it, babe. It'll make you feel better. It'll give you courage."

Atlanta reluctantly took a swig of brandy but the taste made her shudder.

Then Fabio lit a joint and passed it to her.

"Two drags, babe—that's all you get. We'll save the rest for just before the scene. Are you ready for Ritchie, now?"

She nodded, inhaling the smoke deeply. It had a kick like a mule and she gasped. She'd had no experience of drugs before she'd been with Fabio and she still didn't like them.

"What is this?" she coughed. It tasted different from the marijuana joints that Fabio occasionally gave her as a prelude to love-making.

"My own special recipe, babe," he whispered, his lips brushing her hair. "All the way from Colombia. It's the best. One more drag of this and you'll be ready for anything."

They couldn't believe it when they saw the rushes.

As they watched Atlanta's perfect body fill the screen, both men became hard.

"That looks so real. Are you sure she was just acting?" asked Marcello.

With an unaccustomed rush of jealousy, Fabio snapped at his colleague, "Of course she was faking it, you dirty-minded bastard."

"Hot, *damn*." Marcello licked dry lips when the lights came up in the projection room. "We've got a gold mine on our hands—a star is born, Fabio—a fucking star. Congratulations."

Fucking star is right, thought Fabio grimly. He lit a cigarette and stared morosely at the blank screen. Atlanta had done what he'd told her to do all right. Done that and more.

Maybe the little witch had actually enjoyed her sex scene with Ritchie Roberts. They'd pulled out all the stops, just as Fabio had instructed, and Ritchie had looked in seventh heaven as he had caressed Atlanta and nuzzled his head in places which Fabio liked to think of as his own private property.

They hadn't actually gone all the way, but by the manner in which the scene had been shot, it certainly looked like it. Well, it was over now. The final scene—this torrid sex scene—was in the can, the film was finished, and once word got out about what

they had on celluloid, it would make them
rich.

Ever since the love scene with Ritchie
Roberts, Atlanta had felt uneasy because
she could hardly remember anything of that
afternoon. It had all been a haze. She
vaguely recalled that after a few puffs of
Fabio's special joint, she had become
aroused, but she didn't want to remember
what she had done then. She didn't want to
think about anything these days, except for
Fabio.

She was obsessed with him. She couldn't
get enough of him—it was as if she was
drugged with passion. As soon as he came
home he was on her, and she was always
ready. Sometimes they made love for so
long that their bodies ached with exhaustion.
They were both feeling a lust that only the
passage of time would diminish.

"It's so good between us," he whispered.
"You were made for this, Atlanta—made for
love."

But when she looked into the mirror and
her perfect face stared back, Atlanta still
couldn't believe it was really her. In her mind,

she saw Atlanta the ugly duckling. However much Fabio made love to her and told her how much he adored her and how beautiful she was, Atlanta still found it hard to believe.

The assistant editor of *Saturday Night Girl* made another copy of the outtakes, which he spliced together, with the lovemaking scene in its entirety, whistling under his breath as he put them on to reel. This was the hottest thing he'd seen since the legendary Julie Christie and Donald Sutherland lovemaking scene in *Don't Look Now*.

"Why should they be the only guys to make money out of this?" he asked himself. Ritchie was a hot, if fading, leading man, and the girl was a famous heiress, the daughter of Hollywood royalty, a luscious, uninhibited peach. It was a golden opportunity to make some dough, and he wasn't going to let it slip away from him.

The editor sold the twenty-minute reel of film for five thousand dollars to a production manager he knew at Paramount. The production manager went to his brother-in-law, who owned a little editing room in the Valley, who had it transferred to video, and ran off twenty-five hundred copies.

When his brother-in-law discovered who he had on film, he whistled joyfully. "This is worth a fortune." He smiled to himself. "An absolute fucking fortune."

Within a week, everybody who was anybody in Hollywood either owned or had seen a copy of the video. Shock waves ran through the conservative Hollywood community, particularly among those who had been friends of Laura.

"My God, what has gotten into that child?" Ginny Jones sighed. She had moved back to Hollywood after Laura's death and was living quietly in an apartment on Melrose Avenue, comfortably off with the legacy Laura had left her.

"Fabio Di Navaro has gotten into her." Coral Steele was tight-lipped. "Into her head, into her brain and everywhere else. My God, Laura must be turning in her grave."

"I wouldn't like to see Nicholas's reaction," said Ginny grimly.

"He'll probably want to kill her," came the reply.

Although some people had been genuinely shocked by the video, times had changed. In the good old days, a starlet taking off her blouse in front of a crowd on the beach at Cannes would have caused scandalous headlines. Now, in the early 1990s, people needed far more titillating events in order to be shocked.

Naked female breasts were a dime a dozen on beaches, in newspapers and magazines and it had been with this argument that Fabio had finally persuaded Atlanta that she was not being particularly outrageous the day she bared her all for "art."

But the video was a different story. When Atlanta had seen the first few minutes, she had closed her eyes and begged Fabio to turn it off.

"What am I going to do?" Her beautiful face was stricken. "How can we stop people from seeing this? When my father hears about it he'll probably have a stroke." Or probably won't care at all, she thought.

"We'll get hold of that asshole who's released those prints. Offer him a packet of dough and get back the negative," said Fabio.

"But these horrible outtakes he's put in— who else has seen them?"

"I won't lie to you, babe. I'm afraid the

whole town's talking about it, but I'll tell you something funny, your new agent told me that his phone's ringing off the hook for you. You've become a star, sweetie."

"I might believe you about that when the movie's released," she said slowly. "But certainly not before."

There was no answer at the Stephanopolis residences in New York, Paris or Athens, only machines that said they were out, and promised the family would "get back to you." Atlanta left messages for Nicholas to call her, but in her heart she knew he wouldn't, and she realized that she would now probably lose her father completely.

She sighed, remembering her sullen shyness as a child. How she had wished she'd had the guts to be more like her reckless sister. She remembered taking the photographs of Venetia with Alain in the gay disco and felt a shiver of guilt.

Venetia's tabloid scandals were notorious, and she was *still* only a teenager. Was she becoming just as bad—a stranger to civilized behavior? Atlanta was deeply ashamed of what she had done. Embarrassed and disgusted with herself but now also angry with Fabio for allowing it to happen to her.

Venetia, on the other hand, was never embarrassed or ashamed by anything she ever did.

Having started off with smoking pot at the age of twelve, she'd developed an addiction to cocaine after she had first tried it at Madame Jo-Jo's. "It gives me energy," she giggled to Alain.

Although now at school in Paris, she spent every weekend night at Heavenly, a disco, with Alain. They had been lovers now for some time, but he was certainly not her only one.

Venetia adored dancing and she did so wildly, all inhibitions thrown to the wind. Her favorite outfit was a boob tube and a microskirt, and her vigorous dance moves often caused her top to slither down. Since she never wore a bra, this was a delectable sight for Heavenly's clientele.

If she had popped enough Ecstasy that night, or snorted enough coke, she wouldn't notice she was bare breasted, and would continue her solo gyrations while a horde of admirers ringed her in a circle, egging her on.

Venetia, lost in the world of throbbing music, knew nothing and heard nothing except the fevered beat. She was a stupendous hit at Heavenly, especially as she sometimes took the most ardent of her admirers into the dark alleyway outside the club.

Alain turned a blind eye to this as did Roberto, the proprietor. It was great for business and the word spread around Paris that Heavenly was *the* place to go. Soon Roberto was on a first-name basis with Hollywood's wildest male stars, who made a beeline to the club whenever they hit town.

Venetia exhibited herself on the dance floor as carelessly as if she were the floor show. Untamed, wild as the wind and drug-fueled, she unleashed her primitive side. Venetia loved men, and they loved her even more.

CHAPTER TWENTY-TWO

Atlanta saw Kevin Bentley again when he entered Spago, looking as if he were walking onto the deck of the *Queen Mary* in a 1930s movie.

In a sharp white suit, his thinning brown hair brushed back, and flanked by a pair of gorgeous girls in their early twenties—one platinum blonde and the other raven-haired— he gave off an aura of blasé sophistication.

The blonde, dressed in a clinging black Lycra minidress, possessed plastic-perfect breasts and waist-length hair. The sultry brunette wore a similar outfit in white.

As Kevin Bentley loped his way across the

room, tourists paused mid-bite to gape at this living legend, this phallus on legs, this aging Adonis, and from across the restaurant Atlanta observed him too as he swept the room with a pale stare.

He met the ingratiating grins and waves of stars, directors and writers with a lazy half-smile and his eyes were just about to finish their tour when they came to rest upon Atlanta. He did a double take, stunned by her metamorphosis. He'd seen photos of her, but they hadn't prepared him for this vision. He acknowledged her presence with a wave, and then turned his attention back to his companions.

Fabio gripped Atlanta's arm excitedly. "You know him?" he asked.

"I've known him since I was a kid. He was a friend of Mama's. Sometimes they ran their old movies at the house, but I haven't seen him for ages." Atlanta was secretly thrilled by the approval in Kevin's eyes.

"You know he's casting his new movie." Fabio's voice was unnecessarily low, even though no one could ever make themselves heard at Spago in anything less than a full-pitched bellow. "He's looking for the female lead—she has to be young, juicy and hot,

but she also has to have a virginal waiflike
look. Perfect for you, babe, perfect."

"Well, it looks like he's already found
someone." Atlanta noticed Kevin's hand
around each girl's shoulders. "Those two are
actresses aren't they?"

"Hookers," Fabio said succinctly. "I know
'em both."

"You do. How come?"

"They hang out at the clubs all the time—
always with a different guy—they work
together—scenes—partoosies—y'know the
sort of thing."

"Oh." Atlanta nodded vaguely. "Is it true
what they say about Kevin?" she asked casually.

"Y'mean about him screwing every female
he meets? Sure. It's true. Hollywood would
be surprised if Kevin Bentley *didn't* screw his
leading lady or his makeup lady or even his
hairdresser. Kevin Bentley, it is said, sweetie,
has fucked the better half of Hollywood."

"I wonder if he slept with my mother? They
made several movies together and she kept
a picture of them on her dressing table."

"I wouldn't put it past him. So why don't
you go over and say hello? Sounds like Uncle Kevin's practically one of the family."

"Oh, I can't—it would be too pushy." She demurred.

"Listen, Atlanta." Fabio put out a powerful hand and grabbed her wrist. "I *want* you to go and say hello."

Atlanta flinched. She hoped Fabio wasn't going to get in one of his rages tonight. It didn't happen very often and after he'd yelled at her, he always apologized, but it frightened her nevertheless.

"OK." She sighed. "You'd better order me another margarita."

She crossed the room and stood over him, five foot seven of delicious womanhood. Long black hair, firm little ass, legs sheathed in those skintight designer leggings that were such a turn-on, and fabulous boobs just visible through a gauzy white blouse.

A tasty morsel indeed, thought Kevin.

"How are you, Kevin?" she asked politely.

"Atlanta? Is it really you?"

Kevin's table companions exchanged suspicious looks as they took stock of the intruder's assets.

"Yes, it's little old me," Atlanta smiled. "Or rather the new me."

"What're you doing in Hollywood? And how come you look so gorgeous?"

"I'm acting now. I just finished a movie last month."

"Great. Great. Glad to hear it. You look fantastic, amazing, just like a movie star."

The two hookers exchanged looks.

"Thanks." Atlanta didn't want to linger. Table-hopping always made her edgy, and the jealous glares she was getting from the Bobbsey twins were making her feel self-conscious.

"I can't get over how incredible you look." Kevin continued to stare at her with a look she could only interpret as exceedingly interested.

"Thanks, Kevin. Well, I've got to go, now." As she turned he stood up and whispered, "Who's your agent?"

"Argyle Management," she said, and then said good-bye sweetly to the girls, and rejoined Fabio, who was exchanging good-natured banter with Wolfgang Puck at the front door.

"So, how'd it go?" he asked as they walked up the hill toward Spago's parking lot as the paparazzi trained their cameras on them, while stumbling backward. The explosion of flashbulbs was so strong that they could barely see where they were going. "Did he like you?"

"I guess so." Atlanta settled down into Fabio's black Cadillac. "He was very friendly. And he asked for the name of my agent."

"Great! Hey, babe, that's really *great*." Fabio slammed the car into gear, almost running over the foot of an overzealous snapper who was leaning over the hood for a better shot, then he turned the radio on loud to his favorite rock station.

"Tell your agent to get onto this right away and get you an audition with your Mama's old friend. This is Hollywood, sweetheart. Contacts are everything, and you've certainly got the right one for this job."

Three days later, Atlanta's telephone rang at nine in the morning.

"You won't believe this." Her agent Hank's voice throbbed with excitement.

"Try me." Atlanta's head was still fuzzy from sleep.

"Kevin Bentley *personally* returned my call." Hank sounded triumphant. "I'd been trying to get you an interview with him for *Orphans* for weeks and now he just called me back. Wants to see you in his New York office at three o'clock, the day after tomorrow."

Fabio had put the phone on speaker.

"Yes!" Fabio and Atlanta yelled in unison.

"I kid you not, kids!" Hank was now gushing with the news. "He wants you to read for the lead. He'll even pay for your fare. This could be the big one for you, Atlanta."

As she waited to be summoned into Kevin's inner sanctum, Atlanta's heart was thumping. The walls of his waiting room were covered in posters and stills from all his movies—in addition to acting, he had been producing and directing for twenty years.

"Go on in, he'll see you now," a stick-thin secretary didn't look up from sipping her can of Diet Coke.

Kevin sat behind his desk, the afternoon sun glinting on his thinning hair, his face wreathed in its famous boyish grin.

"God, Atlanta, you look incredible."

"Thank you." Atlanta was trying to remain calm. Why did Kevin still make her feel weak at the knees? He was old enough to be her father, in fact she had heard the whispered innuendos that he might even *be* her father.

Kevin's mind was running on a similar

track while he stared at the girl who sat opposite him. He remembered how beautiful her mother had been. How he'd adored Laura, longed to make love to her, but she never would let him.

Now here was her daughter, a veritable miracle of the plastic surgeon's art, which had given her the physical attributes needed for the lead role in his new movie. All he needed to do now was to find out if she had inherited Laura's talent.

Kevin chucked a blue script across the table. "Read it," he commanded, leaning back in his reclining chair, arms behind his head as he observed her through narrowed eyes. "And then we'll talk."

CHAPTER TWENTY-THREE

The instant Atlanta stepped off the plane at LAX, several yapping reporters and paparazzi surrounded her.

"Welcome back, how was New York?" called one.

"Hey Atlanta, look at me," yelled another.

"Atlanta, over here, over here."

Camera straps festooned their bodies like Chanel chains on a Beverly Hills matron, and their multiple lenses were poised for action. Each lens served a different purpose, enabling them to get different angles, most of which were unflattering to their subjects.

The tabloids loved those, because their readers liked seeing celebrities looking the worse for wear.

"So you're going to do a movie with Kevin Bentley?"

"Maybe." She smiled and then looked up to see the rangy figure with the long blond hair pushing his way through the crowds.

"Hey babe—I'm here, over here."

Fabio elbowed people aside and hugged Atlanta. "Congratulations, babe," he crowed. "It's good to see you."

"Wow!" said Atlanta when she saw a gleaming white limousine at the curb. "This is even more vulgar than your last one."

"Vulgar!" He looked annoyed. "It's the height of class. It's the latest stretch Rolls-Royce, there are only a hundred and fifty in the whole world. We're about to hit the big time now, sweetie, we've got to look it."

Atlanta threw herself into the backseat as photographers rapped on the tinted windows trying to attract her attention.

"I can't believe it, Fabio." She turned to him with shining eyes. "Hank called me this morning. Kevin wants me for the movie. I simply can't believe it's true."

"Don't be so insecure, babe. Look at yourself, you're beautiful. Why can't you face that fact and stop acting so shy?"

"I *do not* act shy, Fabio. I may not be Joan Rivers, but I can more than hold my own in a group—will you please stop putting me down all the time?"

"OK, OK. Now listen: you got the part, sweetheart! So nothing can stop you now, even if our movie turns out to be a turkey."

"How could it be a turkey? The script was good. You said it was going to be a great art film."

Fabio turned up the rap music until she could hardly hear him. "Our movie will be just fine—at the premiere next week we'll find out how much audiences like it. Meanwhile, sweetheart, you're starring in Kevin Bentley's next project. Hey, babe, nothing's going to stop you now."

Atlanta could barely control her excitement at the premiere of her first movie.

Enthusiastic fans in the bleachers cheered when the beautiful actress appeared with her handsome producer boyfriend. In his tuxedo, with his pale sulky face, and his blond hair in careless confusion, Fabio looked like a somebody.

Atlanta wore a white lace décolleté dress, and diamond earrings that had been lent to her by the studio that was releasing the movie. It had also supplied the white chauffeured limousine, and afterward would pay for the reception and dinner party at Spago.

The studio had insisted that the limo deliver them to the premiere an hour before the start of the movie because Publicity wanted to make certain that the photographers took plenty of pictures to flood the media. Atlanta exchanged pleasantries with several influential columnists, smiling and waving to the cheering fans and greeting anyone of importance in the foyer. After that, she was allowed to go to her seat.

Although Atlanta had met many famous people in her life, she never tired of looking at movie stars.

"Look, there's your friend Coral." Fabio nudged Atlanta. Chic in a red satin dress with matching accessories and flashing a magnificent ruby parure, Coral clutched the arm of a distinguished attorney as she sashayed down the aisle, bestowing smiles and "Hello darlings" to the more important members of the audience.

"Hollywood is a town where one's lipstick color is more important than one's mind," Coral had warned Atlanta before she started shooting her first movie. But Atlanta had barely listened. It was all thrilling and excitingly new, and tonight she hoped she was poised on the brink of stardom.

What Atlanta didn't realize was that most of the guests were under some kind of obligation. They couldn't care less who was starring in this film. This was Hollywood, where a favor given is a favor one day returned, and who knew when they might need to call in a marker or two from the studio head? That was the movie business. Tit for tat. Measure for measure.

Half of the audience would far rather have been relaxing at home than exchanging animated chitchat in a stifling hot cinema with people they didn't give a damn about.

Atlanta snuggled into her seat and grabbed Fabio's hand as the lights dimmed, the velvet curtains were raised and the opening title credits rolled.

When Atlanta's face, which on film seemed to have an almost extraordinary innocence, appeared in close-up for the first time, the audience applauded, and she shuddered with pleasure.

Playing a girl from an East European village who is adopted by a middle-aged farmer and his wife, she wore a simple cotton dress, her hair in a ponytail, and no makeup. She grabbed the audience's sympathy from the moment they saw her.

They were obviously rooting for her and Atlanta was reveling in the attention. Through the eyes of this audience she was discovering herself again. She could tell by the whispers of admiration, by the sympathetic laughs in all the right places that she was a winner tonight. Fabio squeezed her knee, as excited as she was.

The black-and-white lighting of the *cinema noir* style accentuated the soft angles of her face. She looked like a madonna and, although she possessed a subtle animal magnetism, she was never vulgar.

At least not until halfway through the movie.

Quite suddenly, the film changed from an allegorical fantasy shot with taste and discernment into titillating soft porn.

The scene was set in a barn, where

Ritchie Roberts, playing a rough-and-ready farmer, was keen to relieve the innocent girl of her virginity. The audience sniggered as Ritchie ripped off Atlanta's blouse, announced: "I'll show you what a *real* man is like." They laughed as Atlanta gasped in shock as he began to grab her breasts. Within seconds, the couple were writhing and moaning dramatically on the straw-covered floor.

The rest of the passionate scene, intercut with shots of cows mooing, horses neighing and rearing up on their hind legs, and chickens squawking their heads off, caused the audience to roar out loud, as tears of hilarity ran down their faces.

Toward the end of the sex scene, many of the audience started to file out, muttering, "Disgusting, awful, how could Laura Marlowe's daughter do that? What is this business coming to? Poor Laura will be turning in her grave."

Coral stalked out, grimly muttering to Atlanta, "I'll speak to you tomorrow, dear."

Atlanta huddled in her seat, tears streaming down her face, Fabio's reassuring hand in hers failing to assuage the bitter pill she was swallowing. The audience sounded the death knell for the film and the dreams of Atlanta and Fabio were inexorably smashed.

"Oh God," she murmured, as the auditorium emptied and the realization of how awful the film was hit her. "Oh my God, Fabio, what the hell is my father going to say?"

CHAPTER TWENTY-FOUR

Venetia woke up slowly, stretching luxuriously in her scented linen sheets. She ran her fingers down her firm body and was delighted to discover that her stomach was flat again.

The doctor had done a good job, terminating this pregnancy as efficiently as the one last year. Gone was the slight swelling that had blurred her youthful curves and caused her grandmother Anne to chastise her.

"You've been overeating again, Venetia. You eat far too much pudding, dear—you'll have to go on a diet."

Ha! Venetia smiled to herself. If Grandma

only knew that she'd been two months pregnant, she'd have had a stroke.

In the nightclubs and restaurants in Paris,
Athens and Rome, in shower rooms, gyms
and health clubs, young men gossiped
about the notorious Venetia Stephanopolis.
They regaled each other with details of their
various conquests of her and with tales of
Venetia's sexual prowess, for she possessed such animal magnetism that few
men could resist her when she swiveled her
ravishing aquamarine eyes in their direction.

Venetia closed her eyes and relived that
afternoon with Jake Jones, when she'd
probably gotten pregnant. Of course it could
have been Alain's baby, or the hot guy who
worked as a shoe salesman, or any of the
several men she had slept with recently. As
a tiny pang of guilt swept over her, she
reached for her stash and lit a joint. That always assuaged any negative feelings that
intruded on her consciousness. She knew
she liked men—maybe liked them too
much—and she knew she behaved outrageously sometimes, but there was a streak
of wildness in her that seemed to drive her
actions, probably inherited from her father.

Besides, there were so many gorgeous

men in Paris, and none more so than Jake Jones, the latest American anti-hero. A scowling Adonis in blue jeans. Zeus in a torn T-shirt. Venetia had loved the way the two of them looked together. She, so blonde, he so dark and surly but oh so sexy. At the thought of what they'd done on that early spring afternoon in the long grass behind her father's summer retreat, a smile crossed her face.

He had certainly been a fabulous lover, one of the best she'd known. He had the confidence that came with knowing that he was irresistible to women. Venetia remembered the feel of his skin, his scent, how the sun had glinted on his curly brown hair, and those intense, moody dark eyes.

Jake's rough approach, his take-me-or-leave-me attitude, had excited her, and she had thrown herself enthusiastically into their lovemaking. So enthusiastically, in fact, that her second abortion had been the ultimate result.

But to Jake Jones, Venetia had been just another notch on his bedpost, and shortly after their romance began, he'd flown to Tahiti for yet another remake of *Mutiny on the Bounty*. They had only spoken briefly during his time there, and Venetia hadn't told him about her "accident." She'd told no one.

When Jake returned to Paris three months later, a dainty dusky damsel whom he called his "personal assistant" was on his arm, and Venetia realized their short-lived affair was over. Like most of her "romances," it had fizzled out. Never mind, there were plenty more fish in the sea.

Venetia climbed out of bed and stared at herself in harsh daylight in her full-length mirror. She didn't look too good today. Though she was only seventeen, even she was aware that her looks were going off the boil. The flaxen hair was still lustrous and her figure amazing, but her eyes looked bloodshot, her skin was blotchy and her cheeks were bloated.

Venetia opened a drawer in her dressing table and surveyed the cache of chocolate bars and other delights all arranged neatly, ready for her selection. She took out a Toblerone and ate it quickly, then lit another joint and stared at herself in the mirror defiantly.

So what. All she needed to do was stop drinking and she would look fine again. Besides, her telephone never stopped ringing. She was the most popular girl in Paris. She could do exactly what she wanted, with whom she wanted. She had it all.

She was her father's favorite, pampered and adored, given anything that her heart desired. Venetia believed that her money and her beauty could get her anything in life. So why was it that after she got what she wanted she didn't want it anymore? Venetia had gone through boyfriends and lovers with alarming speed. She had also gone through alcohol, coke, Ecstasy, uppers and downers. She'd tried practically every drug invented at least once.

Sometimes she hadn't known where she was, let alone who she was—or what she was doing. There were whole periods of her life—hours, days, sometimes weeks—of which she had no recollection at all. It was all a blank. But strangely, it didn't bother her. Only making love or dancing all night at clubs felt real to Venetia. Everything else was make-believe.

CHAPTER TWENTY-FIVE

"How could you do such a thing, Fabio? I mean how *could* you?" Atlanta's eyes were swollen from crying.

Fabio sat slumped in an armchair, gazing morosely out of the window at the traffic on Sunset Boulevard, the television as usual tuned to MTV with the volume turned up.

"It's not my fault. It's Marcello's."

"Marcello's! Did you give him final cut? Answer me, Fabio. Did you?" She stormed up to the television and snapped it off.

Fabio's gray-blue eyes were cloudy.

"He double-crossed us, sweetheart. You know I wouldn't do anything to hurt you—or our movie. I'd waited a long time for this. I told him to tone it down." His voice was bitter.

"Then why? Why? How could it happen, Fabio?"

"I told you—Marcello must've got hold of the print from the editor after the final dubbing last week and spliced in our outtakes."

"All those animals, making those barnyard noises. Ugh! I've never seen anything so cheap and horrible. How can I *ever* hold my head up in this or any town anywhere again? How can I?"

"You will, sweetie—you will." Fabio continued staring at the traffic and let out a deep sigh.

This had been a mistake, a bad mistake. When he and Marcello had discussed beefing up the sex scene, Marcello had promised to talk to the editor about it. But he hadn't. He had spent twenty-four hours alone in the editing room doing it himself with all the rolls of film, the outtakes, animal stock shots and the negatives of that ghastly video. The result was a catastrophe for both them and their movie.

"When I see that bastard Marcello again I'll wring his neck," said Fabio.

"What good will that do?" Atlanta sighed.

"Well, at least you've got Kevin Bentley's movie." He comforted Atlanta as cheerfully as he could. "That's a great career move."

"Do you *really* think he's still going to want me after all this? I doubt I'll ever hear from him again," Atlanta said gloomily.

However, within the week Kevin Bentley did call and said nothing about Atlanta's movie fiasco. He suggested that she meet him for dinner at his house in Coldwater Canyon the following night to "discuss the project."

It was an unusually cold California night when Atlanta drove her new Mustang up the long winding drive to Kevin's house.

He answered the door himself, casual and charming in an open-necked white silk shirt and jeans.

"Come in honey," he said, ushering her through the spacious entrance hall into his study. "Good to see you. What can I get you to drink?"

"A Coke, please." Atlanta sat down on the enormous sofa, which was as soft and comfortable as a bed, and studied the dozens of framed black-and-white candid photographs on the walls. There was Kevin with Queen Elizabeth, Kevin with Marilyn

Monroe, Kevin with her mother. There was Kevin laughing and clowning with Frank Sinatra and Dean Martin. There was Kevin on the golf course with Bob Hope and playing tennis with Robert Redford. And there he was in the pits, leaning over a racing car sharing a joke with Paul Newman. There was also a very young Kevin dancing with Ava Gardner at Mocambo and Laura Marlowe at Ciro's. He was "boys' night out" personified, with Presidents Carter, Ford, Nixon and Reagan, and he was even pictured with Margaret Thatcher at Chequers, looking unusually solemn.

What an ego, Atlanta thought. Even bigger than my father's.

"Well now," he said, returning with her Coke, "how do you feel, honey?"

"How do you mean?" She asked warily. He must have heard about her movie's débâcle by now.

"You poor kid. I guess you must be pretty upset by what they did to your movie."

She nodded, unbidden tears stinging her eyes.

"Poor little kid." He moved closer to her on the sofa and started stroking her hair.

She stiffened. Surely this couldn't be the scenario for tonight? Kevin Bentley, the great Don Juan, out to practice his seduction technique on her. She turned to look into his green eyes and was momentarily startled. His eyes were soft and melting and his voice was soothing as his hand made its way up to her cheek, then down to the V-neck sweater. Atlanta had wished for this encounter so many times when she was younger, but now that it was happening she felt uncomfortable and trapped.

"Kevin, please don't." Atlanta moved away, but he moved closer to her.

"Why?" he said huskily. "You want me, don't you . . .? I know you wanted me the first time I saw you at that dinner at your father's. Admit it."

"But you didn't want *me* then."

He smiled. "I've changed my mind, honey, like you've changed your looks."

"Look, Kevin, let's be reasonable." She tried to laugh but only a croak came out. Oh God, how was she going to handle this? She wanted to be in his movie, but if she rejected him, would he still want her in it? She wasn't a whore, she'd leave that to her sister. Venetia's reputation was almost in tatters, but right now it looked like hers was going the same way.

"You love sex, Atlanta, don't you? I knew that night on your island that once you got rid of your virginity, you'd be horny as a little toad."

Atlanta wrinkled her nose at this unfortunate analogy but he seemed not to notice her distaste as he continued his spiel. "I knew for certain when I saw your video that you'd be a firecracker in bed."

"You *did see* that video?" she asked, horrified.

"Sure, honey. Everyone in Hollywood's seen it. And they all think you're hot, baby— real, real hot."

"I was drunk when we shot that scene." She was conscious of the feebleness of her excuse. "Drunk and drugged."

"So what?" Kevin's hand was moving to the buttons on her sweater, his fingers doing walkies up the front of it. "It's the result that counts."

"Kevin, please stop." She put her hand over his. "I really don't want to do this. I have a boyfriend and he's terribly jealous and . . ."

"Fabio Navaro, jealous?" Kevin let out a

peal of laughter. "Fabio's had practically every chick in this town and every other town from what I've heard. Don't be naïve, Atlanta. Wake up and smell the coffee. Your boyfriend's a notorious cocksman. He's just using you, honey. Can't you see that?"

"That's not true!" Her voice was thick with the effort of not crying.

"Ask him," shrugged Kevin. "Ask him where he was last Tuesday afternoon, for instance. I happened to see him myself, going into the Bel Air Hotel with Rebecca Stevens, and they *weren't* about to have a script conference, I can assure you."

"No. It can't be true. He loves me."

"Love!" Kevin scoffed, and took a sip of his Scotch. "Love's only for the movies, sweetheart, love's in romance novels, love's for kids. But I guess you're still a kid, aren't you?"

"I'm twenty-two," said Atlanta, unbidden tears running down her cheeks.

"That's still a kid. There, honey, dry your beautiful eyes and tell me something. Do you *really* want to be in my movie, or don't you?"

"Of *course* I want to be in it."

"Then all you have to do"—he bent close

to her and playfully bit her earlobe—'is be nice to Uncle Kevin. That's not so hard is it?"

"Are you actually saying that if I *don't* sleep with you, then I won't get the role in your movie?"

"It's just business, honey." His hand stroked her hair. "You like me, don't you?"

Atlanta's mind was racing. So this was it, crunch time. Kevin had laid his cards on the table and it was now up to her as to how she was going to play hers. How much did she *really* want to go on acting? The words her mother had said to her father echoed again in her mind, "The life of an actress is actually a very empty one." Then, she remembered something Laura had said in a magazine article: "At twenty-seven, it was all over for the young contract actresses, and when they were fired I saw how much they suffered. There was nowhere for them to go. It was heartbreaking."

Did she really want this show-biz life? This low life, peopled with amoral swine; the Kevin Bentleys and the Marcello Lupes of this world. Did she really want to be hounded by the press and paparazzi, conned, humiliated and drugged for a porno-graphic scene in a movie? She looked at

Kevin, at the raffish, ruthless, smug expression on his once handsome face and suddenly he revolted her.

Her answer was a resounding no. She didn't want him—she didn't want a movie career and, in any case, her feeble attempt to win approval from her father had backfired horribly. If Nicholas wasn't yet aware of her screen humiliation, he certainly soon would be, and he would then disapprove of her more strongly than ever.

Atlanta took a deep breath, and wiping her tears with her sleeve, stood up.

"Thank you for the offer, Kevin," she said quietly, "but I'm afraid I must refuse. Both the movie and you."

She walked with rubbery legs to the front door and heard Kevin yell, "You're making a big mistake, honey!"

Right now she had a bone to pick with Fabio, but when she eased her tense, tired body into their bed beside him he was sound asleep. When she woke at noon he had left. There was a scribbled note stuck to the door of the fridge, "Gone to meet Marcello for lunch. Back around four."

CHAPTER TWENTY-SIX

At a cocktail party in Paris, Maximus Gobbi, the owner of a small Italian magazine that specialized in gossip and interviews with rich and famous celebrities, introduced Venetia to an aspiring actor. Antonio Zorba was handsome in a flashy way, with a weak chin and liquid brown eyes with little behind them. He was bragging about the film he'd appeared in, in Italy.

"Oh really?" responded Venetia in her forthright manner. "I see lots of Italian films, but I don't think I ever remember seeing you in any of them."

"*Return to the Black Lagoon*. Did you see that?"

She giggled. "What did you play? The creature?"

"How did you guess?" he said totally without humor.

Although Venetia liked men, she was unimpressed by this boaster with his wavy hair and overexercised body in yellow trousers and black-and-yellow shirt. They spoke more of a gigolo than of a struggling actor. And he wouldn't stop yapping on about himself.

". . . and when Fellini saw my test he thought I was too handsome for the lead so they gave it to that *putz*—Vittorio what's-'is-name. I had a nice little role, small but nice. I did well. Fellini, he loved me—but unfortunately not enough." He shrugged self-deprecatingly.

Venetia stared at him, blank faced. His charm was falling on stony ground.

"Sadly for me, my whole part ended up on the cutting room floor. That's show business for you, I guess, but it beats washing dishes for a living."

Maximus sycophantically joined in Antonio's laughter, but Venetia didn't. "Yes, well, that's really interesting. But if you'll excuse me, gentlemen, I must be off," and she wandered away to join a group of friends.

"Let's make a toast to your career." Maximus turned to Antonio with a sly look, wondering how long it would be before he got him into his bed. "Which will be launched tomorrow afternoon, with the unwitting help of our pretty young friend." He gestured toward Venetia and both men raised their glasses.

It hadn't been difficult to bring Antonio to Nicholas and Stefania's summer lunch party the following day. Two or three hundred people had been invited and Maximus brought him along as his guest. Stefania Scalerina greeted Max warmly. Her sunglasses were darker than usual to conceal her black eye. Nicholas's sado-masochistic sex games were becoming more extreme all the time— with an emphasis on the sadistic.

Maximus strolled about the beautiful grounds of the great Paris town house, greeting people he knew, for Maximus knew many people. Occasionally he took a snap with his Instamatic.

Antonio had, on Maximus's instructions,

oozed his way close to Venetia and attempted to engage her in conversation, but she practically ignored him. It was a piece of cake for Maximus to stroll over to where they stood, saying in a friendly way, "Hold it, Venetia, I just want a quick shot of you and Antonio."

Antonio edged closer to Venetia in the split second before Maximus pressed the shutter and, as Venetia had half turned with a smile to greet someone behind him, she met Antonio's eyes with what looked, photographically, like a melting glance.

Two days later, Venetia was sitting with Alain at Heavenly's when Antonio came over to their banquette to greet her. As he kissed her hand, while staring meaningfully into her eyes, the club photographer flashed a couple of quick shots.

The next morning, Venetia went for her usual jog through the Bois de Bologne. There he was again in running shorts and singlet, friendlier than a motherless puppy.

"Wonderful to see you again," he cried matching her stride. "What a coincidence!"

"Isn't it," she said through gritted teeth. What was this creep up to?

Panting somewhat more than necessary,

he kept pace with her until she reached the gates of her home. Then with a cheery wave, a blown kiss and a "*Ciao cara*," he jogged away down the quiet street, looking pleased with himself.

The impact of the photographs in the press couldn't have been better for Antonio. Maximus had contacts with at least one major tabloid in every European country, and the pictures of Venetia and Antonio, with snippets of the accompanying story, were dribbled expertly to the eager press—judiciously spaced a few days apart. Venetia was a pot of gold to the media and, with Antonio being an undeniably handsome and young actor, the papers pounced on the story.

Maximus's master plan worked brilliantly. Two weeks after Antonio Zorba had first set eyes on Venetia Stephanopolis, he was being gossiped and written about not only in Europe, but in America too.

"Secret romance of Venetia Stephanopolis and unknown actor." The American *Daily Record* had picked up the story and run with it on its cover.

"Our love is private and beautiful. We wanted to keep it a secret, but now that the news has come out I can only say that I adore Venetia. She is the woman of my dreams," bragged Antonio Zorba to *La Stampa*.

"I love her and I know she loves me," he told the *Daily Mail* as he held up a photograph of the two of them looking soulfully at each other. This photo was a composite picture, brilliantly put together by the art department at Maximus's magazine, *Bravo*.

"What the hell is going on?" screamed Venetia, staring furiously at photographs in several European tabloids of her and Antonio.

"Who does this guy think he is?" she squawked, storming into her father's study.

Nicholas was sitting behind his desk while his secretary juggled three telephones, which were ringing constantly.

"Kitten, you've been photographed together, at least four times, and the press haven't stopped calling." He sounded more irritable than usual. "Miss Jeans has been dealing with them, but they're insisting on a statement."

"He's even giving interviews on TV," said Miss Jeans, hanging up one phone and immediately picking up another.

Venetia was livid. "*Why* is he doing this?

It's not true, *none* of it. I swear I hardly know him. I met him with Maximus and then I kept bumping into him."

"You must learn to ignore the press," Nicholas said. "They love to build you up then pull you down again. I've never believed what's been written about *me* over the years. However, you can't get away from this. Put on the videotape, Mary," he ordered.

Miss Jeans pressed the PLAY button on the video and Antonio's cocky young face appeared on the screen.

"This was live this morning in America," stated Nicholas grimly.

Venetia gazed open-mouthed at the screen as Antonio said: "Venetia Stephanopolis and I come from different worlds. That is why I've now decided to have some time apart," he confided to Joan Lundon on *Good Morning America*. "All this publicity has clouded the issue, which is our pure love for each other. The pressure of our romance being revealed has been too much for Venetia. She has become upset, so now we must be apart for a little while—to give us time to think."

Joan broke in smoothly. "How do you account, Antonio, for the fact that Nicholas

Stephanopolis's spokespeople deny all knowledge of your friendship with his daughter?"

Antonio shrugged, smiling. "What else can they say?" he answered with sincere sickly charm. "Venetia is only seventeen. I am twenty-six," he lied modestly, knocking off only three years.

"She is too young yet for a full-lifetime commitment, which is what I want to give her, eventually, of course. But I too must go on with my life as an actor, in spite of my feelings for my dearest true love."

Venetia ground her teeth and shrieked. "You creep. Don't I have enough to contend with the press, without this shit?"

"Sssssh," admonished Nicholas. "Control yourself."

"And so," the camera was in close now on Antonio's earnest face, "I must go on with my own career, however humble. We talk on the telephone all the time, of course, and soon, very soon, we shall be together again. And I hope for both our sakes that when that time comes, we will be together for always." He smiled intimately into the camera.

"What are your plans now, Antonio?" asked Joan pragmatically.

"I'm going to Hollywood today to meet a very important director who wants me to star in his new romantic comedy film. I think maybe with Michelle Pfeiffer. I hope so. She is beautiful, but not as beautiful as my Venetia."

"Oh, turn it off!" screamed Venetia, slamming her fist into the embroidered Aubusson cushions on the sofa.

Silently, Miss Jeans switched off the TV.

"The bastard, I swear I've only met him twice," said Venetia angrily.

"Kitten, does it really matter?" sighed Nicholas, mindful of the little white lies he had heard from his daughter over the years. "Don't get so upset about it, it isn't important."

"It *is* important," Venetia countered furiously. "I'm going to nail that liar to the wall—he'll be sorry he ever met me."

"Venetia, need I remind you that you are a Stephanopolis. We do *not* make idle threats. We must behave with dignity and accept the fact that some things are said about us that are unfortunate and untrue. But we can't formally deny every story that is ever printed about us, kitten. You have to accept the bad with the good, Venetia, and behave with dignity."

Venetia glared at her father. What he was

saying was right of course. "But it's not *fair*. I have enough lies and scandal written about me in the gossip press."

"I know, kitten," Nicholas soothed. "I admit it's unfortunate. They pick on you because you're so beautiful. Try to ignore it, just get on with your education and with your life, and hope that it'll all blow over and be forgotten. Meanwhile, I'll make a few calls to some of my newspaper acquaintances telling them to take it easy on you."

"Thank you, Papa." She came over to hug him and gave him a lingering kiss on his cheek, and he ruffled her hair lovingly.

Miss Jeans glanced at them from the corner of her eye. Amazing, they almost looked like lovers. It was incredible though, how Nicholas favored this daughter over his other one. Incredible, yet rather sad.

CHAPTER TWENTY-SEVEN

Atlanta took little notice of her sister's new romance in the tabloids. She had enough problems of her own.

Checking up on Kevin's tip about Fabio, she had discovered with sickening certainty that her lover had been cheating on her practically throughout their entire relationship.

She had hired a private detective for a couple of weeks to make doubly sure, but there was no question about it. He seemed to be bedding half of the starlets in Hollywood, and for Atlanta, this was the ultimate rejection. In spite of Fabio's impassioned protests, she moved out of their apartment and into the Chateau Marmont, where she thought hard about her future life and career and waited for the inevitable call from her agent, telling her that she would not be in Kevin's film.

It came a few days later. "Sorry kiddo, I'm really sorry," Hank's voice was doleful. "I just don't understand it. I guess your movie was too raunchy and Kevin couldn't take the heat. All the gossip must've put him off you."

"I guess you're right. Well, Hank, at least I've made a decision," she said calmly.

"And what's that, hon?"

"I'm quitting movies. I don't really like acting, I'm not cut out for it, I'm uncomfortable in front of the camera and I *hate* the people I have to deal with. Not you, Hank, of course," she hastily added.

"But you can't quit now." Hank sounded panicked. "I've got another script for you to read. It's a beaut. Not as good as *Orphans* but you're gonna have to live down your porn movie. Don't worry, hon, this town's got a short memory. Now listen, this is a good script. It's called *The Girl Can't Help It*. It's a remake of an old Jayne Mansfield movie, it made her a star."

"No thanks, Hank. This girl *can* help it, and my acting days are definitely over."

Atlanta flew to New York on the red-eye and holed up in the family apartment on Fifth Avenue. Nicholas and Stefania were cruising on the *Circe,* and who knew what shenanigans Venetia was up to in Paris.

Atlanta sat alone brooding for hours. What was she going to do now? She wanted self-respect and the admiration and love of her father, but why couldn't she get it? Why did he condone and accept anything that Venetia did and yet castigate her—that is, when he wasn't totally ignoring her, which was most of the time?

She went over to the mirror and looked at her perfect face, but once again she saw only that sad, plump little girl with the faint mustache. Maybe that's what Papa sees when he looks at me. I'm just a fat, ugly nine-year-old to him . . . stupid, brainless, and always in his way. Why?

As Atlanta stared at herself, somewhere, deep inside her memory, something stirred. A long-forgotten night when she'd been ill and feverish as a child. She couldn't remember what had happened, but sometimes, in her nightmares, she would dream she was outside the cabin of a boat, where something horrible was going on inside. She always woke with a start before she could see what it was, then dismissed it from her mind.

"I must pull myself together," Atlanta admonished herself. "My life's a mess. What *the hell* am I going to do with myself now?"

A few days later Venetia called to say hello and commiserate over her movie flop. Since Atlanta didn't believe her sister gave a damn, she quickly changed the subject to Venetia's latest exploits, as reported in the tabloids.

"Daddy's been *so* understanding about those horrible lies in the papers."

"I bet he has." Atlanta hated to hear the resentment in her voice. "Didn't he tell you to pull yourself together and behave?"

"Tell me to pull myself together? Why should he? The Antonio story wasn't my fault. It was a setup, and Papa knows it was. But that creep certainly got enough mileage out of it," Venetia said bitterly. "Do you know he actually got a part in a Bertolucci movie." Then gaily: "Has Papa seen your movie yet?"

"*God* no!" The thought was enough to send Atlanta into cardiac arrest. "And I hope he never does."

"Well, he's cruising the Turkish coast right now, with Stefania and a group of wrinklies. But I'm sure someone must've told him about it. You know Papa—he always gets to hear about everything."

"When he hears about my film I think I'll take the next rocket to the moon," Atlanta said gloomily.

That'll *really* put an end to any good thoughts he might have had about me, she thought, after she'd hung up.

CHAPTER TWENTY-EIGHT

When Nicholas finally did hear about Atlanta's movie, he immediately gave orders that all the copies be bought up and destroyed. Then he rang his eldest daughter. "How *could* you allow yourself to be compromised into such a perverted, loathsome situation, Atlanta? Being filmed copulating like a whore? Don't you have *any* self-respect? Doesn't our family and the memory of your mother mean anything to you?"

"Of course it does. You know how much I loved Mama!"

More than you did, Father, she wanted to

say. Much more than you ever did from what I remember.

"Look, I admit I made a terrible mistake in letting Fabio talk me into that love scene, but we were just acting—we didn't actually do it."

"Love scene!" Nicholas was outraged. "Love scene? Atlanta, it was the most abominable thing I've ever seen. A disgusting embarrassment. I couldn't watch after the first few minutes."

Atlanta flushed, but she answered meekly: "I'm sorry, Father. Truly sorry. But it will never happen again, because I'm giving up acting now. I'm going to try my hand at something else."

"Thank God for that. And just what are you going to do to make a living now, may I ask?"

"Well, Father—I—I don't really need to actually *make* a living, do I?" she stuttered. ". . . I mean, I do have my trust fund allowance."

"You *had* your trust fund." Nicholas's voice was ice. "But the trustees and I have decided that because of your shocking behavior we are stopping your allowance with immediate effect."

"You wouldn't do that." Atlanta was shocked. "You couldn't. You can't cut my allowance, Father, you can't!"

"Don't tell me what I can or can't do, Atlanta. I can, and I have!" snapped Nicholas. "You certainly don't deserve five thousand dollars a month. In my opinion you don't even deserve five thousand dollars a year. Not with the way you've been conducting your life lately. So, I've made a decision. From now on, Atlanta, you are going to have to make your own living, until you prove to me and to the trustees that you are a responsible and worthy person who is doing a civilized and proper job. Until then I really don't want to hear from you at all."

"Father . . . No! You can't!"

"Atlanta, please don't try your histrionics on me, because they won't work. You can go on living in the apartment until you get a job, then I will expect you to move out and support yourself, as most normal twenty-two-year-old girls do these days."

"But I . . ."

"I don't wish to discuss it anymore, Atlanta." His voice was so cold that her knees started to give way. "As far as I'm concerned, until you can prove to me that you are a useful member of society, and a worthwhile person, I don't wish to have any contact with you at all."

"What about Venetia's allowance?" she sobbed. "It doesn't matter what she does, does it, Father? She could stand naked on top of the Eiffel Tower and you wouldn't bat an eyelid. She would still be your darling kitten wouldn't she?—your favorite. What about all *her* affairs, Father? All of her rotten scandals?"

"Venetia is still a child," he said coldly. "She's only sixteen."

"Seventeen!" yelled Atlanta. "She's seventeen, Father. And what the hell is she doing with *her* life?"

"She's still a girl, Atlanta. She's too young to know better, and I do *not* wish to discuss her with you. That is not the point of this conversation."

"Oh, but it *is*, Father. That *is* the point!" Atlanta's words were tumbling out now, a torrent of protest. The dam had burst and there was no stopping the flood that for more than a decade had been held back.

"You let Venetia get away with *everything*, Father. You don't care that she's out at nightclubs and sleeping with anyone she fancies. She's got carte blanche for everything she does. She behaves like a slut and you let her get away . . ."

"That's enough filth out of your mouth, Atlanta. Just because you're jealous of Venetia is no reason to malign her."

"Jealous . . . JEALOUS!" Atlanta could hardly breathe, she was so angry. "It isn't Venetia I'm jealous of, Father. It's the fact that you have never had any time for *me*. Never. Ever."

"This conversation is over," Nicholas said coldly and Atlanta heard the long-distant click on the line as her father hung up.

"Oh God!" she screamed, tears of anger and hurt running down her cheeks. "Oh my God. Why, why do you hate me so much, Father?"

CHAPTER TWENTY-NINE

Kristobel's Couture House was thriving. He was now dressing senators' wives and socialites who merited column inches—a far cry from Bruce's original clientele of rich Arabs and minor actresses.

Everyone assumed that Kristobel and Bruce were lovers, but they weren't, for Kristobel had had no lovers—either male or female—in his entire life.

Kristobel was Atlanta's only true friend in New York. Although she had many acquaintances, no one really understood her or could share her pain. She could confide her hurt only in Kristobel.

The young designer stood in front of his easel in his usual crisp white smock, his long black hair tied back with a velvet band, his eyes behind his accustomed dark glasses, enigmatic. As he listened to Atlanta's woes, he never stopped sketching. Although only a few years older than Atlanta, he was wiser in the ways of the world than she was.

"You must get on with your life. Forget about the movies. You cannot live in the shadows, overpowered by your father any longer. Get out of his apartment. You can come and stay with me if you like, but you *must* get yourself a proper job that you can be respected for. But first, you need to go far away, until this horrible mess about your film blows over."

"Well, that won't take long," said Atlanta bitterly. "The reviews were so bad, and audiences so sparse, that the studio was pulling it out of the theaters until Father bought up all the copies."

"That's good. The fewer people that see it the better. Why don't you go to stay in the summer house in the Hamptons, where you told me your mother took you when you were children?"

"That's a great idea. I've got a key and Father won't even know that I'm there—he never goes at this time of year. If my savings run out, I can always sell a few *objets d'art*! The summer house is so secluded and isolated, I could really get my head together there." Atlanta started to feel enthusiastic.

"That's what you need now. Get away. Don't watch TV or read newspapers or magazines. Just take stock of your life and don't think about your father. Even though he is the lover of one of my best clients and pays my bills on time, he's not a nice man, Atlanta."

"I know," she said quietly. Elusive memories swirled like mist in her head. "You're right, Kristobel."

Kristobel raised his glass of apple juice in a toast. "To your future rebirth and transformation. You've done it physically, now it's time to do it emotionally, spiritually and personally. You must develop the confidence in yourself that you deserve. It's time to grow up, Atlanta. You have been waiting far too long."

* * *

After two months of meditating in the Hamptons, taking stock of her life, swimming, listening to music and totally relaxing, Atlanta felt almost reborn. Her morale had improved and she felt healthy and ready to tackle the world; she had decided she wanted a career in journalism. She started by sending the Italian publisher Maximus Gobbi some of the profiles and short stories she had written. He became quite excited by them and called her to set up a meeting.

They were having tea in the lobby of the Waldorf Astoria. "You're a good writer," Maximus said approvingly. "You have a true knack for this. I like how you write about celebrities. It's clever, subtle and a little bit bitchy. It's what people like to read."

"Thanks. Writing stories about real people has always fascinated me."

"Well, that's what I would like you to write for my magazine; in-depth profiles of celebrities, some of whom you know—like Stefania, Kristobel, Sandrelli, Kevin Bentley—maybe even your father."

Atlanta gritted her teeth. "I think *not*."

"Then, on your travels, you can feed my gossip columnist a few juicy tidbits occasionally. Without compromising yourself, of course," he added hastily.

"But won't those celebrities realize that the stories came from me?"

"Being a gossip columnist—a good one mind you, not one of these fly-by-nights writing for supermarket rags—can give you real social cachet these days. Look at Liz Smith and Cindy Adams. Why do people invite them to their parties? Because, my dear, most people in the public eye today *adore* being talked about, they relish seeing their names in the gossip columns. You know yourself that half of those skeletal society ladies in New York have their own personal press agents whose job it is to get their names in Suzy's column as often as possible."

"But Max, I want to be taken seriously as a writer. How can I be if I write gossip?"

"It's a good place to start. Like all magazines, *Bravo* likes a little bit of scandal and gossip, but mostly we like pretty pictures of pretty people doing and saying pretty and amusing things. I promise you that if your first celebrity interview is any good, I will print it. *Bravo* will put you under exclusive contract for three months," he said. "If we like your writing, you will be signed up for a further year. That's how you'll earn your stripes. How does that suit you, gorgeous lady?"

"Gorgeous lady!" Atlanta jumped at the compliment and quickly opened her silver compact to check her makeup.

In the reflection she saw a familiar figure behind her, walking from the concierge's desk, followed by a bellboy carrying a pair of matched Vuitton suitcases.

"My God, talk of the devil, it's Kevin," she muttered. "What's he doing in New York?"

She turned her head, and as if by radar, Kevin looked at her. "Well, well." He grinned boyishly as he sauntered over to their banquette and crinkled his trademark eyes. "What are *you* doing in New York, Atlanta?"

"She works here." Maximus smoothly extended a fleshy hand. "For me. How do you do. I'm Maximus Gobbi."

"Hi." Kevin's eyes didn't leave Atlanta's. "Good to meet you, Maximus."

"Please sit down," oiled Maximus. "Take a coffee, a drink with us—please."

"Thanks, but I can't stay long—my casting director's meeting me in a few minutes." Kevin's eyes swept over Atlanta's body with expert appraisal.

"Ah yes, your new film," said Maximus,

pleased with his inside information. "It's about orphans, no?"

"Something like that." Kevin's capped teeth sparkled in the gloom of the bar.

"There's a rumor that Sharon Stone is going to star," said Maximus. "Is that true?"

"Could be," smiled Kevin, elusively.

Atlanta was dumbstruck. Her heart was beating too fast for her to join in the conversation. She felt a terrible anger toward this man whom she had known since her childhood.

His nerve! Was she supposed to forget that he had tried to make her have sex with him in exchange for a part in his film? Were those the rules of the slick, sick society he inhabited? Well, if she was going to survive in her new career, she had better learn the rules fast. Otherwise Maximus would have no compunction about getting rid of her. And what would she do then?

CHAPTER THIRTY

For her first celebrity profile, Atlanta persuaded Maximus that she could do an excellent piece on Coral Steele.

Four-times-married Coral, a star since she was a child, a close friend of Laura's, and to top it all, Atlanta's godmother, was not averse to the idea, and invited Atlanta to stay at her villa in Cannes for a week.

On her way Atlanta found herself stuck in one of the endless traffic jams that were part of the dubious charm of August in the Riviera. The air-conditioned limousine crawled along the packed Croisette at Nice as she looked out of the window at the teeming masses. Hot and red faced, in crumpled T-shirts and shorts, they made Atlanta feel almost secure in her newfound beauty. But she still couldn't help but identify with some of the obese women who strolled by. Any one of those plain, overweight, badly dressed girls was a mirror image of what she had once been.

That was all over now. She fiddled with the knob to get Riviera Radio. Now the only vestige left of the plump creature she had been was in her mind. Why was it that even though some men stopped talking when she entered a room, and many women envied her, she still felt so plain most of the time? When was she going to feel inside as she looked outside?

Now the time had come to see if her newfound glamour could work for her in the sinful playgrounds of the rich. The limousine left Nice, snaking behind the tiny narrow roads to Coral's villa, situated high in the hills, with the bay of St. Jean Cap Ferrat stretched below like yards of blue satin. Like many of its neighbors, it was built of pale peach-colored stone. Coral stood at the top of the ivy-covered steps dressed in raw silk lounging pajamas, her arms outstretched in an extravagant welcome and a cigarette holder clenched between her lips.

"My darling, I'm *so* happy you could make it," she trilled in her smart Bostonian accent, her multicharmed bracelets tinkling as she waved beautifully manicured hands with long false fingernails. "My God, darling, you look *divine*. The makeover is a triumph." Atlanta followed Coral into a spacious cool room with white-painted wicker furniture covered in blue and white chintz and overlooking a dazzling view of the swimming pool and bay. Small speedboats darted across the water, and the house smelled of lavender from the profusion of bushes that edged the garden.

"Now sit down, darling, we'll have some iced tea and I'll fill you in on the cast of characters for tonight." Coral inserted another Sobranie into her slender coral cigarette holder, which matched her lipstick, as did her nails and beautifully tended toenails.

"You look wonderful, Aunt Coral," Atlanta said warmly.

"Not *Aunt* anymore, dear," admonished Coral. "You're far too beautiful, and I'm far too old. Call me Coral, please, dear. I don't wish to appear more of a geriatric than I already am."

"But you look gorgeous. You really are amazing . . ."

". . . for my age." Coral finished the sentence with a laugh, pouring iced tea into pale peach glasses. "It's true, dear, I am. But it's all maintenance. I told my last husband, poor boy—Frederick, I said, both this house and I need *lots* of money spent on us, for maintenance."

Atlanta laughed and sipped her tea.

"So I'll tell you who's coming," said Coral. "Dean and Jennifer Holden. You know them of course?"

"No, I don't—who are they?"

"Dean is an older but still attractive American gentleman who's involved in some pretty shady arms sales to certain hostile countries," said Coral. "But they have been welcomed with open arms into New York society. Jennifer, his new wife, is forty years younger. My dear, she was a waitress Dean discovered in New York, working at Joe Allen's. Can you imagine! He asked for a hamburger and this little dish threw herself at him. She'd been a model wannabe but as soon as Dean started decking her out in Saint Laurent suits and Fred Leighton jewels she gave up *that* idea pronto."

"Is he the jealous type?" asked Atlanta.

"Jealous! My dear, does Dolly Parton sleep on her back?" Coral laughed. "He spends *hours* questioning her about her movements. If the poor girl so much as takes a trip to Bloomies after lunch, he has her followed. He's crazy about the woman. However, I *have* heard rumors . . ."

"What sort of rumors?" Atlanta wished she had not packed her mini cassette recorder away in her bags. This was the perfect story for Maximus's column.

"She was spotted at a Chippendales show recently."

"That's not so shocking. Everyone goes there, just for laughs."

"I agree, darling, it is *très amusant*. But when she inserted a ten-dollar bill down one young stud's posing pouch, with the phone number of her hotel *and* her room number written on it, it's *not* so *très amusant*."

"How do you know?"

"Joe Boolie was there with her. He saw it all."

"Did she meet the guy later?" Atlanta was mentally making notes.

"No one knows for sure. But you know Joe. He loves to create gossip. He could make a scenario out of you and me having tea," laughed Coral. "Anyway, ask him yourself, he's staying here too."

"Oh good. Is he photographing the party tonight?"

"Of *course* not, darling. Joe is *much* too grand. He only photographs couture for the glossies these days. If I even *suggested* it he'd stalk out in a snit. No, he's here as a guest. With Thierry of course. And then we have the fabulous Kevin coming tonight. That's rather a coup."

"Kevin?" Warning signs flashed in Atlanta's head. "Which Kevin?"

"Come, darling, there's only *one* Kevin."

"Well, there's Spacey and Costner and Bacon," muttered Atlanta, realizing that even the mention of the man made her angry. "It's quite a common name."

"But Mr. Kevin *Bentley* is still the numero uno stud in the world today, in spite of his age. Don't you agree, darling?"

"Mmm, I guess so." Atlanta tried to sound noncommittal. "But I've heard he's constantly on the prowl. Don't you find that awfully unattractive?"

"It's true. He is—shall we say—not very

discerning when it comes to getting female scalps on his belt."

"Isn't he getting a bit long in the tooth for that now?" Atlanta sounded uncharacteristically bitchy.

"Watch it, duckie!" smiled Coral. "Kevin and I are *exactly* the same age. My God, but he was a good lover," she mused. "Back in the sixties when we made our movie together, he was so indefatigable I even left Ralphie for him."

"But you went back to Ralphie, didn't you?"

"Yes, for a while. My dear, I was worn out after a year of living with Kevin. Morning, noon and night he wanted sex. Sometimes I felt I was living with a sexual robot. His libido was so lethal that he couldn't bear to be rejected. After a while, darling, I felt there was something wrong with a man who's almost in a *constant* state of priapism."

"Constant?"

"Well, almost. He's famous for it. Don't just ask me, ask everyone. I mean if you look through a *Who's Who* of female Hollywood, you can bet your Manolos that Kevin has bedded ninety percent of them, and the ones that he hasn't are so old and ugly that even he wouldn't bother."

"So what's his secret?" asked Atlanta curiously.

"Well, first of all I think that he really *likes* women. Not just their bodies, but also their brains. He's made a study of them, handles them as smoothly as an elevator operator. He knows *just* the right buttons to push. I can still remember the heights of pleasure and passion, even after more than thirty years. When I went back to dear Ralphie, I knew it could never be the same in the bed department. That's really why we broke up."

"And you've never had anyone as good since?"

"Of, course darling, don't be silly. My polo player, Juan, was fabulous—so was dear Martino, and of course Gerd," she said loyally. "Anyway, enough about Kevin. Oh dear, I do hope you don't put this conversation in your article. I must go and talk to my staff about tonight and you must have a little rest before the party. See you in your fairy frock at nine sharp. I *know* you're going to knock 'em all dead, darling!"

*　*　*

By Coral's standards it was a small, informal party. Only sixty people. Six tables of ten.

"Sixty is the perfect number," she explained to Atlanta. "Big enough for a grand soirée, and to meet new people, yet small enough not to hurt too many of one's friends' feelings."

Kevin Bentley had arrived alone, as usual, believing that he traveled fastest by doing so. He stood next to the brilliantly lit swimming pool, waiting for the dazzling women to come to him. He had met most of them, but there were still a few he wanted to meet. Soon a steady procession of the Euro-rich, princesses, contessas and tycoons' wives, were drawn to him like iron filings to a magnet. Their couture silk and chiffon gowns fluttered gracefully and beringed hands brushed against his white dinner jacket like delicate moths, while Kevin graciously accepted their attentions as his due.

Atlanta hovered on the edge of various groups, her ears cocked for interesting gossip. Tidbits, information, tittle-tattle, scandal—her tiny mini cassette recorder, which could pick up anything up to ten yards away, was ready. She had it in her handbag, a gossamer creation of silk and golden latticework.

Maximus needed her to deliver the goods. *Bravo* was now the spiciest magazine in Europe, and since he was breaking into the American market this autumn, he needed even more sizzling stories to make his circulation rise.

Atlanta had already recorded a fascinating conversation between Dean Holden and a well-known Lebanese arms dealer which she knew Maximus would love. Selling arms to *that* particular Arab country was a definite no-no. But she needed more fodder. She had noticed Kevin observing her across the terrace, but then she had noticed him looking at every pretty woman tonight. She knew she looked particularly attractive in a black chiffon slip dress, her shapely bosom barely covered by sheer, black lace.

She watched Joe Boolie chatting up a good-looking polo player, famous not only for his exploits with ponies but with ladies too. Casually, Joe touched the man on the elbow, running his hand lightly down his forearm as he told a joke in his outrageously witty way. The polo player was laughing hard.

Then—Atlanta couldn't believe it—was she seeing things? The polo player put his hand up to Joe's face and brushed a lock of hair off his forehead, his liquid eyes giving Joe a definite mating call. She was quite sure that by the end of the evening Joe would have paired off with him.

When dinner was announced, the guests strolled to their tables set with Coral's signature peach tablecloths, fragrant with centerpieces of peach roses massed around ormolu candelabra and accessorized with trailing ivy and white lilac.

"No expense spared tonight." Joe was Atlanta's right-hand dinner partner. "Do you know how much peach roses cost in August? And, of course, she had to have them flown in from Holland."

"Yes, but everything looks so beautiful," said Atlanta. "So does Coral."

"Hmm. Just had her third lift I hear." Joe sucked on a baby asparagus with relish, eyeing the polo player next to Atlanta.

"I don't think that matters. Look at me, I've had everything done. I'm a makeover miracle."

"You certainly are." Joe laughed. "A modern miracle, and that's the best thing you ever did. I congratulate you, doll."

"Thanks."

"Why aren't you eating?" He pointed accusingly at her asparagus soufflé. "It's delish."

"Would I blow this body? Do you *know* how many sit-ups I have to do every day?"

"I know several guys who would like to do things with your body. You're the prettiest here tonight."

"I'd rather just be an observer." Atlanta turned to Eduardo, the polo player on her left, who made some halfhearted eye contact with her, but the secret looks between him and Joe did not go unobserved. Joe whispered to Atlanta. "He will be *mine* tonight, child. I guarantee it."

"I never knew he was gay."

"He's not. He's bi. But he prefers the fruit of the banana to the fruit of the fig. He just can't resist my fatal attraction, doll. Few can, y'know."

Atlanta laughed. It was hard to believe, because Joe was shortish, plumpish, and on the wrong side of fifty, but such was his charm and chutzpah that when he put his mind to it he could have whoever he wanted.

"Oh, it'll probably only be a blow job with protection," Joe said airily. "But who cares? These days, child, a girl can't be too careful."

Kevin was seated between Coral and Jennifer Holden, but since he'd been having Coral on a regular basis for decades, he concentrated on the pretty young trophy wife, who was all bedroom eyes and fluttering eyelashes. When he put his hand on her firm, bare thigh under the table he had felt a frisson of pleasure. This could be a fortunate night indeed.

Los Paraguayos came in to play after dinner while Atlanta watched the guests' activities from the corner of her eye.

She observed Jennifer sauntering casually into the main house followed shortly afterward by Kevin. It wasn't hard to surmise where they had slipped off to, and Atlanta tailed them diligently.

Jennifer's bedroom was two doors from hers, so Atlanta opened her sliding glass doors and tiptoed onto her balcony, and then she nipped over to the next one and eased herself into the shadows outside the window. The curtains were slightly open, and dextrously, Atlanta bent down to look through the chink in the curtains.

Kevin, already stripped, lay on the bed,

ready for action, and Jennifer, unhooking her Lacroix dress as fast as false fingernails would allow, was getting there.

Atlanta didn't want to stick around to witness what was about to happen. She had what she wanted. She'd snapped the two of them going into his bedroom, now she would snap them when they left in disarray. A picture speaks a thousand words.

Maximus would be pleased with her work tonight, but in her heart Atlanta wasn't. Shut up, said her mind. Don't you want to succeed in publishing, to be a writer? This is how you have to start, in the gutter. Besides, no one will know it was you. They'll blame the staff.

Tonight was obviously Joe Boolie's lucky night, as well as Kevin's. Atlanta noticed his absence immediately when she returned.

The dancing was in full swing, Los Paraguayos having been replaced by another Latin-American band, who were blasting out a torrid version of "La Bamba." Half the couples were whirling and twirling in the sticky August heat while the other half sipped drinks and chatted.

With unerring instinct Atlanta headed for an unlit part of the garden, far below the oleander bushes. She was right. Joe had scored all right—and what a score. Six foot three of polo-playing manhood leaned against an olive tree while Joe knelt at his feet. From Eduardo's sighs Joe was obviously no slouch at this job.

Atlanta drew the line at taking a photograph of that and slunk back to the party. She had clocked up three stories tonight for Maximus. She felt rather guilty about it but it was just a job, and a girl had to eat after all.

Maximus was over the moon with delight when Atlanta called him in New York and told him everything.

"Just keep my name out of it, I beg of you. If it comes out that I'm some sort of stool pigeon, my entrée to these kind of parties will be finished."

"Don't worry," soothed Maximus. "The way we will write the stories they will never be able to trace who did it. And, *cara*, I *love* your article on Coral. We'll use it in the November issue. Now, why don't you go to the Volpi Ball in Venice next week? Then I will meet you in New York, and we will start a new plan of action for the autumn."

*   *   *

When Maximus realized what a driving dervish he had on his hands, and what a genius Atlanta was at gathering gossip, he appointed her editor-at-large.

With her prolific capacity for work and her network of international acquaintances, Atlanta now had the opportunity to travel extensively, and she brought Maximus ever more juicy tales of scandal, corruption and decadence in high places.

In January, it was Barbados, Mustique or Acapulco, then Paris for the couture collections, after that perhaps Rio for the Carnival and Mardi Gras in New Orleans. In early spring, she went to New York, where she stayed with Kristobel, hanging out at Mortimer's, Elaine's, Nell's and all the other favorite watering holes of the rich and famous. From spring to midsummer, she stayed in London, at Claridges, and at various country estates for the weekend. The English aristocracy let their hair down more freely in their rural surroundings than they did in London, all of which was reported by Atlanta's sharp pen. She made frequent trips to Paris and Rome; Paris during fashion week was an unending source of scoops, for there were always vendettas between the top designers.

In midsummer she went to Cap Ferrat, where she stayed with Coral, hit all the parties and occasionally helicoptered to St. Tropez. There were wild parties at rich people's villas, with coke, rock stars and pretty girls in abundance, but all in all, St. Tropez had lost its luster, so Atlanta never stayed for long.

In August, she holidayed in Gstaad to get away from the milling holiday swarms, and read and walked and breathed fresh air. Then, in September, it was time for a voyage, the Turkish coast being the beau monde's new favorite, where she saw the same people she had been seeing all year round, only this time they had suntans. After the summer whirl, it was back to New York again for the autumn round of charity events and parties, then to St. Moritz or Aspen for Christmas and New Year's. Then, in January, the whole round started again.

Restlessly crisscrossing the most glamorous spots on earth in search of exclusive stories about exclusive people, Atlanta followed them, the jet set and the Euro-trash. It was an exhausting life but she thrived on it. Her beauty and birthright were her entrée and she was invited everywhere.

Many men found Atlanta dazzling and hit on her, but she turned them all down. She had begun to dislike rich men. During her travels she had witnessed the worst examples of male behavior and had helped to wipe away the tears from many a girlfriend's eyes as she listened to their tales of betrayal. In fact, she observed so few healthy relationships between couples that she despaired of ever having one herself.

"All men are rats and those who aren't are boring," Coral Steele jokingly said on the subject. Except Atlanta wasn't so sure it was a joke. Coral had the upper hand on men. She used them before they managed to use her, and now she had enough money and clout to get away with it.

As Atlanta's career progressed, she realized that she wanted more than just writing monthly profiles of celebrities for *Bravo* and feeding Maximus with gossip. She wanted to have her own magazine, and she thought she knew how to get it.

CHAPTER THIRTY-ONE

Kristobel loosened his black silk cravat, smiling the secret smile that brought his customers to their feet after his shows.

Although it was October, he was perspiring, so he sprayed himself generously with his new signature scent. He had found the potent ingredients, which so enticed the senses, on a recent trip to India, and the recipe for his unmistakably sensual aroma was his alone.

Today, at Bloomingdale's, he had launched this new fragrance. He had stood in the marbled perfume department of the great hall, modestly accepting the praise of the fawning women who had willingly shelled out 250 dollars for a cut-glass bottle filled with half an ounce of his dreams. But he was not interested in women in a sexual way—or in men for that matter. His passion was for fashion and art. Each day he sat in his studio, wearing a fresh white piqué robe, his hair pulled back into a ponytail, his next collection forever fermenting in his brain.

He wanted to stun people with his new visions. He wanted the American fashion world to revere him as the messiah of style for the 1990s. He had done it with his ready-to-wear collection, for years mixing street cred with haute-couture elegance. But his goal was to design exclusively for couture. There were less than a dozen American designers who had achieved this and he longed to join their ranks.

Yes, today he had been a great success. The American fashion press had gushed and cooed with sycophantic delight at each of his *bons mots*, even the dreaded *Women's Wear Daily* were taking him seriously.

It was the right time for him to branch out from ready-to-wear and scent to haute couture, and he had finally found the financial backing.

Yet Kristobel sighed. It was getting hotter. Opening the window of his balcony, he looked out over a serene and moonlit view of the East River. Here and there lay packages. Human packages of dross, gray and brown, sleeping next to the river.

He shuddered. That was a look he was never going to use in his collection. Street cred and rags might be his latest forte, but the homeless and the beggars made him shudder. They should sweep the streets clean of them.

Was the madman who had murdered the major and his wife, Lavinia—those sweet people who would not have hurt a fly—one of those who still wandered the streets, terrorizing the weak?

Whenever Kristobel thought of that killer, a mist of hatred came over him. That the man had got off with a minor sentence was an outrage.

Kristobel stared down at the sleeping bodies for a very long moment. He closed the windows and fanned himself rapidly with his black paper fan, then went into the bathroom to spray his body again with his latest scent.

CHAPTER THIRTY-TWO

"I won't wear this dress, it's absolutely *vile*."

Kristobel shrugged. He'd had about enough of Miss Venetia Stephanopolis, and this was only their second fitting. She might be only twenty, but she was already a first-class spoiled bitch. He summoned his diplomacy and charm, and said, "Look, my dear, *I know* it's not what you usually wear, but since you are going with your father to the White House—you cannot look like a . . ." *trampy little sexpot,* he wanted to say, but he held his tongue.

Venetia pulled disdainfully at the heavy fabric of the couture dress. Kristobel leaned against the wall, his face a study in pained martyrdom, casting his eyes to heaven, and lit a Sobranie as if it were his last treat before the guillotine.

"This fabric's so *scratchy*," whined Venetia, "it's boiling hot, and ugly."

"We will *line* it," sighed Kristobel, "in pure Italian *silk*. Charmeuse, if you wish it, my dear."

His sarcasm was not lost on Venetia, who shot the designer a withering look.

"Your father was adamant about what you were to wear to meet the president," he said firmly. "No minidresses—nothing too tight, or transparent, and no cleavage, or Bill Clinton won't be able to take his eyes off you."

"So what?! He's an old man. Oh hell, this is such a drag. I *hate* this dress."

"It's chic," Kristobel insisted.

"It's awful. It makes me look ancient, I look *thirty*," she wailed.

Kristobel made a moue to the fitter on the floor, who had a mouthful of pins, and then smiled patiently. "Your father will be so proud of you when he sees how elegant you look in it."

"Well, I wish Stefania could've gone with

him, instead of doing some stupid film in Holland."

Venetia was bored and fidgety. God, she wanted a joint or some blow, even though Grandmother had been nagging her relentlessly recently about her habits. Why should she care what she thought? As long as darling Daddy still thought that the sun came up when she entered the room, what did it matter? She could twist Daddy around her little finger. In his mind she could do no wrong and she knew it. No matter how many gossip items appeared about her in the papers, Nicholas never believed them.

Venetia glanced at her watch. Only another two hours until this afternoon's assignation and this one was surely going to be memorable. One of the world's most famous and fuckable men, even though he was far older than her usual conquests. We'll see if you're as great as you're supposed to be, she thought, shrugging off the scratchy dress.

Venetia opened the door wearing a smile and a silky kimono, underneath which he glimpsed a white lace bra and matching panties.

She pulled him into the room like a spider pulls a fly into its web and, before he knew it, her notorious tongue was in his mouth, her notorious hands were pulling down his trousers, and her notorious breasts were being rubbed against his shirt. Within seconds, he was more ready than he had ever been and, so it seemed, was she. Without foreplay or preamble, silently, eagerly, with small gasping sighs, the most notorious cocksman in America pleasured one of the most notorious heiresses in the world, on the thick white carpet of her father's drawing room.

Venetia turned to him as he lay next to her with a satisfied smile. "They were right. You *are* absolutely fantastic."

He kissed her shoulder, patted her ruffled hair and whispered, "Thanks. Let's have some more blow, honey, not that you need it, but I do."

Slowly Kevin Bentley removed the glass pipe from his side of the bed and passed it to her.

She lit up thankfully, drawing the rich fumes into her lungs, then passed it to him. He ran his fingers down her naked spine. The faint pangs of guilt he had felt about sleeping with Laura's daughter were now assuaged.

"Hurry up with that pipe, baby," he said hoarsely, rubbing himself next to her. "I've got something else I want you to blow on."

He made love to her twice more, and then, as soon as it was over, Venetia got up abruptly.

"That was great." She adjusted her robe, avoiding his eyes. "I've got to go now. You know the way out. I guess I'll see you around."

She disappeared into the other room, closing the door dismissively, leaving Kevin surprised and disoriented. He wasn't used to women treating him so cavalierly. She had thanked him as coolly as she would thank a plumber who'd come to fix the boiler. Well, maybe he had at that. If her sighs of delight were anything to go by, he'd fixed her plumbing nicely. But there was something missing from their encounter. He shrugged. It seemed the Stephanopolis girls were both cold fish, in spite of their pretty packaging.

In her dressing room, Venetia got out her Ecstasy, which she knocked down with trembling hands and a mouthful of vodka, then she lit up a joint, and leaning back, inhaled the acrid smoke. As it permeated her being, she felt wonderful, in total peaceful harmony with the world.

It was a peace that she did not receive from lovemaking anymore, or from any of the unfulfilling relationships she had been involved in. She lay back dreamily, feeling no pain—feeling wonderful—feeling exactly like a beautiful, famous heiress should feel.

The fact that she needed to take huge amounts of designer drugs to get that glorious feeling was something she didn't allow herself to think about. Nobody knew how hooked she was . . . besides, everyone took drugs these days. Why should she be any different?

CHAPTER THIRTY-THREE

She watched the dealer's movements with rapt absorption. Her anticipation made the ritual even more sacred. She had seen it nearly a dozen times but each time her eagerness to take what he was concocting made her mouth dry.

He unscrewed the cap of a plastic bottle of water, emptying a third of it into a bowl. With his cigarette he burned a hole in the bottle, then inserted an empty tube from a ballpoint pen halfway inside it.

Two pink dots started to burn on Venetia's cheeks as the dealer placed a strip of aluminum foil over the bottle top. The others moved closer to watch, their addiction to the process almost as strong as the high they were about to receive.

Methodically, the dealer pricked holes in the foil with a needle, then expertly sealed the foil around the bottle neck and the pen with Blu-Tack. He tapped ash onto the foil, placed a small white rock on the bed of ash, and then he flicked his lighter over the crack and passed it quickly to Venetia, hissing, "Draw—honey—draw!"

She felt the effect instantly as she sucked it into her lungs. She felt it tearing into her brain, feeling immediately the exhilarating rush of euphoric happiness it brought.

This was a feeling she could only experience with crack. A feeling that she was already deeply addicted to after less than a month.

She smiled at the others sitting in the crack house with her. She loved them all so much. She loved the world, she saw its beauty so clearly when she was on this wonderful clean high.

The dealer's girlfriend, a pockmarked prostitute wearing only underwear, sat wearily on a broken couch, her head supported by her skinny arms heavily marked by needle tracks, while a two-year-old child crawled listlessly at her feet. The girl looked pleadingly at the dealer as the last of his clients took their fix, but he shook his long Rasta curls.

"You ain't done enough business today to get nothin', girl," he drawled. "You go'n git another couple o' tricks and then Bu-Bu'll give you a fix."

Tears filled the girl's dead eyes but she wordlessly stuck her feet into scuffed pumps and, throwing a torn jeans jacket over her underwear, shuffled out down the stairs onto the street to find a john. The child howled when her mother left, but no one took any notice.

Venetia smiled at the baby girl beatifically. "Beautiful—you're so beautiful, little baby," she whispered as the girl continued to howl.

"Shuddup you," yelled Bu-Bu at the child, who whimpered and retreated into a corner. He had started to make another batch for the six zombielike figures who leaned or lay around the filthy room. Their one aim in life was to get the high that crack, and only crack, could bring them, and Bu-Bu knew that in less than an hour they would be ready for more.

Alain watched in shock. Could this be Venetia? What had happened to her once beautiful young face? Her eyes were closed, her head rocking from side to side, a smile on her lips. She looked like a zombie.

So this was where she went. Since he'd arrived in New York two weeks ago, he had been worried about her. She had become completely different from the wild teenager, full of *joie de vivre*, who would dance till dawn. She was now a haggard wreck. He couldn't believe the change in the beautiful girl, couldn't believe what this drug had done to her.

Venetia had only told him about it after a lot of prodding. She had told him everything, since they were children, and he was surprised she had been so reticent about this. But he had badgered her and finally persuaded her that he, too, was enough of a thrill-seeker to also want to indulge in the dangerous practice of freebasing cocaine. So she had agreed.

"You'll love it," she told him excitedly as they had climbed the graffiti-covered staircase. "It's a high like *nothing* you've ever known, Alain. Once you've done this, you'll realize that spliff and E are just kid's stuff."

He didn't want to say, "But you're still just a kid." Didn't want to burst her bubble of euphoria. Neither did he want to take the filthy plastic Evian bottle, with the embers of crack glowing on top of it, and the ballpoint pen sticking out of the side.

Bu-Bu handed it to him with a smile that revealed several absent teeth.

Alain thought fast. If he didn't take a drag they'd kick him out, but he knew that crack could hook you totally after only three fixes.

"I'll wait," he indicated another corner where Bu-Bu's partner Errol was busily making yet another supply. "I like a fresh pipe," he explained, as Bu-Bu narrowed his cold, black eyes. "I like to go first." He was aware that he probably looked ridiculously preppie in loafers and pressed chinos and shirt, compared to the filthy-jeaned, matted-haired losers slumped vacuously around the room.

"Your first time, man?" Bu-Bu casually lit another cigarette from the butt of his previous one.

"Yeah . . . Venetia . . ." he wondered if she'd given them her real name ". . . my girl-friend told me it's got a fantastic kick, so I decided to try it myself."

"What are you, man—French or some-thin'?" Bu-Bu stared at Alain's stylish clothes. "Foreign, ain't ya?"

Alain tried a casual friendly laugh as he saw Bu-Bu exchange looks with Errol.

"You're very . . . er, intuitive."

"Yeah, we gotta be in this racket, man."

He glanced over to Errol, who was casually placing a mixture of cocaine and bicarbonate of soda in a test tube of water, holding it over a flame until the impurities boiled away.

"You gonna be much longer with that stuff, Fatso?"

"Minutes, boss, minutes," called Errol.

Alain hoped it would be longer. He lit a cigarette casually and, giving the suspicious Bu-Bu a conspiratorial wink, sauntered over to Venetia, who was leaning against the wall.

"Let's get out of here, *cherie*," he whispered urgently.

She opened glazed eyes, in which the whites were now yellow. Her puffy face was wasted, her blonde hair dirty and stringy, and she looked as if she hadn't had a bath for a week. She was barely twenty but she looked almost forty.

"Stop being a spoilsport, Alain. I don't *want* to go—I'm having a ball." She tried to hug him and he drew back. If she kept on like this she would be dead in six months.

"OK, Venetia." He decided to humor her. "OK, you take one more blow or draw, then we're going home. You owe me that, Venetia. You're my best friend, I haven't seen you for a month, we need to catch up—alone."

"OK, OK," her eyes were staring and unfocused now. "I'll go home but only because I haven't seen you for ages."

She staggered over to where Bu-Bu was fixing the paraphernalia for the next session and handed him a twenty-dollar bill, which he threw on top of the piles of dirty twenties in a cigar box.

Christ, was that all it cost? thought Alain. It was so much cheaper than coke and smack. No wonder there were so many addicts in New York.

Bu-Bu gave her the pipe and she drew deeply then handed it to Alain who handed it to the guy next to him.

"Guess I'll take a rain check this time, gotta get the little lady home and get a piece of you-know-what." He gave a salacious wink and Bu-Bu smiled back with his lips only.

"Next time, bro'," his voice was harshly

Misfortune's Daughters

Misfortune's Daughters

menacing, "you gotta blow, brother, y'understand? Otherwise don't come back, motherfucker—OK?"

"OK . . . OK."

"Only 'cos she be such a hot customer is why I'se let you stick around . . ."

"Right. I'm outta here." Alain yanked Venetia, who was so stoned she could hardly stand, across the floor littered with the refuse of a hundred empty take-out cartons and a thousand cigarette butts.

"Nice to meet you."

"Likewise, motherfucker," smiled Bu-Bu. "I'll see your lily-white ass on the line for the stuff next time, motherfucker, don't you forgit it."

"I won't, I won't."

He had her out of the door now and down the stairs as fast as he could half carry her. For a thin girl she weighed a ton. There were no cabs to be had on 123rd Street. So, half dragging his semi-conscious prize, he staggered thirteen blocks down Broadway until he gratefully saw the familiar light of a vacant taxi.

As Alain bundled Venetia into the back, he wondered what her father would do if he knew what she had become. He knew that Nicholas had coldly cut Atlanta out of his life because she had embarrassed him and the family with a sex scene in a movie. Since then, most people had forgotten about it, but not Nicholas. Venetia had told Alain that her father still wouldn't accept Atlanta's telephone calls.

If Nicholas Stephanopolis knew what his precious baby girl had become, Alain was positive not only that the Greek's revenge on Bu-Bu's crack house would be swift and terrible, but that he would punish Venetia as harshly as he had Atlanta.

Even though Nicholas had always turned the other cheek to Venetia's excessive partying and scandalous relationships, if he saw she had become a hopeless addict, would he be so lenient? Alain had to protect sweet, headstrong, crazy Venetia from her killer habit. He had to get her off drugs and into a safe place where she could recover.

The only thing was, how?

CHAPTER THIRTY-FOUR

When her father had cut off her allowance, Atlanta had initially believed he would relent and that after a time the check would be deposited in her account as usual.

She had written to Nicholas to tell him what she was doing, enclosing her first printed story on Coral Steele. A note from Miss Jeans was all she received in return: "Your father acknowledges your letter and the magazine article and hopes you are well. He is away at the moment cruising in the Bahamas."

That Christmas, Atlanta had sent another letter filled with seasonal best wishes and news. In return she received a printed Christmas card of Nicholas on a polo pony. It had no signature.

Her only contact with her father had been through the intermittent conversations she had had with her sister or Stefania, who had unsuccessfully tried to heal the rift.

Atlanta realized that there were no family ties anymore, and as she became busier, she pushed the pain of her father's rejection to the back of her mind.

Atlanta was again staying with Coral Steele, who was throwing another of her fabled dinner parties in Cap Ferrat, when she met her future husband.

"Hi, I'm Phil Kellog."

She looked up into a tanned face that looked like it hid some secret joke. He had tousled brown hair streaked with gray, and an assertive look in his amused slate-blue eyes. She had been told that he owned and controlled some of the world's top newspapers and magazines. "You're Australian, I guess."

"Sure am. And this is my right-hand man, Steve Kelly."

Atlanta shook the firm brown hand of a

handsome blue-eyed man about Phil's age. He smiled a polite "How do you do, Miss Stephanopolis?" She detected vestiges of a colonial accent and observed that he stared at her for a touch longer than necessary.

"Steve keeps me in line," joked Phil, whose own eyes had never left Atlanta's. "If it looks like I'm getting too big for my breeches, Steve steps all over me, don't you, cobber?"

Steve nodded, pretending to observe the dancing couples while covertly scrutinizing Laura's daughter. She looked nothing like Laura. Only the shape of her dark eyes bore any resemblance to the woman he had loved, all those years ago, in South Africa.

This was the girl who was on board the yacht the night Nicholas Stephanopolis had killed his wife. Steve still believed that and nothing that the coroner or anyone else said could make him think differently. The official line was still that Laura had slipped, fallen and hit her head on the marble fireplace. Case closed.

But for Steve Kelly, née Badenhorst, the case had never been closed. From the moment he had heard about Laura's death, he had been determined to discover the truth about that fatal night.

He had not returned to Johannesburg after Laura's funeral but to Sydney, his birthplace, where his mother, Ada Kelly Badenhorst, still lived. He had written several articles about his adventures as a big game hunter and ranger, submitting them to his local paper under the name of Steve Kelly.

The proprietor, Phil Kellog, had been interested enough in his factual yet breezy style to hire him for special features. That had been fifteen years ago, during which Steve Kelly had progressed higher and higher in Kellog's publishing hierarchy until he had become Phil's second in command.

With complete access to all of Phil Kellog's files, dossiers and newspaper morgues, Steve had read endlessly incriminating information on Nicholas Stephanopolis.

His deep abiding hatred for the man who, he was convinced, had killed the love of his life, was like a festering sore. He knew of Nicholas's cruelty to Laura and he was unsurprised to discover numerous clippings chronicling a variety of unexplained injuries that Stefania Scalerina had suffered, along with those of numerous other women who had had liaisons with Nicholas. Lame excuses such as "she slipped in the shower" or "she fell off her exercise bicycle" accompanied the descriptions of black eyes, broken wrists and bruises, but Steve believed none of them.

Phil Kellog smiled at Atlanta and she smiled back sincerely, for he was one of the most attractive men she had met in a very long time.

The disc jockey was playing "Summer Dreams" from *Saturday Night Fever.*

"Want to dance?" he asked and she nodded.

"Oldies but goldies, they still work," Phil said as he took Atlanta's arm.

"Better than all that awful house music, and rap," she agreed.

Everyone was gyrating, the middle-aged wishing they were young again; Phil too felt middle-aged and out of condition as he held Atlanta's slender body in his arms and for the fifth time that year resolved to give up smoking and drinking. There certainly were some beauties at this party, but none appealed to him as much as the cool Miss Stephanopolis.

"I've heard a lot about you," he said, when they returned to their table, and he lit up a Camel. He seemed to be the only person there not afraid to smoke—she even liked that.

"What have you heard?" she murmured, noticing Coral's approving smile across the floral centerpiece. Coral had extolled the merits of Australian men: "They're *real* men, dear. What you see is what you get—and I've seen and had a few."

"I've not only heard but I've observed. You're a bloody good reporter, Miss Stephanopolis, and a damn good journalist. You should be doing better things than writing articles for that sleaze-bag Maximus Gobbi."

"Like what, for instance?"

"Like working for a magazine with a bit of class. Not that piece of dreck. I wouldn't put it in the bottom of my parrot's cage. You've been working there for too long. You're much too good for it. You've done some clever things with those celebrities. Nice twists on the same old boring people. I mean you even made a story about Coral Steele interesting, and I've been reading about her exploits since I was in short pants!"

"Thanks," she murmured, conscious that the man called Steve was still staring at her, although pretending not to.

"I'm amazed that one of the American

glossies hasn't tried to snap you up." Phil leaned forward and she met his slightly cocky grin with a cool smile.

"You're just what *Harper's* or *Esquire* could do with. Smart, young, fresh. I like your style, Miss Stephanopolis, I like it a lot, and that's why you need to be with a class act."

"Oh, like yours, I suppose?" She laughed. "Now, Mr. Kellog, I know that your own magazine might have a circulation of several hundred thousand but . . ."

"Six," he said, succinctly draining his beer. "Six hundred thousand, my dear young lady, and growing faster than a beanstalk, and by the way, the name's Phil . . ."

"And I'm Atlanta." She found herself blushing and said hastily, "But *Comet*'s not exactly the *crème de la crème* of magazines, is it? I mean it's more *National Enquirer* than *Vanity Fair*."

"You're right," he agreed. "But my next one's going to be a zingeroo. It will be the best, the most sophisticated, the most modern magazine in America."

"You're starting a new magazine? What's it going to be called?"

"We haven't announced it yet." He dropped his voice. "But I've just bought *Mercury*."

"*Mercury*?" She raised her eyebrows. "But that's almost as old hat as the *Saturday Evening Post.*"

"Not when I'm finished with it." He spoke with the absolute confidence of a man who knew exactly what he was doing and had the cash to do it. "I'm going to turn it totally around. Make it the hottest magazine going. I'll get top-rated people on board, the most outstanding editors, the greatest photographers and the finest bloody writers we can poach from the other mags. Everyone's going to want to work with us, Atlanta—everyone. We'll be a smash. You just wait."

"It sounds fabulous."

"It'll be the best damn magazine in the bloody world. Everything's ready to roll. We're starting production by the end of the year." He leaned back and surveyed her coolly. "And there are one or two positions I haven't filled yet."

"Really, what are they?"

"Style director. I haven't got the woman I really want, she's too loyal to Tina, but I'll make her an offer she can't refuse. We're still a bit weak in the art department, but my people in New York are taking care of that right now. What I'm *really* looking for . . ." He leaned across the table, almost hypnotizing her with his clear, blue stare. "What I *need now* is a social editor—someone who knows everyone who's anyone in society, gets invited everywhere, and isn't afraid of getting their little white gloves dirty now and again."

He gave her a meaningful wink. He had done his homework on Atlanta Stephanopolis. He knew that she knew where *lots* of skeletons were buried, and he liked the way she operated.

Atlanta smiled her most dazzling smile. "I'll take the job, Mr. Kellog. It sounds absolutely like my cup of verveine."

"Hey, hang on, I haven't offered it to you yet."

"Oh, I'm sorry, I thought that was a proposition." She laughed. Suddenly, she felt as if she had found a soul mate.

"There's one condition, ma'am."

"What's that?"

"Have dinner with me tomorrow night."

She paused for what she thought should be the right amount of time before saying, "All right. I'd love to."

"You won't regret it." Phil winked, and they gazed into each other's eyes.

* * *

Phil took Atlanta to a romantic candlelit restaurant in the hills above Cannes and, after they had laughed and talked about every subject under the sun and agreed and disagreed on everything, she threw caution to the winds and allowed him to take her to bed. It had been three years since she had been made love to—Fabio had been her last and only partner. Phil was a thrilling and excellent lover.

Coral called the next morning, crowing with delight that Atlanta had at last found a "real man."

"I was starting to worry about you, darling." She laughed. "People were beginning to think you were a dyke."

CHAPTER THIRTY-FIVE

Philip James Kellog had been born in a red-brick house in the center of Sydney, six years after his marine father returned from the Second World War.

James Kellog Senior was a husky, sharp-talking Australian who had inherited a publishing empire from *his* father. The Kellog Company controlled practically all the Australian media. Both upmarket broadsheets and the most yellow of tabloids flew the Kellog emblem; it also owned an eclectic selection of magazines ranging from men's soft porn, which James called stroke books, to bodice-ripping romances and home-decorating periodicals.

His was a monopoly that could not be broken, and James Kellog was an autocratic employer who would tolerate no breach of the unimpeachable conduct he expected from his employees.

His work ethic also applied on the home front. He was the master of the universe, and at his manor house in the center of Sydney overlooking the ravishing harbor, his stern words were law.

Young Phil grew up with machismo and guts. Hs ex-marine father was his role model, and his admiration and hero worship of James Kellog was intense.

At sixteen, Phil was apprenticed to the *Sydney Sun* and throughout the years progressed from tea boy to the mailroom, to assistant in the art department and finally to cub reporter. He learned everything there was to know about the publishing empire, and in between he married a nice, ordinary Sydney girl whom he treated with cavalier indifference. Work was his life, and since they never had any children, they eventually divorced.

By the time his father died, there was

nothing Phil didn't know about the world of publishing, and with his monopoly on practically the entire Australian media, he was calling all the shots.

Maximus huffed and puffed when Atlanta gave notice, but then shrugged his big good-natured shoulders and kissed her on both cheeks.

"I wish you lots and lots of luck—you did well for *Bravo*. We got some great stories. You're a clever girl, Atlanta. I'm going to miss you."

"Thank you, Maximus, I'm going to miss you too." She kissed his cheek. "You've become like a father figure to me." God knows she had certainly been in need of one.

For only the second time in her life Atlanta fell in love. In her travels she had been pursued and propositioned by some of the richest and most attractive men in the world, but since her affair with Fabio had ended in humiliation and the sort of pain that doesn't disappear overnight, she had been extremely cautious about giving her heart again.

Now with the feisty, wise-cracking Phil Kellog, she found herself blossoming. Not only did she admire him tremendously, adore his down-to-earth humor, his tough man-of-the-people approach to everything, but she was completely in love with him.

Although at forty-three he was eighteen years older than she was, he was a caring and diligent lover, and Atlanta was a willing pupil, not only in bed, but also about the magazine business. She had finally found her purpose in life.

Phil, realizing that he had an outstandingly talented journalist on his hands, had given her two jobs: She was to be the society editor and the editor-at-large of *Mercury*, which was to be launched in the autumn.

And to put the cherry on the icing, Phil had asked her to marry him. Atlanta was seriously considering his proposal, when the invitation arrived. She knew what it was before she tore it open.

Engraved, embossed, the thick white envelope was exquisitely addressed in black calligraphy:

NICHOLAS
STEPHANOPOLIS

Requests the pleasure of your company
To celebrate his
60th Birthday
On the 17th and 18th August
At Stephanopolis Island

RSVP
Mary Jeans
84 Avenue Foch
Paris VII
33 4250 3631

White tie and
decorations for
18th

Cruisewear and
semi-formal
or 17th

"I'm not missing this one," said Atlanta to herself. "No way."

When the sisters met in the Concorde Lounge at Kennedy Airport, they hadn't seen each other in three years, and hardly recognized each other.

"My God, I can't believe it's you," gasped Venetia, taking in Atlanta's svelte body and chic elegance.

"Ditto," said Atlanta. "But what have you been *doing* to yourself, Venetia? I hate to say this, but you don't look too good."

"It's life in the fast lane. I've been partying a lot lately and I didn't sleep much last night. You know what Nell's is like."

"I certainly do," said Atlanta. In fact she knew intimately what every New York disco, nightclub and low dive was like, and she had been to them too often to be fascinated anymore. "Are you OK? You look exhausted, Venetia."

Venetia took another nervous drag on her Marlboro, then asked plaintively, "Do I look that bad?"

"Put it this way, sister dearest, you look like drugs have become your new best friend." Atlanta knew all the signs of drug addiction—she'd seen so much of it.

"Hell, Sis, I was up all night because I finally broke up with the creep."

"What creep?"

"Alain. I gave him the old heave-ho. It wasn't easy, but the thrill was definitely gone. He was always nagging at me, Atlanta. Never stopped watching over me, telling me what to do, who to see, what to eat."

"And drugs—I hope he nagged you about those?"

"Yes," answered Venetia turning away

sulkily. She had been grateful for Alain's dedication in weaning her off crack. It had been bloody hell for both of them, but they'd done it together and in return she had let Alain become her lover again. It hadn't taken her long to become fed up with fidelity, which Alain soon realized. But he loved Venetia and, as long as she kept off crack, he resignedly turned the other cheek to her escapades.

"I'm *not* glad you left him, Venetia. Alain was good for you and I liked him, even though Father didn't."

"Papa never likes *anyone* I'm with," sighed Venetia. "No one was good enough for his little girl. Nobody."

This time Atlanta didn't answer. She hadn't seen her father for five years now and had been surprised to be summoned for his sixtieth birthday, but she had to go. Not only was it a royal command, but she was curious to see how he would react to her.

The sisters sized each other up as they waited for the flight to be called. Venetia looked enviously at her sister. Photographs hadn't begun to do her justice.

Both girls were wearing denim, but while Venetia was in ripped jeans and a battered old jacket, Atlanta was wearing Chanel's beautifully tailored denim jacket with gold buttons, a black turtle-neck and black leather trousers and boots. Around her neck and waist were black leather and gilt chains, and black Ray-Bans completed her stylish look.

Venetia, in contrast, looked bedraggled. Her blonde hair was dirty and stringy and her white shirt grubby, and she chain-smoked. The other passengers nudged each other as they noticed the difference between the two sisters who chatted away until the Concorde was called for boarding.

"I hope these birthday festivities aren't going to be a total drag," sighed Venetia as they walked to the plane.

"They'll be OK. It'll be interesting to see how Father is," said Atlanta, wondering again how he would react to her.

They entered the cramped high-tech plane and took their places in the bulkhead seats.

"My God, so much has happened in three years." Venetia sighed, longing for a cigarette.

"You can say that again." Atlanta buckled her seat belt, smilingly refused the attendant's offer of champagne, and requested a club soda instead. "I just hope that we're all going to have a good time this weekend and that Father doesn't get mad at me, or ignore me as usual."

"Oh, I'm sure he won't." Venetia knocked back her glass of champagne and signaled for another. "I think he's mellowed recently."

Atlanta glanced at her sister. It was obvious that she was completely stoned. And those clothes! How could she look so awful, have so little self-respect?

Atlanta wondered if it were true that Venetia was still obsessed by men. Didn't it ever enter her brain that a woman can do very well without a man? If she's clever and dedicated to her job, she can often do much better than if she's involved with one. Men can screw you up, take your mind off really important things, like work, your career, your own ambitions. Atlanta's thoughts turned to Phil and how lucky she was to have found a man like him who really cared about her work. Because of him her ambitions were about to be fulfilled and her career was, like the Concorde, ready for take off.

As the magnificent airplane started its rapid journey down the runway, then took off into the clouds like a rocket, the sisters clinked glasses.

"To Stephanopolis Island." Atlanta smiled. "May the weekend be peaceful and fun."

"And to Daddy," said Venetia. "May he have a happy, happy birthday."

"And many more," Atlanta added, with an enigmatic smile.

PART THREE

Nicholas and Atlanta

CHAPTER THIRTY-SIX

It was one of the most glittering parties the beau monde had seen in years. The *crème de la crème* of the worlds of high society, big business, show business and even royalty had been invited, and remarkably, they all turned up. Princes and potentates, kings and movie queens, cavaliers and contessas; the free world was represented by all colors and creeds.

Nicholas's security forces were augmented by agents who also worked for the CIA, Scotland Yard and Interpol. Teams of undercover men and women disguised as staff members would be keeping a wary surveillance on the celebrated guests, paying particular attention to the three not-so-benign dictators who were present.

Atlanta had only managed the briefest of words with her father, who had behaved in his usual autocratic manner, but Stefania had been, as usual, effusive toward her protégée.

"Atlanta! *Carina,* you are *bellissima*," she exclaimed, air-kissing vigorously, her piled red curls bobbing. "She is beautiful, no, Nicholas?" Stefania turned to Nicholas, who was holding Venetia's hands and smiling tenderly at her, oblivious to her haggard face. Then he turned to face his eldest daughter.

"How are you, Atlanta?"

"I'm extremely well, Father." She tried to sound adult and sophisticated, but in Nicholas's presence she as always felt insignificant.

At sixty, Nicholas's once jet-black hair was almost totally silver, but his eyes still burned and the sardonic set of his lips in his dark, intelligent face still gave him an imposing look.

"Good, I'm glad. You look well." He turned impatiently to Stefania. "What time did we invite everyone?"

Stefania patted his arm, with a placatory smile. "Nine o'clock, *caro*, we have time for a glass of champagne with the family." She slipped her arm through Nicholas's and Venetia took his other side. Atlanta observed the happy family scene, trying not to feel bitter. She now knew for sure that whatever she might achieve or become, her father's lack of interest in her was never going to change.

Tonight's opulent party gave new meaning to the word "extravagance."

In a Kristobel gown of gold and red lamé, its flaming colors matching her hair, Stefania stood beside Nicholas in the great hall greeting his guests. A dozen triple-decked Empire chandeliers, each holding a hundred candles, cast their magical light on the paneled walls. Great ormolu wall sconces held aloft scented beeswax candles, filling the enormous rooms with the faintly ecclesiastical fragrance of honey and pine. The vaulted ceiling, painted with frescoes of gods and nymphs, was a vision of soft blues, pinks and peaches.

Among the paintings around the walls hung several portraits of Nicholas, two of Laura and one of Venetia. The floor was inlaid with parquet squares edged with crimson, white and dark blue tiles, which formed an enormous mosaic of Nicholas's family motto, "Death Before Dishonor." But there were so many people standing on it that it was impossible to see the floor at all.

Stefania wore an exquisite necklace that had belonged to the Empress Josephine. Her hair was skillfully twirled around a tiara, and on her gloved wrists were several diamond bracelets. Lady Anne stood next to Stefania, imposing and erect in spite of her advancing years. As befitted her rank, she was festooned in almost twice as many diamonds as Stefania, and huge brooches clung to the ruffles of her black dress like dazzling limpets.

Next to Anne stood her granddaughters. Venetia was wearing a pink Lacroix dress, the bodice cinched tightly at the waist, the skirt an enormous pouf of taffeta and tulle. In spite of the stylish gown, her carefully painted face looked garish and puffy, and her delicate features coarse.

Beside her, Atlanta looked chic and beautiful. In a black chiffon gown sprinkled with tiny silver beads, her breasts were framed by a froth of black lace and her sleek hair was sculpted to her head like a Renaissance madonna. The contrast between sisters was startling.

Nicholas tried to greet each new arrival warmly but was already finding the whole affair boring. His mother and Stefania had insisted on throwing this party, but he had never even met some of the guests before. Besides, he had other things on his mind.

Stefania smiled seductively at Kevin Bentley, who shot a come-hither smile back in her direction. They had had brief encounters over the years, and the heat still seemed to be there for both of them.

After dinner there was dancing and then a staggering display of fireworks over the sea. Each explosion of brilliant light and color was followed by another still more dazzling, and the whole island seemed ablaze in thousands of sparking prisms of light.

The *pièce de résistance* was a colossal full-length "portrait" of Nicholas with the words "Happy Birthday Nicholas" in silver and gold sunbursts—at which point the crowd burst into what could almost have been mistaken for genuine cheers of affection.

CHAPTER THIRTY-SEVEN

When Dr. André first told Nicholas the news, Nicholas had refused to believe it. Not heart disease, that was for old men. He was in his prime, powerful and feared—invincible, or so he thought. How could this disease have struck him, of all people? He rarely smoked now, he played racquetball or tennis every day and he rode his horses vigorously. Why him?

"I don't believe you," he hissed at Dr. André, who nervously fiddled with his pocket handkerchief. "There must be a mistake. You must have mixed up my tests. I'm only sixty; that's no age these days. How could I have a bad heart? I feel fine—just a little breathless now and again, but nothing serious."

"I'm very sorry, Mr. Stephanopolis, but you have a serious heart condition."

"Well, what can be done about it?"

"Mr. Stephanopolis, if there was something we could do, we would start immediately—but your condition has remained unchecked for too long, and unfortunately, at this stage, there's nothing we can do."

Nicholas was incredulous. "Why the hell not?"

"I'm afraid that we are still at the research stage regarding a cure for heart disease. But if you watch your diet carefully, take your medication, stop drinking and avoid stress—"

"How long have I got?" Nicholas interrupted.

"A year if you're careful, maybe eighteen months at the most," came the reply.

"So you see there's absolutely nothing anyone can do. That's it. It's terminal." Nicholas's daughters sat in stunned silence on the sofa. Neither had uttered a word while their father had told them the grim prognosis.

It was a typically hot and sunny late summer day on Stephanopolis Island, but in Nicholas's study it was cool. Nicholas stood before the fireplace, his back to his daughters.

"Papa, I don't believe it. There just has to be a cure. *Something* we can do, someone we can find to help." Venetia struggled to hold back the tears that threatened to engulf her.

"But it's 1994," Atlanta said quietly. "They can cure just about anything today."

"No they *can't*," snapped Nicholas, "they can't cure AIDS, they can't cure poverty and starvation, they still can't even cure the common cold."

"But Papa . . . heart disease . . . they've had tremendous breakthroughs, in American research—I'm sure I've read about it. In Houston, I think," ventured his younger daughter.

Nicholas shook his head. "My darling, I, more than anyone, wish it were true. But I've seen the results of my tests, and I've had second and third opinions in New York and in Paris."

"But Papa—what's going to happen when you . . ." Venetia couldn't continue.

"When I die." Nicholas calmly finished the

sentence for her. "That's what I intend to talk to you both about.

"Because your mother is no longer alive, and because I have only a short time to live, we have to make some decisions about the future of my empire, my holdings and my companies. I have had lengthy discussions with your grandmother, who is the only other person, apart from the doctors, who knows of my condition. If your mother had produced a male heir, this would all, naturally, be a different story." He turned toward them, his eyes as black and penetrating as ever.

Venetia started to sob loudly.

"But unfortunately, I have no male heir, which is why I am having to do this."

Suddenly his voice hardened, and he looked at both girls with contempt. "I'm ashamed to have to admit that you are my daughters. One thing I have learned in life is that people of importance, people in the public eye, must always retain an element of dignity, of mystery. They should not be seen too much, or be too accessible, and they should remain on the gilded pedestals where money and power have placed them. If they get too familiar with the media, any person of importance will inevitably lose their mystery and therefore their influence. Both of you in the past few years have behaved in a manner that has caused your grandmother, myself, and indeed everyone associated with the Stephanopolis family, the greatest possible embarrassment."

"But Papa," Venetia protested, wiping her brimming eyes. "You have always forgiven me. Whatever went wrong, you always said it wasn't my fault, that the media was judging me too harshly."

"Well, I was wrong," Nicholas snapped. "Things have come to light recently that have convinced me that you are just as bad, if not worse, than your sister. At least now she is making an attempt at some sort of a job."

Atlanta winced. Some sort of a job! Was that really all that being an editor of an important magazine meant to him?

"I have been embarrassed, not to mention horribly disappointed by your behavior, Venetia." Nicholas's voice was increasingly cold. "Don't for one moment imagine that all your little deceptions have hoodwinked me, that you can pull the wool over my eyes that easily."

"But Papa . . ."

"Shut up, Venetia," said Nicholas coldly. "Shut up and listen to me. I have now discovered many of the things you have done. Do you remember your little trip to that gay bar—with your friend Alain?"

"Yes, but we didn't do anything wrong, Papa." Venetia wondered what was coming next.

"Perhaps not by other people's standards. But by the standards of a family like ours it was appalling behavior.

"And you, Atlanta, compounded the vulgarity of Venetia's sordid little outing by taking those photographs that appeared in the press. You did, didn't you?"

Atlanta gasped. "How did you find out?"

"It was you who sold those pictures of Alain and Venetia wearing your mother's clothes to the press, wasn't it? That's what started the media pack howling after Venetia," he said coldly. "Admit it, dammit. You did, didn't you?"

"I admit I took the photos for a joke, but I never sold them to anyone. I don't know how they got into the newspapers. I left them lying around in my bedroom and one of the maids must have taken them. I'm sorry," whispered Atlanta.

Nicholas replied coldly, "Whether you *actually* sold them or not is immaterial. The result was the same. My God, Venetia was only fourteen. It was bad enough that she should be involved in such a sordid stunt, but for her own sister to betray her was unforgivable."

"I said I'm sorry." Atlanta suddenly felt as if she was nine years old again.

"And that's not all you did to Venetia," said Nicholas. "It was you and that appalling Maximus Gobbi who took those photographs of her with that ridiculous Italian actor, wasn't it?"

"I did *not*. I never did that, Father. How could you think such a thing?"

"Don't lie to me, Atlanta."

"I'm not lying—I swear it."

He ignored her.

"Then, as if that wasn't bad enough, Atlanta, you go off to cause trouble with many of my friends. My God, when I put two and two together, I came up with dozens of transgressions. You've almost destroyed some people's lives with your vicious innuendo in Maximus Gobbi's piece-of-shit magazine."

"I can explain, Papa. It isn't what you think."

"Oh, I am sure you can explain brilliantly. After all, you have become an expert liar, but I don't want to hear your excuses," snapped Nicholas. "And as for your so-called screen career—there can be no possible explanation for what you did in that ghastly movie, Atlanta. None. To perform sexual acts, to allow yourself to be used in such a degrading manner, was for me absolutely the final straw."

"I'm sorry," Atlanta mumbled. Why did this man have such power to frighten her? Horrible images flickered like an old movie in the back of her mind whenever her father released the full throttle of his anger toward her. Memories stirred but were then lost in the mists of her subconscious as Nicholas's remorseless tirade began again.

"It wasn't my fault—it was Fabio's . . ."

"Shut the hell up, Atlanta. You wouldn't be imprisoned for any of your acts of betrayal because they're just malicious, dishonorable and deeply contemptible, and anyone who perpetrated them simply isn't fit to inherit any of the responsibility that goes with great fortune."

Venetia's spirits rose. Did this mean that her father was appointing her as his successor? She hadn't done anything really bad. Not that he would know about—or would he?

"As for you, Venetia," Nicholas turned. "Your behavior over the past several years has been worse than the cheapest of whores."

"Papa," gasped Venetia, "how can you say that?"

"I know everything now," said Nicholas dispassionately. "Don't forget I have friends everywhere. When I first saw those dreadful stories in the tabloids, I didn't believe them. Just more newspaper trash I thought. Horrible fabrications." Nicholas picked up a small file from his desk.

"But I was wrong. The media only scratched the surface where you are concerned, Venetia."

Venetia held her breath. How could her father possibly believe those things? She'd always been able to twist him around her little finger. What had happened to change him?

Nicholas flicked through the file he held in his lap. "I'm not going to list the names of all the men . . . and God help us, the occasional woman, that you've slept with. You know who they all are, that is, if you can remember them. Being the sort of people they are, they're only too happy to tell anyone who cares to listen about their sordid flings with Venetia Stephanopolis. I couldn't *believe* that my own adored daughter could do such things. I'm not a fool, but I couldn't believe it. Frankly, it sickened me." Nicholas turned away from his daughter's shocked gaze. "Prancing about almost naked on tables at nightclubs in Paris, in front of hundreds of people. You were like an obscene free cabaret. What is wrong with you, Venetia?"

"I had a coke problem then," Venetia mumbled, "I had a habit, a real bad habit, Papa. I was hooked—you can't understand what that's like. I didn't know what I was doing."

"Well, all I can say is you certainly must have been drugged out of your mind all day long, because that can be the only excuse for your appalling behavior." Nicholas sat down heavily.

"So now—what a pretty pair you are, my daughters. To think I was so proud of you when you were born. Now you are nothing more than a drug-addicted nymphomaniac and a slandering, plastic-faced bitch."

Then, rising from his chair, he confronted them, blazing-eyed. "Both of you are immoral and corrupt," he spat. "Neither of you has deserved the endless privileges of wealth that have been showered on you all your lives, but sadly for me, you are all that's left of the Stephanopolis family. The future of my companies and my empire lies in your hands, and how it breaks my heart to realize it. God help us all now." He shook his head slowly. "Because no one else can."

"Papa, I've kicked the habit, really I have," sobbed Venetia. "Alain is helping me. Papa, I'll change, really I will. I'll go to detox again—I'll even go cold turkey."

"You're going to have to, because that's what this meeting is all about." Nicholas paused to take a sip of forbidden whiskey.

"I have the unenviable task of appointing one of you as my heir and successor and my decision is irrevocable. Since neither one of you is fit to run any of my companies at the present time, if ever, I have decided that the first one of you to bear a male child will inherit everything."

"What?" Atlanta was aghast. "That's the most sexist thing I've ever heard. You can't be serious, Father."

"Oh, yes, my dear—I'm deadly serious. The world has always preferred that men run everything. That's the truth, whether you like it or not. So don't start up with your stupid feminist views. Women are inferior to men, you may as well face it, Atlanta, because it's true, whether you and all your liberal flag-waving females like it or not. For centuries it's always been the tradition in every country that men rule and that is one of the many reasons why I have come to this decision."

"What decision?" asked Venetia weakly.

"You will both have to marry, if anyone will have you. Someone suitable, I hope to God. Then the first one of you to give birth to a male child will inherit and run my companies, my empire, the shipping, the conglomerates and all the various businesses. When the boy reaches his majority, he will then of course take over. As you know I have a handful of trusted advisers who will instruct the boy's mother . . . and of course the boy himself during his formative years, until he is twenty-one."

There was a shocked silence as both girls tried desperately to digest this news, realizing only too well the ramifications of what their father had said.

"Do you understand what this means?" Nicholas questioned. "The one of you who produces my heir will automatically be ac-

cepted as one of the richest and most powerful women in the world. You will have almost unlimited power. You will appear to run
my companies, with the assistance of my
advisers, but you will actually be under their
jurisdiction until you prove you can do it
alone. You will receive immense admiration
and envy and perhaps, if you earn it, even
respect. All this would be yours for the
twenty-one years until your son comes of
age."

Atlanta was rendered speechless by her
father's chauvinism. She had always known
he was a dyed-in-the-wool misogynist, but
now he'd proved it beyond doubt.

But this was an opportunity filled with
such golden possibilities that immediately
each girl knew that she should grab it.
Power, money, influence—a lifestyle beyond
a mere mortal's understanding. It was unbelievably tempting.

After a long pause Nicholas said, "Well,
my daughters, what are you thinking about?
Am I to assume that my proposal is acceptable to you?"

"Yes, Papa," said Venetia meekly. "I promise
you faithfully that I'll kick drugs forever. Alain
has been begging me to marry him, so I will."

"Good," said Nicholas. "Alain has turned out to be a good young man and if he's helping you to get over your problems, so much the better. And what about you, Atlanta? Is there a suitable man in your life at the moment?"

"Yes, Father," said Atlanta quietly, "there is. His name is Phil Kellog. He's asked me to marry him and now I shall, as soon as I get back to New York."

She looked down into her lap so that her father and her sister might not see the eager glitter in her eyes. Atlanta's mind started racing. Her sights were suddenly set on the twin goals of power and money. With her father's colossal wealth, they could entice the best writers, artists, journalists and photographers to *Mercury*, making it the number-one magazine.

She would tell Phil immediately. Why had she been stalling him? Had she been punishing Phil for Fabio Di Navaro? Well, he was history. It was time to go for the power and the glory. Atlanta wanted it all: She would marry Phil, have a child, and run the most fabulous magazine in the world. Suddenly she knew she *could* have it all.

CHAPTER THIRTY-EIGHT

"Have I got a surprise for you." Phil grinned when Atlanta walked into his impressive high-rise office on the northeast corner of Park Avenue. Two of the four walls were nothing but huge sheets of glass affording a dizzying view of the concrete superstructure of Manhattan.

Everything about the office seemed to match Phil himself. Tough and sinewy, his brown hair flecked with gray framed a deeply tanned face lined from years in the sun. Blue eyes full of amusement and an expression of quizzical interest gave him the look of a man who never allowed boredom to enter his life.

He was wearing a slightly rumpled tweed jacket, and as usual his tie was loosened and the top two buttons of his gray-and-white-striped shirt were open.

The surface of his desk, sculpted from a huge piece of metal, was almost obscured between the stark unblinking screens of several computers and piles of magazines and newspapers.

In front of his desk several chrome and leather chairs were neatly regimented. The room contained no flowers or decorative objects of any kind, so it perfectly reflected the character of Phil Kellog—geared to nothing but business.

"What d'ya think, sweet face? You like?"

"Like it? Oh Phil, it's wonderful."

"Wait till you see this." He took her hand, guiding her into the corridor. Then, triumphantly, he opened the door to the office next to his.

Atlanta took in the pristine perfection of her new office. "It's absolutely divine. You're an angel."

"And you, my princess, are my special partner." He breathed in her fragrance as she threw herself into his arms.

She pulled back, looking straight into his

eyes. "Does this mean we're really partners now?"

"It sure does. You're now the official editor in chief of *Mercury* magazine. All you have to do is answer to me—the chairman of the board and your publisher. Congratulations, princess."

"I don't know how to thank you, Phil. I'm going to make you proud of me, really I am." She looked around at her new office, a feminine version of Phil's. Beyond the blond maple-wood desk, bare now except for the computer, an enormous window looked out over Park Avenue. The room was a symphony in beige but at the same time a completely businesslike workroom. The only sybaritic object was the large, comfortable-looking sofa.

"And now, my darling, *I* have another surprise for *you.*" Atlanta took Phil by the hand and sat him down next to her on the sofa. "I accept."

"What do you accept?" He pretended puzzlement.

"Weren't you the man who was inundating me with proposals of marriage before I went away?" she said innocently. "Correct me if I'm wrong, but I seem to remember you saying something about wanting me to be your wife?"

"You're *on*, cupcake." Phil laughed and, scooping her up in his arms, covered her face with kisses. "Right on. I'll make an honest woman out of you as soon as you want. When shall we do it?"

"Soon, very soon," said Atlanta huskily as she started unbuttoning Phil's shirt buttons and moving her fingers down to the buckle of his crocodile belt. "But for now I want to do *this*."

"For God's sake let's lock the door first, sweet face. I don't want our newly hired pencil pushers to see their editor and chairman *in flagrante*!"

"I don't give a damn," breathed Atlanta, wriggling out of her dress, "I haven't seen you for a week. That's much too long, darling . . ."

They were married at City Hall the following week.

The bride wore a white shantung suit created in a hurry by Kristobel. The groom was in Ralph Lauren gray.

It was a brief ceremony attended only by Steve Kelly, and by Atlanta's new personal assistant, the recently divorced Jennifer Holden.

Atlanta had said she didn't want a honeymoon. On their wedding night, Phil took her to dinner at Le Cirque, and then couldn't wait to get her back to their apartment, where he was surprised by her sexual ardor.

She had told him that she'd only had one lover before him, Fabio Di Navaro, even though she knew that Phil was so comfortable in his own skin that he wouldn't give a damn about who his damn wife had bedded before. Atlanta really turned Phil on. She was so exciting in bed that his usual quizzical expression was replaced with a permanent grin of satisfaction. It excited him that when they were in the middle of a passionate session of lovemaking, she would suddenly stop, look at him seriously, and say, "Do you *really* think we should take those cigarette ads? Or do you think it will offend our readers?"

Phil became her Svengali. He had a deep understanding and love of the whole magazine business and was instilling it in Atlanta. He was determined that *Mercury* was going to be the new arbiter of taste for the nineties, and wanted to break new ground. "It's going to have the latest trends, fads and vogues," he told his editorial staff. "We'll show our readers how to share in that enviable celebrity lifestyle, yet we'll give them serious in-depth political and social comment too. We'll get interviews with people who've never given press interviews before." He was investing heavily to get *Mercury* off the ground.

He wanted *Mercury* to be at least one step ahead of every other glossy monthly and was going to print stories and unearth facts that no other magazine had yet dared to do.

Phil knew that upmarket glossies only make 25 percent of their revenue from their cover prices, articles and pictures. The other 75 percent comes from advertising, which is what Phil was brilliant at getting.

"Making money and all its vulgar trappings still means instant success and social desirability for those who have it. We're giving our readers journalism of excellence with just enough inside info that they haven't heard before. That's how we get that cutting edge—that's what *Mercury* is all about." Phil repeated this mantra daily to his editorial staff.

*   *   *

Sometimes Atlanta went to Phil's office during the day, locked the door and slowly
stripped for him. She would hardly let him
say a mumbled "I don't want to be disturbed"
to his secretary before leaping on him. Phil
Kellog had nothing to complain about in that
area.

"Forget honeymoons. Who needs 'em?
I'm worn out," Phil confided to Steve one
morning.

"Aren't you getting a bit long in the tooth
for all that, mate?" joked Steve. "You better
watch it, an old geezer like you, your heart
might give out."

Phil grinned. "No worries, Steve. Atlanta's
the greatest woman in the world and I love
her to death."

"Love sucks," said Steve laconically.

"You're just jealous. How come I've never
seen you with a pretty young thing?"

"I haven't met the right girl yet." Steve
smiled halfheartedly as he thought about his
two magical weeks with Laura. He had never
even found another woman he cared
enough about, let alone fallen in love with.

Phil had come uncomfortably close to the
truth when he'd mentioned jealousy. Steve
had found Atlanta's beauty and style—mixed

with insecurity, which she tried to disguise—
quite endearing. She was certainly her
mother's daughter in that respect, and he often studied her surreptitiously in the office.

Laura's mysteriously tragic demise, seventeen years after that of another hugely popular icon, Marilyn Monroe, spawned many
speculative articles, but the final conclusion
was always that Nicholas Stephanopolis
bore no blame for his wife's death, and no
charges were ever filed against him.
    "I know that bastard murdered Laura,"
Steve muttered, every time he read a news
story or heard gossip about Stefania Scalerina. "Actress unable to continue filming due
to bathtub injury." That tabloid headline was
also corroborated in some of the more upmarket newspapers. It had happened four
years before in Rome. The insurance company had been called in to verify the authen-
ticity of the claim and, apparently satisfied,
had paid up and the movie was recast using
another actress.
    Studying the photos that had appeared of
Stefania around that time, Steve could see
heavy bruises on her unbroken arm that
looked more as if they came from a human

hand rather than from a bathtub, even though she had obviously done her best to cover them with makeup.

"Stefania takes overdose." "Sexpot actress tries suicide." More headlines in the gutter press. This particular story had been categorically denied by all parties concerned, but carefully studying photos of her around that time, Steve noticed a glazed, defeated look in Stefania's normally sparkling eyes.

He'd spread a bunch of Stefania's stills on and off camera on the floor. He could almost chart the downhill slide of her looks and personality.

The pain that sometimes showed in her eyes didn't come from age; she was only forty-one. They both obviously drank too much. There were countless photos of her and Nicholas in nightclubs worldwide, always with a bottle of Krug on the table and Stefania with a cigarette in her hand. Examining them closely, Steve could see that several of the photos showed Stefania looking furious while Nicholas's eyes were focused on some other woman in the picture.

Steve had never seen one picture in which Nicholas seemed to be the slightest bit out of control. But one night he must have been.

He must have been totally out of control the night Laura had told him about her love for Steve, as she had told him she would. Had she told Nicholas his name? When Steve had first asked himself this question he had realized he needed to change his identity.

"Steve Kelly will look better on the bylines of my stories," he told Phil, by means of explanation. "There's a lot of prejudice against *white* South Africans too, y'know."

"Damn," breathed Atlanta, slinging her panties into the laundry basket. This was the second time that "the curse" had proved true to its name. In spite of satisfying sex sessions with her husband, she still wasn't pregnant. "Maybe I'm working too hard," she muttered.

There were many things on her mind, the magazine being uppermost. With only a month left before *Mercury*'s first publication day, the atmosphere on the 65th floor of the Seagram Building had become totally frenetic. Atlanta had such a compulsion to succeed with this publication that maybe that's why she couldn't get pregnant.

The stick-insect women who controlled rival publications had laughed their dyed heads off when Atlanta had been appointed as the editor, but they weren't laughing so hard now. The competition in the New York publishing world was fierce, and those older and more manipulative female editors were now gnashing their teeth over this upstart magazine, already worried that it could affect their sales, their advertising revenues and, most important, their prestige.

Phil, working on the tried-and-true assumption that money can, and does, buy anything, had installed a couple of "moles" in the two publishing houses that he considered to be their most serious rivals.

When they reported back that the other editors didn't consider *Mercury* to be a potential threat, Phil said to Atlanta, "You're six years younger than one of those bitches, and thirty years younger than the other. You've got more energy, more contacts, and I've certainly got more money than both of them put together. They don't stand a chance, sweet face."

CHAPTER THIRTY-NINE

Venetia and Alain flew to a remote village in the Scottish Highlands and were married immediately. Since no banns or blood tests were necessary, they had escaped the onslaught of the press. They had then flown to Vevey, a little town in Switzerland where Charlie Chaplin had once lived. There, Alain checked Venetia into a detox clinic once again.

High on a grassy hill, the spa specialized in drying out very rich—and in particular infamous—celebrities. The clinic's list of successes in getting people off alcohol, barbiturates, coke, heroin or even food, was impressive, but their regimen was famously tough.

Venetia had promised Alain that she was determined to kick the habit and he believed her; he had also had a serious drug problem which he had overcome. Alain had been overjoyed when she had finally accepted his proposal of marriage, and Venetia had made no bones about getting pregnant as soon as possible. When she told Alain the reason, he became equally keen. But first she had to clean up, rid herself of her craving for cocaine and Ecstasy. In spite of countless previous attempts to go straight, the slightest stress had always sent Venetia back to her drugged nirvana, a victim of her own insecurity.

Dr. Kempel could tell by her contracted pupils and her hyperactive giggles that Venetia was stoned even now.

Venetia had never confronted her addiction realistically before, justifying it to herself as merely recreational and unaware of how seriously it had progressed.

"I don't want a drug-addicted baby," she told Dr. Kempel at their initial meeting, as they sat in his pleasant office with a cool breeze ruffling the chintz curtains.

"From what you've told me, you've been a longtime user of so-called soft drugs, and it's obvious to me that your cocaine habit is exceedingly grave too. If you want to get well and get pregnant, you're going to have to be strong and do exactly what we tell you, because you're well on your way to complete mental and physical self-destruction."

"I do know that, doctor." Venetia looked at him beseechingly. "What I've been doing is wrong. I'm a junkie, but now that I've faced it and accepted that I need help, I want to clean up my act. I really do. And after I've kicked the habit, I want to have children and live a normal life. As normal as Nicholas Stephanopolis's daughter's life can be," she muttered to herself.

"Then we can help you—but only if you're willing to help yourself. It isn't an easy regimen at our clinic. Many patients have found themselves unable to stay the course, but if you're willing to obey the rules, I think I can say with some certainty that we can cure you. But nothing here will work for you unless we have your complete and utter cooperation."

"Whatever I need to do, I'll do it, doctor, I give you my word. This means everything to me."

*   *   *

Eight weeks after checking in, Venetia was released from the sanatorium. Dr. Kempel said, "You've done extremely well, my dear. I know it's been hard, but you've achieved it, and you should be proud of yourself. The next two or three months are probably going to be extremely difficult for you. Although we've virtually cured your body of its physical need for drugs, your subconscious mind still remembers the feelings you had when you were on them. We call it 'euphoric recall'—it would take very little to trigger a craving again, unless you're extremely strong willed."

"I still remember all those feelings very clearly, doctor, but that doesn't mean I'm going to get strung out again." Venetia shuddered. "I remember some of the things that I did when I was high, and I can't believe I did them. I can't *believe* I was so stupid. Never again. I mean it, doctor, never, *ever* again."

"I strongly advise you try to live as simple a life as possible for the next few months. Avoid stress of any sort, although I realize how difficult that can be these days. And, of course, please do not go to places where people who take drugs are likely to congregate."

"You mean clubs, discos, that sort of thing?"

"Exactly. There's nothing worse than those places for the recovering addict. You would find yourself open to very strong temptations all over again. Here, it has been relatively easy for you, given that you have been sur- rounded by others in the same situation as yourself. But now you're on your own. You're going out into the real world, the hard cruel world that we must all cope with as best we can in our own ways."

"Oh God, I wish I could just stay here, it would be so much easier." Venetia sighed, looking through the window at the flocks of sheep grazing on the gently rolling hills. "It's so wonderfully peaceful, I think I really do prefer the simple life."

In the distance a church bell tolled six times. Dr. Kempel stood up, extending his hand.

"Well, good-bye Venetia, and good luck. I'm always here to help you, day or night. If you're ever tempted, or if you have any prob- lems at all, just pick up the telephone. Re- member that, and don't forget to go to the Narcotics Anonymous meetings."

"I will, and thank you, doctor. You've all

been wonderful." Venetia shook his hand warmly. "I'm going to make it now. I know I am."

Alain had gone back to Paris to prepare for Venetia's arrival. His parents had given him an apartment on the Rive Gauche, which he was transforming and decorating. He had taken a job as assistant to a well-known antiques dealer in the Rue Bonaparte, around the corner from the apartment, and although he liked his new status as husband, he sometimes became bored by domesticity. But the apartment was close to some interesting bars where he often whiled away the lonely weeks, waiting for his wife to return.

Venetia was happy to see Alain again. "You're not only my husband, but my best friend too." She smiled.

"I'm going to take care of you now. You look wonderful." Alain admired her slim figure, the fresh bloom on her cheeks, the sparkle that had returned to her blue eyes.

"I'm cured, darling," she whooped, "one hundred percent cured, and I feel so good about myself. I've kicked the habit once and for all and I'm *never* going to touch so much as an aspirin ever again. I'm fit and I'm healthy and now I'm going to jump all over you and start making that baby!"

CHAPTER FORTY

As the weeks passed by, New York's magazine editors seethed while their best staff were poached. Soon *Mercury* became perceived less as a parvenu and more as a serious rival.

New York's most exclusive and expensive PR company had been hired to hype *Mercury*'s image.

"It's quicksilver. Just when you think you understand which direction it's going in, it goes off in another" went one of the ads heard on every major radio station and TV network. Phil had bought bus backs featuring a plain silver poster printed only with

MERCURY. NO ONE CAN HOLD IT DOWN. Others, in the subways, proclaimed ELOQUENT, ACTIVE, EVER CHANGING, EVER FASCINATING. MERCURY. THE MODERN MAGAZINE. FOR MODERN PEOPLE.

The media started buzzing. Aware that more press interest equated to more public interest, Atlanta and Phil were convinced that the success of their precious brainchild was now assured. Atlanta's other goal was to produce a son. Yet she was working like a dervish. Twelve-hour days at the office, an hour of grooming, an hour at the gym and lovemaking every night left her with precious little time for eating or sleeping. Obsessed by the twin goals of pregnancy and commercial success, she was becoming a driven woman, but with the magazine set to go to press and in the fourth month of her marriage, Atlanta was still not pregnant. Why? She was young, healthy and strong; could it have anything to do with her?

She went to see her gynecologist, who told her that fertility tests on women are fairly complex and invasive. He suggested that Phil should get his sperm tested first, to see whether the problem lay with him. This sadly turned out to be the case. Phil had been married before but he and his ex-wife had never had any children, even after fifteen years. Now that his test results were in, this made perfect sense.

Atlanta was faced with a dilemma. She truly loved Phil. He had become the father figure that she had never had, the confidant and friend she always craved, the perfect lover; but she wanted to be the first of the Stephanopolis daughters to have that son. After four months without a sign, when the *New York Post* hinted that her sister might be expecting, she knew it was time to take a radical step. If her beloved husband was unable to impregnate her, she needed to turn elsewhere. After a number of heartfelt conversations with Phil, Atlanta was reassured that he was relaxed about her using a donor to try and become pregnant. She made another appointment with her gynecologist immediately.

The day *Mercury* hit the stands was one of joyous celebration at the office, and everyone was ecstatic when they heard the magazine had sold out at newsstands across New York. Such was its controversial content that Atlanta and Phil Kellog became the talk of Manhattan, the latest in a long line of golden couples. Overnight, the media couldn't get enough of them.

Although Phil never considered himself a social climber, it was hard to resist the blandishments of Mrs. Trump, or Mrs. Astor, or Mrs. Kempner when asked to join the glitterati at a benefit, ball or Broadway opening. Phil liked to think that he wasn't affected by these glamorous occasions or scintillating company—that he could take or leave the constant round of cocktail parties, lunches and charity balls to which they were now invited. Not that they always accepted, by no means were the Kellogs an easy social conquest. Their very elusiveness made them all the more desirable as guests. They were catapulted not only into the most enviable position in the publishing world but also into the sparkling social scene that had always been Atlanta's birthright and that she now began to actually enjoy.

"We're on our way," crowed Phil as he studied the sales figures.

"So what do we do for an encore?" asked Atlanta.

"We steal," he said. "We need a hipper gossip columnist, Teddy's too old guard; no one wants to read about wayward English duchesses and impoverished pretenders to the French throne anymore. We need someone like Taki or Suzy—someone with a cutting edge that Americans can relate to."

"Well, let's get Taki," said Atlanta.

"No—I tried, but he won't budge. He's happy at the *Spectator*. I think we can get Suzy. She'd do it if we pay her enough and buy her enough frocks."

"Are you sure?"

"It's hard to resist our lovely greenbacks, sweetheart. She can still do her daily columns in *WWD* and the *Post*, as long as she saves all the best stuff for us."

"Brilliant. Now I know why I married you, you're just a genius."

"And I thought it was for my devastating movie-star looks." He grinned.

Mercury was causing such a sensation that the advertising department couldn't keep up with the demand for space. Phil immediately instructed them to raise their rates by 30 percent, but it did nothing to slow the advertisers from buying. *Mercury* found itself in the unique and enviable position of having top companies and prestigious products vying with each other for full color pages and offering huge premiums for the privilege.

The day after the third edition hit the stands, key staff sat around the polished oval table in their conference room.

"What's our next move, boss?" Phil asked Atlanta.

She raised her eyebrows. "Boss? You're the boss."

"No longer, sugar-pie. From now on the ball is in your court and I'm just going to be an adviser. So shoot from the hip, sweetie."

She had learned a great deal in the months he'd been teaching her. She was an excellent pupil. Now it was time for the bird to leave its nest and fly alone.

Atlanta looked nervously at Phil and he nodded approvingly. "Resentment is curiously fashionable these days," she said slowly. "Have you all noticed recently that it seems to be what makes our daily life turn more and more?"

"It's an interesting premise. Explain," said Phil.

"Well, the poor resent the rich, and the rich resent the poor. The public adores movie stars and celebrities, but they envy their lifestyles and often hate them for having them."

"What exactly are you getting at, Atlanta?"

"I think that we should do a piece on the bubbling cauldron of hatred and envy that exists right here in New York City," said Atlanta. "The mayor is loathed by black and white, Jew and gentile, rich and poor. He can't put a foot right. Let's profile him, the *real* him—not the way he likes to portray himself, as a sort of benign, put-upon uncle, but as he really is."

"Heavy stuff, Atlanta," said Steve. "We stand to alienate a lot of the readers we've just taken on board."

"Why should we alienate any of our readers if we're telling the truth? That's what's wrong with magazines today; they're all full of lies and half-truths. Look at these. Just take a look at these ridiculous puff pieces."

She threw the latest issues of several glossies down on the table. "Do we really want to read any more about how much the cast of *Friends* are getting per episode? *Must* we see that pop creature ravenous for publicity stroking her crotch and dyeing her hair a different color each week for publicity?"

She flipped open another publication and held it up. "Here we have a story on a well-known actor—well known except that no one goes to see his films, even if he does get two million dollars a flick. But this guy is an *active* supporter, and *heavy* contributor of funds, to the IRA, for God's sake! And this sycophantic trash doesn't even mention it."

"And they put him on the goddamn cover," said Phil.

"So who do you suggest we do our next celebrity piece on?" asked Steve. "You know if we pan any celebs, their press agents will blacklist us from their other celebrity clients."

"Maybe, but I believe that the American public is tired of reading the same old hype about the same boring twenty-five celebrities," said Atlanta. "I'm sick of Julia Roberts and her serial boyfriends, although I agree she's the flavor of the decade. Let's bring people into *Mercury* that the public are not yet sated with. Mrs. Clinton, for example."

CHAPTER FORTY-ONE

Naturally inquisitive, when he and Atlanta first got together, Phil had gone to the "morgue" of one of his newspapers and spent a fascinating hour flipping through yellowed newspaper clippings about the Stephanopolis family.

It wasn't hard to imagine how difficult life must have been for Atlanta as a child and even worse as a teenager. The contrast between the chubby child with the prominent nose, fleshy lips and ungovernable mass of black hair and the golden-haired, chocolate-box prettiness of her mother and sister was all too obvious. It must have been hell for her.

It was hard to reconcile the image of his dazzling wife, the slender epitome of elegance, with that odd-looking child, whose brooding expression emphasized by the dark circles beneath her eyes only further accentuated her look of intense isolation. But it had been an iron will coupled with the miracles of cosmetic surgery that had turned that sow's ear into a ravishing silk purse.

She worked out for two hours every day. He'd watched her with her personal trainer— she even made him sweat. She was dedicated to keeping that racehorse-sleek body in perfect shape. Poor darling girl. He felt a great rush of pity for her and the agony that she had endured to achieve her flawless face and figure, as she now lay beside him, sleeping softly.

He put one hand tenderly on Atlanta's belly, where their child was forming. He had suspected that he couldn't father a child during his last marriage, so when Atlanta suggested the donor program, he had agreed. Atlanta had become pregnant swiftly—one of the lucky few. It would be *their* child even if he wasn't the biological father.

Then the alarm's shrill beep interrupted his musings and woke Atlanta.

"Yeltsin," she mumbled in that shadowland between sleep and wakefulness.

"What did you say, sweet-face?"

"Boris should be our cover story for April."

"I think he's got enough problems at the moment."

She sat up, pushing her thick hair out of her eyes. "I think it's ripe now for a sympathetic story about what really happened during the coup.

"Gorbachev got all the world's sympathy because he was kidnapped. Poor old Boris was just a second banana, apart from that great scene when he jumped onto the tank in Red Square. If we could get an interview with Boris Yeltsin, we'd have one helluva story, wouldn't we, darling?"

"Don't you ever think about anything else except work?" laughed Phil as his valet gave him his tray containing a hearty breakfast and Atlanta's maid placed a tray containing a sparse repast onto her lap. He stuffed half a buttered croissant into his mouth, saying: "You're one helluva workaholic, y'know that?"

She turned to him, her eyes burning fiercely. "We're a great team, Phil. Everyone thinks our fourth issue is going to be even hotter than the first three. Don't you see, if we're going to annihilate the competition, we've *got* to be continually ahead of the game."

"Maybe Yeltsin is a good idea," he conceded, flipping through the mail and morning papers. "Hey—hang on—what about *him* if you really want some controversy?"

He pointed to a grainy picture of the latest serial killer, an ordinary-looking man who'd admitted to murdering, then eating, twenty-six young boys.

"Why not?" She grabbed the paper and stared at the murderer's face with interest. "He's quite a good-looking guy, really. We could send Helmut to photograph him in jail, we could talk to the mothers of some of the boys he's killed, it would be a great story—absolutely mind-boggling."

"Atlanta, sometimes I think you are absolutely sick!" Phil spluttered. "I was only kidding. You can't *seriously* imagine we could put a serial killer on the cover of *Mercury*? We'd be the laughingstock of the industry, not to mention the bleedin' scandal. Jeez! We'd probably get picketed."

"Well, it's not a bad idea," she said smiling, "controversial as hell."

"Well, I won't allow it. Enough already. Much as people may like to read about these sickos in the gutter press, they do not want to see them glamorized as cover boys in their glossies. I absolutely draw the line. No go, princess."

"Yessuh, bossman," she said, pulling a mock subservient voice. "Let's go to work on Boris Yeltsin then. He'll be our next. OK with you?"

"Do that," he said, opening the *Wall Street Journal*.

"Helmut'll do the session so he'll look almost as good as Brad Pitt. Eat your heart out Tina Brown, this one's hard to beat."

CHAPTER FORTY-TWO

Venetia was in her element. Being a Parisian housewife had given her a new and excitingly different life. Mundane things, which she had never even contemplated doing before, were suddenly interesting. All the minutiae of daily life, grocery shopping, cooking and cleaning the apartment were a sudden source of endless fascination. She loved being a hausfrau and, although her cooking left much to be desired, she experimented constantly and vowed to improve. Alain left for work each morning, usually after they had made love, and he often came back for lunch, after which they made love again.

Most nights followed the same pattern, and within a few weeks of arriving in Paris, Venetia was pregnant. She was overjoyed.

The telephone rang and she heard Ginny's voice when she picked it up.

"Darling Venetia, I'm here for two days staying at the Place Athénée with Coral," said her godmother. "I would adore to see you. Are you by any chance free for lunch tomorrow?"

"Of course," said Venetia. "I'd love to see you too and I'm as free as air."

"One o'clock at Le Relais Plaza tomorrow, darling. See you then."

Coral and Ginny had remained close friends since their child-star days. They had come to Paris for the winter collections. Ginny's once wild red hair was now gray and cropped short, and since her weight had hit the two-hundred-pound mark she mostly wore comfortable tracksuits and caftans. But she had kept her freckles, and her round face was usually wreathed in smiles. She had never married, and had little interest in either sex, in contrast to Coral.

Still a stunner, Coral Steele looked years younger than her age, and her beauty and elegance ensured that she didn't sleep alone often.

The previous night the two women had dined with some dull old friends at L'Ami Louis. Having drunk several bottles of excellent Haut-Brion, they decided to explore some of the seedier areas of Paris.

"I hear there's a street near here that has some very interesting clubs and bars," said Ginny. "Even raunchier than New York."

"Rue Napoleon," she told the cabdriver. "The street is near there somewhere. We'll just have to look for it."

"*Merde*," cursed the cabdriver when he realized the street was so narrow that he couldn't drive through it. "If this is the street you want, madame, you will find everything you want here. Drugs, sex, rock and roll. And all sorts of people doing all sorts of things." An expression of resigned disgust was on his face.

The effects of several glasses of wine had loosened Ginny's inhibitions. "I want to see it all. Let's go!" Coral sighed. This wasn't her scene at all. She looked strangely out of place in this seedy back street in her gray silk dress with matching turban, gloves and shoes, and her signature diamond, ruby and emerald parrot earrings. But she was a good sport and always ready for an adventure.

The dimly lit street was lined with bars and clubs, most of them sleazy, some quite expensive-looking, others merely pokey holes in the wall. Outside, burly bouncers hustled for business, extolling the sexiness of the girls and the boys inside.

"How about this place?" Ginny's eye caught the color photograph of a seductive transvestite. Wearing a pink bustier, fishnet tights, and a "skirt" of two dozen plastic bananas slung around ample hips, she was sucking on a real fruit while pointing another lasciviously at her crotch. "Banana Joe's! Now that sounds like fun. Let's give it a whirl, darling."

"I've heard it's just a clip joint for the Tour D'Argent crowd, darling, forget it." Coral wrinkled her elegant nose.

The bouncer and shill for the club, a pock-marked youth, dressed like a twenties pimp in black-and-white-checked trousers and cap and a black turtleneck sweater, grabbed Ginny's arm giving her the low-down on Banana Joe's talents.

"What she do wiz ze banana—*c'est fan-*

tastique—you 'ave nevair seen anyzing like eet before."

"Nor do we want to," said Coral emphatically, pulling Ginny's arm away. "Come on, Ginny, let's go."

A few doors down they were riveted to a billboard featuring a collage of photographs of women in various stages of undress, clinging to an enormous Afghan hound. They all seemed extremely affectionate toward the hound, who just stood looking bored in spite of the lustful smiles of the women and the glowing prose that spelled out just exactly what the dog did with his eager female admirers.

"No! No! My dear Ginny, doggie love is *not* my scene," Coral insisted. "In fact, just the thought of seeing a dame with a dog would make me throw up!"

They continued strolling, warding off the solicitations from hookers of both sexes and Moroccans selling a variety of drugs, until they spied a hole in the wall with a sign that said "Dicks." There was no doorman outside. Old paint had peeled off the narrow doorway in mottled stripes and the brass name plaque was black with age. Most tourists would have passed it by without a second glance.

"This is it," said Ginny excitedly. "*This* is the club Morris was telling us about. He said it's the wildest, most bizarre joint in town."

"It doesn't look like much of a club," said Coral.

"Oh, it is. Morris told me the password to use. Damn, what was it?"

"Maybe this password will be enough." Coral produced a hundred-dollar bill and rapped on the ancient door. "It usually works."

A suspicious eye peered out through a narrow grille.

"*Oui? Qu'est ce que vous desirez?*"

Ginny suddenly remembered the magic words. "We've got a date with Dick."

A bolt was pulled back, the door opened and an enormous hulk of a man, in black leather, grabbed the bill then said, "*Deux cent francs.*"

He frisked them both quickly, then smiled broadly, revealing a huge silver tooth, and gestured behind him. "*Ça va—entrez.*"

In the tiny nondescript bar there was a light buzz of conversation. A few men with hookers sat listening to Elvis from an ancient jukebox, and a couple of boys in tight jeans and a lot of makeup were sipping beers. No one looked up as the two women entered. To this clientele Coral, in her sophisticated clothes, and Ginny, in her mannish attire, were simply another lesbian couple.

"What can I get you ladies?" The barman was polishing a glass with a dirty rag.

"Two Scotches—doubles," said Ginny as Coral looked around in disappointment.

"Is this it?" said Coral.

"Wait." Ginny nodded her head sagely. "Just get your drink, then you'll see."

As soon as their drinks arrived, Ginny raised painted eyebrows at the barman and he gestured for them to follow him.

They walked through a dark, narrow passage that stank of urine, and then the barman unlocked a door from behind which they heard faint sounds of music and laughter. At the end of the room was a heavy black leather curtain covered with metal studs that their guide threw wide open with a theatrical flourish; they were practically knocked down by the blast of acid rock that howled at them from huge speakers in each corner of the tiny, dimly lit room.

The smell of hashish, alcohol, sweat and

urine was overpowering, and both women suddenly wished that they were back at the hotel.

Directly ahead of them, in the center of the room, beneath a flickering blue neon light, about twenty people were clustered watching some sort of performance, for there was much movement, excitement and shouting, which could barely be heard above the loud music.

"Morris wouldn't tell me exactly what happened here, only that it was very, *very* unusual."

"From the sound of things it doesn't sound like a cockfight," whispered Coral. They moved closer, and stood on the edge of the circle peering between the jostling bodies.

Stretched out in the middle of a narrow table, a smile on his painted face and obviously doped to the eyeballs, lay a young man. Golden haired and handsome, he was naked except for garlands of black leather and chains around his neck and wrists. Crawling over and around him, almost humming like insects as they did so, were half a dozen of the most degenerate-looking men and women Coral or Ginny had ever seen. Drag queens in full makeup and wigs, bull

dykes with forearms bigger than a steve-
dore's, transvestites and half-naked gay
hustlers, they were all intent on doing something to the inert body. Some were kissing
him or fondling him, one was even mastur-
bating over him.

"Oh my God!" Ginny couldn't keep the disbelief out of her voice. "What the hell are
they doing to him?"

"Everything," said Coral grimly. "Don't look.
Let's get out of here. This scene is definitely
not my idea of a fun evening out."

"Oh Christ." Ginny grabbed Coral's arm. "I
can't believe it—do you see who it is!" she
gasped. Coral turned to stare at the painted,
gilded creature who lay still as stone while
the pack crawled over him like maggots on
rotting fruit. Then she drew in her breath with
a sharp shocked hiss.

"Oh my God," she whispered. "It's Alain."

When Venetia was told about that evening
by a stony-faced Ginny, she felt she was going to faint. They were lunching at the Relais
Plaza, which was packed.

"Are you sure?" Venetia stammered. "Are
you absolutely positive it was Alain?"

"I'm afraid so. One hundred percent sure,"

said Ginny grimly. "Coral and I stuck around a little while longer to make quite certain. We even asked the barman his name. He didn't even lie."

"But *why* is he doing this? *Why*?" Venetia's weeping caused diners nearby to look at her curiously.

"Come, let's go to my room." Ginny signed the bill. "We can talk more freely there."

"I'm so sorry, Venetia—really sorry," she said as they entered her suite.

Venetia sat down heavily into a Louis XVI *bergère*. "Have you told Papa?" she asked.

"Of course not, darling. I only found out last night, but obviously I had to tell you as soon as possible."

"He did go out." Venetia spoke slowly. "Last night after dinner, and I must have been asleep when he came home—but . . ." Her lower lip started trembling.

"But what?" asked Coral, putting a comforting motherly arm around Venetia's shoulder. "What is it, darling?"

"Recently, he's been going out practically every night," blurted Venetia. "I don't even know where he is or what he's doing."

Venetia's mind was racing. She thought of all the times in the past few weeks when she'd begun to notice signs of drug addiction in Alain, which she herself had fought so hard to overcome.

"I pretended to myself that I didn't notice what was happening. When we went to the cinema, or to dinner with friends, every half hour he would get up and go to the bathroom. Oh my God, do you think it's *true*? Do you *really think* he's on the stuff?"

"Honey, I don't know that much about the drug scene. I can only tell you that at that club, or whatever the hell it is, Alain was on another planet. He was totally out of it. Have you seen his arms lately?"

Venetia was silent, her eyes huge and full of fear.

"Have you?" Ginny insisted.

"No, I haven't. That's another thing I haven't wanted to think about, Ginny. I've just put it all to the back of my mind. He's started wearing pajamas at night. He said he's cold. But we have the heating on and it's only November." She began to sob and Ginny passed her a box of tissues.

"Did *you* see his arms?" Venetia asked.

"Yes, I'm afraid I did. Coral and I saw them quite clearly, covered in needle marks. Some of the group around him were mainlining, passing a needle to each other as if it was a packet of peppermints. It was horrifying."

Venetia's hand flew to her mouth. "Oh God, no—sharing needles? But that's crazy—it's suicide these days."

"I know." Then Ginny said quietly, "Venetia, I hate to bring this up, but since your mother was my best friend, I feel that you're almost like my daughter . . ." She stopped and took a sip of water.

"What are you trying to say? Please don't hold back now."

"If Alain has been sharing needles, and if he's been with men he could have . . ." Ginny's heart was hammering.

"I know what you're going to say, Ginny. I know." Venetia almost screamed. "You think that Alain could have AIDS?"

Ginny nodded, her face ashen. "I suppose you still make love?" she asked hesitantly.

"Make love?" Venetia's eyes were blazing and two red spots had appeared on her pale cheeks. "Make *love*! Of course we do. For the first few months after we got married we were making love all the time. You see, we've been trying to have a baby."

Ginny's ears were ringing. She felt as

though she was in the middle of some sur-
real nightmare.

"We both wanted a baby—we tried so
hard—and now . . ." She swallowed hard and
looked away, studying the pattern of the
carpet. "We succeeded. You see, Ginny—I'm
three months pregnant."

The two women stared at each other with
looks of horror on their faces.

CHAPTER FORTY-THREE

Atlanta strode down Park Avenue, her beige cashmere cape billowing behind her, the November wind whipping her hair into disarray. A few pedestrians turned to stare at this arresting sight, whom some thought they recognized as "somebody." She had been in a state of emotional turmoil for some time now—worrying about whether she would succeed in winning her father's empire by producing a male heir. The truth was she didn't even really want a child. She was beginning to realize that her maternal feelings weren't strong. She never felt the remotest quiver of broodiness glancing into baby carriages or observing tiny toddlers teetering about. Photographs of beautiful babies bored her. Kids left her cold. There was one reason, and one reason only, why she had wanted a child: to continue the Stephanopolis empire. But now she wasn't so sure. Did she really want to give up her new life? She'd worked so hard for her position on *Mercury*—and she loved being with Phil and being part of the glamorous social set. She knew that a baby would change everything.

What to do? What to do? She stopped at a red light at 60th Street, glancing at the newspaper kiosk, where she was pleased to see that *Mercury* was featured in a fine and flashy display. A caption in a tabloid caught her eye and she tossed down two dollars and picked up the paper.

"Both Stephanopolis Heiresses Expect Babies!" blared a headline in the *National Raker*. Beneath it was an old photograph of a smiling Nicholas, flanked by Atlanta and Venetia.

Oblivious to the scurrying crowd, Atlanta read the story and then crumpled the paper and threw it into the gutter, ignoring the chinchilla-swathed matron who cursed, "Damned litterbug—you should be ashamed of yourself!"

*   *   *

So the papers were saying that Venetia was pregnant too? Atlanta had to face the fact that she might now lose the Stephanopolis empire, yet still become a mother in the process. God, how she *hated* this idea of being a baby machine. She walked more slowly, trying to analyze her thoughts. Since his illness, her father had started to sound gentler, more malleable. His telephone voice was no longer harsh, it sounded almost kind, concerned, even considerate. Was he mellowing because of his condition, or because he knew he would soon have an heir?

Atlanta didn't feel the icy wind as she wrestled with her thoughts. She was a happy and successful woman now. *Mercury* was a sensation and her marriage was flourishing. But if Venetia had a little boy before she did, what would *she* gain from this idiotic race? Nothing. If she and Venetia both had girls they'd have to start this charade all over again.

"I can't, I can't go through with it," she mumbled to herself, as she strode down Park Avenue. "I don't care about Father's empire any more. He can have it. I've got everything I want—a brilliant career and a loving, wonderful husband. I'm not going to sacrifice any of it."

CHAPTER FORTY-FOUR

Venetia lay back on the antique white lace bedspread that Alain and she had found together one rainy afternoon in the Marché aux Puces. That happy time now seemed so long ago but it was only a few months.

Longing desperately for oblivion, Venetia had taken two sleeping pills to block out the vile images that Ginny had conjured up for her of Alain in that awful club, but her mind was spinning like a Catherine wheel. The dim light from a bedside lamp glittered on the brass headboard of the huge Spanish bed they had recently bought together from an antiquaire on the Rue Jacob. Every stick of furniture in this bedroom, in the whole apartment in fact, had been chosen by the two of them together. Like giggling children, with money burning a hole in their pockets, they slapped down their platinum Amex cards and thick wads of five-hundred-franc notes to buy furniture, objects and pictures for their love nest.

Love nest! Once more a tear trickled down Venetia's cheek. It felt more like a viper's nest to her now. Her husband was the viper whom she had harbored in her breast. And she had loved him. Truly loved. He was her best friend. Yet even now she could be diseased by the poison he had sown in her, maybe passed it on to their unborn child. Oh God, she couldn't bear it. How could he have done that? How could he? Alain had never given her a clue about his proclivity for his own sex. They had both taken drugs on and off since they were fourteen, but how could he have been so devious, so destructive, to their relationship? Had he literally gone mad?

She had wanted this baby desperately; it held the key to acceptance in her world, finally giving her the respectability she so craved. No longer would she be Venetia

Stephanopolis, the wild-child heiress, the bimbo, still the butt of tasteless jokes. Even yesterday, while flicking through some racks at Galeries Lafayette, Venetia had heard some blonde smirk to a friend, "I hear she's had more pricks in her than a secondhand dartboard." Did they think she was deaf as well as dumb?

This tiny speck of humanity growing inside her was her only way to escape the quagmire of her past and she wanted to do that more than anything; then she could do what her father expected. Take over the reins of the empire that he had handled so brilliantly. She knew she could do it. With Alain's help she could do anything, or so she'd thought. He was the half who had given her the courage, the strength and willpower to kick her killer habit and embrace a normal life. But *why* had he betrayed her? Was Ginny's story to be believed? Alain had always been wild and crazy, a boy who loved the bizarre. Venetia knew in her heart that it must be true.

So where was her honeymoon husband now? Was he once again at that depraved den allowing unspeakable acts to be done to his body?

Venetia's sapphire blue eyes, exact replicas of her mother's, stared unblinkingly at the ceiling until she heard Alain's key turn softly in the front door.

She glanced at the clock—four o'clock—then closed her eyes, pretending sleep as stumbling footsteps and muffled curses announced Alain's shuffling presence. He tiptoed over to the bed, but Venetia kept her eyes tightly closed. Even if she couldn't see him, she could smell him. A mixture of cigarettes, sweat, marijuana and something else, something strange, that she couldn't identify.

He paused by her for a few seconds before lurching off toward the bathroom. She heard the shower running, the faint sound of a scrub brush against flesh, and when he came to bed in clean pajamas, the nauseating smell was gone.

She moved over to her side of the bed as far as possible, praying he wouldn't come near her.

"You've got to talk to him," her inner voice said, as she drifted into troubled, nightmarish sleep. "You've got to have it out with him." Tomorrow she would. Definitely.

CHAPTER FORTY-FIVE

"I want a termination." Atlanta stared challengingly at the doctor across his desk.

"Have you really thought this through? It's not a decision to be taken lightly."

"This is New York State, Dr. Elly," said Atlanta matter-of-factly. "Abortion is legal here, and for whatever reason the mother specifies. Quite frankly, it's none of your business what my reasons are. If you don't wish to perform the operation, I'll go to someone who does."

She lit a cigarette with a slightly trembling hand in spite of the No Smoking sign on the doctor's desk, and gazed across at him with calmness she didn't feel.

The silence was broken only by the doctor softly drumming his fingers on the desk while he stared out of the window.

"Are you absolutely sure about this?" he asked finally.

"Absolutely, one hundred percent sure. I'd like you to do it today, if that's possible."

"It's not possible." He flicked through his appointment book. "Thursday is the soonest."

"That will have to do. That's perfect, thank you, Doctor."

"Have you told your husband?" he asked, scribbling the appointment in his book.

"Yes. Actually he's quite relieved—he doesn't really care that much for children either."

That was, in fact, true. When she'd first told Phil she wanted to try for a baby, he'd said, "I sure hope having a kid won't interfere with your work, sweetie. You're an ace editor. I just hope being a mum won't change things for us."

She had assured him that it wouldn't, but now she knew with absolute certainty that she didn't want a baby. Oh, yes, it would have

been exciting to run Nicholas Stephanopolis's empire, but she was quite content with
Phil Kellog's empire. Motherhood could wait
a long time as far as she was concerned.

Atlanta leaned forward and asked the doctor, "Can you do this termination in your office, in the evening or early morning, without
your nurse having to be here?"

"I could in theory perform a termination
without a nurse being present, but it isn't
ethical. And it's against the law."

"Oh, pooh—you and your old Hippocratic
oath," she said in her best Scarlett O'Hara
manner and, reaching into her handbag,
brought out a check, which she placed
faceup on the desk.

"I believe you are on the board of the Manhattan Hospital for Children, an organization
involved with research into brain-damaged
babies and children?"

He nodded, a slight frown on his face.

"This is a check for a hundred fifty thousand dollars, made out to the hospital. If you
can perform the operation for me next Thursday, without anyone present, the check is
yours, doctor—for the hospital, for the sick
children."

Unblinkingly, she held his gaze across the

desk and, in spite of himself, he felt a grudging admiration for her guts and her absolute confidence in doing and achieving whatever she wanted.

"*No one* must ever know," she said coolly. "As far as everyone is concerned I shall have had a miscarriage. You must realize, doctor, that as a modern woman I have the right to choose if I wish to have a child or not. And you as a modern doctor can surely respect my choice?"

The doctor picked up the check and examined it. A hundred fifty thousand dollars would go a long way toward buying the new scanning equipment for detecting pre-birth brain defects. It could help many children and many parents, for that matter.

"OK, Atlanta, I'll do it," he said brusquely. "Be here at six thirty sharp on Thursday evening. But you'll have to bring someone with you to take you home afterward."

"Thank you, Doctor. I appreciate it, I really do." She rose, turning back to him when she reached the door.

"I want you to know, Doctor, that I am doing exactly what I feel is right for me to do. It is, after all, my body and I should choose what I want, don't you agree?"

The doctor nodded. "Yes, Atlanta, as a matter of fact I happen to agree with you, as do many of my peers. Having said that, abortion is not an easy choice and can lead to serious emotional repercussions—I hope you've given it a great deal of thought."

"I have, Doctor. And you can rest assured that my husband will support me—he'll be coming to take me home afterward. I'll see you next Thursday," said Atlanta gravely.

Venetia was waiting for Alain. With suitcases packed and an overflowing ashtray on the coffee table beside her, she had been sitting in the drawing room for hours, staring blankly into space, smoking and thinking. How she would have loved to have a joint; she craved the blessed relief that a line of coke or an E would give her. But she had to be strong and get the truth out of Alain. He arrived home at seven thirty, a normal time for a husband to return from work, except that now she knew that her husband was far from normal.

"Why are you sitting in the dark?" He laughed, switching on the overhead light.

"Because I want to." Was this the man she had loved on and off since they were teenagers? The husband whom she'd promised to love and honor until death parted them?

Venetia stared at him dispassionately. Alain looked puffy and decadent. She noticed that there were lines on his face. His suit was crumpled and his shirt open untidily as if it had just been done up.

"What have you been doing at night, when you go out, Alain? Tell me the truth, because I know."

"What do you think you know, my little kitten?" His face was the picture of boyish innocence.

"Don't call me your little kitten," she said savagely. "I'm *nobody's* little kitten anymore. Yours least of all."

"What's gotten into you, *chérie*?" He laughed, pouring himself a huge glass of Stolichnaya. "And where's the ice?"

"Find it yourself," snapped Venetia. "I've got better things to do than to worry about fetching your fucking ice."

"What's gotten into you? What's wrong, *chérie*?"

"It's what's got into *you*, Alain. You're homosexual, aren't you?" she said calmly.

He stared at her with doleful blue eyes,

then drained his vodka and poured himself another.

"You still like men and, after all this time, all those promises, you're still doing drugs, aren't you?"

"Who told you?" he murmured. "How did you find out?"

"Ginny went to that horrible club. God, Alain, how could you do this to us? To our baby?"

Venetia had promised herself to stay calm, but she couldn't control her mounting hysteria.

"Ginny saw us?" He looked horrified, then horribly embarrassed. "At the club?"

She nodded numbly.

He sat down heavily. "I'm sorry—I—I don't know what to say, Venetia. I can't explain why I do it. It's—it's like a drug. It's because it's forbidden, such a taboo." He hung his head while Venetia stared at him in disbelief.

"And I suppose . . ." he continued, "that the drugs make me lose my self-control."

"Drugs?" She felt numbed. "You're back doing drugs? After you promised to quit? You promised faithfully. When I was drying out at the clinic you said you were clean, that you'd kicked it forever. You've even taken me to Narcotics Anonymous meetings, dozens of times. How could you *lie* to me like that? How *could* you?"

"I don't know, *chérie*. Maybe because I'm just weak—or just no good. But I know one thing for sure, I love you, Venetia, I really truly love you."

"Oh, for God's sake—how can you lie to me? How can you love me when you let those people—when you let them . . . Oh God, I can't believe what Ginny told me."

"It's the drugs, *chérie*. You of all people should understand, and now I can't help myself."

"So what fucking drugs are you using?" Her voice was hard and accusing. "What are you on?"

"Oh my God, Venetia, I'm sorry." Alain's face crumpled and he sat heavily onto the sofa.

"Uppers? Coke? Ecstasy? *What* are you taking?"

He started to weep and then took off his jacket, unbuttoned the pink shirt she'd bought him for his birthday and stripped to the waist. Then he held out his arms toward her. She drew back with a sickening jolt as she saw the needle tracks.

"How could you be so *stupid*?" Venetia's voice was little more than a whisper. "What have you done?"

"I'm stupid, *chérie*—you should never have married me. I don't know *why* I do it but I've started taking smack again." His body heaved with wracking sobs. "I've been mainlining."

"Oh my God!" Venetia stood up, her heart pumping wildly. "*Heroin?* Alain, what the hell do you think that has done to our baby?"

PART FOUR

Venetia and Steve

CHAPTER FORTY-SIX

Atlanta knew something was very wrong when she awoke in the cold dawn with agonizing cramps.

"Something's wrong. It's the baby," she gasped to Phil as she staggered into the bathroom. "You'd better get me to the hospital."

Although Atlanta had been planning on having a termination, she wasn't prepared for this, so when she awoke in the hospital, it was with a mixture of sadness and relief.

"I'm sorry, babe," said Phil. "I was so worried about you."

He handed her an exquisite bunch of her favorite flowers—lilies of the valley.

"It was obviously definitely not meant to be," said Atlanta, putting on a brave face. "At least this way I didn't have to make the choice. Now I know where I'm meant to be, working at *Mercury*."

Phil smiled at his tough, beautiful wife, his eyes shining with admiration. "That's my girl."

As soon as he opened his eyes, the first thing Nicholas noticed was that he ached all over. Summoning every ounce of willpower, he rolled to the edge of his bed and made his way gingerly to the bathroom. Holding the basin tightly, he stared at his reflection in the mirror.

Beneath his tan, his skin was gray. His lips were pale and his eyes seemed out of proportion; he could see the hollowness in his cheeks and there were deep lines on his face. His clavicles stuck out sharply and there was scrawniness to his neck. He looked and felt fragile—and this was not something that he was used to experiencing.

So this was the effect of the disease? This unrelenting ebbing away of his strength and vitality? He felt too exhausted to even lift his toothbrush.

He leaned over to splash cold water on his face and, not for the first time, felt a diamond-hard agonizing ache in his chest, which made him break out in a cold sweat.

He gave a low moan as the pain pierced him again and, sitting down heavily on the edge of his black marble bathtub, he pulled the bell cord for a servant.

The doctor had assured him that the pain would only be transitory. Sometimes it would strike for an hour or two, then there would be days, weeks even, during which he would feel nothing and could go about his life normally. But today was not one of those days and he looked every one of his sixty years. He had to be at an important meeting that morning in Athens. From his bathroom window he could see the waiting helicopter on the pad outside, so he gulped down four painkillers as his valet knocked and entered in his usual deferential manner, his bald head gleaming in the morning sun.

"Coffee," snapped Nicholas. "Strong and black."

"But the doctor has forbidden you coffee, sir."

"Fuck the doctor and fuck you. Fetch it if you want to keep your job."

The valet glided out, then Nicholas started to shave his pallid and sagging cheeks carefully.

"I'm not going to give in to this," Nicholas had told Dr. André.

The astute doctor, experienced and skilled in his field, had never seen such a determined fighting spirit as Nicholas's. But he noted his patient's alarming loss of strength and advised him to drink half a liter of fresh carrot juice with breakfast and some freshly squeezed beetroot, courgette and parsley juice with lunch.

"Balls," growled Nicholas. "I hate fucking vegetable juices—I'll go on drinking my claret, thank you, doctor, and you can give me some more of these miracle pain pills."

The doctor stared at Nicholas and then said, "I received a call last night from an American friend of mine, a consultant at the Mayo Clinic. He tells me that they've been conducting research into this particular disease and that they have been having some measure of success with a revolutionary form of therapy. It's fairly radical, but I think it could be worth a try. Would you be interested?"

"Of course I would be. I'm much too fond of life to give it up so easily, Simon. I'll accept any new form of therapy if there's a chance it'll work," he said grimly.

"I'd hoped you'd say that. I'll be talking to the specialist later today and I'll order some of the serum to be sent from the States immediately."

"I'll send the jet to pick it up. And . . . thank you, André. There's still plenty of life left in me; I'm not about to abandon this sinking ship quite yet."

CHAPTER FORTY-SEVEN

Because Venetia didn't know what to do or where to go, she went home to Daddy. She told him that Alain was on a buying trip to Russia and that she hadn't wanted to be alone in Paris. She moved back into her childhood room on Stephanopolis Island and Nicholas was so delighted to see his favorite daughter that he started to feel a little better. Welcoming her with open arms, he seemingly forgave her for all her transgressions, and was thrilled she was going to give him an heir.

Stefania too was looking far happier than she had in years. The bruises that could often be glimpsed on her body were no longer apparent. She was about to leave for Los Angeles to play a cameo role in a new Martin Scorsese film. She was excited about playing an opera diva, even though the role was small, and she hummed Italian arias all day with infectious gaiety. But Stefania was increasingly concerned about Nicholas's health. His brow seemed now permanently furrowed in pain.

Day after day, Venetia lay on her luxurious canopied bed, staring miserably at the pale gilded ceiling. Thoughts tumbled over one another inside her confused mind, as she remembered what Alain had told her when *he* was helping *her* to beat her addiction.

"Darling, I was completely addicted to smack. After you left me I got so depressed I started experimenting with it. I was wiped out all the time because I only wanted to see reality through a haze, so I stayed in bed all day, snorting coke and smack. I convinced myself I wasn't doing myself any harm. Several friends, all addicts of course, told me it was quite safe—it was just a recreational kick, they said, just as long as it only went up my nose."

He had clasped Venetia's hands, and said fervently, "But I didn't listen. I started mainlining and got hooked fast and my greatest kick was when I connected. I was stoned all the time. I never went anywhere without a deck of gold dust or white on me. I shared it with my friends and, as you can imagine, I suddenly had lots of new friends. I was rich so I could always afford free fixes for them. Then one day I finally saw the light.

"Do you remember Elyse? She finally knocked some sense into me, got me off the stuff and helped me toward recovery. Believe me, it wasn't easy, and now that we're together I promise I'm going to help you quit, my darling."

And he had. Venetia had come out of the sanatorium she'd nicknamed "The Final Solution" clean of drugs and eager to begin married life. A new life that would, she hoped, include regaining the respect of her father. A baby would help, the baby that was now starting to move faintly inside her. Her perfect child. But was it?

When Venetia had confronted him, Alain had confessed that he'd regressed and shared needles, as well as having sex with strangers. "Men, women, I can't remember them. *Chérie,* I'm so sorry." He had sounded mortified, but Venetia couldn't bear to think of how he had jeopardized the life of their unborn child.

Before she left Paris, she'd asked her doctor about the chance of a fetus contracting AIDS given that the father was bisexual and a needle-sharing drug addict.

"Tragically, we're seeing more of this kind of thing," he said. "I'm afraid that if what you tell me is true, there is a strong chance that you and the baby could be infected with HIV."

"Oh my God," Venetia stammered. "Isn't there anything you can do?"

"We would, of course, test you and do our best to control the disease should you have it. And we will test your baby when he or she is born. But it's all so new. It's a disease still in its infancy."

"Oh God, how terrible." Venetia had the sudden dreadful conviction that her baby was HIV positive. What kind of life would the poor mite have? She'd heard about HIV babies that had been born with the most terrible physical disabilities and her heart went out to them. How would she cope with a baby that needed such special care?

Venetia knew only too well that her father

would blame her for her baby's illness and would probably never forgive her.

Venetia then thought about the race to produce a Stephanopolis heir. If Atlanta had a son and her child was a girl, the race, of course, would be over, but while Venetia still had a fighting chance, she would take great care of her health to give her baby the best chance. She couldn't bring herself to find out the baby's sex before the birth. She would love her baby whatever its sex. Venetia decided to spend time each day with Nicholas's advisers learning all she could about his business, in the hope that she would be the one to inherit it.

But now there was nothing to do except wait. She wouldn't think about what Alain might have done to her and to their child. She couldn't.

CHAPTER FORTY-EIGHT

Atlanta examined her reflection while she put the finishing touches to her toilette. Exquisite perfection stared back at her, which she still couldn't accept. That overweight, pudgy-faced child with unmanageable wiry hair, heavy brows and a downy layer of fine black hairs on her lip stared back at her.

However beautiful she appeared to others, Atlanta could never see the ravishing creature that they saw. Inside she still felt like "the Blob," the nickname she had overheard herself called at school. She had never forgotten it, or the girl who had christened her with it. Neither had she forgotten what she'd heard Ginny saying to Coral on another long-ago day. "Isn't it sad that such a ravishing couple should have such a plain child."

Atlanta adjusted the *décolletage* of her Galliano gown, as Phil tapped lightly on her dressing-room door.

"Come in, darling." She turned to greet him with an exalted smile. "What news from the front?"

He grinned and kissed her. "Sales are up, advertisers standing in line to buy space and every press agent from London to LA is on the blower begging to get their clients in our mag."

Atlanta hugged him gleefully. "Oh, darling, did you ever imagine that *Mercury* would do so well so soon?"

"Of course I did—that's why I hired you, when I read those profiles you wrote for Maximus's 'Excrement Monthly,' and I was more and more impressed by your writing, not to mention that OK face and body. My poor old ma said that if you get a bright enough Sheila to run things, she'll usually make a better job of it than a bloke."

Atlanta grinned. "Your mama was obviously an early women's libber. Listen, I've had a brilliant idea." Atlanta's eyes were shining. "I want to do a story on the unfortunate down and outs who live in this city."

Phil looked less than enthusiastic. "Who wants to read about them?"

"I think people are fascinated by individuals who sink so low they have nowhere left to go except the gutter."

"OK," said Phil reluctantly. "If you want to spend a lot of time researching."

"I do, darling." She kissed him on the nose. "So what else do you have to tell me?"

"Steve's come up with a humdinger of a story for the next issue. Ostensibly, he wants to do a cover story on Stefania Scalerina, but what he *really* wants to do is Nicholas Stephanopolis—your dear old dad—cornered in his island lair. What do you think about that, my darling?"

"But Father never gives interviews— maybe once in a blue moon to some financial newspaper, but that's it. And he'd never allow Steve to interview Stefania on the island."

"Listen, sweetie, don't underestimate Steve Kelly. In the past few weeks he's become, let us say, *close* to that Italian bella donna," he winked.

Atlanta's eyes opened wide. "Are you

telling me that Steve's been seeing Stefania on a—well, on an intimate basis?"

"Not quite, sweetheart. He hasn't gone all the way yet. You may not believe this, but Steve's quite a lad. Many a lady has fallen for his low-key Aussie 'Shucks, I'm just a boy from the outback' approach."

Stefania. That sly fox. Atlanta was still quite close to the fiery beauty, but *Mercury* had taken up so much of her time recently that the shopping and girly lunches that she used to share with Stefania had all but ceased.

"When did this all start?"

"Stefania's in LA making the Scorsese movie and Steve was out there trying to interview that gay rock chick—who's more slippery than a bar of soap. So he meets the Scalerina *signorina* at some Hollywood party and she takes a bit of a shine to him. He gives her his fabled Aussie chat-up and she gets even keener."

"She *does*?" Atlanta was genuinely surprised. "I guess Steve is good-looking, but he's always seemed so laid back. I'm surprised to hear about him chatting up women."

"Yeah? Well, you've never seen him in action," Phil continued. "So he takes her off for a cocktail at the Beverly Hills Hotel, which is where she's camping out, in the biggest bloody bungalow, of course, and I guarantee you it's *not* Mr. Scorsese but your dear old dad who's paying for it. Anyway, Stevie hustles her into the polo lounge and plies her with heavy doses of charm, not to mention three or four champagne cocktails, and suddenly she's begging for it."

"You're kidding me!" said Atlanta.

"I kid you not, kiddo," grinned Phil. "Now, Stevie doesn't take the lady up on her invitation to a nightcap in Bungalow Six. Oh no, he brings out that classic line that you ladies have always used for years, 'not tonight dear, I have a headache,' and tells her that sleep is the only thing that cures his migraines and, besides, he has to take the first flight back to New York in the morning."

"She must have gone *crazy*. Stefania's a lady who always gets her own way, and she *hates* rejection."

"Sure looks that way. So this Sheila is really interested in Steve now, and she keeps ringing him day and night at his apartment, and he keeps giving her the sexy come-on and the 'You're so beautiful I can't wait to see your gorgeous face' line until finally he's got her practically creaming her panties, and she screams that she's got to see him pronto. Got to have him for breakfast, lunch and dinner."

Atlanta smiled. "Sounds like Stefania."

"She likes a bit of dick, sweetie, say it like it is. After a week of lovey-dovey verbals on the phone she was panting for Steve. So, when she finishes the film, she drops off in the Big Apple, at the Carlyle, and she's all ready to meet lover boy. But, can you believe it, the clever bastard tells her he has to go to Ireland, to interview fucking Gerry Adams, if you don't mind!"

Phil doubled up with laughter and Atlanta joined in.

"She must have been furious."

"'Course she was. She was in a right bate. She cursed and called him every name under the sun and he played the 'nose-to-the-grindstone-I've-got-to-do-my-job' card. Then eventually she calms down, and thanks to Steve's brilliant acting, she realizes she might lose him for good, so she says, "Why don't you make *me* your job?" and she practically has to *force* him to come and visit her on Stephanopolis Island to write a profile on her. Can you *believe* it?"

"It's amazing. No journalists have ever been allowed on the island, not even friends of Mama's."

"Well, Steve's flying to Athens next week. Stefania's sending the chopper to pick him up. She'll probably have his boxers off before he knows what hit him."

"But how on *earth* did she persuade Father to let him onto the island?" asked Atlanta.

"All I know is he's got the OK, and he's going to write a really detailed, probing piece on your father. Is that fine with you, sweetie?"

Atlanta thought for a few moments. Her father was very ill and for that she was sorry. The doctor had told them that six months, at the most, was realistically all that Nicholas had left.

"Can we hold the story until . . .?"

"Sure, sure, sweetie." Phil stroked his wife's hair sympathetically. "We'll wait until he's no longer with us. But it will attract massive interest."

"*Caro mio, amore* of my life." Stefania ran her fingers through Nicholas's hair as they lay in her imperial-sized bed in her mirrored, brocade-draped boudoir, but her mind was full of Steve Kelly. Mr. Kelly was good-looking, mysterious and enigmatic, and Stefania liked that a lot. He intrigued her more than any man had done for years, and the fact that he seemed almost impervious to her charms acted on her like an aphrodisiac.

Nicholas was making love to her but not in his usual rough way. The doctor had told him not to exert himself, so it was a gentler Nicholas who pleasured his long-term mistress. As he did, erotic visions of Steve flashed through her mind.

She faked pleasure as Nicholas thrust inside her while she held the image of Steve in her mind. She had to have him. It was obvious that the only place she was going to be able to was on the island. She and Nicholas were spending at least the next six weeks here while he was taking the new medicine, and he would also be occupied with battalions of businessmen, accountants and lawyers.

"You are fantastic, *caro*," she murmured, lying back with a sigh. "Thank you."

Against doctor's orders, Nicholas lit a cigarette. "In spite of my stupid heart, I still seem to be able to please you."

"More than ever, *caro*." She licked the sweat from his brow with a delicate tongue. "Much more than ever."

She rested her hand on his chest. "Since you are so busy, *caro*, and my new movie is opening in America in three months, I thought it would be all right if I asked one or two of the most important American magazine journalists to interview me here?" she murmured. "It would be so convenient, *caro*, and it would mean I wouldn't have to leave you. The studio have said that if I agreed to do just a couple of interviews here, they will let me off the hook for that awful promotional tour of America which is in my contract." She sighed dramatically. "I think it would kill me to tour the States—ugh—the dreadful food, those appalling hotels and those awful journalists, who *all* ask me about you and your business. Always saying bad things. I do think, *caro*, that one or two nice reporters here doing favorable stories would make both our lives so much easier, don't you?"

She held her breath, hoping for the best.

Sometimes the only way to get anything from Nicholas was to come right out and tell the truth—or something close to it. She stroked his chest, looking up at him beguilingly.

Nicholas's mind, severely overtaxed by his illness and keeping track of his business, tuned in to Stefania. Something about someone to come and visit her? Why not? The house was swarming with accountants and lawyers as it was. One or two more people weren't going to make that much difference. Besides, she didn't ask for much really, other than clothes, jewels and plenty of sex.

"The publicity is very important to me, *caro*—I'll make them promise not to mention you in the articles—what do you think?"

"Of course, *carina*." He kissed her then and turned away, ready for sleep. "Whatever you want. Ask your friends—I've a great deal on my plate just now, so I'd be happy to know that you're being kept amused."

"*Grazie, caro*," she breathed, brushing her lips on his cheek and snuggling down with her back to him on her side of the bed. "You're so good to me." Stefania's dark eyes glittered as she looked up at the mirrored ceiling to admire her luscious hair and tawny body, sprawled across the satin sheets and lit by the faint moonlight.

She knew that once on the island, Steve Kelly would never be able to resist her. No one ever had.

CHAPTER FORTY-NINE

It was a spectacular spring day, and Atlanta, buzzing with elation about the morning's editorial meeting, decided to walk to the restaurant, excitedly thinking of whom to cover-profile for the next issue. Suddenly a filthy tramp lurched into her, almost knocking her off balance. Automatically, Atlanta plunged her hand into the pocket of her mink-lined coat for one of the single dollar bills which she always made sure she carried. Everyone in New York kept loose dollar bills in their pockets to escape the torrent of abuse from beggars. She proffered it but the man threw it back in her face, shouting at

her, "Fucking bitch. You'll get yours, bitch—
I'm warning you." Then he spat at her.

Shuddering, Atlanta walked away rapidly,
pretending to ignore the man, obviously one
of the many schizophrenics the administra-
tion had recently released from the state
mental hospitals due to severe budget cuts.
Now these pitiful human beings wandered
the streets and subways, gibbering to themselves, weaving drunkenly, discarded by a
society that no longer wanted to know of
their existence.

It was interesting that there were always
more male vagrants than female. Was it because women were tougher and more re-
silient than men? She believed that they
were. Undoubtedly females had the greater
tolerance of pain. Yet, in her experience, even
the most enlightened of men held the subconscious belief that they were the superior sex.

Atlanta had started hearing epithets about
herself in the office. Only this morning she'd
overheard one male voice saying to another:
"If that bitch gets any tougher, she'll start
growing a pair of balls."

"She's already copped Phil's!" another had
sneered. "He lets her run the joint—why
doesn't he put his foot down?"

"Let's face it—he brown-noses her because of the big bucks from her daddy."

Atlanta had listened, then stuck her head around the door and said a cheery, "Good morning, gentlemen. Are we working like little beavers today? Or are we just jerking off?"

The two had gaped at her. She had looked at the shorter man. "Geoffrey, isn't it?" He'd nodded, his fear only showing itself in the slight trembling of his hands.

"For one who was so outspoken a few seconds ago, you seem to have lost your tongue." She had taken another step into the office. Nicholas would be proud, a little voice had whispered.

"I just want to tell you guys, I *will not tolerate* any kind of disloyalty at *Mercury*. There's enough street fighting and double dealing in the magazine world without it going on in our own ranks. Right?"

"Right, Mrs. Kellog," they'd chorused.

"And it's Atlanta. We're a team here, a democratic one, and we support each other. I *won't* have treachery in this company. If I hear any of you bad-mouthing anyone else here, you'll be out on the street with the other bums, OK?"

"Yes, Atlanta."

"Good." She'd surveyed the two men and smiled. "I'm glad we understand each other."

Atlanta possessed the survivor's ability to expunge unpleasant thoughts from her mind whenever she chose and after walking the couple of blocks to Mortimer's, she had soon forgotten about the malodorous stranger and her altercation in the office. Glen Bernbaum, the proprietor, had greeted her with his usual affability and she had table-hopped briefly, saying warm hellos to friends and cooler ones to acquaintances.

Her guests were already seated at the best table in the window alcove, savoring their pre-lunch cocktails of designer water with lemon slices. This was Atlanta's lunch, so she sat with her back to the room, facing the bay window that looked out on Lexington Avenue.

"Darling, you look gorgeous." Coral, chic as ever, was in buttery yellow leather, her enormous sunflower earrings glistening as brightly as her lips.

"Heaven, as usual, honey," said Coral's equally chic friend Betsy. "Whose is that *divine* dress?"

"Kristobel's, of course. For the past three

years I haven't worn anybody else." Atlanta patted the cheek of the enigmatic pony-tailed designer, who sat beside her. "Well, if you don't count Karl and Valentino."

"It's only because she can't be bothered," Kristobel drawled. "She's really deeply lazy."

Everyone laughed. If there was one thing Atlanta Stephanopolis Kellog was not, it was lazy. She was the embodiment of the nineties woman—tough, clever, bright and climbing fast to the pinnacle of her profession.

"If you want to know the truth, she really can't afford me," joked Kristobel, usually not noted for his humor. "So I give her freebies. Some people ply her with dinners and dia-monds; I ply her with frocks—and why not, with a magazine like hers? It's going to be number one by next year.

"Look over there." He gestured toward Lexington Avenue, where two matrons, faces and bosoms lifted to the limit, were clumsily climbing out of a yellow cab. Both wore copies of a Kristobel design from last season—a tight-waisted tweed jacket and a long skirt, slit to mid-thigh. "You know my fashion comes from the street, but when it goes *back* to the street, that's when I must change it.

"*Quelle horreur*," he muttered. "What can one do with women like that?"

"Women like *that*, darling, ensure that you are one of the most successful designers in New York," said Atlanta.

He allowed a rare smile to cross his somber features. "Look at the short one. Her skirt's so tight she's almost fallen out of the cab."

Atlanta turned, and then found herself eyeball to eyeball with the same wild-eyed vagrant from earlier, who was leaning insolently against a lamppost and staring straight into her eyes. Although the restaurant was warm, she suddenly felt icy cold.

None of the other lunchers seemed to notice the strange man, and Atlanta's guests were all giggling at the other woman, who had now become hooked by the chain handle of her fake Chanel bag to the door handle of the taxi.

They were all inured to vagrants anyway. The city wasn't going to do anything about them, so they might just as well pretend the poor creatures didn't exist, like the cockroaches that infested the kitchens of some of their favorite restaurants. Atlanta was working on her article about them, but had begun to think that the only way to get the real nitty-gritty was to disguise herself as one of them and infiltrate their ranks. Would that be possible, she wondered?

Atlanta stared at the man again. Was he following her? What did he want? Beneath the rags and matted hair there was something familiar about him, but what was it?

She forced herself back into the group's conversation about Kristobel's first haute-couture collection. He had invited the fashion pack from Europe and if the show turned out to be as successful as he was hoping, he intended to launch himself in the couturier's heaven on earth—Paris.

Atlanta raised her glass. "To Kristobel, and to his continuing success." Then Kristobel raised his glass and said, "To *Mercury*. May every issue be as big a sellout as the first ones."

A cute blond waiter came to take their order and for the rest of lunch, Atlanta didn't raise her eyes to the window. But all the time she sensed that the man was there outside. Watching her. Waiting. For what?

CHAPTER FIFTY

Steve Kelly jumped out of the helicopter and, in spite of his dark glasses, squinted into the glare of the blazing afternoon sun, which was reflecting off the shining silver metal and the white gravel of the path leading up to the enormous villa.

A white-gloved manservant relieved him of his suitcase and led him toward the house. Steve's journalistic eye was already taking notes.

A vision in turquoise greeted him, as great carved front doors were heaved open by two more manservants in crisp white uniforms.

"*Caro*, I'm so happy you came—welcome, welcome."

"Hi Stefania, how are you doing?" Steve grinned, shaking her exquisitely manicured hand, noting that her crimson nail polish exactly matched the color on her lips. Several ropes of carved turquoise and silver beads were swathed around her throat and her red hair was all but hidden under a turquoise turban.

Stefania's lounging pajamas were tightly draped across the bodice, accentuating her still extraordinary breasts. Her pajama bottoms were cut like wide-legged palazzo pants, and a floating sleeveless coat swung lazily around her body as she walked. She looked straight into his sunglasses, whispering meaningfully, "You have no idea how glad I am that you've finally made it, *caro*. Come, I'll show you to your room."

Steve had been in enough lavish houses and luxurious dwellings to know how different the rich were from ordinary mortals, but this villa bore no relation to anything he had ever encountered before.

In contrast to the brilliant sunlight, the enormous entrance hall was cool and dim;

although the house was old, the temperature was perfectly regulated and comfortable.

"First, I want you to rest, take a shower, then later I will show you everything," trilled Stefania, ushering him into the largest and certainly the most sumptuous guest suite he had ever seen.

It was dark and cool, until Stefania pressed a button, and the metal shutters over the windows slid up silently, flooding the room with the brilliant late-afternoon sunshine and revealing a view of picture-postcard perfection.

On the walls hung lithographs by Picasso and Matisse and a large abstract painting by Leger dominated the room over a pearl-colored imported seventeenth-century stone fireplace. The floor was covered by a Portuguese hand-stitched rug depicting coral poppies and peonies on a cream background.

"And now, the bedroom!" announced Stefania, and with another meaningful look she threw open double doors to reveal a vast womb of cream and white dominated by an enormous four-poster bed covered and swagged in cream and peach brocade.

"You like?" asked Stefania.

"I like," he smiled, taking off his dark glasses, and looking her straight in the eye. "I like very much."

"Good, it gives me pleasure to please you." With a sharp pink tongue she licked her glossy lips. "Perhaps we do the interview here, no?"

"I think perhaps not. I'm sure I wouldn't be able to concentrate on my work."

"Of course. I understand. So, when shall we start?" she asked huskily, continuing to stare into his blue eyes. "Tomorrow?"

"Sure, why not?" Steve felt he was picnicking on the edge of a volcano. This woman was an experienced and famous temptress, and here she was, making no bones about her fancy for him. He knew her reputation for conquest and felt sure that Nicholas must be aware of it too. Then again, Steve wondered if Nicholas really loved her, or indeed if he'd ever been capable of love at all. Certainly, from everything Laura had told him, he'd never really loved his wife. Who had said, "Love is a kind of warfare?" As Steve stared at the bedposts, he wondered if the gossip was true that Stefania was into the whole bondage thing. If she were, she was certainly barking up the wrong tree, as far as Steve was concerned. He liked his sex straight up and nothing kinky.

"Now, *caro*, I must go and change for dinner. After you have rested, we shall meet on the terrace for cocktails at nine o'clock. I want you to meet Nicholas."

And so do I, thought Steve grimly, as she blew him a smoldering kiss from the door. You have no idea *quite* how much, lady.

The sun was setting in a fiery glow behind the hazy mountains of the Peloponnese as Steve arrived at the terrace. The vast expanse of white marble, interspersed with huge ornate stone pots filled with heavily scented jasmine, was already half full of gray-suited men with matching faces nursing tumblers of Perrier and chatting quietly.

Yanks, Steve realized. American executives, high ranking, obviously important, and all terrified of their cholesterol levels and potential heart attacks. Steve never bothered about either although he was around the same age as most of these characters. Living in the jungle for so long had taught him the inevitability that when your number was up, it was up, and there wasn't a bloody thing you could do about it.

Stefania was already onstage, flitting from group to group, dazzling in semi-transparent white chiffon harem pants scattered with pearls and a heavily embroidered silver-and-pearl bustier. Her breasts were now even more prominently displayed, and Steve noticed with amusement that the American executives couldn't keep their eyes off them. He smiled to himself with the secret knowledge that this dazzlingly desirable woman could be his—maybe just for one night, but it would be a night to remember.

She wafted over to him on silver stilettos, the warm breeze blowing her luxurious hair into casual disarray. Even though she wouldn't see forty again, she was certainly a gorgeous woman, and Steve was looking forward to whatever it was she was going to offer him. But he wasn't about to forget he was here on business—*Mercury*'s business—and to settle a secret score with the man who, he was convinced, had murdered the love of his life.

"I hope you rested well, *caro*?" Stefania smiled sexily, taking his arm with an imper-

ceptible squeeze and handing him a frosted
goblet of champagne which she had taken
from a uniformed waiter.

Steve couldn't believe that he was seeing
liveried servants on a Greek island. Serious-
faced in their eighteenth-century white
breeches and their dark blue frock coats
with silver buttons, they attended to everyone's needs with dedication, and no one
else seemed to find anything out of the ordinary in it.

Stefania dragged him across the terrace
saying, "I want you to meet Mr. Samuels, Mr.
Gold and Mr. Powell . . ." She quickly introduced him to the guests, the names tripping
effortlessly off her tongue. She was obviously an expert at remembering names, and
Steve shook half a dozen stalwart hands as
he murmured pleasantries. Then when Stefania said, "Steve, this is Venetia, Nicholas's
daughter," his heart almost stopped beating.

She looked like a carbon copy of Laura.
Younger than when they'd been in Africa, but
the perfectly shaped, wide-apart blue eyes,
the retroussé nose and the long, fine blonde
hair were an absolute facsimile of her
mother.

Why had he never noticed before the uncanny likeness when he'd looked at press photos of her? Perhaps it was because in most of them she'd looked so dull-eyed and stoned, or her beautiful face had been twisted into gargoyle expressions to irritate the photographers.

She was now a delicate vision, the mirror image of the woman he had loved and lost. Steve held her hand, staring into her beautiful face.

"Hi, how d'you do?" Her accent was more European than Laura's had been. He detected the clipped tones of an English nanny as well as a faint American twang.

How old would she have been when Laura died? Four? Five? In any event too young to have any real depth of memory of her lovely mother. Who had brought her up? Who had taught and trained her? Who had given her the inner strength she needed for today's unforgiving world? Certainly not Nicholas, he was sure of that. He would have been far too preoccupied with business and women. No—she had probably been raised by nannies and governesses. He recalled the stories of her wildness, her drug abuse and her nymphomania. Poor little soul, how could she help herself with a father like hers?

Steve felt he wanted to take care of this fragile creature, to protect her from this world full
of danger and evil.

He looked into her eyes and felt himself
sinking. This was insane. He was fantasizing
about a girl he'd just met when five minutes
before he'd been actively contemplating going to bed with her father's mistress! He held
Venetia's hand longer than necessary and
she smiled at him. He was attractive, this
tanned Australian with the intense blue eyes
and endearing smile enhanced so charm-
ingly by that tiny chip on his front tooth. He
looked vaguely familiar.

"I'm . . . a friend of your sister's," Steve
blurted lamely, never wanting to let go of her
hand. "Actually, we work together."

"At *Mercury*. Oh, of course." She smiled a
genuine and devastating smile. "Isn't it great
that Atlanta's doing so well? Can you believe
it? I hear she's got Tina Brown and Helen
thingummy all of a twist, is that true?"

"She certainly has." He glanced down at
her body in the loose pink dress and noticed
her bump.

"I'm just a little bit pregnant, as they say."
She smiled an enchanting smile, just like her
mother's.

He racked his brains for a comment that wouldn't sound facile. "Congratulations."

Then Venetia started to move over to where a flurry of activity was occurring at the doors that led inside from the terrace, and her face lit up.

"There's Papa!"

Steve stared at Nicholas Stephanopolis. A wave of jealousy and rage, which he'd been fighting for years, engulfed him. He drained his champagne and watched as Venetia ran to hug her father, who returned her embrace eagerly. They clung to each other as the crowd wandered over to pay their respects.

"They adore each other, no? I've never seen two people love each other so much." Stefania had slithered over, outwardly cool, yet emanating waves of sexuality so strong that Steve felt like some jungle animal catching the scent of the female's lust. "Nicholas worships the ground his daughter walks on. Venetia can do no wrong."

"How do you feel about that?" asked Steve, unable to take his eyes off father and daughter: the gray-haired tree trunk of a man and the ravishing blonde who clung to his arm adoringly.

"How do I feel?" she shrugged, arranging

her diaphanous trousers, surreptitiously caressing the curve of Steve's buttocks with a delicate hand. "Except for a short shift, that's the way it has *always* been between Nicholas and Venetia. Just look at them."

He stared harder, fascinated, his mind swirling in confusion. Could it be true that this man had killed his adored daughter's mother? Steve intended to find out.

CHAPTER FIFTY-ONE

"So how come you've never married Nicholas then?" asked Steve. They were strolling around the sumptuous grounds of the island, the air was warm and a faint breeze carried the scent of pine and gardenias.

Stefania shrugged. "If I told you that he'd never asked me, I wouldn't want you to put *that* in your article. The truth is that once a rich man marries his mistress it creates a job vacancy and I wouldn't want some younger conniving beauty to step into my shoes. Nicholas is extremely generous, and besides, I'm happy as I am."

"Are you?" He looked at her with candid

blue eyes which seemed to bore into her soul. "Are you *really* happy, Stefania?"

She sank down onto a stone seat, half hidden by clumps of flowering gardenias and honeysuckle.

"What is happy?" she murmured, staring across the sea, which glittered green and oily, to the mountains beyond. "Happiness is a relative state, *amore*. No one can ever have it all. No one. But we all hold the key to our own survival—every one of us. And my key happens to be Nicholas."

"Meaning?"

"Meaning, *caro mio*, that my film career was successful when I was young, slim and gorgeous. Now that I am older and plumper . . ."

"And still gorgeous," he finished with a smile.

"*Grazie, amore*—but I know that the reason I'm still employed on a more or less regular basis at the age I am now, which I shall not reveal to you"—she made a girlish moue—"is because of my affair with Nicholas Stephanopolis. Any film company knows they will get big publicity because of it. Nicholas is media bait, so because of him, so am I, still. Which is why you're here, isn't it?"

"Only one of the reasons." Steve placed the tape recorder on the seat between them, then followed the direction of her gaze to Nicholas's magnificent yacht.

"But don't you think money has a lot to do with your happiness? Being rich is a damn sight better than being poor, and being mega-rich is even better. Tell me about what it's like, Stefania, to live in the world of the mega-rich."

"Nicholas always says that to be very rich is like belonging to some terribly exclusive club," confided Stefania. "A small club with a restricted membership, whose members know everything about each other whether they've met or not. They know the size of each other's fortunes and the size of their houses and yachts. Most rich people spend a great part of their lives in the pursuit of luxury and pleasure. It's a club, where only the very best will suffice and whose members only share their knowledge with each other. They all know the best dealers for their pictures and their furniture, the finest craftsmen and decorators for the boats and houses, even where to get the best deals when buying jewels for their mistresses, or who is the latest, most expensive florist who always comes to the scene just when the parvenus have discovered the old one, thus making him no longer fashionable. They let each other in on the secrets of where the finest wines in the world can be found, or which particular shoemaker can construct a pair of shoes of leather so supple that wearing them is like walking on air. Ah yes, the world of the ferociously rich is a world that few will ever be allowed to understand. Even those who, like me, climb on to the—how you say—gravy train of that lifestyle can still never be *truly* a part of it."

She stopped, tracing a manicured finger across Steve's lips. "I love your mouth," she whispered. "It's so strong."

"Don't change the subject." He laughed and tapped the tape recorder. "Your every word is on here."

"I forgot." She smiled and for a second he looked at her not as a hardened journalist but as her lover of the past three days. She was certainly indefatigable. On the pretense of recording her entire life story on tape, each afternoon they had taken long walks across the island. At some point Stefania, usually wearing only the flimsiest and most tantalizing of designer sportswear, would drop her guard along with her clothing and he would join her. Making love outdoors had always heightened Steve's sexuality, and it had been some time since he'd been with a woman.

And Stefania was an expert in the art of love. He had heard the term "Cleopatra's clutch" but he had never before come across any woman who had perfected the art of bringing her partner to fulfillment by the skillful manipulation of just one muscle in her body.

"Where on earth did you learn how to do that?" he had gasped after their first night together.

"Shanghai, *amore*," she whispered mysteriously. "In a brothel. We were shooting one of my first films there. I was playing a young prostitute, so I decided to learn exactly what it is they do."

"My God. That's carrying the Stanislavsky Method to the ultimate."

"Don't put that in the story."

"Of course not, you know I wouldn't."

She lay back on the bench, clicked off Steve's tape recorder. "I need a little rest from all this talking, *caro*."

Slowly she slid her hand down his open-necked shirt until it came to rest below the waistband of his jeans; she slipped the silk wrap off her shoulders until she was naked except for her sunglasses.

As Steve entered her, he muttered, "What if someone sees us?"

"Don't be silly, *caro*," she whispered huskily. "Even if they did, they wouldn't tell Nicholas. They know the shock would probably kill him."

When Steve had noticed deep scars on Stefania's back, he had asked questions. She had at first demurred, but having had a little more wine than usual at lunchtime, she had confessed at his insistence that Nicholas had once beaten her so badly that she'd had to have stitches.

"It's what he does—or did—for kicks," she said sadly. "I went along with it at first, even liked it, I admit. But sometimes it got really bad, *caro*—please let's not talk about it."

"Do you love him?" Steve asked.

"*Caro*, what is love? It's *this* I love, you know," and she bent her lush body over his to end the conversation.

On the fourth evening, when Steve was seated next to Venetia at dinner, she asked,

"Have we met before? You do look awfully familiar."

"I do?" He gave her a quizzical half-lidded glance. His "Mel Gibson look," as Phil called it.

He felt strangely uncomfortable next to Laura's daughter, yet strangely at home too. Her pert profile and frank aquamarine stare were so familiar.

"I don't think we've ever met, but I'm certainly glad I've been given the opportunity now." And he continued talking to Venetia throughout dinner in spite of Stefania's jealous stare.

The exotic dishes that were served were new to him. The turtle soup *en gelée*, topped with a heaped tablespoonful of glistening beluga caviar, he found impossible to appreciate, and he noticed that the six American executives felt as he did, although two did try to rescue the caviar. The salad was one of the most expensive and unusual salads in the world. Tiny ovuli mushrooms, yellow on the inside and white on the outside, were sliced and served with thick slivers of pungent white truffles. The lobster thermidor flown in from Maine on Nicholas's plane that morning and garnished with a *mélange* of tiny pink crayfish and prawns was truly superb.

But Steve couldn't concentrate on eating. He remained fascinated by Venetia. He found it almost impossible to believe that this was a girl the gossips had viciously christened "The Greek Open." This could be no nymphomaniac. This was a sweet, charming young woman who was becoming more and more intriguing to him.

When most of the executives had returned to the mainland, after dinner one evening Stefania suggested that they should all take a midnight swim outdoors.

"It's so unusually hot, *tesoro*," she said to Nicholas. "It'd do us all good."

But as they were finishing their coffee and liqueurs, ominous thunderclaps were heard and a light rain started to fall, so Stefania suggested that those who wished to should swim in the indoor swimming pool.

The two remaining businessmen patted their paunches and groaned, saying they'd rather take a rain check and get a good night's sleep.

But Nicholas was in an expansive mood,

so he, Steve, Stefania and Venetia all went down to the enormous underground pool. The cavern in which it was situated was as big as a ballroom, with three huge skylights in the roof. The stone walls were decorated with *trompe l'œil* frescoes of mythical scenes, above which ran a wide minstrels' gallery. Steve was stunned by the detail in the vast murals and by the grandeur of their subject matter.

Poseidon sat high on a golden throne encrusted with coral and pearls, holding aloft a jeweled trident, surrounded by sea nymphs and fauns. Mermaids, twined sinuously around craggy rocks, combed their flaxen hair, while strange impish-faced sea creatures with dragonlike bodies swirled slavishly at their silvery tails. Ancient Greek gods and goddesses—Zeus, Hera, Eros, Aphrodite and Apollo—all looked down at the pool with the kind of piercing eyes that always seem to follow the onlooker's every move. The pool was Olympic size, and faint curls of steam rose lazily from the water into the humid air.

It was cloyingly hot in the painted room, in spite of the height of its high-domed ceiling. As Steve dived into the warm water, he felt strange, as if the eyes of a strangely malevolent spirit were following him as he swam.

Stefania and Venetia had decided to play backgammon, and sat together sipping wine and giggling.

Steve watched from the pool as Nicholas walked out of the changing room, his valet trailing behind him. In black swimming trunks, his bronzed and toned body did little to betray Nicholas's sixty years. Only his face, lined and weary, revealed his age.

"Bring us a bottle of Krug," Nicholas commanded, before diving into the deep end. Venetia smiled at Steve, who grinned back at her, but she immediately looked away. He was certainly attractive, she had to admit that, but she was finished with men right now. She was pregnant and married, albeit to a drug addict. Her flirting and screwing-around days were gone—forever.

Nicholas climbed out of the pool and shook water from his head just like a dog. "How about a game of backgammon, Steve?"

"You're on!" answered Steve.

"A dollar a point?" suggested Nicholas as he shrugged into a terry-cloth robe.

"You're on again," said Steve.

*   *   *

Both men were fiercely competitive back-gammon players. They finished one bottle of Krug and Nicholas called for another. "A magnum this time," he ordered. "Leave it in the ice bucket and then you can go. We won't need anything more tonight."

The servant bowed and withdrew silently.

"*Caro*, I am *exhausted*." Stefania sighed. She stood behind Nicholas, pushing half-exposed breasts against the back of his head and caressing his neck while her eyes met Steve's across the table. They were eyes filled with promise, but he was deeply involved with beating Nicholas Stephanopo-lis right now, and Stefania's demands were starting to become more than a little wear-ing. He glanced at Venetia, who kissed her father lightly on the cheek as she whispered, "'Night, Papa. Good luck."

"Good night, kitten. *Buena notte*, Stefania."

Steve rose as each of the women kissed him on the cheek, then in a flurry of chiffon they were gone.

"Now we can get down to some serious drinking," said Nicholas. "And some serious gambling. How does ten dollars a point grab you?"

"Grabs me just fine," said Steve, already three hundred dollars ahead. "Just fine, sir."

"Call me Nicholas," he said brusquely as he shook the black alligator dice-box and threw a pair of threes onto the board. "Ten bucks a point it is then." And he filled their glasses of champagne once again.

Nicholas put a CD into the state-of-the-art hi-fi system. It was Jessye Norman singing "The Death of Isolde."

"It's the most erotic piece of music ever written," Nicholas said, "almost orgasmic."

The rafters shook with her passionate voice, and then, as if arranged by an opera director, they heard another great crack of thunder outside.

"A storm—we've been waiting for this for days—the gardeners will be pleased." Nicholas shook the backgammon cup and threw a six and a three. He moved his piece across the board and leaned back, squinting at Steve through the haze of smoke from the cigar clenched between his teeth.

There was a further loud clap of thunder, which was eerily amplified by the acoustics of the pool area, then a bolt of forked lightning lit it up. Nicholas filled their glasses with more champagne.

Each of the men was determined to win, each bent on proving something to the other.

During the game Nicholas drank steadily and Steve pretended to, but surreptitiously emptied his glass into a potted plant whenever possible.

They played evenly and, though Steve was an excellent player, he finally allowed Nicholas to beat him, for political reasons.

After polishing off most of the magnum, Nicholas suggested it was time for another swim. Steve was now behaving as if he was in his cups and he lurched toward the pool's edge. "Ready or not here I come!" he chortled. He tipped the bottle of champagne to his lips, then dived into the deep end.

Nicholas was already in, water glistening on his black eyelashes, his silvery curls sleek on his head.

"Right. How about a race, my boy? Are you ready for it?"

"Am I ready? I am steady!" Steve hiccuped. "Steady as I'll ever be."

"You've got nearly twenty years on me but I'll still beat you," said Nicholas confidently. He started swimming toward the shallow end with a smooth thrusting crawl.

Steve lumbered along, pretending he was trying to keep up, splashing and breathing heavily.

"Good at this aren't you?" He faked breathlessness as they simultaneously reached the shallow end.

"Come on, come on, you can beat me." Nicholas turned and swirled rapidly back toward the other end, cutting cleanly through the water. "You're a young man, Steve, show me what you're made of."

He swam proudly and swiftly and was half a length ahead of the younger man when he gave a sharp cry, "Christ, I've got a cramp in my arm."

The thunderclaps were now almost directly overhead, and a bolt of lightning hissed as it crashed down into the forest nearby. Nicholas looked up at the cruel demon face from a mythical scene illuminated through the skylights by the white-green light of the flashes. It loomed over him, mocking him with its jeering, unforgiving grimace. With the rushing in his ears and the harsh erratic thumping of his heart he imagined he could hear the devil's laughter. Maniac cackles seemed to echo in the murky green gloom of the vast cavern. The demon face seemed to be moving toward him, its gaping mouth stretching open as if to devour him.

The Wagnerian sounds of Jessye Norman's pure voice soared to a climax just as a second jolt of lightning cut the electricity. Everything was blackness, save for the candles burning on the tables. Suddenly it was silent as a tomb. Nicholas felt disoriented and drunk in the warm black water and his arm was throbbing. I'd better get out, he thought, drifting and confused in the darkness. Then there was another deafening crack of thunder, a flashing blaze of lightning, and the emergency power kicked in.

Nicholas started flailing desperately in the center of the pool, the pain in his left arm becoming more intense every moment. "For God's sake, help me."

Steve, no longer pretending to be drunk, blithely ignored his cries. "What's the matter, Nicholas?" he asked innocently.

"For Christ's sake. Please, *please* help me!"

Then the water choked his words and his head went under. He flailed his right arm in a frantic attempt to stay afloat but the rest of his body refused to move. It seemed as heavy as lead and the pain in his other arm was now excruciating.

"Come on Nicholas, hurry up. I'm beating you." Steve streaked past him, a couple of feet away but remaining deaf to his screams.

Nicholas's head disappeared under the water for the second time. The pain in his arm had moved to his chest now, in pounding, agonizing torment, and all his limbs seemed to be disconnected from the signals coming from his brain. He swallowed more water and bobbed up again, gasping for air. The water was choking him and suddenly he knew with complete certainty that he was going to drown.

Suddenly Steve swam very close to Nicholas. So close that Nicholas could see those cold blue eyes boring into him. They were the eyes of an avenging angel, full of hatred and loathing.

"Help me, for God's sake!" Nicholas went under again and screamed beneath the bubbling water, a silent, choking scream that filled his lungs with liquid: "No!"

The pain was so intense now and his fear so great that Nicholas felt his only escape was to sink to oblivion beneath the foaming water. His mind was a red mist of pain and

the inevitable acceptance of death. It was almost with gratitude that he felt the water
starting to engulf him for the last time.

He was losing the battle, sinking. His heart
was beating erratically, far too fast. It was
throbbing wildly in his chest, fit to burst.

Venetia heard the muffled cries as she was
crossing the minstrels' gallery. Unable to
sleep, she suddenly had an irresistible craving for ice cream. There was a fully stocked,
old-fashioned ice-cream parlor in the base-
ment, next to the swimming pool, and Venetia was dying for a scoop of Häagen-Dazs.

She stopped dead when she heard the
sounds of screaming and splashing. Then
she ran to the edge of the gallery but froze
when she saw the scene beneath her—her
father flailing in the water and Steve struggling to pull him out.

"Daddy!" she screamed. "Oh my God—
Daddy!" Without hesitating, Venetia climbed
onto the balcony rail and jumped into the
churning water below.

When the police arrived from the mainland
an hour later, they found a hysterical Venetia
kneeling and weeping over her father's body.

It lay on the tiled edge at the shallow end of the pool. His bronzed limbs were splayed out on the shiny turquoise tiles.

Wrapped in a terry-cloth robe, sobbing and shivering, Venetia was being comforted by Steve, who was informing the police about the tragic turn of events.

"We were having a race," he said, "I tried to save him. But we were both so drunk . . . I'm so sorry. I realize I shouldn't have let him drink so much—I didn't know about his heart problems."

Venetia's sad blue eyes looked over at one of the detectives, who felt a surge of compassion. Poor kid, she'd obviously tried to revive him by giving him the kiss of life after she and the Australian guy had pulled him out. And to dive fifteen feet from that balcony to save her father had been an act of incredible bravery. The more so because of her condition.

Suddenly Venetia doubled up in agony.

"What's wrong?" Steve was horrified by the expression on her pinched white face. "What is it?"

"Get me to the hospital," she gasped, "I think the baby's coming."

CHAPTER FIFTY-TWO

Immediately on hearing of her father's death, Atlanta and Phil took the first plane out of New York.

The following day, they went straight to the villa, where the family gathered in Nicholas's book-lined study. Lady Anne was ramrod straight in a tall bergère. Stefania and a very pale and weak Venetia were sitting side by side on the sofa. Steve, sitting behind them, was suffused with an overwhelming concern for Venetia's welfare. They hadn't been able to save her premature baby.

"It was my fault. I should never have agreed to that race. If I hadn't, he'd still be alive," Steve had told Venetia the night before as she was lying on her bed.

"Don't blame yourself," she said softly. "It wasn't your fault. I'm sure he knew how hard you tried to save his life."

Steve looked at her. She was like a jewel, a pastel drawing by Rossetti. He was trying hard not to give in to his feelings of guilt and revenge. He hadn't actually killed Nicholas, just as Nicholas hadn't actually killed Laura. But Steve had concluded from the autopsy reports that Laura must have lived for some hours after falling against that marble fireplace, precious hours in which Nicholas should have gotten help as her life left her body. They had both been accidents. Steve had had his revenge, finally, but at what cost?

"I talked to the police," said Venetia. "They told me how you struggled to save him. It must have been terrible."

"Thanks, Venetia," he said softly. "I only wish I could've saved him." Steve lowered his eyes and sighed. "I did my best. I think you should rest now, you look exhausted."

It was true, she was tired. The baby had been a little boy. Venetia felt a pang of sadness as she realized that if he had come to full term she would have inherited the empire. She tried not to think about the baby. She would never know if he was HIV positive. Never mind. It didn't matter now. She was so exhausted and nothing seemed important anymore, now that Papa was dead.

They buried Nicholas Stephanopolis in the family plot between Laura and Constantine, his father.

At the funeral, Lady Anne, gray faced and uncharacteristically shaky, had mumbled, "Too many funerals. There have been too many funerals."

Atlanta, dry eyed, held tightly to Phil, while Venetia, close to tears, clung to the arm of Steve Kelly. Stefania, wreathed in black veils, was sobbing next to him.

Well, he'd gotten his story all right. He had finally avenged Laura for the crime he believed Nicholas had committed. But now, with Laura's daughter clinging to him, admiring him for the way he'd tried to save her father's life, he felt an overwhelming spasm of remorse.

Once again the family gathered in Nicholas's study, this time for the reading of his will. Afternoon sun dappled the walls with zigzags of vivid light and, in spite of the light breeze coming through the half-drawn curtains, there was a damp, musty smell, as if no one had been in there for years, even though Nicholas had spent every day there for the past three months.

How quickly we all turn to dust, thought Atlanta, glancing above the fireplace where a portrait of her mother by Pietro Annigoni hung, painted at the peak of Laura's beauty. In the neoclassical picture, Laura was wearing a simple white Grecian-style gown, her golden hair cascading over pale shoulders and a serene faraway look in her aquamarine eyes.

Steve couldn't keep his eyes off the portrait, which captured her ethereal beauty to perfection. He wondered how many people noticed the uncanny similarity between Laura and her youngest daughter who, still weak from her ordeal and with eyes swollen from weeping, sat beside her sister.

Only immediate family were present to listen to the somber tones of Samuel Newman, Nicholas's legal representative, as he read the will. Stefania and both Atlanta and Venetia had insisted that Steve stay, so he now found himself in a tremendous quandary. Everyone believed that he'd tried to save Nicholas when in truth he'd done nothing of the kind—he had let him die. Steve shuddered. Did that make him a murderer? He had encouraged Nicholas in his drinking and then accepted his challenge. He hadn't known that Nicholas had a heart condition. For it wasn't until after Nicholas's death that Steve was told he'd been warned not to drink, smoke or overexert himself. But it was Nicholas himself who had chosen to do those things, and he had paid the ultimate price for his folly.

But as much as he agonized over the Greek tycoon's death, Steve couldn't help but feel it was a fitting punishment for what Nicholas had done to Laura. He felt vindicated that he had finally avenged her death.

Then his thoughts turned to his new predicament. The beautiful, frail mirror image of Laura had been clinging to him practically the entire time since the double tragedy of the deaths of her father and baby. In spite of the fact that a haggard Alain had arrived, Venetia had turned not to him for comfort, but to Steve.

Although she'd known Steve for barely a

week, his strength was helping her get through this nightmare. She was also starting to be attracted to him, despite their age difference. He was becoming her rock, her tower of strength, and she had poured out to him her grief and sorrow as she had never been able to do with anyone else. Most of the time Alain hadn't seemed to care—he was far too busy grappling with his own demons. After a few days, Venetia encouraged him to leave.

"I need time on my own to grieve. You'll be better off back home taking care of your health, Alain."

Grateful for the out, Alain returned to Paris, where he continued with his dissolute lifestyle despite being diagnosed as HIV positive.

Stefania, draped in black lace from top to toe, was weeping dramatically. Even her handkerchief was edged with black. But she hadn't been weeping the previous night when she'd come to Steve's room. Neither weeping nor dressed in mourning. Unless one counted the black chiffon lace teddy that she'd worn beneath her satin peignoir.

"*Caro mio,*" she had whispered theatrically, closing the door and leaning against it in an attitude of the deepest despair. "*Caro mio*, I have missed you so much. Why have you not come to visit me? To bring some cheer to poor Stefania?"

"I'm sorry, Stefania, really I am." Steve looked up from his work and ran a hand through his tousled hair. The very last thing he wanted right now was an erotic tumble with a grieving mistress.

"I've got a deadline for my story on you and I'm burning the midnight oil to finish it." He gestured at his battered computer and the desk littered with papers. "Got work to do, Stefania. A ton of work."

"I know," she said softly, wetting her already glistening lips with a predatory tongue. "I know you have, *amore*, but I'm so lonely and so sad."

"It's only been three days since Nicholas's death. It's natural that you should feel like that, Stefania."

She floated over to the sofa and threw herself down on it dramatically. Her robe parted as if by magic to reveal her sumptuous body. She laid her head on the back of the sofa, looking at him with soft beseeching eyes.

"I'm so very lonely, Steve."

"I know, I know you are, Stefania," he said, not daring to come too close to her. She had a potent aphrodisiacal effect on him. Despite the fact that he was falling under Venetia's spell, Stefania's crackling sexuality usually managed to arouse him. He gestured helplessly at his papers.

"Look, you've just lost your lover—you're virtually a widow, for God's sake—and the two of us . . . it . . . it wouldn't be right," he finished lamely, watching her as she started to caress her breasts through the dark chiffon. He watched transfixed as she made her nipples stand out up against the thin fabric. She moved one hand up and down between her legs, her eyes never leaving him.

"Help me, *caro mio*, please," she whispered. "Help me to forget my sadness."

And so he did. After all he was only a man, and she was more than a woman.

The expressionless Mr. Newman cleared his throat and began reading the last will and testament of Nicholas Stephanopolis.

There were the usual bequests of lavish amounts of cash to Miss Jeans and other faithful employees, and then finally . . .

Here it comes, thought Atlanta.

"To my mother, Lady Anne, I bequeath the sum of ten million dollars, Stephanopolis Island and everything contained therein for her personal use as long as she shall live."

Which doesn't look as though it'll be for much longer, from the look of her, thought Phil, glancing over at the old lady still dry eyed and the model of old-fashioned dignity. But the signs of old age were barely disguised by the excellent posture and the couturier's art. Lady Anne was an incredibly well-preserved eighty-nine now, but her grief at losing not only her son but also her two expected grandchildren, although well concealed, had aged her dreadfully.

"After my mother's death, it is my wish that ownership of Villa Stephanopolis be shared equally between my two daughters, Atlanta and Venetia, their husbands and their heirs."

The girls glanced at each other ruefully. There were certainly not going to be any heirs in the near future.

"To Stefania Scalerina, I bequeath my Avenue Foch house in Paris and all the furniture, paintings and valuables therein. My estate will provide her an annuity of one million dollars for life."

Newman continued. "All of my business holdings, including my controlling interest in Transglobal Shipping, my stock holdings, bonds, real estate holdings in North and South America, properties in London, Gstaad, Cap d'Antibes and Tuscany, my collection of eighteenth-century French furniture, jewels and *objets de vertu*, my paintings, my motor yacht *Circe* . . ." the list droned on and on.

When Newman finished, Atlanta could hardly believe what she had heard.

He had left it to *her*—the conglomerates, the shipping business and all the glory and kudos yet to come! The entire Stephanopolis empire would be hers. There was, of course, a stipulation that Nicholas's battalion of advisers would guide and oversee her. Their chairman had passed the reins of power exclusively to his eldest daughter, who was not yet thirty.

Venetia looked dumbstruck, pale and close to tears. She was starting to feel faint. *She* had always been her father's favorite— so how could he have left everything to Atlanta? He never even *liked* Atlanta! It wasn't fair. She felt unaccustomed anger toward her father. If her baby had lived, it would have been different. What the *hell* am I going to do with myself now? she thought grimly.

Venetia received several million dollars, fifteen Impressionist paintings and the New York penthouse, but with the current slump in the Manhattan property market, that mammoth apartment, with its twenty-four rooms and spectacular views over Central Park, would be worth nowhere near the ridiculous price her father had paid for it.

The only bright spot was that Steve lived in New York. She glanced at his craggy profile and brown hair flecked with gray, which still flopped on his forehead boyishly. He caught her eye, gave her an encouraging grin and squeezed her hand.

Then Venetia turned to look at Stefania. Had those whispered rumors been true that her father's mistress had taken more than a liking to Steve Kelly? She felt something akin to a faint flicker of jealousy, but then, returning his smile, she squeezed his hand tighter.

"Do you realize that if I hadn't lost my baby in trying to save Papa I would have inherited *everything*?" Venetia paced across the thick carpet, puffing angrily on a Marlboro.

Steve had been startled to find Venetia at his door after the reading of the will. He knew that the doctor had insisted she rest as much as possible.

"Calm down. You mustn't berate yourself." He watched her, delicious in a short yellow sundress that matched her hair.

"What am I going to *do*, Steve?" She threw herself into the same sofa on which Stefania had seduced him the night before, looking at him with huge supplicating eyes.

"You could get a job."

"A job? How? I've never worked a day in my life. I don't know how."

"Most people learn." He grinned. She could be a spoiled brat but adorable nevertheless.

"I'm frightened, Steve, and I'm weak. I know I am."

"You're not, princess," he said firmly. "I think you're much stronger than you imagine. Look at how you tried to save your father's life. And look how you kicked your drug habit. Those aren't signs of weakness."

"But I'm afraid, I don't know what to do with my life, and I know I could easily go back to drugs again if I don't have some direction. Oh Steve, it's awful to be rich."

"Sure, tell me about it." He started to laugh.

She hastily added, "No, I don't mean it to sound like that. I mean to be so rich that one doesn't need to have any motivation in life. Knowing that every day, when you wake up, there's going to be someone to put the food on the table, someone to lay out your clothes and to run your bath." She giggled suddenly. "Once, I had a personal maid who put toothpaste on my toothbrush for me! Can you imagine?"

They laughed, then her face clouded again. "It's not funny, you know. Not really. People always feel sorry for the poor but they never feel sorry for poor little rich girls— like me. Oh God, Steve." She started to sob and he went to her and stroked her bare shoulder. This moment reminded him vividly of the night Laura had wept while confessing to him the truth about Nicholas's vicious cruelty. Then he had confessed his love for her and after she reciprocated fully, they had bonded together that night. They had had just two short weeks together and then he'd never seen her alive again.

Suddenly he felt himself teetering on the verge of exactly the same all-consuming passion. It was crazy, but what he had felt for the mother he was now feeling for the daughter. The warmth from Venetia's shoulder on his hands made him tingle but his touch seemed to calm her. She turned to look at him with brimming eyes.

"If I come to New York and live in the apartment, will you help me, Steve? Help me find some direction in my life. I *know* I could have run Daddy's business, I would've been good, I know it. But . . ." she shrugged. "*C'est la vie.* Maybe if I'd had the baby I'd have found my direction."

"Don't torture yourself," Steve said, while the proximity of Venetia and the tenderness he was feeling toward her were torturing him.

"Oh, Steve." She leaned toward him, her pink lips parted, eyes like twin pools of desirability. "I'm going to make something of myself. I am. I'm absolutely determined now. But I need to have support. I never really got it from Daddy, except in one way."

"Which way was that?" he asked.

"Money, of course. He left me plenty in the will and he threw money at me all my life and gave me anything I wanted except direction and guidance. Will you be my friend, Steve?"

He nodded. He hoped that one day she would want to be more than just his friend. Until that day came, this beautiful girl would be his crusade and he would do his utmost to help her reach the pinnacle of whatever it was that she wanted.

"I came to your room this afternoon but you were busy," rasped Stefania, her eyes flashing with fury, a dervish in purple chiffon. "Busy with Venetia."

"I was just calming her down," said Steve.

It was all turning into a nightmare. He needed to get away from the claustrophobic confines of this island. Since Nicholas's death, the island seemed to have taken on sinister undertones. Suddenly he wanted to breathe the stale air of Manhattan. He needed New York, in all its noisy sulfurous, unsurpassed glory.

Above all, he had to get away from Stefania. He had become the current object of her erotic obsession, and for him any kind of long-term relationship with her was just not on. He felt not the remotest pangs of love or even affection for her. She was a self-obsessed actress, outrageously oversexed but, unfortunately for him, with the seductive allure to back it up. Now, filled with the memory of Venetia's sweet face and her honey-scented skin, he was resolute. He was not going to succumb to Stefania's charms.

It was midnight. Everyone had retired shortly after dinner, wanting an early night before leaving the following morning.

"Oh *caro mio*, let's not do this to each other," she murmured. "It's our last night here but when I finish my new movie I'll come to New York and I promise you, *amore*, we'll begin again." She wafted closer to him, rubbing herself against his body. "*Amore mio*," she whispered. "*Mi grande amore.*"

Sure, thought Steve wryly, until the next one, who she'll probably find on her new movie. Well, his little fling with Signora Scalerina was over. He moved away from her questing lips and maneuvered her to the door. "I've *got* to finish this story on you by tonight's deadline," he said firmly. "So *ciao*, Stefania. I'm really sorry, but I must get to work." Giving her a peck on the cheek, he almost pushed her out of his bedroom door and breathed a huge sigh of relief.

CHAPTER FIFTY-THREE

"Power. You've either got it or you ain't," muttered Kevin Bentley through gritted teeth. He'd just been stood up for a power breakfast meeting at the Four Seasons by the twenty-eight-year-old tracksuited head of production, who, having green-lighted his new movie last month, yesterday canceled it and was now causing him this humiliation.

The maître d' had informed Kevin with a phony smile that Mr. Greene had been forced to cancel. So now he was stuck at the entrance of the Polo Lounge feeling exposed and paranoid, while the roomful of agents, producers and studio brass witnessed his ignominy.

Kevin managed a rictus grin and a cheery "That's OK, Pasquale. Don't worry about it. I'll just eat at the table by myself."

"I'm sorry, sir, but Mr. Greene canceled the table, and we're completely full." Pasquale had the decency to sound embarrassed at least.

Craig Greene had *canceled* the table! Kevin Bentley had been a mega-star when that little prick had been slurping pureed spinach. How dare he treat him with such contempt!

Padded shoulders back, black shades balanced on the tip of his nose, Kevin left the Polo Lounge with as much *savoir faire* as he could muster. He sauntered through the newly decorated lobby, past polyester-clad tourists who whispered, "Isn't that . . .?" "No, it can't be, he looks too young—Kevin Bentley must be pushing sixty."

He tried not to wince as he signed a scrap of paper that a gray-haired mama in a muumuu had proffered.

"I've loved you since I was a little girl," gushed the woman, gripping his lapels so that escape was impossible. Hell, she looked old enough to be his fucking mother, for Christ's sake, but she was probably his age—shit.

"Could you write 'To Evangeline with all my love.'" Kevin scribbled while a couple of backcombed hot-panted hookers strolled by, leering. "Hi Kevin, how're ya doin'?"

Then he escaped into the sanctuary of his ice-cool Mercedes and felt the sweat trickle down the inside of his seven-hundred-dollar shirt.

So this was it. Hollywood hell. A star is shorn—of his glory. He'd tried hard not to face it, but he'd known it was coming. Knew when the invitations to the important parties dried up, knew when girls he'd tried to hit on giggled or pushed him away dis-interestedly—one had even sneered, "Get lost, Grandpa."

He hadn't even been able to get a slot on *Oprah* for his last two movies' publicity tours. And she was a *friend*, for Christ's sake—he had tons of friends, hadn't he? No, you haven't, asshole, said his vicious inner voice.

You've never had a lot of fucking friends. You've had a lot of friendly fucks and a lot of business colleagues, but you've been short on the old friendship, and now it's crunch time. His last three movies had been gigantic flops. In one of them he had tried to regain his lost youth by using flattering, soft-focused lighting and working with a nineteen-year-old leading lady. But almost overnight, the fabled Lothario had become a joke, the butt of Jay Leno's sarcastic wit on the *Tonight Show*.

Kevin sped angrily down Sunset Boulevard. Where the fuck could he go now at eight fucking thirty in the morning? The horribly empty day stretched ahead of him with hours and hours to fill. But with what? Tennis? He hated tennis. Golf? That was a game for old men like Bob Hope and Dean Martin. Work out at the gym? He couldn't stand the competition any more, all those actors with their young, optimistic faces, their oily, rippling muscles and their heads thick with healthy, untinted hair. Just you wait, you morons, he'd thought when he'd last seen all those self-satisfied studs flexing, pumping, hoping for their big break, it will happen to you too.

He'd been the smartest, the hottest, the cleverest of all of his generation of film actors. De Niro, Pacino, Redford, he'd been up there with all of them, but they were all still up there, while for him the gig was up.

Suddenly Kevin heard a cop siren behind him, saw flashing lights, and pulled over to the corner of Foothill to wait.

"Do you know how fast you were going, sir?" The cop looked no more than twenty.

"Sorry, officer." Kevin removed his shades and flashed the famous dynamite smile, as he produced his license. The cop glanced at him and it, then without recognition, began writing out a ticket.

Shit. At least this was one way to pass the morning. He leaned back, flicked a Camel from the pack and lit up. "Would you mind not smoking, sir?" The cop didn't even look up. Would he fucking mind? It was his fucking car, for Christ's sake. The world was going crazy. The other cop came over to take a look.

"Jeez, didn't you used to be Kevin Costner?" he said.

"Bentley." Rage rose like bile in his throat. "Kevin *Bentley*."

"Yeah, of course. Kevin Bentley. My mother loved ya. Hey Frank, it's Kevin Bentley."

"Uh." Frank, unimpressed, continued writing the ticket and handed it to Kevin with a curt, "Cool it on the road, sir. You know we've got a speed limit here in Beverly Hills."

"Oh really?" Kevin couldn't stop the Jack Lemmon impersonation. "I *never* knew that, officer. My. My. My. I've lived here, man and boy, for most of my life and I *never* knew we had a speed limit." But the young cop had turned away to his partner.

"'Bye, Mr. Bacon. See you on the late late show."

"And fuck you too," muttered Kevin. Fuck you, the industry and all the rest of the putzes in this stinking company town. May the lot of you rot in hell.

That night, Beth, who was one of his main squeezes, came over. She was a looker, an aspiring but talentless actress whom he'd spotted in a soft-porn flick and insisted his agent get her number. After sex, which Beth had endured with her usual theatrical moans, he went to the bathroom and inspected his face. He looked his age. No, he looked seventy. He looked older than George Burns, and soon it would be time for a toupee like his. Oh God, could he ever manage to play character parts? Should he try? His accountant had told him that things weren't good at all. His high-flying lifestyle needed a high-flying salary, and that hadn't been forthcoming for a long time. Thirty-five years in the business and almost broke. It wasn't fair. Maybe he should consider doing that piece-of-shit Italian movie that was the only thing on the horizon. Savagely, Kevin threw open his bathroom cabinet and took out the magic pots. He stared at his newly lifted eyes which, unfortunately, had given him a startled-rabbit look, then rubbed sixty-dollar cream into his wrinkles, extract of placenta on his neck and, kabuki white, returned to bed.

"Don't touch me, babe," he said as Beth's eager young arms tried to enfold him. "You mustn't crease my creams."

CHAPTER FIFTY-FOUR

Steve had never before been so happy to see the scurrying pedestrians in the streets of Queens as they drove in from the airport. He breathed in the stale air as he and Phil settled down into the back of the limo.

"No place like New York." He grinned.

"Too right, mate. Now it's back to the grind for you."

Steve was strangely silent, staring out of the rain-soaked window with a distant look.

"Are you in love with Stefania?" asked Phil.

"Don't be bloody stupid, you think I've got rocks in my head?"

"I heard that you had a big rock in your pants for her when you were on that island. A right lady-killer, weren't you? Casanova of the Antipodes."

"Stefania is attractive, I must admit, and quite sweet and caring underneath all that actressey bullshit, but she's *not* for me. No way."

Steve glared at Phil and pulled a mock rueful face.

"OK, OK, OK, I was just pulling your leg. Of *course* you're not in love. How could you be? You don't know how. You've never been sweet on a girl in your life." Steve was still staring at the steamy streets. How way off the mark Phil was. He was in love, all right, and he knew it. For only the second time in his life, Steve Kelly had fallen head over heels, and this time for the daughter of the first love of his life.

Atlanta's mind seethed with questions as she entered the mammoth glass building on Fifth Avenue. The head offices of Nicholas Stephanopolis's companies were situated inside the tower. She felt a fog of gloom descend as she walked into the main reception area to be greeted by an elderly receptionist.

The sour-faced woman pressed a buzzer and a door opened into the directors' offices. This atmosphere was completely different from the camaraderie, creative energy— even the wisecracking bitchiness—of the publishing scene. The *Mercury* offices crackled with life, dynamic activity and laughter. Her employees seemed invigorated, functioning with vitality, doing hard work, but enjoying every second of it. Mailroom lackies, star writers, photographers and stylists alike all loved what they were doing, and it showed in their joyful attitude.

By contrast, the heavily curtained offices of the Transglobal Shipping Company were dry as dust, dark and dank, and the employees seemed dull, stuffy and humorless. Who did this decoration—Charles Dickens? thought Atlanta. Why had her father given her this prize, which on closer examination didn't seem such a wonderful prize after all? Was it because his favorite daughter had been a drug addict, or had he finally forgiven Atlanta for all the grievances he had held against her for most of her life?

Nicholas's New York second-in-command, Franklyn Forsyth, yellowing teeth too big for his thin pinched mouth, scraps of hair plastered to a bony skull, Uriah Heeped her to her father's inner sanctum.

"If you don't mind, I'd like to be alone here, Mr. Forsyth," she said pleasantly. He backed off, bowing obsequiously. Without knocking, a secretary poked a pompadoured gray head around the door. "Would you like a cup of coffee, Miss Stephanopolis?" she asked.

"No thank you, Miss Briggs," said Atlanta. "And by the way, it's Atlanta, or Mrs. Kellog."

Miss Briggs withdrew disapprovingly and Atlanta sighed, sitting down at Nicholas's ugly, gargantuan English eighteenth-century partners' desk, which featured carved gargoyles for feet. Her father had always had good taste; who on earth had persuaded him to purchase this monstrosity?

The desk was bare except for a computer, a telephone and three thick red folders marked "For the urgent attention of Ms. Stephanopolis. Atlanta shrugged. So they were determined to keep her to her maiden name, were they? Well, they'd better think again.

The walls were lined with leather-bound tomes on shipping, technology, business and commerce. An oil portrait of Nicholas's father, Constantine, glared down, beetle browed, from over the mantelpiece. Photographs of Nicholas with his children and family, and various luminaries from the Niarchos, Onassis and Goulandris clans were all prominently displayed in Tiffany frames.

Atlanta opened the curtains and watched the heavy gray clouds skim along an even grayer sky and a few dirty raindrops spatter the windows.

"What a dump," she muttered in her Bette Davis voice and opened the first folder, which was labeled Monthly Market Fiscal Analysis Reports/Global Re-insurance Reviews.

In spite of her crash course with Nicholas's closest advisers, the columns of figures and financial statements still seemed like double Dutch. She flicked open the second, then the third, then, sighing heavily, chucked all three across the desk.

What was she supposed to do? Was she supposed to buy and sell tankers? Do a bit of corporate-raid acrobatics? Turn a company around into profit by sundown? She lit a cigarette and stared grimly into nothingness.

"Now I've finally got it, I don't want it," she whispered to herself. "It's dull and soul destroying. What the hell am I supposed to do with it?"

Atlanta smiled to herself. *Mercury*. She belonged there. Loved the hard-won respect and admiration which she had begun to see on the faces of her publishing peers. Loved the constant buzz of excitement.

Now that she could afford them, important authors and journalists would pass her lunch table at the Four Seasons to say hello. *Mercury* was on a roll, a red-hot roll; did she really want to give that up to simply be a tycoon? Could she ever be interested in shipping, stocks, bonds and the intricacies of international sky-high finance? In becoming a clone of her father?

Since the reading of her father's will, she had tried to learn—about the oil business, commerce, how to transact deals, how to organize the million and one things necessary to run her father's complicated operations.

One thing she knew—it could never be a labor of love—for her that was *Mercury*.

CHAPTER FIFTY-FIVE

There was no one left on the island except Venetia, Lady Anne and the servants and workers, who had all been well provided for in Nicholas's will. There were still the vineyards, the olive groves and orchards full of fruit to be tended and harvested, the flower beds, vegetable gardens, roads and beaches, all of which made Stephanopolis Island a tiny kingdom to itself and which needed constant maintenance.

The two women lunched together every day on the dazzling marble terrace, looking out at the incomparable view of the sea on which the *Circe* still lay at anchor. Her crew, immaculate in crisp white uniforms, went about their business as usual, although they knew that the yacht was already on the market and that there had been keen interest in it from various billionaires.

"But, Grandmama, you can't stay here all alone," protested Venetia. Her grandmother, still an imposing and autocratic figure, was seated upright in her chair. Although the temperature was well into the eighties, the old lady was dressed in full mourning: a long black bombazine dress, almost Edwardian in cut, with lace at the collar and cuffs, a discreet string of pearls around her neck. On her arthritic hands she wore fingerless black net mittens and her white hair was piled elegantly on top of her head. Considering that she would be ninety next year, she still possessed unusually luxuriant tresses, Venetia thought ruefully, twisting a strand of her own delicately fine hair through her fingers.

"Of course I can, my dear," said Anne briskly. "Don't be ridiculous. This is my home; I've lived here for almost sixty-five years. You can't expect me to leave now. Where would I go? Don't forget that all the servants here are my friends, and most of my own friends are dead. Even if they're not, I must confess that whenever I see any of them I find them all elderly and extremely irritating."

Her pale blue eyes, only a little less bright than when she was a girl, twinkled across the table at her granddaughter. "Ah, Venetia, you're so young. It's hard for you even to imagine the changes that age can bring to one."

"But, Grandmama, you've hardly changed at all—ever since I can remember," said Venetia. She sipped at the delicate rosé wine from the island's vineyard, admiring the old lady's stiff yet elegant posture and exquisite manners. Venetia realized for the first time that she had deliberately eschewed the Old World behavior and superficial manners and attitudes that her grandmother and a barrage of governesses had tried to instill in her. She had been far too busy being a rebel to want to emulate any of those antiquated ways.

But now, looking over at her tranquil grandmother as she daintily cut her *poulet à l'estragon* and baby *haricots verts* and blotted her lips with an embroidered linen napkin, Venetia couldn't help but admire the breeding and true refinement of the old lady.

"Of course, I'm almost the last of a dying

breed," Anne said matter-of-factly. "When the women of my generation and class die, there will be very few others left to take our places. Manners, breeding, values, consideration and compassion for others, no matter what creed, class or color, will all turn to dust.

"With few exceptions, the generations of the future will have very poor role models from whom to learn their manners and their behavior. Just ugly, vulgar people on the television. Those awful films you watch. Everyone killing each other and crashing cars. That's the kind of entertainment that your generation appears to like. And the way you all dress." She indicated Venetia's clothes.

"But, Grandmama, I'm a modern girl—and this is how we dress in the nineties."

"Well, I think that your clothes verge on the anarchic, my dear."

"Grandmama, I'm far from being an anarchist. It's just a T-shirt. All the kids wear them now."

"Exactly my point, my dear," said Anne dryly. "All 'the kids.' First of all, Venetia my dear, I think it's high time for you to realize that you are no longer a 'kid.' You will be twenty-two next birthday."

"What are you getting at, Grandmama?"

"I am merely trying to offer the advice of a wise old lady who has lived a long time. You must get on with your life and find a direction as soon as possible." Anne laid a mittened hand on Venetia's tanned arm. "I know all about the sterling job you did on stopping smoking those cannabis cigarettes—so did your father."

"It was much more than just that, Grand-mama. Cannabis is for kids—beginners, novices on the drug scene. I kicked the hard stuff, Grandmama—coke and crack—and believe me, it was no picnic. If I'd gone on taking crack it would've killed me."

"Yes, I imagine it must have been difficult for you, but now I think it's high time you returned to New York and got on with whatever it is that you want to do with your life."

"But I don't *know* what I want to do. The only thing I'm any good at is painting and art. I haven't been trained for anything, Grandmama."

"You were at school for years."

"Oh sure. Most of that time I was completely strung out in a drug-induced stupor."

The old lady refused to allow herself to register shock, calling to the silent servant who stood a little way from the table in the shadow of an olive tree.

"Some pudding wine please." She took another bite and then continued. "What is happening between you and Alain?"

"We're divorcing." Venetia gazed up at the cloudless blue sky. "There's no bad feeling or acrimony. It's best for both of us. We'll still be friends, like always."

She didn't tell her grandmother that Alain's doctors had told her that he was not responding to the new wonder drug AZT. Why burden her with any more sadness? Thank God her own HIV test had proved negative.

"I was always fond of Alain." Anne took a sip of syrupy Sauterne. "Such a nice young man, from a good family, in spite of his occasionally wild ways."

Occasionally! thought Venetia. Gran, if you only knew how wild his ways were you'd probably have a seizure.

"Well, you won't find any suitable young men here," said Anne briskly. "And whatever you modern girls may think today, work, marriage and motherhood should still remain a woman's priorities."

"I know, Grandmama, I know that's what

you think. Look, I just need to stay here a few more weeks, get my head together, then I promise you I'll go to New York and try to figure out what to do with the rest of my life."

"Perhaps you could become a model," said Anne brightly. "Like the lovely girls on the covers of those fashion magazines. You're certainly pretty enough."

Venetia let out a peal of laughter. "Darling Grandmama, I'm *far* too old for that. Most of those girls start modeling at fifteen and they're at the end of their careers when they're my age. No, don't worry, Grandmama, I'll think of something to do. I know I will."

After lunch, Lady Anne went for her siesta, and instead of spending the afternoon by the pool, Venetia decided to wander around the villa.

Nothing had changed or been moved since Nicholas's death. His book-lined study was exactly as he had left it, with the exception of his empty desk. Somebody had even put fresh flowers in crystal vases on the Chippendale tables, and from the mullioned windows, Venetia could see the profusion of Technicolor blossoms of the hundreds of flowers and shrubs that led down to the sparkling sea.

She walked through the enormous ground-floor reception rooms, her footsteps echoing noisily on the marble and parquet floors. Although the temperature was well into the nineties, it always remained cool inside the thick walls of the house.

At the top of the curved staircase was the door to Nicholas's suite. She hesitated a moment, and then turned the door handle and went in. She could still smell the lingering aroma of his aftershave, and tears pricked the back of her eyelids as she closed the door and turned on the lights.

Nicholas's huge four-poster bed was hung with heavy caramel-beige draperies shot with gold and the matching curtains were tightly closed against the strong afternoon sun. She examined the mahogany and ormolu empire dressing table and the objects displayed on its marble surface, which included several Fabergé eggs, silver and tortoiseshell frames containing candid photographs of his women—predictably herself and her sister, his mother, his mistress and his dead wife—and a twenties Cartier carriage clock, whose golden pendulum still moved with metronomic precision.

She walked through into his paneled bathroom with its black marble sunken bath and brass fittings. On the marble-topped sink, his silver cutthroat razor lay next to his shaving soap and three ivory-handled hairbrushes, as if all waiting to be used by their owner. She picked up one of the monogrammed brushes and lifting it to her nose, inhaled her father's familiar fragrance.

Memories came flooding back. Memories of an afternoon long ago. This same smell had filled her nostrils and she had inhaled it deeply while her father had . . . what? She had been aware of this memory once or twice before, and each time that she had felt something approaching panic, a kind of automatic shut-off took place in her mind. This time it flooded through her.

She had been playing hide and seek with her nanny in the rose garden and had managed to hide herself very well behind a rose-bush. She had heard the voices of her mother and father coming toward her. They were raised in anger. As they came closer, she scrunched farther down. Then she

heard her father call her mother a terrible
name and heard the sound of a slap. Laura
started to cry and Venetia joined in the wailing with all the power of her four-year-old
lungs until her father lunged behind the bush
and shook her like he would a dog. Her
mother was lying on the ground sobbing and
her father screamed at Venetia something
she couldn't remember—something horrible. It had frightened her so much she had
banished the memory—until now.

She shuddered and dropped the brush
with a clatter, staring at her frightened face
in the mirror. But what was there to be frightened of? She'd been Papa's little kitten,
hadn't she? His golden girl. She didn't want
to think about it anymore, so she closed
Nicholas's door and opened the connecting
door to Laura's suite. She'd half expected it
to be locked, but it wasn't. It had been left
completely untouched (except for cleaning)
since she had died and would probably remain so until Grandmama died and she and
Atlanta took over the villa. All creamy gold,
with a painted cerulean ceiling and tiny white
clouds scudding across it, the walls were intricately draped with delicate ice-blue silk on
which hung a dozen or more pictures by De-

gas, Renoir and Rossetti. There was a beautiful Waterhouse oil of a girl in a pink dress with long blonde hair that didn't look unlike Laura.

The slim white and gold columns of her four-poster bed supported laughing gilded cupids who held aloft the silk canopy. The creamy carpet continued into the dressing room. Venetia had always thought of Laura's dressing room as one of the Seven Wonders of the World. It was a gigantic L-shaped room and the long corridor of wardrobes that led from it was covered in mirror-fronted sliding doors, as was the main section of the bathroom.

She sat down on the needlepoint Louis XVI stool, opened one of her mother's cosmetic drawers and stared at hundreds of lipsticks, all regimentally organized by color, from almost colorless wands to pale pinks and graduating to deep reds. Venetia applied a smudge of carmine to her pale lips and studied the result; she removed the stopper from a Lalique scent bottle and inhaled the nostalgic smell of her mother; she took a swansdown puff out of a box of Coty face powder and applied it to her faintly tanned skin. Then she opened another drawer, where dozens of eye pencils and crayons of every color lay in neat rows.

She drew black "doe eyes" around her eyes, exactly as her mother had done in her movies, penciled and thickened her brows, and brushed her cheekbones with pink rouge. She swirled her blonde hair up onto the top of her head and secured it with a diamond-studded comb. Then she compared her reflection with the framed photo on the dressing table of Nicholas and Laura. Yes, it was true. Her resemblance to Laura Marlowe was extraordinary.

What was it that Steve Kelly had said to her? "Uncanny. You look uncannily like your mother." Steve Kelly. She half closed her eyes and looked at the thousand reflections of Laura Marlowe.

"It's true, I really do," she whispered. Relishing the game she was playing, Venetia ran a bath, pouring a generous amount of foaming bubbles into the water, and then examined the contents of her mother's closets.

Every great couturier and designer was represented there: Balmain, Valentino, Dior, Saint Laurent, Balenciaga. The contents of Laura's closets would have filled a dozen boutiques, even clothes museums. There must have been a thousand dresses there, ranging from black cocktail frocks to the most extravagant and lavishly beaded and embroidered ball gowns. Underneath each gown was a carefully labeled box containing the correct shoes and bag for the ensemble and again every major shoemaker was represented.

She threw her clothes onto the floor, stepping into the scented water. Her mother's old-fashioned portable cassette player, which she had always taken everywhere with her, was next to the bath. Venetia switched on PLAY and closed her eyes, drifting luxuriously in the scented foam to the sounds of Laura's favorite song, "Aquarius." Venetia smiled, remembering her grandmother telling her how cross Nicholas became that in spite of the most modern and up-to-date sound equipment he'd had installed in the house, Laura still preferred to listen to tapes on her battered old Sony.

Then the music stopped abruptly, and she heard footsteps on the tape, as though someone had entered a room.

"So, you're finally back." She immediately recognized the voice as her father's. "You've certainly been gone long enough."

"I know, I'm sorry, Nicholas," responded the cool dulcet tones Venetia knew were her mother's. "Ginny and I were having such fun. Oh Nicholas, we had a wonderful time. I wish you could have seen all the animals we saw . . . elephants and rhino and . . ."

"Oh, I'm sure it was fascinating." Was there a faint sneer in his voice? "And I suppose you were up every morning with the larks, bagging lions and tigers right, left and center? Did you become a crack shot, my dear?"

There was a pause and Venetia heard the sound of moving water, then her mother's voice again.

"There's no need to be sarcastic, Nicholas. Please, can we discuss all of this after dinner, on the boat?"

"I thought we were supposed to *meet* on the boat?" He sounded full of anger. "That's what I instructed you to do."

"I know, I'm sorry." Serene and angelic, her voice had the placatory note of one who has to placate often.

Venetia felt freezing cold, even though the water was warm.

"I went to the boat as soon as I got here and I saw Atlanta. She seems so much better. She recognized me and we had a little talk. Then, since you weren't on board yet, I thought I'd come back here for a bath before dinner. You know, the one thing you miss on safari is a long, hot bath."

"Well, bloody well hurry it up," he snapped. "You could've had a bloody bath on the boat. It's almost eight now. Dinner's at half past and I'm starving."

"Yes, Nicholas," Laura said. "I shan't be long."

Footsteps—a door slammed and then the feminine voice whispered, "Fuck you, Nicholas Stephanopolis," there was a click and the music of "Aquarius" came back on again.

Venetia was stunned. She stared at the machine as though it was an alchemist's box.

When Nicholas had come in, Laura had obviously pushed the INSTANT RECORD button instead of the PAUSE, a mistake easily made.

Venetia played it back again and then mulled over the conversation she'd just heard. It must have been recorded on her mother's last evening alive. Where Venetia now lay was where Laura had taken her last bath.

Icy cold, Venetia jumped out of the bath

and hurriedly dried herself on soft towels with her mother's initials embroidered on them.

She strode over to one of the wardrobes, and picking out a pink chiffon empire-style dress, slipped it on. It was a perfect fit, as were the matching satin slippers. She must also be the same size as her mother. But something was missing. What was it?

She threw open drawers searching for some jewelry to wear. There were drawers full of hair ornaments, lingerie and hosiery, some still in packets, and one drawer crammed with the kind of junk accumulated after trips. Stubs of airline tickets, packets of matches and brochures from faraway places, old photographs, receipts, sun-glasses, postcards of Africa and a packet of Kodak negatives. Venetia picked these up idly, holding the negative strips up to the light. The pictures appeared to be of Laura and several others somewhere on location with assorted foliage and animals in the background. One of the women looked like Ginny. Venetia squinted but it was hard to see from the negative precisely what the positive image was. Obviously these were taken on Mama's trip to Africa. Maybe she'd get them printed one day. She threw the negatives back into the cluttered drawer and opened the next one. Success! It was crammed with exquisite costume jewelry of every description. Earrings, necklaces and bracelets of gold, silver, pearl, rhinestones, spilled over their compartments in profusion. Ruby, diamond, topaz, amethyst and emerald fake pieces, some of which looked startlingly authentic, filled at least three more compartments.

Venetia picked up a bottle of Fracas, her mother's favorite scent, and sprayed herself vigorously. Disappointingly, the perfume's scent had almost completely evaporated and there was only the faintest hint of fragrance left. Never mind, she had become the daughter of the goddess, with every bit of allure. She didn't need the perfume.

This magical transformation of hers should be shown. Should she wake Grandmama? No, she might die of shock seeing her daughter-in-law suddenly walking around again.

Should she pay a visit to Ginny in LA or to Coral in the South of France? "Hello girls, guess who?"

No. Venetia shrugged. She would save

this magical metamorphosis as a surprise for someone special, she knew not who.

Actually, seeing herself transformed into the legendary Laura Marlowe in her prime seemed to instill in Venetia the ambition and confidence that she needed to pull herself out of her lethargy.

"It's time to get your act together, girl," she whispered to her reflection. "Pick yourself up and get off to New York. I'm sure I'll find *something* to interest me there, I know I will."

Venetia kissed her grandmother good-bye. The black-gowned figure stood watching her at the door, waving her black-edged hand-kerchief until the helicopter had risen high into the sky.

"Please come to New York soon, Grand-mama," Venetia begged her grandmother as they had hugged good-bye to each other in the paneled entrance hall.

"My dear, I'm much too old to travel."

"But why not come for your birthday? Come next February and we'll all have a ball together. Just us three girls—and we'll invite a wonderful escort for you. Please, Grand-mama, please come."

"My dear Venetia," said Anne softly. "I shall

not be making any more social appointments after January."

"What does that mean?" Venetia had asked but Anne had shaken her white head, stroking her granddaughter's cheek.

"We'll meet again soon. But I want you to do well in New York, my dear. Do your best, try hard and believe in yourself, for in the end that is all any of us can do."

CHAPTER FIFTY-SIX

Kristobel was finally going to show his first haute couture collection to the world press. Autumn fashion week in New York turned the city into more of a madhouse than ever. There would be intense competition among the American couturiers to outdo each other for the most column inches in trade and daily publications and particularly in the glossy magazines. Most designers' egos were bigger than their bank balances and they vied with each other as to who would get the most celebrities and influential magnates of the fashion pack to attend. John Fairchild of *Women's Wear Daily* was top of the most-wanted list. With its ultimate power, his daily could make or break a collection or a designer, which it often had in the past.

Seventh Avenue was a seething cauldron of activity. Racks of designer clothes were wheeled at speed into trucks and kamikaze delivery boys wove in and out of traffic, disregarding their own or others' lives and limbs. Hordes of eager buyers crammed the lifts, each wanting to be the first to paw through each designer's collection.

Invitations to the shows were strictly limited and highly prized. The New York Fashion Council was strict about the hour that each designer was allowed to show and, although there were hundreds of designers, only a select few interested the press, and less than a dozen would be showing haute couture.

The final collection was Kristobel's, and anticipation was running at fever pitch, for the fashion pundits all believed his was going to be the highlight of the seven insane days.

The world-famous models, their fabled ten-thousand-dollar-a-smile faces more gorgeous than ever, their bodies impeccably emaciated, descended on New York from Paris, London and Milan.

"Claudia, Christie, Linda, Carla, Helena, Naomi and Karen are more famous and admired than most movie actresses today," Atlanta announced at *Mercury*'s weekly editorial meeting. "I think we should do a group picture of all of them together for our Christmas issue."

"And where do we get the money to pay? They cost a bleedin' *fortune* for print. Even we couldn't afford those little Sheilas," said Phil.

"They did it for *Vogue*, why shouldn't they do it for us?" asked Atlanta.

"Because *Vogue* is in a class of its own and being on a cover has always been the ultimate accolade," said Phil. "Those girls who get ten grand for a catwalk show will pose for *Vogue* for tuppence. It's for the power and the glory."

"We've got power and glory too," defended Atlanta.

"Not enough yet," said Phil. "But we're getting there, sweetheart, slowly but surely."

"I've the perfect headline," said Atlanta. "Is Fashion out of Fashion?"

"What the hell does that mean?" asked Phil.

"I believe that these supermodels are the

only reason some clothes sell at all. Let's face it, look at Miss or Mrs. Average in the street. What's she wearing? Jeans or tracksuit, trainers and T-shirt. Who buys fashion today in Middle America? Who gives a damn about it anywhere today really? It's passé.

"There are too many designers and not enough clients. Look at how early the big department stores start their sales now."

"'Is Fashion Dead?' might be a more grabbable headline," murmured Steve.

"Yes—we'll hire Claudia or Linda, body paint her in black and white to look like a skeleton and have her lying in a coffin with a shocking-pink satin lining."

"Pretty fuckin' hot," said Phil. "I like it."

"So, if fashion's dead, then what's alive?" asked Jenny, one of their top journalists. "Where will the pendulum swing to next?"

"Who knows?" sighed Phil. "If every magazine knew what the public wanted, we'd all get killed in the stampede. So, 'Is Fashion Dead?' will be our next cover story."

"Right." Atlanta glanced at her Cartier watch. "And we'd better get over to the armory for Kristobel's show or they'll give our seats away."

* * *

Kristobel was trying to give an interview in the center of the backstage bedlam of the communal hair, makeup and dressing room. Packs of paparazzi roamed the room hoping to get a topless shot of one of the gorgeous, languid models whose already flawless faces were being covered with the season's current colors.

Battalions of hairdressers wielded their paraphernalia like lethal weapons. Mounds of human hair extensions—plaits and pony-tails, painted in day-glo colors—lay on a trestle table. Another table held dozens of pairs of earrings, chains, necklaces and leather bracelets, some studded with colored stones, some with nail heads.

Ignoring the cacophony around him, Kristobel spoke earnestly to a reporter. "I'm tired of fashion for fashion's sake," he said. "There has been much too much fashion and people are getting sick of it."

"What do you mean exactly?" she asked.

"Consumerism is no longer politically correct in today's politically correct world. Therefore I shall show fashion—yes—but the *way* I show it will be completely different, revolutionary."

"And how will that be?"

"You must wait. I hope to surprise you." He smiled, fanning himself hard. He moved to a nearby table, picked up a swath of black tulle embroidered with tiny jet spiders and, like a conductor picking up his baton, started to drape it around a model's enormous conical hat.

He'd taken over the armory because media and client interest had been so immense that the original venue, the Plaza, hadn't been big enough to hold the huge crowd expected. The press and social stick-insects constantly expected more of him as he was the latest wonderchild of style, America's answer to Lacroix and Versace.

He had personally and carefully chosen the music to accompany his clothes and was having it performed live at astronomical cost, by the current number-one pop group, Vanilla Band. It started with a rap version of Chopin's funeral march, accompanied by anarchic lyrics.

The seats were crammed with the media, the beautiful people and the spiteful, who couldn't wait for Kristobel to fail. Since he aspired so arrogantly to the halcyon heights of the greats of American fashion, he'd better be good. And Kristobel knew there was much at stake this steamy afternoon.

"What are we waiting for?" whispered Bruce. "The place is packed to the rafters and we're already way behind schedule."

"We're still waiting for Vanilla Band."

"*Screw* Vanilla Band. We've got to start. The photographers are getting pissed off."

"Screw the photographers," snapped Kristobel. "They don't run our show."

"They fucking well think they do," said Bruce. "They gave Mackie the slow handclap yesterday, and he was only twenty minutes late."

"We won't start until Vanilla Band is here," insisted Kristobel.

"Shit, here comes the slow clap!" Bruce was panicking now. "Oh hell, Kristobel, we've gotta start now. *Now*."

"We *wait* for Vanilla Band." Kristobel's stubbornness was legendary.

"How do we know they'll even show?" snarled Bruce. "These fucking rap stars are a law unto themselves."

"They promised they'd come. They won't let me down."

"Oh, shit," said Bruce again as the clapping, started by the hundreds of photographers banked in bleachers, was taken up by the impatient audience. Although fashion shows always began twenty or thirty minutes late, it was now nearly forty-five minutes past the starting time.

"The natives are really getting pretty fucking restless," warned Bruce. "It's not a good omen, Kris."

The models knowingly raised artfully penciled eyebrows at each other. At ten thousand dollars a show, they didn't worry about a collection being late. This was the second gig of the day for the five most beautiful and popular of the girls. After this there would be one more show, and they would have earned a cool thirty thousand dollars for a single day's work.

Then a mega-wattage of flashbulbs exploded and the clapping stopped.

"They're here!" cried Bruce. "Vanilla Band have arrived—we can start. Oh thank you, God, you exist after all."

Security guards tried to shoo away the paparazzi, who descended on the twins like flies on a corpse as they took their places.

Vanilla Band was a current show-business phenomenon, and since they hadn't been seen at a fashion show before, this was a major photo opportunity. Implacably, they sat side by side, Jan and Jon Vanilla. It was hard to tell them apart, hard to tell which sex they were—no one could quite figure it out. Identically dressed in white silk trouser suits with several dozen diamond crosses hanging around their necks, they looked like mirror images of each other. Their milk-pale faces were the same shade as their outfits, their eyes were heavy with kohl and their thick, penciled brows almost met in the middle. Their painted carmine lips wore identical trancelike smiles, but it was their hair that truly gave Vanilla Band their out-of-this-world appearance. Peroxided white blond, it hung in dreadlocks onto their foreheads and around their powdered faces like yellow snakes.

Atlanta held her breath and clutched Phil's hand as the first model stepped down the black satin-draped steps and into the spotlight.

"Oh God," breathed Atlanta. "Please let it be good. Please give Kristobel the success he deserves today."

*   *   *

"Why? Why? Why the hell did he do it?" Atlanta raged in the car going back to the office. "How could he have been so *stupid*? Doesn't he realize that the press are going to bury him? I can't bear it—it's just too awful." Atlanta buried her head in her husband's shoulder and he poured her a slug of Scotch from the decanter.

She took it, looking from Phil to Steve to Jenny.

"Well?" she asked softly. "What did you guys think?"

"It was the worst thing I've ever seen," said Jenny. "Diabolical and ridiculous—no other word for it, I'm afraid."

"The whole thing was one of the biggest pieces of shit I've ever seen in my life," said Phil succinctly, never much a fan of fashion shows in the first place. "Right, Steve?"

"Right," answered Steve, who hadn't really been concentrating on the show. The blonde model Karen Mulder had reminded him so much of Venetia that every time she had sashayed down the runway in one more god-awful outfit, he'd felt his heart lurch.

"Those clothes were absolutely *horrendous*," said Jenny. "Kristobel must be out of

his mind. No question about it. He's committed sartorial and commercial suicide. The
press are going to kill him."

It had all started well enough. Karla had
strutted down the catwalk to great applause
and popping flashbulbs.

Then came Valentina, her hair covered in
a thigh-length "wig" made of what appeared
to be pieces of rope yarn dyed in lime and
cyclamen stripes.

To the pulsating beat of jungle drums
mixed with Vanilla Band's explosive fuck-you
lyrics, she showed off a costume that
wouldn't have looked out of place on a character in a pantomine act. Black rubber
sneakers with high wedge heels, diaphanous black chiffon trousers over thick
black wool stockings attached to an old-
fashioned elastic garter belt. Her beautifully
tailored black tweed jacket, curved to fit her
tiny waist, was covered by a three-quarter-
length cloak of murky olive tulle, on which
were embroidered in black beads enormous
spiders and bats. More huge jet-black spiders, this time on a "web" of silver chain
thread, hung from her ears and crawled up
one sleeve to her shoulder.

There was silence as both buyers and celebrities digested this dreadful outfit, glancing surreptitiously at each other to see if anyone looked as if they'd yet committed themselves to an opinion.

Karla was followed by Linda in a similar creation, but wearing hideously shaped seventies bell-bottomed tulle pants and a black plastic "sou'wester" hat atop her thigh-length silver lurex wig. As each beautiful model sashayed down the runway in costumes progressively more hideous, the audience started to titter. Then, when Claudia appeared in a black leather corset so low cut and tightly laced that her nipples were completely exposed, a few of the photographers laughed derisively.

Many of the elegant women in the audience tried desperately to find something to like as one ghastly creation followed another, but it was proving impossible. There was nothing remotely wearable.

Then a fanfare of rapping beats indicated that the *pièce de résistance* of the grand finale was about to appear.

"Here comes da bride, pregnant and wide," the singers rapped and "the bride" entered to gasps of disbelief and disgust.

"He's gone too far this time. The establishment will have his guts for garters," said Phil grimly.

"Oh Kristobel, what have you done?" breathed Atlanta.

The pregnant "bride" wore a "gown" of black leather and nail-heads. A corset pushed her bosom so far up that it almost touched her chin and a shiny black circle was stretched uninvitingly over a false stomach. She sat side-saddle on a silver Harley-Davidson. The bike was ridden by "the groom," a muscular coffee-colored Trinidadian giant, naked to the waist except for dozens of black leather strips crisscrossing his rippling and oiled muscles.

The happy couple wore garlands of black leather and orange blossoms on their heads and a green tulle veil framed the bride's face, her left eye obliterated by yet another beaded spider.

She carried a bouquet of black leather flowers and as the Harley-Davidson turned at the end of the runway, she threw it in the direction of Vanilla Band, who both caught it with other-worldly smiles, to the feverish snapping of the photographers.

Then to some grudgingly weak applause,

the models dragged a reluctant Kristobel to the catwalk and the photographers took a few shots and left, as Chopin's funeral march blared out yet again from the speakers.

When Atlanta returned to her office she found she had two voicemail messages. One was from Venetia, excited and breathless. "Hey Atlanta, it's Venetia. I'm finally here, in the Big Apple. Maybe we can have dinner tonight or soon?"

Atlanta was delighted to hear from her sister. They had been talking regularly on the telephone since the reading of the will and Atlanta was pleased that Venetia had in fact not seemed too upset by losing out on their father's empire. "I'd have been lousy at it anyway," she had told Atlanta. "I'm much too lazy to be any good at big business."

Atlanta hadn't really believed her but she was glad Venetia wasn't hostile. There was no time to analyze it further—she always seemed to be rushing, too busy to think properly. Before she called Venetia back to accept the dinner date, Atlanta listened to the second voicemail message. The guttural snarl made her go cold with fear. "Won't be long now, you whore. Thought you'd get away from me by changing your number, huh? No such luck. I'm out there, and I'm watching and I'm gonna get you, bitch, before you get me in your stinkin' rag."

Atlanta banged her finger down on the OFF button. What did he mean? How did this man know about the article she was writing? How could he?

Phil had liked her first draft on the homeless, but suggested it needed more material and sharper detail. "I want to feel we're there. I think you've got to go out into the field again, Atlanta. We need just that cutting edge more."

Atlanta thought about getting a different angle by delving into the lives of the homeless people who were once well off, even rich. People who'd made their way up life's slippery slope, then been struck down by its vicissitudes. Dorrie, the wretched woman who camped next to the meat market during the day and under the Triboro Bridge at night, had confided her sad life story to Atlanta and then told her about some Hollywood big shot who'd lost everything and become one of them. I must find out his name; his story would be just what we need, thought Atlanta.

*   *   *

Steve certainly didn't need to be asked twice to make up the foursome for dinner at Le Cirque. "It's a welcome-to-New-York meal for Venetia," said Atlanta. "I hope you can make it."

It had been several months since he'd seen Venetia, and apart from his work, during that time he had thought about practically nothing else.

They met for drinks at the Stephanopolis apartment. Steve thought she was, if anything, sweeter and more beautiful than ever.

Venetia hugged her sister and Phil but, to Steve's disappointment, she only shook his hand. However, the dazzling smile she gave him almost made up for it.

They drank martinis and gossiped and giggled together in the chic white drawing room. Venetia was such a vision, pearls at her throat and in her ears, her hair swept up with tiny tendrils blowing across her cheeks, that Steve could hardly take his eyes off her.

Atlanta commented on her sister's appearance as they walked to the car after drinks. "I can't *believe* how much like Mama you look tonight," she whispered, as they climbed into the car, huddling in their furs against the chill autumn wind.

"Do I?" Venetia seemed surprised. "You know I was only five when she died, I don't remember what Mama really looked like in the flesh—just in those films. Do you?"

Atlanta nodded. "Vaguely. But I was only ten, so I guess what I really remember is her scent and her soft skin." She leaned closer to Venetia in surprise. "That's it! That's Mama's perfume. What is it?"

Venetia laughed. "It's called Fracas, and I'm wearing the same face powder she used, Coty. It seems they haven't changed the formula since then." She pulled up her beige mink collar so that it framed her face and Atlanta gasped.

"Oh my God, you look *just* like that still of Mama's from that "caper" movie she made with Cary Grant. What was it called?"

"*Harlequin*," answered Steve, who'd been listening to their every word.

"Why Steve, I didn't realize you were such a movie buff," teased Atlanta.

"He's an expert on everything, aren't you?" said Phil. "Our Steve may be a diamond in the rough, but he's a ten-carat diamond nevertheless."

"Well, I wish I had half your money, mate," said Steve.

"And I wish I had half your hair," grinned Phil, whose *bête noir* was his thinning patch.

"Atlanta's got enough for both of you," replied Steve with a smile.

As the quartet descended from the car, Sirio Maccioni himself came to the door to escort them to the most favored table on the right of the main room. The girls sat against the banquette, surveying the action in what was considered to be the buzziest *boîte* in New York, while the haute-couture brigade at the other tables studied them curiously.

Venetia was discomfited by the women's stares. "Sis, this is a geriatric joint. Why couldn't we have gone to Planet Hollywood?"

"Venetia, don't you ever grow up? People like us don't go to Planet Hollywood. Joe Allen's, or maybe a diner, but when you're a New Yorker, you go with the pack. You eat at Mortimer's, Grenouille or here."

A skeletal social X-ray had not taken beady kohl-rimmed eyes off the sisters while keeping up a whispered running commentary in her escort's ear. Venetia suddenly crossed her eyes and waggled her ears at the woman, who turned away with a moue of disgust.

"You'll get used to it, darling," Atlanta

grinned. "New Yorkers love to gawk, even in the best restaurants. Don't forget they must ring at least five friends tomorrow to tell them that they were here, and so were you, and what you were wearing, and *doesn't* she look amazingly like her mother?"

Steve raised his glass in a toast. "To you, Venetia. May you take New York by storm and I believe you will."

"As long as you don't capsize." Phil winked.

They had *carpaccio* of snapper, then *filet de boeuf*. After coffee was served, Venetia said, "Let's go dancing."

"Sorry dear, the night is young, but I'm not," sighed Phil. "Time for bed, for us, I'm afraid."

"Early meeting tomorrow, darling," Atlanta smiled. "And we're an old married couple now."

Steve was determined to keep close to Venetia, so he chimed in: "I'd love to go dancing."

They all kissed their good-byes as Phil and Atlanta headed off, then Steve turned to Venetia. "Alone at last. Where to, princess?" He smiled.

"This is your town." She snuggled close to

him. "I'm just a country girl. I haven't been in New York in years. Take me to where it's all happening."

It was their anniversary. A week after they first went to bed together, they were still in it. It was as if they had been made for each other. Their lovemaking was tender, passionate and committed. "This feels so right," Venetia murmured, cuddling up to him like a kitten.

"It couldn't be more right," said Steve, stroking her hair.

Venetia smiled up at him, thinking that the twenty-one-year age difference suddenly didn't matter a damn anymore.

Steve had encouraged Venetia on their first date when she told him she wanted to be a painter. "I'd like to go to art school here. I've heard of a good one at NYU and Grandmama thinks I have some talent."

"Did you bring any of your paintings with you?" he had asked the next day.

"A few. Do you want to see them?"

Steve was impressed by her work: "Obviously years of living with priceless Impressionist pictures on every wall has made its mark. I think you've got talent, princess. You've got to go for it, these are great."

A week later, as they lay together, Venetia smiled and said, "You're so good to me."

Steve twined a golden curl around his finger. "And you're *too* good for me. Marry me. I know it's probably too soon, darling, too fast, but I love you so much and I want to be with you forever."

"I don't think I'm very good at marriage, darling."

"With me you will be. You're fabulous at everything you do or say. You're wonderful, Venetia. You make me so happy."

She looked intently into his eyes and said slowly, "It's still too soon, darling, let's not rush things. I'm so happy as we are."

"Did you know that for a guy to propose to a girl is almost as difficult as committing suicide?" said Steve playfully.

"Let's talk about it more when I get back from LA." She sat up and gasped. "Oh God, look at the time."

"LA?" He looked surprised. "Now?"

"I forgot to tell you, I have to go to Los Angeles today. I just heard last night. A friend of mine is very ill."

"I'm sorry to hear that, sweetheart. Who is it?" He lit his first cigarette of the day, admiring Venetia as she sat unself-consciously naked at the dressing table, brushing her hair the requisite hundred times, as Nanny had taught her.

"Oh, you wouldn't know her, she was a great friend of Mama's; she and Mama were under contract together years ago. Then when she married Papa, Ginny became her personal assistant. After Mama died, she moved back to LA and now she's very sick. Coral says it's not looking good, I'm afraid."

Suddenly Steve's cigarette tasted like ashes. Ginny. Venetia was going to visit Ginny Jones. Ginny was the only person in the world, other than Ed Hardy, who knew about his romance with Laura.

He had forgotten about Ginny. Fun-loving, flame-haired Ginny, with her raucous laughter, her loyalty to Laura, and her intimate knowledge of everything that Laura had ever done. He knew Laura had told Ginny about their love affair and, even though that had been sixteen years ago, Ginny would remember all too well. Supposing she had photographs and decided to show them to her god-daughter?

"What's the matter, darling? You look as if

you've been turned to stone." Venetia had finished brushing her hair and was staring at him curiously.

"It's nothing, sweetheart, nothing." He jumped out of bed with a youthful vitality he didn't feel. His heart and legs filled with lead and suddenly he felt every one of his forty-five years.

"D'you want me to come with you—keep you company?"

"No, darling, I'll be fine, I'm only going to go for a couple of days," she said. "Coral's staying with Ginny and she's sending her limo to LAX to pick me up."

"So what's the matter with this, er— Ginny?" He tried to make his voice sound casual.

"Cancer," she answered sadly. "Coral told me that she doesn't have much time left. She said that Ginny's got something important she wants to tell me though, about Mama. That's why I have to leave right away."

CHAPTER FIFTY-SEVEN

The day after his disastrous show, Kristobel's offices were inundated with phone calls and faxes.

"The good news," said Bruce brightly, "is that we're on the front page of every fashion paper and in all the dailies, from here to Milan."

"And the bad?" Kristobel was staring out of the window at the bleak street.

Bruce sighed. "The bad, I'm afraid, is worse than our worst nightmare."

"Don't beat about the bush," said Kristobel. "Tell me."

"We haven't taken one single order, private or commercial," Bruce said bleakly. "Not only that, but Saks, Neiman and Bergdorf have all called to cancel the stuff they'd already ordered from Ready to Wear."

"But they can't *do* that." Kristobel's eyes were riveted to the street, where he was watching a homeless man rummaging from dustbin to dustbin. "They can't."

"They can and they have. I'm afraid it's back to making fairy frocks for the Middle-Eastern set if this goes on. You've been turning them all down recently—maybe you shouldn't have."

Kristobel didn't answer but continued staring with concentrated hatred at the street beggar.

"Listen to me, Kristobel, we can't afford to turn anybody down anymore. Jesus, we can't even make our payroll this week. That show cost us a fucking fortune and for what? The worst reviews since Burt Reynolds in *Smokey and the Bandit.*"

Bruce went to the window to see what Kristobel was staring at, but only saw just another deadbeat eating lunch from a garbage can. Not interesting enough to waste a glance on. But Kristobel seemed mesmerized by the pathetic creature as he hissed, "I *won't* do wedding dresses for rich bitches or Las Vegas bimbos anymore. I'd rather file chapter eleven. I'd rather die."

"Hey! I don't think death's an option, but if we don't get our asses in gear and pay off some of our creditors, it will certainly be chapter fucking eleven for all of us, my dear, in spades."

"Going for the gold!" Phil burst excitedly into Atlanta's dressing room. "Steve's story on your father is a winner. Our sales are fantastic, we've got a hundred ninety-seven pages of ads and a thirty-seven percent market share. We're flying faster than a speeding bullet, sweetie."

Atlanta turned and gave her husband a gap-toothed, brown-gummed smile.

"Jeez, you look like shit, sweetheart," Phil recoiled.

"Like the teeth?" Atlanta opened her mouth wider, revealing a mouthful of brown-snaggled fangs.

"Sweetie, you haven't been flossing properly!"

Atlanta giggled, as Goldie rubbed more grease into her straggly wig.

"Would you give me a quarter, if I asked you?"

"I'd give you more than a quarter to get out of my sight. It's an amazing disguise, babe— unreal—I'd never know it was you in a million years."

"Isn't it brilliant? Jenny helped me with the clothes, and Goldie did the makeup and this gorgeous hair."

Jenny and Goldie turned to bask in Phil's nodding approval. Goldie, the current pros-thetics queen of the New York movie scene, had transformed many actors and collected several Oscar nominations along the way. It had taken her over three hours to transform the twenty-six-year-old beauty into a sixtyish hag but it was an astonishing metamorpho-sis, and one of which she was justly proud.

The hooked rubber nose and double chins, cast from a mold of Atlanta's face, were a masterpiece. Phil peered closer to see if he could see where the edge of the rubber met Atlanta's own skin, but it was practically undetectable. Her skin was stained a weather-beaten red, which Goldie guaranteed was indelible for at least forty-eight hours, and straggly thick gray eye-brows hooded her eyes.

Phil wrinkled his nose. "Jeez, babe, even your stink's authentic, eau de New York sewer."

"Well, you've got to get everything right," replied Atlanta, as she examined her weather-beaten, wrinkled complexion closely, grimacing horribly at herself. "Otherwise they'll smell a rat. They're not stupid, you know."

"Just you be careful, babe, and don't take any chances out there."

"Mirror, mirror on the wall, who's the fairest of them all?" Atlanta murmured at her reflection.

"Certainly not you, babe." Phil patted her huge padded rump. "Now get out there, girl. Bring us back loads of material for our story." He looked at his watch. "I've gotta hit the trail myself, otherwise I'll miss the plane."

"How long will you be in Sydney?" Atlanta asked, as she fussed with a stained collection of plastic bags containing all her worldly goods.

"Only four days, my darling. I can't stay away from you longer than that, even though you do stink. Two days of travel, two days to sort out the problem, then I'll be back in your loving arms—and I hope you'll have had a bath by then."

"Does she really have to stay out with them all night?" Jenny sounded anxious. "It could be dangerous, Phil. Particularly with all those weird phone calls she's been getting lately."

"Don't worry, I'll be fine," assured Atlanta.

"She did it last time for two days and nobody tumbled," said Phil. "If you ever get tired of writing, my love, you could give Meryl Streep a run for her money in the acting stakes."

Atlanta gave him a hug, her filthy duffel coat flapping around her.

"That coat looks like it's about to die of a terminal disease," Phil teased. "How can you stand the stench?"

"All in the name of art, me dear," Atlanta cackled and let a sliver of saliva drip from her drooling lips. "Now, give us a kiss, me lovie." She presented her raddled face to his. "Or I'll breathe all over yer."

"Jesus, babe." He recoiled. "I'm outta here and, if you ever want a divorce, you know how to get it."

* * *

As the plane taxied down the runway, Venetia went over again every detail of Ginny's telephone conversation with her.

"I want to tell you about your mother." Ginny's voice had been weak, not at all as Venetia had remembered it. "There are so many things about her that I think you should know, darling. Her gentleness, her kindness, her sensitivity but, above all, her loyalty toward all of her friends. I need to tell you all this and more before I die, because sadly you never really knew her."

"Ginny, you're not going to die. You *can't*," said Venetia.

"Don't worry, my dear. With this illness, death's a friend. I've had a great run and it's time to drop the curtain. I want to tell you about a man who was in your mother's life toward the end of hers. He's the only man, I believe, who truly loved her unconditionally and in spite of being married to your father, she reciprocated his feelings totally. I really think it's something that you should know about."

"Who was he? What's his name?"

There was a long pause, in which the only sound was the long-distance hum on the phone. Then Ginny's voice came on again, weaker, almost halting.

"This man your mother loved, he was from . . ." Then she started coughing in harsh wracking bursts and Venetia heard mumbled voices in the background and the coolly efficient tones of a nurse.

"I'm sorry, ma'am, but Miss Jones can't talk anymore right now."

"Of course—I understand," whispered Venetia. "Please give her my love and tell her I'll leave New York as soon as I can."

After the seat belt sign went off, Venetia leaned back in the reclining chair, turning up the sound on her state-of-the-art headphones to drown out the sound of the jet engines. She removed her case of cassettes from her bag and took out one that had a handwritten label, the ink faded. It was titled "1970s Mixture." Venetia studied the writing for a moment. Who had made this collection of ancient hits? Her mother? Her father? Ginny? The capital letters gave no clue as to the authorship, so she slipped the cassette in and pressed the rewind button. She wanted to hear it all, from the beginning. Maybe there would be other conversations her mother had inadvertently taped in the bathtub. She sipped her champagne and settled down to listen.

Venetia was enjoying a parade of golden oldies, including songs from the Jackson Five, Diana Ross and Sammy Davis Jr., when during "Aquarius," the music stopped abruptly and she heard footsteps. Venetia listened to the conversation she had heard once before in the bath. A conversation recorded sixteen years ago, which still made her blood freeze.

Coral's limo picked Venetia up at the airport as planned and drove her to Ginny's rambling ranch-style house at the summit of Mulholland Drive. Ginny had always joked that Marlon Brando and Jack Nicholson were her closest neighbors and she could always borrow a cup of sugar from them. Venetia didn't glance at the movie stars' heavily protected houses almost hidden by thick vegetation. She couldn't wait to see Ginny and to hear what she had to say.

The limousine pulled into the graveled driveway and she jumped out as the front door opened and Coral, pale faced, eyes hidden behind giant sunglasses, slowly emerged. Venetia could see traces of tears on her otherwise flawless face.

"I'm so sorry, my darling." Coral hugged her tightly. "I'm afraid you're too late—Ginny passed away early this morning."

"Oh no." Venetia stared at the upstairs bedroom window, as though willing Ginny to return. "I . . . I hope she didn't suffer too much."

"No, not at the end—she had lots of lovely morphine to help her. Believe me I wish I could have had a bit of it myself. I'm a *wreck*—look at me!"

To Venetia, Coral looked no different from her usual, immaculate chic self, sheathed in yellow from turban to toe. They walked into the cozy paneled living room, cluttered with the memorabilia of a show-business life. A giant TV screen dominated the room, surrounded by hundreds of videos on shelves.

"Every one of your mama's films is up there," Coral said.

"Wow, look at the photos!" gasped Venetia.

Two walls were covered floor to ceiling with photographs of Laura and about half of them were of Laura and Ginny, some going back to when they had been teenagers and

Laura was in the first flush of her honeyed beauty.

"God, you must be bored of hearing it, but the resemblance—it's astonishing," Coral said, as the nurse brought them mugs of instant coffee and gave Venetia a curious stare.

"I can't *believe* all these photos. So many more than Mama had. She hardly kept any pictures of herself from her movies or her early life."

"*Most* unusual for an actress," said Coral. "One thing your mother was not, on top of all her other wonderful qualities, of course, was a narcissist."

"Mmm." Venetia was intently studying all the pictures, most particularly the informal ones with her mother and friends.

"Ginny seemed to be with Mama a lot."

"Ginny worshiped the ground Laura walked on," Coral said softly. "Oh, not in a soppy fanlike way; she just adored and admired her. I think when your mother died, a light went out of Ginny's life. She was never again like the old Ginny, boisterous and fun loving. It was as though the electricity had been switched off inside her."

Venetia sat down on the sofa and sipped her coffee. "So tell me, Coral, what was it that Ginny wanted to tell me?" Venetia's eyes were wide and urgent.

Coral shook her head, and her ruby-and-emerald parrot earrings shook along with it.

"Darling, I wish I knew. She was mumbling so much—she was almost incoherent by last night."

"Did she say *anything* at all about me?"

"No, darling, I'm sorry she didn't. I promise you I would tell you if she had. She was so concerned about you. That *terrible* business with Alain in Paris—oh dear."

"I know, I know." Venetia didn't want the subject to change.

"But who was this man Mama was in love with just before she died? Did you ever meet him?"

"Darling, all I know is that he was South African, quite a bit younger than Laura and they met on safari. It was a location romance—nothing could ever have come of it, but it was apparently very heady."

"Surely you must remember his name?"

Coral sighed. "Darling, you know my poor brain is getting addled in my old age. I remember Ginny telling me all about him, after she came back to LA. He even came to Laura's funeral."

"Then you *saw* him?" Venetia asked eagerly.

"Unfortunately not, darling. I was in India with Binkie. We never even knew Laura had died until a week afterward. I was mortified. She was one of my best friends. I went to the memorial service, of course," she added hastily.

"But you *must* remember his name? You must."

Coral wrinkled her perfectly matte nose and, closing her eyes, said, "It was Sam, I think . . . or Steve . . . some simple name like that—oh, Steve, yes! That was it—Steve Baden . . . something or other."

"Baden?" asked Venetia. "Steve Baden? Doesn't ring a bell."

"Oh, it's a South African name, almost as common as Smith out there, tons of them have it. Ah yes, of *course* . . . *Badenhorst*—Steve Badenhorst. That was his name. And there he is!" She gestured to a plastic-framed collage of photos on the wall. "Taken in the jungle in Mala Mala. He's there somewhere. I know he is."

Venetia stood up to examine the photographs, yellowing from the California sun. They were mostly of Ginny and Laura in safari clothes, looking happy, but there was one photograph of the two of them with their arms linked around a young man. He was wearing a khaki shirt, shorts and a slouch hat tipped down over his eyes, which were covered by sunglasses. It was taken from quite a distance; the man's profile was turned to Laura and they were both laughing.

"It's hard to see what he looks like." Venetia sighed, replacing the collage on the wall. "But I'm glad he made Mama happy."

"Oh, indeed he did, dear. According to Ginny he made your mother happier than she had ever been in her life." Coral glanced fondly at Venetia, who looked sad and forlorn as she curled her bejeaned legs on the sofa. "So what about you, darling? Is there someone in your life now?"

"Yes, there is." Venetia's face brightened. "He's wonderful, Coral. He works with Atlanta and Phil at *Mercury*. He's an Australian writer, very funny, very lovable, very clever. In fact, he's got all the qualities a girl needs to make her very happy." She smiled reminiscently.

"And what's this marvelous creature's name?"

"He's called Steve too, Steve Kelly. The only drawback is he's about twenty years older than me."

"Oh, what does that matter?" scoffed Coral. "Most of my lovers have been fifteen or twenty years *younger* than me. Who the hell cares anymore?"

"Well, I don't think I do. He's asked me to marry him, and you know what?"

"What, darling?" asked Coral with an affectionate gleam in her eye.

"I'm going to take him up on it!" smiled Venetia. "As soon as my divorce is finalized I'm going to become Mrs. Steve Kelly."

CHAPTER FIFTY-EIGHT

They gathered beneath the arches of the Brooklyn Bridge, their bodies pressed close to each other for warmth. They were mostly male; some actually enjoyed their alternative lifestyle, hunting and foraging for food, much as their ancestors had done.

The homeless group, which had befriended Atlanta, were clustered around a fire in a rubbish bin over which they were warming their hands. Several hundred souls lived rough in this encampment, but they behaved as civilly toward each other as the residents of a Boston suburb. If they wanted to be among the lucky ones to live here, there were strict rules to be obeyed and, with a few exceptions of excessive drunkenness, crack smoking and occasional fist fights, the residents of Sun City, as they had euphemistically named their camp, were a companionable bunch.

Dorrie, the cross-eyed crone who had become Atlanta's friend the last time she had stayed, waddled over when she saw Atlanta limping from the shadows.

"Well, if it isn't Lady Lizzie. Where've you bin, Liz? We've all bin wonderin'?"

"Miami," huffed Atlanta. "Jeez. It's a long way away by bus, Dorrie." It had been nearly four weeks since she had last been here. She needed a good excuse as to why she'd been gone so long.

"That South Beach—ha!" Atlanta cackled so loudly that even Dorrie was forced to take a pace backward, for Atlanta, ever the method actress, had chewed three cloves of raw garlic that morning. "It's overrated if you ask me. All them skyscrapers—shit—you don't ever get to see the sun, and them skinny models ain't so hot either."

"'Least it was warm." Dorrie helped Atlanta across the rough terrain, a minefield of rocks, smashed bottles and broken furniture.

"Gettin' fuckin' cold here now. Why'd ya come back, Lizzie?"

"Missed ya'll." Atlanta grinned again, and grabbed Dorrie's birdlike arm as they approached the group around the fire.

"Missed New York—ain't no place like it— you can keep Miami, and all of them high rollers—I like it here in the Rotting Apple."

Dorrie joined in her cackling. "Good for ya, gal. Hey, look who's back, boys," cried Dorrie. "It's Lizzie."

"Hi ya, Lizzie," "Yo, Lizzie," and "What's up with you, Liz?" were called to her by men who, she noticed, were too busy getting blasted to pay much attention to her.

"I brought you a present," Atlanta whispered, presenting Dorrie with half a bottle of Old Crow. "Don't let the others see."

"Where'd ya get this then?" Dorrie tipped the bottle to a mouth full of brown teeth.

"Grabbed it from a john at the terminal." Atlanta looked around and noticed a tramp nicknamed Red Pete hadn't taken his piggy eyes off her.

"Don't give him any." Dorrie grasped Atlanta and moved away from the fire. "He's a juice freak. This whiskey's the real McCoy. Don't want that piss-artist to get any of it."

"It's just for you, Dorrie," said Atlanta. "I didn't even touch a drop myself."

The two women arranged their plastic bags, full of belongings, on a relatively clear patch of ground, away from the group but still in view. Dorrie lugged a heavy supermarket trolley everywhere, that looked as if it contained every object known to man. She never let it out of her sight, even sleeping with a length of rusty chain tied several times around the bundle on the cart and then around her waist.

"So—what's going on?" asked Atlanta, accepting a cigarette butt that Dorrie proffered from an ancient, oversized matchbox with "Hotel Mamounia, Marrakesh" written on it. "Things quiet or what?"

"Well, the fuzz bin around a lot. Ole Jerry got wasted y'know. We was all sad about that. Then they came around asking their fucking stupid questions. Like if we'd known one of us'd done it, do ya think we'd tell them?" She spat disdainfully into a rag, inspecting the contents with interest.

"Wasted? How?"

"We think maybe it *was* one of us. Old Jerry wasn't doing no one any harm. Asleep, he was, like a dog, next to the river. Some freak gave him the one-way ticket. Stabbed him—dozens of times. Jeez!" She puffed on her stub until it glowed bright orange in the dark, then took another swig of Old Crow.

"D'ya know who did it?" asked Atlanta.

"I got my susses," Dorrie said darkly. "But we'd never tell the bogeys. Red Pete never liked Jerry, always doing fist jobs with him. No love lost there. Or that one over there. He's a dark horse. He *thinks* he's a big shot." She tittered, and leaning to Atlanta whispered, "He was famous *once*. He tries to pretend he's just one of us, but some of us knows who he really is!" Her squinting eyes glinted in the glow from her cigarette.

"Tell me about him then." She gestured to the "famous" bearded mystery man. Tall, completely covered in gradations of rags, he could have been any age from thirty to sixty; his face was almost covered, hidden by hair that was so filthy and matted that it was impossible to tell its color. He was so hirsute that he was almost unrecognizable as a member of the human race, but as he lifted his can of beer to his mouth, a sudden shower of sparks from the fire illuminated his profile quite clearly. Atlanta felt the hairs stand up on the back of her neck.

It couldn't be him—it simply couldn't. But as she continued to stare, the man turned and looked straight at her with a knowing grin, and Atlanta realized with sickening dread that it was him. The man who had been stalking her. The man who had left those disgusting messages on her answering machine, who had threatened unspeakable things and that he wanted her dead. Suddenly she realized, with a rush of horror, who he was.

Kristobel was unable to sleep, so at dawn after a restless night, he threw on a tracksuit and decided to take a run around Central Park. He hoped that it would make him stop obsessing about his reviews. But there was a glimpse of hope on the horizon. Yesterday he had heard that the monthly glossies *Vogue*, *Harper's Bazaar*, and of course *Mercury*, had given him favorable reviews and that the collection was becoming something of a cult phenomenon.

"Please, God," he thought.

While he was running he thought about the design for the gown Stefania had commissioned. She had called from Rome, last night, full of news, jabbering excitedly. Briefly commiserating about his reviews she'd said, "But, *caro*, you must forget the critics. I always forget. Critics are scum, *caro*—absolute scum. If they weren't they would be creating something themselves, instead of criticizing. Now, *caro*, listen, I want you to make the most fabulous dress in the world for the LA premiere of my Scorsese film. Red, with *lots* of embroidery, big décolletage and a skirt with a train, maybe?"

"But, Stefania, no one wears big gowns to movie openings anymore. They dress simply now. Maybe they wear a slip dress or bustier, but gowns are out in Hollywood, *carina*."

"*Stronzo*, what *stupidos*!" She laughed. "Do you really think that Stefania Scalerina gives a *shit* about what those silly little starlets wear? I am a *great* movie actress. I am starring in a Martin Scorsese movie and I am showing up at that premiere wearing what *I* want to wear, which is red chiffon with *lots* of cleavage, and *not* what is politically correct in Hollywood."

"Your wish is my command, *carina*." Kristobel was pleased. He preferred designing glamorous gowns for women like Stefania. The trouble was too many women nowadays were trying to emulate six-foot teenage models, which was a tragedy for fashion.

"Always be true to yourself, *caro,*" Stefania had said, wisely. "That's why your show failed. You did things you thought the public wanted, but they didn't, they hated it."

"You're right," he said ruefully. "I became known for glamorous dresses and I went too far."

A thought occurred to Kristobel. "It's only a few months since Nicholas's death. Shouldn't you be in black?"

"Don't be silly, *caro.* I was only his mistress. Life has to go on, darling, you know that."

"Right," he said. "So who are you taking to the opening?"

"I am going to the premiere with Kevin," she announced proudly.

"Kevin *Bentley*?" He couldn't keep the surprise out of his voice.

"We're in love," she said simply.

"You and Kevin *in love*? I can't believe it. When did this happen?"

"*Caro*, when I went to Rome for the movie, Nicholas had just passed away and I was *molto* sad. I did love him, you know. Giancarlo Giannini was set for the film, so I was happy because Giancarlo and I are old friends—we go back a long way."

I bet, thought Kristobel, yet another one of Stefania's ex-lovers?

"Anyway, sadly Giancarlo was working on another movie, so the producer asks Vittorio, then Fabrizio, but they were all busy with other projects."

"So how did you end up getting Kevin? I can't believe he'd do a spaghetti western."

"*Thriller, caro*, not western," Stefania said coldly. "It's a spaghetti *thriller*. And Mr. Bentley was very glad indeed to get the job. He hadn't worked in America for nearly two years, in spite of his reputation and fame. He was, as he told me, un-fucking-employable, reduced to drinking tap water."

"Lovely place, Hollywood."

"Don't worry about Kevin, *caro*," she cooed. "He's fine. He's got the movie and now he's got me, although we've known each other for years, of course. We're all over the Italian papers and magazines. Did you see *Gente* this week?"

"No, *carina*, I didn't."

"Well, buy it, darling. Kevin and I have an adorable at home layout. I'm wearing your

clothes, of course. We look very happy together—and we are."

"I'm glad for you," Kristobel said, sincerely.

"Keep thinking about my dress and wish
me luck with Kevin," she trilled. "I think we
may get married. It'll be our first marriage."

"I wish you all the luck in the world, *carina*," he said. "I'll make your wedding dress
as a gift."

Kristobel smiled to himself at Stefania's
childlike optimism.

There were too many derelicts in the park,
sleeping, scratching their lice-ridden bodies.
Kristobel couldn't stand the sight of them.
When one of them came begging, he
averted his eyes and rage filled him as he
remembered his mother's attacker and the
major and his wife's killer. The triumphant
leer as he was led away from the courthouse
to freedom.

Now Kristobel always carried a gun because you could never be too careful jogging
in the park. There were maniacs out there,
crazy men, and even crazier women. There
were packs of "wilders," ready to pounce on
a lone runner and beat him up or kill him,
just for the fun of it, not to mention pickpock-

ets, perverts and the scum who called Central Park their home. Oh no, Kristobel never took any chances, and a small Smith and Wesson was always tucked in the body belt around his waist.

After his run, Kristobel started to jog home. As he passed Atlanta and Phil's brownstone on 75th, he saw a figure creeping inside the front door, which the doorman had carelessly left open.

Kristobel stopped. There were only four apartments in that brownstone. He knew that two of the occupants were away at the moment, and the third, the elderly lady who owned the dogs, was practically bedridden and lived alone. He knew too that Phil was in Australia, which meant that Atlanta was at home alone. Kristobel's heart pounded. A homeless vagrant had slipped unnoticed into Atlanta's building. He had to do something fast.

Atlanta was bone weary. She had been so busy talking she hadn't been able to sleep all night. Dorrie had told her some fascinating anecdotes about the human dross who were her cronies and, after Atlanta had pro-

duced an almost full bottle of gin, she became even more talkative.

Eventually Dorrie had fallen asleep, then
Red Pete had sauntered over and made
such a crude pass at Atlanta that she had
called on all her acting talent to remain
pleasant. The other person whom she'd recognized seemed to have disappeared and
she was extremely relieved about that.
Knowing his identity had made Atlanta desperately uncomfortable.

Did he know that she had recognized
him? How did he know who she was? Or did
he? She thought about the messages he'd
left and realized she was putting herself in
jeopardy staying there. She'd get out as casually as possible and alert the police about
this man. She pretended to fall asleep for a
couple of hours, and then, at six thirty, when
the pack awoke and started to move off to
begin their day's activities, she meandered
off in the direction of her apartment.

She entered the cool haven of the hallway
so exhausted that she could barely totter in.
She peeled off the layers of filthy clothes and
threw them onto a sheet on the floor of her
bedroom, relieved that she would never

have to wear such disgusting rags again. She'd finally got her story and it was a good one. Atlanta stripped down to her panties and bra and was unstrapping the enormous padded stomach when a hand shot out from under the bed, and she felt a viselike hold on her ankle.

She screamed as the hand tightened its grip. She lost her balance, falling half forward onto the bed. The ragged man grabbed hold of her legs for support as he squirmed out from under the bed and pinned her to it with his full weight.

Atlanta stared at him in horrified fascination, as he breathed his foul breath in her face. "Hi sweetheart," he wheezed. "Long time no see—how ya doin'?"

The plane landed at Kennedy on schedule where Steve was anxiously waiting to meet Venetia. She was more thrilled to see him than she could have imagined, and by the look in his eyes, that feeling was more than reciprocated.

In the limo, on the way back into town, Steve asked as casually as he could, "So what secret did Ginny want to tell you? Had she said anything to Coral?"

"No—she died without saying anything to Coral, poor darling."

"I'm sorry, princess." Steve breathed an inner sigh of relief.

He told Venetia that he had something for her and handed her a small red leather box. Venetia's eyes sparkled as she opened it to reveal a heart-shaped diamond ring, nestled in a bed of red velvet.

"Oh, Steve darling, it's gorgeous." She slipped it on her finger. "It's absolutely beautiful—but darling, this is from Cartier. It must have cost you a fortune."

He smiled his chip-toothed grin and hugged her. "I'm not a total idiot, sweetheart. There's a recession on, don't forget. The ring is Cartier, but I bought it from an estate sale for quite a bit less. Sorry baby, I guess it's not very romantic to have let you into my little secret," he said ruefully.

"Steve darling, that's what I love about you. That you always tell me the truth." Venetia's aquamarine eyes gazed into his, shining with love and trust. "I love you, Steve, I really do and I'm going to try to make you the best wife I possibly can."

"Oh baby," he breathed, "you're not going to have to try too hard on that score."

As they embraced, the limo driver looked back at them in his mirror with an approving smirk. But Steve couldn't rid himself of the nagging feeling that he was pulling the wool over Venetia's eyes. He had lied to her many times: about his background, about his real name, and about trying to save Nicholas's life.

But the worst lie of all was that he hadn't told Venetia about Laura and himself. If he confessed that he had been her mother's lover too, would Venetia still want to marry him?

CHAPTER FIFTY-NINE

Atlanta managed to tear the man's hand away from her ankle and scrambled crablike on her hands and knees across the bedroom floor but, before she reached the door, he was on her, both hands squeezing her neck, leering into her face with those hatefully familiar eyes.

"What the hell are you doing here?" Atlanta could hardly breathe and couldn't tear her eyes away from his face. "You promised to leave me alone, after we split."

"Promises are for children," he sneered. "And I ain't no kid." He gave a poisonous

smile and dimly she could see the faint vestiges of the man she'd once loved.

"Fabio. Why in God's name are you here?"

Fabio just stared at her, his bloodshot,
mad eyes smiling, as she tried to escape
from his grip on her throat.

"Is it money?" she gasped. "Tell me what
you want, please Fabio, I'll give it to you, I
promise."

Releasing his hands from her neck, Fabio
savagely ripped the concealed microphone
from around her waist.

"Your promises have never been worth
shit, kid. That sap Dorrie told you everything,
didn't she? And you were going to print it,
weren't you? In that dirty rag of yours."

Atlanta shook her head. "No, Fabio—
when I heard it was you, of course I wouldn't
print it—how could I? After all we . . . we
were—lovers."

A vile grating sound, which could have
been a laugh, rose from his throat. "Yes, we
were lovers, weren't we? I had you when I
was handsome and successful." He pressed
his noxious face closer to hers. "And you
were the perfect little virgin, all shiny and
new, weren't you? And you liked it, didn't
you, Atlanta? That first night in Cannes

when I fucked you, you loved it, didn't you? Admit it, you bitch." He shook her violently like a terrier with a rat.

"You liked it so much you wanted to do it on screen, in front of the world, showing yourself off. A real slut—just like your mother, weren't you? I've heard stories about her that'd curl your fuckin' hair."

"Fabio. Please, please stop." Atlanta moaned as he banged her head against the wall even harder.

"Papa didn't like seeing that, did he? Papa didn't like his poor little rich virgin daughter showing her tits to everyone for the price of a movie ticket."

"Fabio, you know what happened. You made me drunk and drugged me when I did that." She was sobbing, wondering why she should have to make excuses to this travesty of a human being. "It happened years ago. Why are you bringing it up now?"

"Because you ruined my fucking *life*, you selfish *bitch*." He shook her so hard she could almost hear her teeth rattle.

"How could I have ruined your life? What did I do?"

"You left me and went traipsing around the world. The great reporter. You were gone for years and your fucking father made quite sure I never got a job again. Every time I was near to closing a deal, Mr. Nicholas Stephanopolis made certain the door got slammed."

"Papa wouldn't do that."

"Oh no?" His hands tightened and Atlanta felt she was blacking out. "I found out. Your father's got connections all over the world and he used them mercilessly. After I lost everything, I tried to find you, but you were always away, in Marbella or St. Tropez, or some other fucking flesh pot."

"You were looking for me all that time?" gasped Atlanta.

"Sure, I was looking for you. Marcello and I tried to make a couple of flicks in Italy, but the financing fell through—your fucking father made things real bad for me."

They were nose to nose now. He stopped shaking her, and his eyes seemed to be getting heavy. "Then Marcello fucked off with the last of our money, every fucking cent. So then I had nothing."

"How did you survive? What did you do then?" Atlanta felt she had to keep him talking. She could feel him softening, becoming more human, his grip on her throat loosening.

"I did time," he barked. "Eighteen months in the slammer. Ever been in jail, Atlanta? Know what it's like?"

"No, no, I haven't."

"Of course you fucking haven't. You wouldn't be sent to prison anyway, even if you got caught. Your Daddy dearest would never let his darling daughter go to the pen, would he? Even if you killed somebody, he'd get one of those white-bread lawyers and he'd get you off, wouldn't he? Nicholas Stephanopolis's precious little girl would never be allowed to rot in a stinking hellhole."

His face contorted and his hands crept back to her neck.

"Fabio, you know Papa never cared for me . . . you know that better than anybody. And besides, he's dead now." Her voice was weak.

"Good," he snarled. Then, with a faraway look in his eyes, Fabio whispered hoarsely, 'You'll never *believe* what those pigs did to me when they sent me upstate. Never. A re- fined little lady like you couldn't imagine the horror I went through in that pit."

He put his mouth close to her ear, whis- pering the vile things other prisoners had done to him. It was a litany of sodomy, degradation and humiliation. Atlanta couldn't bear to listen anymore.

Suddenly she saw at the end of the hallway that the front door was slightly ajar and her heart leaped. She must have been so exhausted she hadn't closed it properly. She tried to pull away from Fabio's fierce grip and make a run for the door, but he was too strong for her.

He clapped a stinking hand over her mouth, slamming her head against the wall again. "Listen up bitch, listen to me. I was good-looking then wasn't I, Atlanta?" She didn't answer, so he smashed her head against the wall again and again until she felt it would split open like a watermelon.

"Yes you were," she whispered through a mist of pain.

"You *bet* I was. The best-looking stud on the Veneto, they called me. I was tall, blond and handsome, and all the women wanted me. Then, in that rotten hole, all those cons wanted me too . . . the bastards."

His voice rose to a scream, his hands tightened around Atlanta's throat and he started choking her. She struggled, but his body had her pressed to the wall and he was strong. She tried to scream.

"Where the fuck were you, Atlanta? Why didn't you help me, you selfish rich bitch? Why? Answer me!"

Kristobel stopped outside the Kellogs' apartment, where he could hear the sound of raised voices. Was that Atlanta screaming? He could hear a woman yelling, the muffled sounds of a struggle and a guttural male voice too.

Kristobel pushed open the front door, his hand tightening around his gun. Slowly he tiptoed toward the sounds, holding the gun close to his chest as he'd seen movie heroes do. His finger released the safety catch, his shoulders were hunched, his body crouched, then he froze when he saw the tableau that confronted him.

He only recognized a half-naked Atlanta by her voice. Her face, deformed by prosthetics, was set in a mask of fear as a filthy beggar screaming obscenities was trying to strangle her. She was clawing feebly at him on the floor.

The spectacle was so horrific that Kristobel was dumbstruck for a second. Then, as if of its own accord, he pointed his gun at the creature's head and his finger pulled the trigger again and again as the man fell to the floor, a scream dying on his lips.

"Oh my God, oh God, Kristobel." Atlanta staggered into Kristobel's arms sobbing incoherently and in spite of his revulsion at the disgusting way she looked and smelled, he hugged her and tried to soothe her.

Kristobel stared down at the body with shock and loathing. All of the pent-up rage he'd been filled with since that day the murderer of the major and his wife had been freed was gone. Suddenly Kristobel felt that he had avenged the murder of his friends. He felt purged and cleansed and he experienced no feelings of guilt as he comforted Atlanta, listening to her tell him everything about the man he had just killed—Fabio Di Navaro.

CHAPTER SIXTY

"So you see I can't cut it, it's as simple as that. I love what I do at *Mercury* so much that anything else that takes me away from it, even for one day, gives me a real sense of loss."

Atlanta smiled at her sister, who asked disbelievingly, "Are you *serious*? After everything you've gone through, after what we've *both* gone through for that matter, to get control of Papa's empire, you just want to chuck it all?"

Atlanta nodded. "Darling, it's hardly chucking it, is it? Not if I'm handing it over to you.

It's still in the family, it will still be the Stephanopolis empire."

Venetia looked at Steve, who looked at Phil, who gave a shrug of approval. Then they all looked back to Atlanta.

"I just can't edit *Mercury* and give it my undivided attention, if I have to be in Father's office all day. I *know* how much you wanted it, Venetia, so the Stephanopolis empire is yours, darling. Lock, stock and oil barrels."

"But what about the trustees? The stockholders? How will they feel about this?" stammered Venetia. "Surely they must have some sort of say in how Papa's businesses are to be administered?"

"She's already talked to all of them," said Phil, "and as far as everybody's concerned, *and* according to Nicholas's will, as long as the business is administered by a Stephanopolis heir, that's fine by them. They've enough advisers, consultants and big-shot execs to run the whole shooting match themselves really. Having a Stephanopolis at the helm is really only a figurehead."

"But you'll still have loads to do," said Atlanta. "Contracts to sign, decisions, resolutions, zillions of things. It really is a full-time job."

"It's a bit like being president of the USA, actually," Phil joked. "Everybody else does all of the work but he gets all of the glory."

"And you really want me to do it?" Venetia's eyes were aglow. "*Really*?"

"*Absolutely*, darling. If you still want to." Atlanta looked at her sister, who couldn't seem to disentangle her fingers from her fiancé's. "And I hope Steve will help you."

"You bet. Do you think I'm letting her out of my sight, now that I've finally hooked her? She's mine forever now, aren't you, sweetheart?"

"I certainly am." Venetia twisted her platinum band. "Forever."

"Well, that's settled then." Atlanta leaned back in her chair and smiled at the ecstatic couple. "So where will you two be going on your honeymoon next year?"

"Greece," answered Venetia. "We were thinking of using the *Circe* to go on a cruise of the islands, but then Steve suggested 'Why cruise the Greek islands when your family already owns the best one of the lot?'"

"Of course," said Atlanta.

"And we belong to each other." Steve hugged his future wife. "That's all that matters, isn't it, sweetheart?"

"Oh yes, darling." She snuggled closer, running her hand through his curly brown hair. "It's the only thing in life that does matter."

Lady Anne was overjoyed, not only to see her favorite grandchild again and now remarried to such a charming man, but that Venetia was to become the new chief executive of the Stephanopolis empire.

"I told you you'd find something to do. Your father would have been proud," she said.

They sat under an umbrella on the terrace looking out at sea, where tiny white sailboats scudded along in the breeze.

"Nicholas was always very proud of you, Venetia."

"Even though I gave him little cause to be," Venetia said bitterly. "I know I behaved horribly, Grandmama. I'm amazed that Papa put up with my shenanigans for all those years."

"Well, he did, because he loved you so very much." The old lady's eyes were half closing and she looked drowsily at the late afternoon sun.

"I'll help you up to your room, Grandmama," said Venetia. "It's time for your nap."

Venetia tucked Lady Anne into bed then went to her old room. Languidly she looked at the watercolor paintings on the wall, the girlish knickknacks and mementos on her dressing table, the piles of books, tapes and cassettes. It was a pretty room for a young girl and she'd been happy in it, but she'd grown out of it now. After all, she was no longer a young girl. She was now a married woman, second time around, and she needed a grown-up bedroom, an appropriate setting in which to start her wedded life.

So what could be more appropriate than her mother's suite with its sitting room and bedroom, both looking out onto glorious views of Stephanopolis Island?

For some reason Steve hadn't been too happy about staying in her mother's suite. They almost had their first fight about it, but she had prevailed upon him that he was being silly not to want to stay there for their honeymoon. After all, Mama had been dead for a very long time.

Venetia had carefully supervised the servants in the almost reverential removal of Mama's clothes and personal possessions to the vast storage rooms in the cellar. There were just a few more drawers full of private letters, papers and photographs to go through, and Venetia was going to apply herself alone to that task this afternoon while Steve was indulging one of his favorite pursuits of fishing.

She sat in front of Laura's satinwood desk, reputed to have once belonged to Marie Antoinette, and removed a pile of what looked like faded holiday snaps from a drawer. She glanced up at the Louis XVI clock, quietly ticking away. Only four o'clock. Steve had said not to expect him back from fishing until at least six thirty. She had plenty of time to sort all these things out.

Venetia hardly touched her food at dinner that night. She seemed far away, almost removed, as servants placed course after course before them. After they finally left, Steve leaned forward and, clasping Venetia's hand in his, asked, "What's the matter, sweetheart? What's wrong? You look as if you'd seen a ghost."

Slowly Venetia turned to him, her eyes filled with questions. "Steve," she said in a measured voice, "I need to ask you something. How well did you know my mother?"

EPILOGUE

The Present

Under the watchful eye of their nurse, the two children frolicked on the lawn. The little girl, flaxen haired and blue eyed, looked just like her mother. Her older brother had light brown hair that tumbled carelessly over his forehead, exactly like his father's.

Under the portico of the marble terrace Venetia and Atlanta sipped their chilled rosé and discussed their past, a subject of which they never seemed to tire.

As they reminisced, the combination of afternoon sun and wine making them drowsy, Atlanta decided to broach the delicate subject that she had been mulling over for some time.

"I still can't understand how you were able to put it all behind you. I don't know if I would be able to forgive Phil, if he'd lied to me like that."

"He didn't actually *lie*, Atlanta—he just left things out. Imagine if the shoe were on the other foot. I know I'd want Steve to forgive me for hedging the truth, if I'd had my reasons. Wouldn't you expect the same from Phil?"

"Guess so," replied Atlanta.

Atlanta took a sip of wine and said, haltingly, "Sometimes I can't believe how selfish I was when I was young, I was thoughtless and unkind to a lot of people, including you, Venetia, and I sincerely regret that. In no small part thanks to Phil I've changed, for the better, I hope. He's so wonderful to me, I could never knowingly hurt him."

"But whether we like it or not, we *do* hurt our husbands, just as they sometimes hurt us, even if they don't mean to," Venetia said slowly. She had removed her sunglasses and was gazing out to sea with a faraway expression.

"But since he confessed, has Steve ever

hurt you? It's always seemed to me that he worships you."

"Oh, he does and I adore him, but on that terrible day on our honeymoon I thought his love for me was for all the wrong reasons."

"So how *did* you find out that Steve was our mother's lover?" Atlanta asked.

"I found pictures of them together in Africa and I confronted him with them. Ginny had told me that Mama had fallen in love with someone before she died and it emerged that it was Steve. Steve told me about how they fell in love and had a brief affair when Mama and Ginny were on safari. Apparently it made Mama finally realize how unhappy she was with Father and she decided she was going to leave him. Steve believes that Papa killed her because of that."

Atlanta's face grew darker and she drew a deep breath. "I don't know whether Father meant to kill her," she said in a tiny voice. "I interrupted them when they were fighting that night."

"What?" gasped Venetia. "But you never told anyone about this when you grew up. You didn't even tell me, your sister. *Why*?"

"Father made me drink up some champagne to make me forget—I ended up unconscious. It came back to me later in snatches, but I was so scared, upset and confused. I didn't want to believe that my father had killed my mother. Father threatened me afterward when I tried to bring it up—he said that if I ever told *anyone* what I had seen no one would believe me, and I would be sent to prison for the rest of my life for telling terrible lies. Can you imagine how that made me feel? I was only ten. Afterward, strangely enough, I totally forgot. I suppressed it from my memory."

"So how *did* you remember?"

"Bizarrely, when I wanted to quit smoking recently. I'd tried everything and nothing had worked, so eventually I went to that new hypnotist, Dr. Li. When he put me under, he said he believed I had some dark issues I needed to deal with and asked whether I would like regression therapy. I agreed to try that night and blurted out everything that I remembered." She shuddered and closed her eyes.

"What did you see?" Venetia's face was white with shock.

"Dr. Li had his tape recorder on, and I've played it over and over again. I was in my room on the *Circe* and I heard Mama and Father arguing, he was screaming at Mama and she was yelling too. I'd never heard Mama yell back before, so I got out of bed and went to the salon and stood outside. Then I heard the sound of a slap and a thump, as if someone had fallen."

Atlanta stopped, her face was white and her eyes glazed with fear.

"Go on," said Venetia. "What did you do then?"

"I was so scared I ran back to my room and tried to go to sleep. I tossed and turned for what felt like hours but I couldn't sleep. When dawn came and everywhere was so quiet I crept back and peered into the room. Papa was just sitting, staring at Mama, who lay very still on the ground with blood coming out of her mouth. Mama was dead, Venetia, and Father just sat and watched her die."

"The bastard," Venetia cried. "How could he? I never realized what a terrible man he was . . ."

"More terrible than either of us will ever know or ever want to know." Atlanta sighed. "Stefania told me she was badly beaten by him several times when going along with his perversions, but she said Mama never would. Poor Mama, it's too late to do anything now. Tell me more about Mama and Steve, Venetia. You must have been devastated when you found out."

"Oh I was, at first, you can imagine. I thought Steve's love for me was just based on the fact that I looked so like Mama. But he convinced me otherwise, then he told me everything . . . How he'd changed his name from Badenhorst to Kelly and how he believed Papa had killed Mama. He was frightened that if I knew the truth about him and Mama's relationship I wouldn't have wanted to have anything to do with him."

"And would you?" Atlanta asked delicately.

"Probably not at first, but after we were married, I became certain he really loved *me*, Venetia Stephanopolis, not Laura Marlowe, movie star. And when I faced him with the evidence of those photos he seemed so relieved to be able to tell me everything at last. He was totally honest. He said that although he had been in love with Mama, that had been seventeen years ago, when he was only twenty-six, and that his love for me, now, as a mature man, was deeper and more intense and real, not just the passion of a two-week fling on safari, and that he realized that our love was forever."

When she finished, Atlanta looked at her admiringly and Venetia smiled appreciatively.

"I'm so happy you and Steve found each other and I'm glad that Mama found a little bit of happiness in her life. That's all that matters, really . . . happiness and the love of your family."

"I guess I've got a lot of apologizing to do to you, Venetia—I was so damn jealous of you, even when you were a baby. You were always father's favorite."

Venetia smiled. "And I thought you were so stuck up and superior with your nose always in a book, and you seemed so clever."

"Clever!" Atlanta gushed. "I wasn't even clever enough to make my father give a hoot about me. I spent half my childhood eating, and the other half resenting. And what about that awful thing I did to you after I photographed you kissing Alain in drag!"

Venetia giggled. "Remember how furious Papa was after the papers printed them?"

"It was stupid of me to leave them lying around."

"Never mind, it's all in the past now—it's made us stronger."

Venetia put her hand on her sister's shoulder.

"And now we truly are all a family, and not just in name."

"How are my two favorite girls?"

The sisters looked up as Steve strolled across the lawn, holding out his arms to his children, who rushed up to him. He walked toward the women, his children clinging to him and chattering away.

He smiled, his chipped tooth as endearing as ever.

"We're fine, darling, just fine."

Venetia's face glowed as she looked at her little clan, and seeing her joy, Atlanta felt a jolt of envy. Although she had tried again to have a baby with Phil, after extensive tests, they had been told that it would never be possible. Atlanta often wondered if this was some kind of retribution for the baby she had been planning to abort and had then miscarried. But she tried not to dwell on that. Now at thirty-five she was content, secure and happy in her marriage, and running one of the most successful magazines in America. There was nothing more she wanted in life.

Venetia, too, had everything she'd dreamed of and being at the helm of her father's empire with Steve had proved extremely satisfying. The sisters had come through the jungle alone and now they were reaping the fruits of their labors. But their biggest achievement was in overcoming the terrible death of their mother and their unfortunate upbringing by a harsh, uncaring father.

Shortly after Laura's funeral, Atlanta had overheard Ginny talking to Lady Anne. "I dread to think what's going to become of those poor little sisters," she had said sadly, "for despite all the Stephanopolis wealth and power, I really believe Nicholas doesn't really care for those girls at all. They really are misfortune's daughters . . ."

Well, not anymore, thought Atlanta with a smile. Those poor little daughters have it all now. We've won, Father. We've *both* won, and wherever you are, I hope you know that.